P9-CFS-027

Raves for *Goblin Quest:*

"*Goblin Quest* is a hilarious 'good read.' One of the funniest dungeon-delving epics ever!"
—Ed Greenwood, author of *Elminster: The Making of a Mage*

"Most fantasy gamers read fantasy novels. Most fantasy gamers like to slay goblins for fun and profit. After *Goblin Quest*, most fantasy gamers are going to have a very hard time doing that. Jim C. Hines has given us a wonderful adventure from the goblin's point of view, and it's fantastic! I haven't had this much fun reading a book in ages." —Wil Wheaton, actor and author of *Just a Geek*

"Need a book that will make you smile, then grin, then laugh out loud? If your tickle spot's the same as mine, *Goblin Quest* is the book you're looking for. I love an unlikely hero and Jig the goblin is my kind of unlikely love! New kid Jim C. Hines is already an expert at the unlikely but lovable . . . who could beat Jig's pet/sidekick/companion animal Smudge, the fire-spider? Bonus 1: How to manage when your companion animal sets your hair on fire. Bonus 2: How to choose the right god to pray to. Bonus 3: Why you should never challenge a goblin to a duel. —I'm still laughing."
—Janet Kagan, Hugo-winning author of *Hellspark* and *Uhura's Song*

"If you've always kinda rooted for the little guy, even maybe had a bit of a place in your heart for the likes of Gollum, rather than the Boromirs and Gandalfs of the world, pick up *Goblin Quest*—just make sure you keep well away from Golaka's stewpot." —*The SF Site*

"This exciting adult fairy tale is filled with adventure and action, but the keys to the fantasy are Jig and the belief that the mythological creatures are real in the realm of Jim C. Hines." —*Midwest Book Reviews*

Tales of Jig Dragonslayer

GOBLIN QUEST
GOBLIN HERO
GOBLIN WAR

and coming soon in paperback,
a new fantasy from Jim Hines:

THE STEPSISTER SCHEME

GOBLIN QUEST

JIM C. HINES

DAW BOOKS, INC.
DONALD A. WOLLHEIM, FOUNDER
375 Hudson Street, New York, NY 10014

ELIZABETH R. WOLLHEIM
SHEILA E. GILBERT
PUBLISHERS
www.dawbooks.com

Copyright © 2005, 2006 by Jim C. Hines.

All Rights Reserved.

Cover art by Mel Grant.

DAW Book Collectors No. 1383.

DAW Books are distributed by Penguin Group (USA).

All characters in this book are fictitious.
Any resemblance to persons living or dead is coincidental.

If you purchase this book without a cover you should be aware that this book may have been stolen property and reported as "unsold and destroyed" to the publisher. In such case neither the author nor the publisher has received any payment for this "stripped book."

The scanning, uploading and distribution of this book via the Internet or any other means without the permission of the publisher is illegal, and punishable by law. Please purchase only authorized electronic editions, and do not participate in or encourage the electronic piracy of copyrighted materials. Your support of the author's rights is appreciated.

First paperback printing, November 2006
4 5 6 7 8 9 10

DAW TRADEMARK REGISTERED
U.S. PAT. OFF. AND FOREIGN COUNTRIES
—MARCA REGISTRADA
HECHO EN U.S.A.

PRINTED IN THE U.S.A.

GOBLIN QUEST

"We may be outnumbered. They may have magic and muscle on their side. But we're goblins! We're tough, we're mean, and we're more than a match for a few so-called heroes. Some of us will die, but for the survivors, this will be a victory to live forever in goblin memories."

—Goblin captain (name unknown), shortly before his death by multiple stab wounds to the back.

CHAPTER 1

❧❖❧

Muck Duty

Jig hated muck duty.

He didn't mind the actual work. He liked the metallic smell of the distillation room, where week-old blood and toadstool residue dried in their trays. He never complained about having to scrape the pans as clean as possible and mix the residue with boiled fat, spiderwebs, and a dark green broth that smelled of rotting plants. He liked the way it all went from a lumpy soup to a smooth, gelatinous slime as he forced his stirring stick around and around in the giant bowl.

Walking around with the muck pot hanging awkwardly from his shoulder as he doled out gobs of the slow-burning stuff wasn't so bad either. True, if he got careless, it would be easy to splatter a bit of muck onto his skin. Even when it wasn't lit, the mixture could raise blisters in a matter of seconds. When burning, the yellow and green flames were almost impossible to extinguish, which was why they used muck to light the lair. But Jig was careful,

and unlike most muck workers, he had survived for
several years with all his fingers intact.

Jig would have been perfectly happy if he
weren't the only goblin his age who still got stuck
with muck duty. It was a job for children. Goblins
Jig's age were supposed to be warriors, but the few
times Jig had gone on patrol had only sealed his
reputation as the clumsy runt of his generation.

He adjusted the thin handle on his shoulder. The
goblin lair held forty-six fire bowls. Each one was
little more than a hole in the dark red obsidian of
the walls, with a palm-size depression at the bottom
to hold two days' worth of muck. Jig squinted at
the fourth fire bowl, the last in the corridor that
led out of the distillation room and into the main
cavern.

To Jig the flame was nothing but a blur. He could
bring the fire into better focus by squinting, but
that required him to put his face closer to the fire
than he liked. The triangle of flame flickered as
his breath touched it. The bowl was nearly empty.
Whoever made the rounds yesterday had been lazy,
and Jig would have to relight many of the bowls
before he was done.

"Lazy children," he muttered angrily. He dipped
a metal spatula into the muck pot and carefully
scooped out a large blob. This he scraped into the
dying fire bowl, where the flame whooshed and
grew as it touched new fuel. He scraped as much
muck from the spatula as he could, then extinguished it in the sack of sand on his belt. It
wouldn't do to return a still-burning spatula to
his pot.

He passed into the main cavern, a roughly circular, high-ceilinged cave of hard obsidian. The walls
felt greasy to the touch, the polish of the rock hidden beneath years of grime. While the muck fires

gave off very little smoke, several centuries of
"very little" had led to a blackened, soot-covered
ceiling. The sweaty odor of five hundred goblins
mixed with the powerful scent of Golaka's cooking.
Jig's mouth began to water as he smelled a batch
of pickled toadstools boiling in Golaka's great
cauldron.

Jig kept close to the wall as he worked. The
faster he could finish his duties, the sooner he
could eat.

But the other goblins weren't going to make
things easy. Five or six large goblins stood bunched
around the closest fire bowl, watching him. Jig's
pointed ears twitched. He was too nearsighted to
make out who was waiting there, but he could hear
their amused whispers. Porak and his friends. This
was going to hurt.

He thought about starting with the other side of
the cavern. If he worked his way around to Porak's
spot, which would take at least an hour, maybe
they would get bored and go away.

"And maybe Porak will make me honorary captain of his patrol," Jig muttered. More likely they
would circle around to meet him, and whatever
they planned would be worse for having to make
the effort.

Jig hunched lower and walked toward the group.
Most of them were still eating, he noticed, and he
tried to ignore his hunger. Porak grinned as Jig
approached. Long fangs curved up toward his eyes,
and his ears quivered with amusement. Several of
his friends chuckled. Nobody moved out of the
way.

"Cousin Jig. Muck duty, is it?" Porak asked. He
scratched his bulbous nose with a clawed finger.
"How long before you're ready for *real* work?"

"Real work?" He kept out of their reach, ready

at any moment to continue the long goblin tradition
of running away.

"Glory, fighting, and bloodshed." The goblins
puffed up like rock lizards competing for a mate.
Porak smiled, a warning sign if ever there was one.
"We want you to come along on patrol."

"I can't." He held up the muck bucket. "I've
barely started."

Porak laughed. "That can wait until they mix up
a new batch of muck, one that hasn't been
contaminated."

Jig watched Porak closely, trying to guess what
that laugh meant. "The muck is fine," he said
cautiously.

Fingers seized Jig's arms from behind. He
squealed and twisted, but that only made the claws
dig deeper. Stupid! He had been so intent on Porak
that he ignored the others. "What are you doing?"

Porak held up a black rat by the tail. "Look at
that," he said. "I don't know who's more frightened, the rat or the runt."

The goblins laughed as the rat flipped and
jumped, trying to free itself. Jig forced himself to
relax. They wanted him to struggle like the rat.

Porak stepped closer. "Everyone knows rat fur
makes the fire bowls smell awful. A shame someone let this one into the mix."

The rat struggled harder, prompting more laughter. The hands holding Jig relaxed. As fast as he
could, Jig grabbed his spatula and flicked muck
over his shoulder. A few drops landed on his arm,
and he cringed as the skin blistered. But the goblin
behind him took a far worse splash in the face. He
howled and tried to wipe the muck off.

Had Jig been in a better mood, he would have
reminded his captor that wiping would only spread

the muck around. A louder howl told him the goblin had figured that out for himself.

The laughter of the others had only grown at this display. Jig glanced around for the easiest escape route, but before he could flee, Porak lunged forward.

"Not so fast, cousin." He dropped the panicked rat into the muck pot. "Meet us for duty in two hours. Don't make me come find you."

The rat clawed toward the edge of the pot. Half its body was trapped in the muck, and its squeals grew higher as the muck burned through the fur. Jig couldn't have saved it if he wanted to. Even if the pain-crazed rat escaped, all it took was one open flame and Jig would have a frantic, flaming rat on his hands.

"Sorry about this." He put the spatula into the pot and grabbed his weapon, an old kitchen knife with a loose blade. Not much, but enough to put the rat out of its misery.

He cleaned off the blade, being extra careful to make sure no muck remained, then tucked it back into the sheath on his rope belt.

Well, at least he wasn't on muck duty anymore. This was what he wanted, right? He was going on patrol. A clear step up in the world. So why wasn't he happier? Goblins spent years waiting for the day they could go from lighting fire bowls to helping protect the lair from adventurers.

Maybe that was it. Odds were, if you spent long enough looking for adventurers, sooner or later you were going to find some. Adventurers didn't fight fair. They brought magic swords and rings, wizards and spells, and warriors who cut through goblin patrols as quickly as Golaka's spicy rat dumplings passed through the old chief.

Which reminded him, he still had a rat to dispose of. He headed for the kitchens.

Golaka herself was gone, but one of her helpers was there, chopping up an unidentifiable animal who had made the mistake of snooping around in the tunnels. Jig tossed the muck-soaked rat onto a nearby table.

"What are you doing with that slimy thing?"

Jig projected innocence as hard as he could. With a shrug, he said, "One of the others stole it from the kitchen. They wanted me to give it back before you noticed, so they wouldn't get in trouble."

The goblin poked at the greasy, shiny rat with a fork. "That's muck! We can't eat that." His eyes narrowed. "Who was snooping around the kitchen, anyway?"

Jig shook his head. "Porak said he'd kill me if I told." He covered his mouth and tried to look stupid. "Oops."

"Porak, was it? Golaka will want to get her hands on that one."

"Can I go now?" Jig slipped out of the kitchen without waiting for an answer. As he crossed the main cavern, he allowed himself to smile.

Surface-dwellers had an expression about the wrath of the gods. Since goblins didn't really care for gods, they had an alternate expression—they called it the wrath of the chef.

" 'Rat or the runt' indeed," Jig said with satisfaction.

Jig stopped by the privies on his way to meet Porak and the others. Waiting until nobody was looking, he knelt and grabbed a red-spotted spider the size of his hand. The spider crawled up his arm and onto his head. It gave one of Jig's ears a sharp nip before settling into his hair.

"Ow." Jig rubbed his ear. "Stupid fire-spider."

Smudge, the stupid fire-spider in question, ignored Jig's complaint. He was probably upset that Jig had neglected him all day. But since taking Smudge along on muck duty would have been unwise, Jig refused to feel guilty. The last thing he had needed was a spider who grew hot when he sensed danger. If Smudge had been around when that goblin surprised Jig from behind, they all could have gone up in flames.

Jig met the others near the cavern exit. Of the twelve goblins, Jig was easily the smallest, and he tried to avoid the worst of the shoulder-punching and mock fighting.

"Ah, Jig, there you are." Porak grinned. "Jig's going to be joining us tonight."

Unfriendly laughter spread through the group, and Jig forced himself not to cringe. Everything was going to be fine. He just had to prove himself. He could do this.

"Should we grab something to eat first?" someone asked.

"No." Porak's smile slipped, and Jig kept his face still to hide his amusement. "I think we'll avoid the kitchens tonight."

Jig wondered if anyone else guessed the origin of Porak's black eye. Not that he was going to tell them.

"Let's go," Porak ordered, cutting off any protests.

They passed through a long tunnel until they reached an old glass statue of a goblin, the marker that defined the edge of goblin territory. It had stood there for generations, and was probably as old as the mountain itself. Nobody knew who had carved the statue. Being goblins, nobody particularly cared, either. A big rock would have marked the spot equally well.

Two large goblins stood guard, if boasting about their latest sexual conquests could be considered standing guard.

Jig shivered as they passed into neutral territory. He hoped nobody had seen, but he couldn't help it. The underground inhabitants divided these tunnels among themselves. The goblins held the southern warrens. The larger hobgoblins took the warmer caverns to the west, farther from the entrance. Past the hobgoblins was the cold lake of the lizard-fish.

The lizard-fish were the worst, and goblins avoided them if they could. When food grew scarce, the chief would occasionally send goblins to the lake to hunt. This served two purposes. While the white-eyed creatures weren't pretty to look at, they *were* edible, and food was food. Since several of the hunting party usually managed to prick themselves on the lizard-fish's poisonous spines, these hunting parties also resulted in fewer mouths to feed.

Fortunately, the lizard-fish couldn't leave the lake, and an uneasy truce kept the hobgoblins out of goblin territory. Simple fear kept the goblins from trespassing in hobgoblin territory.

Jig glanced back at the statue. *That* was a true goblin warrior, one who had supposedly killed no less than three humans before an angry mage turned him into a green stain on the wall. Made of molded, and in many places chipped, black glass, he was as tall as most humans, with huge fangs that nearly touched his eyes. The nose was round like a lakestone, and his single eye was narrow and mean. A glass rag covered the other eye, which stories said had been lost to a human's sling stone. His ears were perked and wide, alert to the slightest sound. He was a *real* goblin, and even Porak paled in comparison.

Jig barely came to the statue's shoulder. His only scar was a torn ear, and that "battle" had been with another goblin who wanted to rip off Smudge's legs for fun. Jig's arms and legs were like thin sticks, and his constant squint was nothing like the mean glare most goblins wore. On top of that, his voice was too high, and he had some sort of fungus growing on his toenails.

"Torches," Porak ordered.

"This is dumb," Jig grumbled as one of the others handed out torches. "Why not run ahead to warn any intruders that we're coming? Maybe we should sing, too, in case they're blind."

Yellow nails closed on the blue-green skin of Jig's shoulder, and he yelped. Smudge grew warm and scampered to Jig's other shoulder.

"Because, young Jig, we're going to send a scout ahead to make sure everything is clear." Porak wasn't smiling. "That's called tactics." He raised his voice so the others could hear.

"You have to be smart to stay alive down here. Look at our cousin Jig, talking to himself and so distracted that I walked right up without him noticing. If I were a human, I could have killed our scout while he babbled. Then where would we be?"

Jig cringed as the others laughed and nodded. So much for proving himself.

"We have to be alert. We have to be strong. We have to be tough." With each pronouncement, Porak's grip tightened, so that by the end, Jig squirmed to get away.

"You hear me?" Porak glared at Jig. "You have to be tough." He shoved Jig into the wall.

With a harsh laugh, he added, "But even the weak have their uses. This one's going to run ahead to flush out any game. Our own little hunting dog."

Porak pulled out a set of dice, which brought

cheers from the others. "We'll stay here, to protect the lair. If you find anything, we'll be along to do the fighting. All you have to do is stay alive long enough for us to rescue you. Go get 'em, dog."

The other goblins quickly picked up the chant, some barking while others punched and kicked at him. Jig covered his head and ran, Porak's loud voice following after.

"If you see anyone, make sure you scream before they kill you."

Jig's bare feet slapped against the tunnel floor. His ears burned as he put distance between himself and the others, but their jeers seemed to follow on his heels.

"Do we really want to send a runt to do a dog's job?"

"Scrawny bitch, isn't it?"

At least now Jig understood what was going on. He knew why he had been chosen to go with the patrol tonight. They wanted him to check the tunnels so they could play their games. This way they could carouse through the night without, technically, ignoring their duty.

Actually it wasn't a bad idea, which made Jig suspect someone other than Porak had come up with it. Porak was tough and mean, but he would lose a battle of wits with his own shadow.

Jig reached up to make sure Smudge was still there. He scratched one of the spider's legs as he walked. "Too bad I can't teach you to burn on command. I'd love to slip you into Porak's trousers one of these nights."

He reconsidered. Some things were too evil even for a goblin. He couldn't do that to poor Smudge.

"If Porak were smart, he would have brought me in on his plan. How does he know I won't tell the chief what he's up to?" Jig stopped to rest for a minute. "No, even Porak isn't that stupid. If he gets in trouble, he'll know who told. Next time he'll put *me* into the muck pot."

He extinguished his torch on the floor and started walking again, taking a left at the first fork, then two rights. He let his ears and his memory guide him through the dark tunnels.

"Maybe I could blackmail him instead. Threaten to tell the chief if Porak doesn't do what I want." He grinned. Porak was big and important. If Jig could get Porak on his side, life would get a lot nicer. No more sleeping by the entrance, where the draft froze his feet every night. No more waiting at the end of the food line so that his meal was nothing but bones, gristle, and the occasional lump of fat.

"No more getting sent ahead on patrol while the others gamble."

Maybe he'd even get a real sword instead of the stupid kitchen knife he carried now. He pulled the knife out of his belt and swung at an imaginary foe. He could almost hear the hiss of the broadsword. He ducked, thrust, and attacked again.

"Help me," Porak would say as two adventurers backed him into a corner. Jig grinned and crossed the tunnel to rescue his captain. He took one adventurer from behind. The other was meaner. He put up quite a fight before Jig's sword caught him in the chest. Jig raised his weapon in triumph as the adventurer gasped and died. Back in the lair, everyone would talk about his heroic battle. They would ask him to lead patrols of his own, and say things like—

"Be patient, lad. You've gone and made me lose count. I'll have to start again."

Jig jumped. The reality of his small kitchen knife replaced his daydreams of battle and luxury. He pressed himself against the wall and swiveled his ears forward to better hear the voices ahead.

"By all the gods, do not allow me to interfere, oh wise one. Perhaps you'd like to wait while I summon a calligrapher to assist you. And you'll want an artist to paint another scene of old Earthmaker."

"Enough. We're not going anywhere until I finish my map, and I'll not be able to do that until you get out of my way."

Jig clutched his knife in both hands. Two voices. The first one sounded old and gravelly. The second was definitely human.

So what should he do? Screaming was out of the question, despite Porak's orders. Sure, it would alert the others about the intruders. It would also alert the intruders about Jig. That was a problem. Humans had longer legs, and therefore longer strides, so Jig's chances of making it back to the other goblins were slim.

He knew how long he would last against real warriors. About as long as the average fly lasted once Smudge trapped it in his web.

Speaking of Smudge, Jig didn't know if the fire-spider could sense Jig's own anxiety, or if he had heard the intruders down the tunnel, but the top of Jig's head was growing uncomfortably warm.

"It's okay. Don't worry." Jig backed away from the voices as quietly as he could. His free hand went up to pet the spider.

That turned out to be a mistake. Smudge apparently didn't see Jig's hand coming, and when his fingers touched the spider's fuzzy thorax, Smudge curled into a frightened ball. With an audible whoosh, Jig's hair lit up like oil-soaked rags.

The knife clattered to the floor. Smudge leaped away. Jig yelped and tried to beat out the flames.

Crazy shadows danced on the walls and floor, and he spotted Smudge racing toward the opposite wall. "Stupid spider," he shouted. He wasn't worried about the intruders anymore. Not with his hair ablaze. If they caught him, maybe they'd at least extinguish his head before they killed him.

"Ow, ow, ow." He smacked at the flames, trying not to burn his hands. The fire had died down when Smudge fled, and Jig soon managed to put himself out. Unfortunately the blaze had taken most of his hair with it. His scalp was tender and blistered, but he didn't seem to be bleeding.

Jig leaned against the wall and closed his eyes, trying to block out the pain. "What's the matter with you?" he whispered in Smudge's general direction. "You have eight eyes. Eight! How could you not see my hand? I'm the blind one. What were you doing up there, daydreaming? I should let Golaka make a pot pie out of you."

Smudge skittered back and climbed up his leg. As he reached Jig's waist, Jig snagged him and lifted him to eye level. The spider waved his legs and pincers, almost like he had understood Jig's halfhearted threat. Which was possible, Jig admitted. The spider was at least as smart as Porak. "That's the last time I bring you along on patrol."

Smudge's head and legs drooped.

With a disgusted sigh, Jig set the spider on his shoulder. "Just try not to set me on fire again, okay?"

Only then did it occur to Jig to wonder why he could see everything so well. His own aborted blaze had lit the tunnel well enough, but it should have ruined his dark-vision. In fact, if it weren't for the torchlight behind him, he would be completely blind.

His first theory was that Porak and the others

had come to see what was wrong. But they would have started laughing at Jig's misfortune. Since Jig heard no laughter, whoever had come up behind him wasn't a goblin. What was the expression surface-dwellers used at times like this?

"Oh, dung." He turned around.

It was the human he had heard earlier. In one hand the human held a blazing torch. The other pointed a long sword at Jig. A long, gleaming, very sharp sword. Jig bet the blade didn't wobble in its handle either.

"Draw a weapon or cry out for aid and you'll never draw breath again."

Jig blinked. What was he going to do, scramble for his kitchen knife? He should probably call for help though. Porak's orders. He had to warn the others. It was his duty.

It was an awfully big sword.

"A wise choice. Turn around, and walk into that room up there."

The human followed him to the room Jig had always thought of as the shiny room. Tiny glass tiles, no larger than his fingernails, covered the entire ceiling in sparkles of color. The ceiling domed upward, and the swirls of blue, green, and red all merged into a spectacular fireburst at the center.

Even with a sword at his back, Jig couldn't help but look up as he entered. The adventurers had a small fire going, and the reflected firelight danced on the tiles, turning them into a thousand jewels.

"What's this?" It was the gravelly voice Jig had heard earlier, and it came from a four-foot tall mountain of muscle, armor, and tangled black hair. In other words, a dwarf.

"I found him snooping up yonder passage." The human sheathed his sword. "Not much of a spy. He set himself aflame in his panic."

The dwarf laughed. In barely understandable Goblin, he asked "You lived here long?" Without waiting for an answer, he jumped to his feet and waved a large sheet of parchment in Jig's face. "We've got ourselves a room here that's thirteen and a half paces by twelve paces with a door in each wall. I don't suppose you'd be knowing which of those doors will take us to the deep tunnels?"

Jig shook his head and backed into a corner. "I was lost myself," he lied.

The human laughed again. "Probably true, Darnak. Even for a goblin, he has the look of a kitchen drudge. Perhaps a bit thick in the head as well."

Darnak shook his head. "I've thought the same of you from time to time, Barius Wendelson. That doesn't make you any less dangerous."

"How dare you speak to me in such tones?" All traces of mirth vanished from Barius's face. He started to take a step forward, but Darnak beat him to it, leaving him with one foot in the air and no place to put it if he didn't want to step on the dwarf.

"I've known you since you were a stripling," Darnak said, grabbing an iron-banded club and waving it under Barius's nose. "Prince or no, I'll still crack your skull if need be."

While they bickered, Jig took the opportunity to look around. He had no doubt that their quarrel would end instantly if he tried to run, but at least he could get a better idea what he was up against.

The human was . . . polished was the best word Jig could come up with. His chain mail gleamed silver, every link a mirrored ring. The jeweled hilt of his sword was wrapped in gold wire, and the pommel had been molded into the shape of a lion's head. His knee-high boots were soft black leather, and the purple velvet tights looked as expensive as the rest of the outfit. They also looked ridiculous and uncomfortable, but who was Jig to criticize human fashion?

Barius was strong, broad in the shoulders and trim around the waist. What Jig had first taken to be a black hat was actually his hair, cut in a perfectly straight circle around his head. His goatee was trimmed into a point so sharp you could use it for a weapon.

The dwarf looked the meaner of the two. The scale mail he wore under his white robe appeared battered but well cared for. Jig could see where many of the scales had been replaced over time. Likewise, his war club was nicked in several places, as though it had turned aside sword blades or crushed more than a few skulls. As for Darnak himself, a black tangle of hair hid most of his face. His skin was a leathery brown color. A crooked nose, almost as large as a goblin's, poked over a bushy mustache and beard. Jig could see two piggish eyes hidden beneath caterpillar brows.

Jig saw a third member to their party as he looked around. A skinny elf sat by the fire with his knees to his chest. He ignored the argument, the goblin, everything but the flames. His old trousers and torn shirt were as poor as Barius's clothes were fine, and his red hair was cut short and ragged. His face was odd, and it took several seconds for Jig to figure out why. Surface types insisted on wearing at least eight layers of clothing, which made Jig wonder how many hours they spent dressing themselves. All those clothes made it harder to tell, but if he wasn't mistaken, "he" was actually a "she."

What her role in the group was, Jig hadn't a clue. She was clearly the least threatening, but she could still be dangerous. She looked nothing like the graceful, slender elves of legend. For a second, he

wondered if she might be some subrace he had
never heard of. He knew there were different types
of elves: forest elves, mountain elves, and so on.
But urchin elves?

"So what do we do with him, Your Majesty?"
Darnak asked.

That caught Jig's full attention. Since the elf was
a she, there was only one "him" they could be
talking about.

"Safest to slay him," Barius said slowly. "Though
perhaps he could be of use to us. Idiot or no, he
knows more of these tunnels than we do. At worst,
he can precede us to lull the suspicions of any creatures we encounter. Still, I dislike the idea of a
goblin in our group."

Jig crossed his arms and clung to hope. As long
as he was alive, there was still a chance. Porak and
the others might still find him. The other goblins
were armed, and they outnumbered the intruders
four to one. Even goblins might triumph at those
odds. All they had to do was come looking. If they
bothered to notice Jig hadn't come back. If they
weren't too caught up in their games. If they had
the brains to figure out what was going on.

Jig groaned and sat down on the floor. He was,
without a doubt, a dead goblin.

CHAPTER 2

Barius's Vital Weakness

Jig had endured many unpleasant things, from cleaning up after drunk goblins who didn't make it to the privy in time to those nights when Golaka decided to sing as she cooked. None of it had prepared Jig to sit helpless while his captors debated whether or not to kill him.

"He could help us," Darnak said. "Look at Riana. She picked the lock on that gate just as neat as you could ask. Rumor has it the path we want is 'cloaked in watery darkness'—maybe he knows where it is."

"Perhaps he does. But a world of difference exists between an elf, even one of her status, and a goblin." Barius glanced at Riana, who listened to the conversation as intently as Jig. "You should be watching for other monsters, girl."

Other monsters. That they thought of Jig as a monster cheered him up a little. Monster was a step up from "nuisance," which was how most adventurers categorized Jig's kind.

"To invite a goblin to join us is to invite treachery, cowardice, and deceit into our beds," Barius pronounced. "What help he could provide does not justify the risk."

"Ha. As if you've ever gotten anyone into your bed without flashing around your gold and your title."

Jig tried to bite back a laugh and wound up choking instead. Barius whirled while Jig coughed and fought for breath. The human's pale lips thinned, but then he shrugged and turned back to the dwarf. *He doesn't know I understand their language,* Jig realized, thankful for the days when the older goblins would sit around and test the younger ones' use of Human, the dominant language of the surface-dwellers. Each misspoken word earned a kick to the behind.

"Knowing what your enemy says could keep you alive," one goblin had said as Jig lay sprawled on the floor. With a hard laugh, he added, "But it probably won't."

More to protect his bruised body than to gain an advantage over his future enemies, Jig had learned quickly.

Before Prince Barius could resume his argument, Darnak held up a meaty hand and said, "I'd just as soon send him to hell, Your Majesty, as I would a snake who slipped into the palace. But even a snake has its uses. You've always been quick to throw things away without thinking. This is no game, and we could get killed down here faster than you can piss yourself."

"Granted," Barius said, sounding like he wanted to hit something. "But perhaps you've not heard your own words? That is precisely the reason I feel we should eliminate the goblin."

"Aye. Kill the snake if you want, but then tell me how you plan to find its hole?"

Barius started to answer, then stopped himself as the dwarf's words sank in.

"That's right," Darnak said. "Damn me if I'm not starting to chip through that granite skull of yours. Who knows how many of them are hiding up these tunnels? For myself, I'd rather know a bit more about what we're walking into. Otherwise you're likely to find yourself stepping in something unpleasant."

Jig kept his face still as they glanced at him. They wanted to use him as . . . what? A guide? If so, they would likely be disappointed.

He knew some of the tunnels, of course. Every goblin did. Every goblin who survived past their twelfth year, that was.

That was the age when each goblin was taken up to neutral territory and abandoned. It was a trial to see who had learned the layout of the tunnels and corridors that twisted and branched back on one another. Many spent days wandering in the darkness. Jig himself had taken nearly eight hours to find his way back to the lair. But he had been smart. A few weeks before, he had bribed several of the older goblins with food swiped from Golaka's kitchen. In return, they told him the tricks of the tunnels. He learned how to feel the slope of the ground and to listen for the echoes that told of open caverns. He learned the general layout well enough to avoid the hobgoblins or the lizard-fish and their lake.

He also heard many stories of the horrors that guarded the hidden tunnel to the lower caverns, and the gruesome death that waited for any goblin foolish enough to wander alone and lost through the tunnels.

"Worse than lizard-fish?" he had asked, trying not to tremble.

The older goblins laughed. "When your skin shrivels up and your bones tear out of your flesh, you'll wish you'd died a pleasant death among the lizard-fish."

Forty-one goblins, including Jig, went into the darkness that day. Nineteen made it back. Those with torches died first, since torchlight served as a beacon for hobgoblins and other creatures. Patrols found the bodies of a few, some killed by hobgoblin swords, others by arrows or the occasional beast that roamed the deeper tunnels. But the ugliness of those deaths was nothing compared to Jig's nightmares about the others, the ones who were never found. There were many stories about the inhabitants of the lower tunnels. Not a single one ended happily, and most made murder by hobgoblins sound like a pleasant way to spend an afternoon.

Jig had memorized everything he could learn about these tunnels, and he could find his way blind and deaf. He had moved through the darkness, one hand always on the wall, relying only on his memory. That day, memory had proven stronger than fear and confusion, and Jig had made it home.

But the adventurers wanted him to lead them beyond goblin territory and the neutral tunnels. Once he crossed those borders, he would be as lost as any surface-dweller.

What could he do? He wouldn't lead them back to the goblin lair. His job was to *protect* the lair. Even if Porak and the others had sent him off on his own, he still had to try to stop the adventurers.

Unless he could trick them. He rubbed the tip of one fang as he considered an idea. If he lured the adventurers to the lair without saying where they were going, it wouldn't matter how powerful or strong they were. The goblins would overwhelm them with sheer force of numbers. Many goblins would die, of course. Goblins always died. That was a defining trait of goblinhood.

Wait—maybe he didn't have to risk goblins at all. What if he led them west, toward the hobgoblins? Hobgoblins were bigger, stronger, and better fighters. Jig could escape in the confusion and run back to the lair. By then Porak would have returned as well. He'd probably be laughing about how Jig had run off and gotten himself lost. Jig could imagine the look of shock on Porak's face when Jig not only turned up alive, but told them all how he had single-handedly led *three* adventurers to their deaths. Not even Porak had that kind of victory to his name.

What was the best way to lure them into hobgoblin territory? He needed to find out what they wanted. Treasure, obviously. Every adventurer wanted treasure. They seemed to want it more than food or water or air to breathe. But what else? From the gems on Barius's sword, this lot was already wealthier than the average adventurers. What reward would fuel their greed so they would rush to their deaths without a thought?

His ears shot straight up. Finding out what the adventurers wanted would have to wait. If he wasn't mistaken, those faint voices he heard from the tunnel were coming closer, and they sounded like goblins. His heart sank. They sounded like *drunk* goblins. Soon the others noticed as well.

"So what's this, then?" Darnak asked, turning toward Jig. "More of you? Planning to wait until your friends come along to take us on, were you?"

"We should slay him now, before he can warn his comrades," Barius said.

"No!" Jig cried before he could stop himself.

Their eyes widened. "The little bugger speaks

our tongue." Darnak laughed. "Thought you'd sit there and spy on us?"

Jig knew what a real hero would do. A hero would scream something defiant, wrestle Darnak's club away, and use it against the dwarf and the human. A hero might even slay them both before making his escape. Of course, Jig knew all the goblin songs, so he knew what happened to goblin heroes. While he was busy going for Darnak's club, Barius would stab him from behind, and that would be the end of Jig. Unless he was lucky enough to make it into a song.

He had no desire to be a hero. He only wanted to go home, curl up with a hot bowl of lizard-egg soup, and feed dead cockroaches to Smudge.

The spider had resumed his perch on Jig's head, where he grew uncomfortably nervous. Jig didn't worry too much about the heat. Goblin skin was thick, and now that his hair was gone, he should be a bit more fireproof. Still he stroked the firespider with one finger to calm him.

"Well? Have you anything to say in your defense?" Barius strode across the room and looked down at Jig, a sneer of disgust wrinkling his aristocratic features like a prune.

A real hero would muster up something clever on which to spend his last breath. He would face death like a man, with courage. He certainly would *not* kick the young prince square in the vitals.

Jig was no hero. As Barius tumbled to the ground, Jig whirled and sprinted up the corridor as fast as he could. Behind him the dwarf swore, the prince moaned, and the elf giggled.

He had to catch the others. If he could reach Porak in time, they might have a chance. Because these were the tunnels Jig knew. Three of the doorways in the shiny room led down passageways that eventually merged into one. The fourth led to the surface.

From what Darnak said, they hadn't explored the other three passages yet. They would expect Jig to return with help, but they'd expect that help to come as single mad rush.

Twelve goblins. Three passageways. That meant four goblins through each doorway. If they timed things right, the adventurers would face an attack from three directions at once. Even goblins couldn't mess up a plan of such beauty.

He wished Porak and the others would stop singing. They would call their deaths down upon their heads if they didn't shut up.

"Quiet!" Jig shouted as he neared the group. "Intruders. Adventurers, three of them behind me. We need to head back to the junction." He stopped to catch his breath.

The song broke off in midchorus. "Who's that? Jig? Running back with his tail between his legs already?"

"Jig! We thought an ogre had gotten you," someone said, giggling.

"No, I thought a bat had mistaken him for a bug."

A deeper voice said, "But it couldn't be Jig. Jig would never be foolish enough to tell me what to do."

Jig saw orange torchlight on the tunnel walls up ahead. "Porak, you don't understand. There are intruders back there!"

As Porak came into view, Jig bit back everything else he was going to say and retreated toward the wall. He had forgotten how mean Porak got when he was drunk. He was mean sober, too, but alcohol made him even worse. Bottle in one hand, Porak stomped up the tunnel and grabbed Jig's throat.

"Intruders or not, you don't command here. Not unless you want to fight me for it." He squeezed. "Well?"

Jig shook his head, feeling stupid. What had he been thinking? That Porak would be grateful for his help? That everyone would thank him for his advice and follow his plan? That wasn't the goblin way. The goblin way was to charge in like idiots, following whoever was biggest and loudest, and in this case, drunkest. Being this close to Porak meant his every breath filled Jig's nostrils with the scent of fungus-distilled klak beer.

"Come on," Porak shouted. "Most likely our little pup got too close to the entrance and was frightened by his shadow. But we'll check it out anyway. Weapons ready."

Porak's hand moved to Jig's shoulder. He shoved the smaller goblin so hard that Jig nearly fell. "And you can lead us, pup. Take us to these intruders of yours."

He considered trying to explain his plan again, but one look at Porak's angry, bloodshot eyes killed that idea. There would be no clever ambush. No, they would fight like goblins and die like goblins, the latter being the inevitable result of the former.

He looked at Smudge, who still emitted dry waves of heat from Jig's shoulder. He thought about tossing the fire-spider into the shadows. No sense letting him get squished in the upcoming massacre. But he changed his mind.

"After all, if it weren't for you, I wouldn't be in this mess," he muttered. Smudge lifted his head as if to protest, then turned so he could see where they were going.

"Come on," Jig said wearily. "They're up this way." This was turning into a very bad day.

* * *

Where were they? Jig had almost reached the shiny room, and still no sign of the adventurers. Some of the more intoxicated goblins had begun to snicker, and a few were even singing again. Jig's heart beat so fast it was like a buzz in his chest. On top of that, he was going to have eight heat blisters on his shoulder, each the size of a certain spider's foot. This wasn't right. Something should have happened by now.

Behind him, the goblins started in on the chorus for the third time. Jig folded his ears forward, trying to block out the sounds of "101 Deaths for a Goblin Hero," but it didn't help. What kind of stupid song was that, anyway? He bet dwarven songs didn't all end with the dwarves getting their heads cut off or being trampled by horses or catching a poisoned arrow in the eye. "Only goblins," he grumbled.

The tunnel ahead was dark. "They must have put out their fire."

Porak shook his head. "Hear that? Jig's invisible friends are hiding. Maybe he frightened them off."

The laughter of the goblins briefly interrupted the song, and Jig flushed so hot he felt like a firespider himself. Trying to ignore Porak and the others, he found himself singing along as he crept up the tunnel.

> *He can run into battle and fall upon a spear.*
> *He can peek around a corner, catch an arrow in the ear,*
> *Or be chewed up by a dragon he just happened to offend,*
> *There are oh so many ways a goblin hero meets his end.*

His mouth dried out from fear. Every step he took was torture. What was their plan? Whatever it was, Jig guessed it would result in a lot of dead goblins. As "101 Deaths" continued, Jig found himself thinking of new lyrics.

The human's shining sword could slice off my poor head,
Or the dwarf could use his club; either way I end up dead.
Only a few more steps and every one of us is doomed.
Why oh why oh why did I go into that room?

"What's the matter Jig, afraid of the dark?" Porak raised a torch and shoved past Jig. "Nothing to worry about. Let a real goblin go first to show you that—"

Jig didn't get to hear what Porak wanted to show him. With a loud grunt, Porak spun and fell. The shadows flickered as his torch dropped to the ground. Suddenly the others were rushing forward, swords and clubs waving in the air as they charged. Porak himself had an arrow sticking out of his shoulder as he pulled himself up and stumbled toward the room ahead. Jig tried not to think about how close he had been standing to the goblin captain. A foot to one side, and that arrow could have hit him. He backed into the wall and waited for the rest of the goblins to pass by. If they were the "real goblins," let them be first to the slaughter.

But only four or five goblins made it into the room. Where were the rest? Jig looked back, confused.

He saw one of the drunker goblins stumble to the ground, not an unusual thing by itself, but at least half of the group had fallen, and nobody was getting back up. He couldn't see well enough to figure out what was causing their collective loss of balance, though.

Hurrying back, he grabbed a fallen goblin and shook him hard. His fingers touched warm blood on the goblin's back. Slowly, Jig released his grip. He could shake and prod all he wanted, but this goblin wouldn't be joining the fight. Jig had never been in battle before, but he was fairly certain this was one dead goblin. The arrow sticking out of his back like a roasting spit provided all the evidence Jig needed.

Sticking out of the back . . . Jig flattened himself to the floor as that sank in. Something buzzed over his head, and another goblin fell. The few who had survived long enough to enter the room weren't doing too well either. Jig heard Darnak the dwarf shouting merrily, stopping only to punctuate his war cries with the crunch of wood against bone. He also heard Barius yelling, "Back, you unwashed creatures, you monstrous cowards of the dark. Back, I say!"

Even if Jig hadn't recognized the prince's voice, he doubted anyone else could sound that pretentious and swing a sword at the same time. But if the prince and the dwarf were both up ahead, who was behind them in the dark? The elf? Elves were supposed to be fearsome archers, but the girl hadn't carried a bow.

Another arrow shot past, and Jig decided perhaps this wasn't the best time to ponder such mysteries. He dropped to the ground and crawled toward Porak's dropped torch. His ears were useless with all the shouting and dying going on, and he could barely see a thing in this blasted darkness. Not that he'd be able to see much better in the

light, but maybe he would at least know which way
to run.

He crawled past several more bodies to get to
the room. Every time an arrow shot past, he
cringed and stopped moving. Just a little farther.
Once he made it to the doorway, whoever was back
there would have to stop shooting, or else risk hitting their own party. *Unless they're a really good
shot.* He tried not to think about that.

After an eternity of crawling through blood, bodies, and the occasional squishy thing he didn't want
to identify, Jig finally made it. He pulled himself
into the room and rolled away from the doorway.

Of the goblins who had made it this far, most
lay senseless on the floor. Senseless, and in several
cases handless, armless, or headless. A few groaned
and swore in the general direction of the
adventurers.

To Jig's shock, three goblins were still up and
fighting. One sounded like Porak, still attacking and
shouting despite the arrow in his shoulder. The
other two were too busy with the dwarf to say
much.

Jig wondered how long it would take for the last
few goblins to die. When Barius slipped in a puddle
of blood, Darnak moved close to protect him. The
dwarf knocked Porak's sword aside, deflecting a
blow that could have split the prince's head. Before
Porak could recover, Darnak dropped his club,
caught Porak's arms, and flung him into the other
goblin, knocking them both off balance and giving
Barius time to regain his footing.

Before the fight could continue, Jig heard two
sharp twangs, and both goblins fell. One thrashed
about on the floor, but Porak groaned and tried to
rise. Two arrows stuck out of his body, but he still

lived. As Jig cowered in the corner, all he could think was that being a "real warrior" seemed to involve a great deal of pain and blood loss. Darnak kicked Porak's sword away, then walked over to greet the archer in the doorway.

This wasn't the elven girl. Jig couldn't tell exactly what the shimmering form was, but it was too large to be Riana. He stared, rubbed his eyes, and tried again to focus. The outline of the archer ran and shifted like water, blurring into the shadows. No wonder none of the goblins had noticed him. If he was this hard to see in torchlight, he would have been all but invisible in the dark tunnels.

As he entered the room, the shadow-shimmer vanished as if a curtain had been drawn back, revealing a slender human. He looked around, nodded curtly at Darnak and Barius, and set about unstringing his bow.

"Nice shooting, Ryslind," said Darnak.

Barius sniffed. "Though as always, brother, your approach to battle leaves much to be desired in the way of honor."

The one called Ryslind began to examine the fallen goblins. Those few who were still alive he dragged into the center of the room. The rest he left as they were. "If you prefer, I will let you seek the rod by yourself. Don't worry, when I see our father again, I'll be sure to tell him you died with your precious *honor*."

His voice was similar to Barius's. Both spoke in a clear, polished baritone, both had the same slight sneer—though that sneer was much more pronounced when they spoke to each other. But there was something more in Ryslind's voice . . . more power, a presence and self-assurance Barius lacked. It was that same dangerous edge Porak had always tried to project. But for all Porak's bullying and threatening, Ryslind made him look like a harmless kitten.

Ryslind's hand shot out and grabbed Jig's ear. As he was jerked to his feet, he had the unwanted opportunity to study the newcomer up close.

He smelled of strange spices, and Jig tried not to sneeze. Ryslind was as tall as his brother, but of a more slender build. He wore a loose black robe, tied at the waist with a simple white rope. A short sword hung from one hip, a quiver of arrows from the other. Green tattoos covered the backs of his hands and vanished into his sleeves. They looked like writing, but the spiking, angular characters were no language Jig had ever seen. Not that Jig was much of a scholar. Ryslind was completely bald, lacking even eyebrows or eyelashes. Jig wondered if he owned a fire-spider.

Ryslind's eyes ran the length of Jig's body, and the goblin stiffened. His fear grew stronger, if that was possible, for those eyes glowed with a soft red light. Taken with the robes and the tattoos, those eyes meant Jig was standing far closer to a living wizard than he wanted to. He wondered if he could subtly put a bit of space between himself and Ryslind. A hundred miles or so should suffice.

"No wounds on this one." Barius shoved Jig into the middle of the room. On his shoulder, Smudge flared again, and Jig thought he smelled burning skin. "Probably lost his weapon and spent the whole fight hiding in the corner."

"This goblin shows more sense than yourself, brother." Ryslind clasped his hands together. "Had the one who escaped you before been armed, you would have far worse than bruises to show for your carelessness. As is, you are fortunate I was in place before he led his fellows to attack."

"Here now, we won and that's the only thing

that matters when you get down to it," Darnak interrupted. "Let me tie these three up before they try anything else. Barius, why don't you go find out where Riana's hiding herself?"

"Find her yourself, friend dwarf." Barius strode over to face the surviving goblins. "One of these creatures will pay for his assault on my . . . dignity."

"So that's what they're naming it these days," Darnak muttered.

Beside Jig, Porak groaned. "What's he talking about?" The third goblin shrugged, then groaned as the movement aggravated the arrow wound in his gut. Jig tried to look invisible. The prince was close enough for Jig to see the hatred in his eyes, and he wondered what sort of revenge Barius had in mind. Knowing humans, it probably involved sharp knives, hot coals, and a great deal of pain and unpleasantness. Pain for Jig, that was. Barius would no doubt enjoy himself immensely.

"Stupid coward," Porak grumbled. "You led us into a trap. An ambush. Why didn't you warn us about the archer?"

"I didn't know," Jig protested.

"You didn't know. Most of my patrol wiped out, and you didn't know." He snorted in disgust.

"Silence," Barius snapped.

"Silence yourself, human," Porak said.

Jig groaned. He didn't think the prince spoke Goblin—he probably considered it beneath him to learn such a "primitive" language—but there was no way he could have missed the contempt in Porak's voice.

Barius's jeweled sword moved slowly through the air to point at the goblins. Behind him, Ryslind sighed. "You haven't lost your penchant for melodrama."

Melodramatic or not, that sword dripped blue-black goblin blood, and Jig wasn't about to laugh.

"Answer me one question, goblins." Barius paced back and forth, studying each of their faces. "Which of you assaulted me in your cowardly attempt to escape?"

Without thinking about the consequences, without seeing anything but the tip of that blood-soaked sword, Jig's hand raised as if of its own will. Raised, and pointed at Porak.

"What?" Enraged, Porak lunged at Jig.

Jig squealed. Smudge leaped from his shoulder and scurried into the corner. But Porak never finished his attack.

Barius's gloved hand caught Porak by the belt and flung him back onto the floor. He landed next to one of the bodies. Dazed, he clutched his head, and his eyes fell upon the hatchet the dead goblin had dropped. Snatching up his new weapon, Porak charged.

Jig scooped up his fire-spider and set him on his unburned shoulder as he watched Barius take one step back, then another, flicking his sword out of the way of Porak's mad swings. On the third step, that sword dipped beneath the axe, then snapped back up to throat level. Porak either didn't see it or was moving to fast to stop. Either way, the result was the same, and even with Jig's poor vision, he could see blue blood spray the prince's tunic.

The other surviving goblin yelled in panic and fled. Jig started to follow, but movement to one side made him hesitate. The wizard walked with grim purpose after the goblin.

"Stop him!" Barius yelled.

Glowing eyes glanced at Jig in passing, saw that he wasn't moving, and snapped back to the retreating goblin. One hand flicked lazily at his quiver. An arrow floated into the air, rotated to point down the tunnel, and shot off after the goblin. Loud cursing signaled the accuracy of Ryslind's magic.

Jig wondered why Ryslind even bothered with the bow. Perhaps killing people with magic took more energy. Or maybe the bow was simply more fun.

"What are you waiting for?" Barius demanded. "Finish him off. Slay him before he can warn his fellows."

Ryslind shook his head. "Mage-shot such as this has a limited range." He held up his hand before Barius could answer. "And before you protest, dear brother, I suggest you try to fling an arrow three hundred yards up a tunnel that takes at least two sharp turns, and see what you can hit."

"But he'll tell the others," Barius said, his polished voice turning nasal, almost whiny. "Within the hour, we'll face a swarm of the vile things."

"Not bloody likely," Darnak said from the tunnel. He stepped back into the room, dragging the elven girl by her thin wrist. "Not after the pasting we gave 'em. Ryslind just handed them one more reason to avoid us." He surveyed the carnage, counting corpses on his fingers. "No, they won't likely bother us again. My thinking is that we'd best be getting ready for the real monsters."

He scowled when he saw the prince standing over Porak's body. "And what might have happened to that one while I was gone, Barius?"

" 'Twas an honorable fight. The prisoner grabbed an axe and attacked. I had no choice but to defend myself."

"True," Ryslind said. "A fair fight, despite the fact that the goblin had been shot twice. Likewise,

I expect it was pure chance that my brother flung the prisoner within arm's reach of a weapon. Most noble indeed."

Barius whirled. "What about you? Sending magicked arrows after fleeing prisoners?"

"Simply following orders. You are the elder, after all." His voice was flat, but Jig sensed more menace in those easy words than anything else the wizard had said so far.

Darnak sat down and stared at the ceiling. "Earthmaker, if you wanted penance out of me, why couldn't it be something simple? Send me to move the Serpent River or chase the orcs out of the northlands. How did I offend you so that you led me here with these two louts?"

That quick prayer finished, he grabbed a leather knapsack and rummaged through the contents. Jig saw rations, clothes, a whetstone, a bedroll, a large hammer . . . the dwarf carried an entire shop on his back. "Aha." Darnak plunged a hand into the pack and seized a length of rope. He cut off about ten feet or so, which he tossed to Barius.

"Tie that last one up before he runs after his friends." With that, he began the momentous task of cramming everything back into his pack.

Jig's hands were jerked behind his back and bound tightly enough to scrape skin from his wrists. When Barius was done, six feet of rope stretched out behind Jig like a leash. The prince grabbed the other end and dragged Jig toward the rest of the adventurers.

In passing, he kicked the body of Captain Porak. "That's the last goblin who tried to flee from me. Keep that in mind if you're harboring thoughts of escape."

Jig noticed that Barius didn't say anything about *how* his prisoner had escaped. He still couldn't believe his luck at the adventurers' mistake. If they had recognized Jig as the goblin who had escaped before, nothing would have stopped Barius from killing him.

On further thought, their mistake wasn't as surprising as it appeared. After all, Jig wouldn't have been able to tell the two humans apart if they weren't dressed so differently. And to them, goblins were little more than pests. If a bug bit you, you slapped it. You didn't stop to see whether *this* was the bug with the torn ear, or if it was bigger than the other bug who had been buzzing around your ear an hour before.

"Easy there," Darnak said. "He's a prisoner now, and the gods expect civilized treatment from folks such as us."

"I doubt very much that they would treat us with the same courtesy," Barius said.

Jig thought he heard the girl snort, but he wasn't sure. Still Barius was right. If the situation had been reversed, there would have been none of this tying of the wrists or honorable combat. Goblins didn't waste time on that nonsense. Especially when they were hungry.

"Your friend spoke Human, goblin," said Darnak. "Do you?"

Jig nodded.

"Excellent. I'm called Brother Darnak Stonesplitter, tutor and scribe to their majesties Barius and Ryslind Wendelson, seventh and eighth sons of King Wendel and Queen Jeneve of Adenkar." With a nod at the girl, he said, "That's Riana.

"You try to betray us, we'll kill you. Same holds true if you try to escape. I don't like it, but we can't have you running loose, telling everyone we're here. But if you cooperate, I'll do my best to see you're still breathing at the end of the day."

"Enough of this," Barius said. "We should get moving. The rod would be in our hands already if you hadn't been so determined to map out every inch of this underground tomb."

"Never underestimate the usefulness of a good map," Darnak snapped. "Try walking through the iron mines of the northern peninsula and you'll quickly come to appreciate my quill. If you ever find your way back out, that is."

Very tentatively, Jig asked, "Will you let me go when you find whatever it is you want?"

"Of course."

Jig nodded as if he believed it. If it were just Darnak, he might have taken the dwarf's word. He seemed to take this honor stuff seriously, and so far, he had argued for keeping Jig alive. Of the four adventurers, that made him Jig's favorite. But the others clearly didn't want a goblin around. Not that Jig blamed them. Were he in charge, his first move after the battle would have been to kill the prisoners. Much simpler that way.

Still, how hard would it be to wait until the dwarf went off on another errand? Then it was a matter of letting Jig "accidentally" get his hands on a weapon, just like Porak.

"So what is it you're looking for?" He hoped they would say gold and treasure, but he didn't expect anything that simple. Treasure would be so much easier to find. Jig knew where at least one goblin hid his collected coins, and there had to be more tucked throughout the tunnels. Of all the adventuring parties who came into the mountain, most were satisfied with stealing the treasure their fallen predecessors had left behind. He could lead them to a few stashes and maybe they would let him go.

But there were a few groups for whom treasure

wasn't enough. Barius had said something about a rod. Jig had a very bad feeling that he knew what they wanted.

In a voice so respectful that Jig didn't recognize it, Barius said, "We seek the Rod of Creation."

CHAPTER 3

History and Harmony

"The Rod of Creation," Jig repeated. Every goblin knew of it, but no goblin knew anything *about* it. Or rather, they all knew the same three things. First, the rod was ancient, powerful magic. Second, it had been hidden in this mountain ages ago to keep it safe. Finally, trying to steal the rod was an elaborate but foolproof way to commit suicide.

"Surely you've heard the song," Darnak said. He had been attempting to sketch the ceiling's design onto his map. Setting quill and parchment aside, he coughed to clear his throat, took a drink from his wineskin, and began to sing in a low, rumbling voice.

> *There was a mage named Ellnorein*
> *Who lived in times long past.*
> *A merrier man was rarely seen,*
> *For he made magic last.*
>
> *One day he met a lonely queen,*
> *A lass as pure as gold.*

His eye for beauty was quite keen,
So he said in this bold:

A wizard am I, whom many dread,
With power like a God.
So come with me to yonder bed
And see my mighty rod.

"Darnak, please," shouted Barius, drowning out the dwarf's song. "What is this dwarven nonsense of which you sing?"

"It demeans the very memory of the wizard Ell-norein," added Ryslind.

Jig blinked. Truth be told, he had been looking forward to the next verse. Maybe he could convince Darnak to sing the rest of the song later, when the humans weren't listening. Goblins would like this kind of song. Assuming he ever made it home to share it with them.

"Allow me," Barius said. His voice was pure and perfect, a silver bell to Darnak's hunting horn.

Ages past, the high gods clashed,
The skies turned black and lightning flashed.
We men were naught but pawns who fought
And oh the terror that was wrought
As war swept o'er this world so vast.

The gods chose nine from all mankind
To be wizards of the blackest kind.
They pooled their might, from darkest night
They summoned dragons to roam and fight,
And in their wake the widows pined.

The gods' war ended, their quarrel they mended,
And mankind their victims tended.
But wizards' greed had fed their need,

For power greater than dragon steeds.
And so another war portended.

But in that age of the bloody mage,
There came an old and tired sage,
Who raised his eyes toward blackened skies,
And spoke a spell to terrorize
Those butchers born of gods' own rage.

The dragons fled, the nine fell dead,
The power from their broken bodies bled
Into a wand, which he had planned
To bury deep in a faraway land,
That it would stay safe once he lay dead.

Barius let his voice trail off on the final note, and his eyes closed, as if overwhelmed by the beauty of his own voice. Ryslind immediately broke in, saying, "First of all, as any tome will tell you, there were *twelve* Mage-Gods, not nine. You're confusing Ellnorein with a completely different tale. Furthermore, that last stanza should begin, 'The spell was spoke, their powers broke, the mages died in sickly smoke.'"

"Nonsense," Barius snapped. " 'The spell was *spoke*?' What bard would dare set such a clumsy rhyme to song?"

"Pah. Neither has the gut-ripping style of the dwarf version."

Jig looked from Barius to Darnak, then to Ryslind. "So what you're saying is that Ellnorein was a wizard?"

They stared at him.

"Did you not hear my song? The *Epic of Ellnorein* is famous. Surely even here you've heard of the great mage who healed the world after the God-Wars."

Jig didn't know what to say, so he just stood there.

Barius started to protest further, but Darnak interrupted. "The gist is this. Ellnorein was a mighty wizard, but he's dead now. Before he went, he trapped a goodly bit of power in his wand."

"Rod," Ryslind corrected. "The bards said 'wand' to make the rhyme work. But it was a rod, about three feet long and made of simple wood."

Darnak rolled his eyes. "So he put that power into a rod. The Rod of Creation. The power in that thing was the same magic the gods used to bring dragons into the world. According to legend, Ellnorein used it to make this whole mountain out of nothing. Pulled it out of the ground in a single day, then carved out these here tunnels to protect the rod after he was gone. Didn't want anyone else to get their hands on it, you see. Earthmaker only knows what guards the rod today."

"A dragon," Jig said.

Silence.

"What . . . what did you say?" Darnak asked softly.

"A dragon," said Ryslind. "Ironic, yet there's a certain logic to Ellnorein's choice. The magic used to create dragonkind could also destroy them, so what creature would have greater cause to keep the rod safe?"

Not everyone reacted to Jig's revelation with Ryslind's cool appreciation. Riana's wide eyes stared at Jig in disbelief, and Darnak whistled softly.

"We knew we faced an opponent of some power," Barius said.

"An opponent of some power?" Darnak glanced heavenward. "Lad, you've either got the greatest gift of understatement ever seen in a human, or else you've not the slightest idea what you're talking about. You'll be lucky if your precious sword doesn't snap like a twig against a dragon's scales. As for Ryslind, he may know how to toss magic about, but a dragon *is* magic. Throwing spells at one is like pissing on a forest fire. Either way, you're going to burn. We'll need Earthmaker's blessing to steal the rod from one of those beasts."

There was that name again. "Is Earthmaker another adventurer?" Jig asked.

This time it was Darnak's turn to stare at Jig. "Is that a joke? For if so, it's in poor taste."

"Silas Earthmaker is his god," Riana explained.

"Will he help you fight Straum?" When nobody answered, Jig added, "That's the dragon's name."

Darnak shook his head. "Earthmaker expects every man to prove himself. He'll not interfere in a fight, even when the odds are against us."

"Oh. He doesn't sound like much help." He saw Riana cringe.

His hand resting on the handle of his club, Darnak asked, "What would you be knowing of gods, goblin?"

Jig started to answer, but closed his mouth when he saw Riana shake her head. "Nothing," he said meekly. That seemed to satisfy the dwarf. Darnak turned back to the humans, leaving Jig to study Riana and wonder again what she was doing here. To judge by the way the others ignored her, she wasn't a friend. She had done nothing during the fight, so she wasn't here to help during combat. In fact, the only thing she *had* done was hide and stay out of the way. Which wasn't a bad example for Jig to follow.

So he sat down against the wall and tried to wrap his brain around exactly what this party wanted to do. To steal the rod from Straum's own hoard was unthinkable. As Darnak had said, their best efforts would do little more than annoy the great beast, and the most they could hope for was a swift death by flame, tooth, or talon. If the dragon was in a bad mood, he had other ways to dispose of those who annoyed him. Jig knew of tales wherein Straum had stolen the very souls of his enemies. Others he simply turned over to the Necromancer, the sorcerous master of the dead who some said dwelled beneath these very tunnels.

This would make a marvelous song: "The Raiders of Straum's Lair and Their Long, Painful Deaths." Goblins everywhere would sing about this quest as they ate their evening meals. Insanity. Jig had wondered about Barius's state of mind from the moment he heard the prince speak. As for the wizard, well, all wizards were a bit crazy. That much was common knowledge. So Jig understood how these two might believe they could successfully raid Straum's lair. But the dwarf looked sane. For a dwarf, at least. And what could have convinced an elf to throw away the virtual immortality of their race for such a futile—no, such a *stupid*—quest?

"Ellnorein placed the rod here to keep it safe?" Jig asked.

"Now you're getting it," Darnak answered.

"And Ellnorein was a smart man?"

"The wisest mage of his time," Barius said. "Indeed, perhaps the wisest man in all of human history."

"And you want to take the rod away, even though Ellnorein went to such lengths to keep you from doing that?"

"Er . . ." The dwarf glanced away.

"That is precisely our intention," Barius said. "To rescue the rod is my quest. Tradition and honor require me to prove myself to my father the king, as well as to his subjects. My six brothers before me each undertook such a quest, but by retrieving the Rod of Creation, I shall prove myself a man of more courage and strength than the best of them."

Jig tried to understand this. Less than half of all goblin children survived into adulthood. Scavengers claimed many, and others died the first time they ventured out of their territory. The rite of adulthood claimed plenty as well, but that tradition was a matter of survival. The goblin who couldn't find his way through the tunnels was a danger to everyone, and bound to get himself killed sooner or later. Better sooner, so he wouldn't take anyone else with him. But the tradition Barius described was like teaching a child to swim by throwing him into a lake full of lizard-fish.

"How many of your brothers survived these quests?" he asked.

"Four."

"Three," Ryslind corrected.

"Untrue. Thar survived."

"Thar believed himself to be the god of the sea. He fought a master mage to the east," Ryslind explained. "The mage died, but he took Thar's mind with him. So our brother lived, but he developed the unfortunate habit of running nude through the palace, searching for his giant starfish. He drowned in the moat six months later. It seems that our god of the sea never learned to swim."

"Enough," Darnak said. He tucked his map into a long leather tube, which he slid into his belt. "We get no closer to the rod by standing here telling old tales. Goblin, which way leads to the deeper tunnels?"

Jig stopped himself before he could answer truthfully. As the saying went, truth caused more trouble than humans and hobgoblins combined. The last thing he wanted to admit was that he knew no more than they did. They wanted a guide, and a guide they would have. Anything to keep himself breathing a bit longer.

"This way," he said, trying to sound decisive. He would have said more, but he didn't know if he could keep his voice steady. Besides, it didn't matter which of the three doorways they took, since all three tunnels merged anyway. Maybe this would give him time to figure out where to go once they reached hobgoblin territory.

The dwarf had said the way was cloaked in watery darkness. The only water Jig knew of was the underground lake, where the lizard-fish lived. He hoped that wasn't where they needed to go, but considering his luck, he wouldn't be surprised. Glancing at Smudge to make sure the fire-spider was still safe on his shoulder, Jig marched toward the doorway where he and the others had entered . . . only to be jerked short when Barius grabbed his rope and wrenched him back.

"Your enthusiasm is admirable," Barius said wryly. "But we prefer to be prepared before charging into the shadowy bowels of the earth."

Jig sat down and tried not to think about that image.

Darnak grabbed a lantern out of his seemingly bottomless pack and handed it to Barius. Jig stared, fascinated by the device. The lantern was a small metal box with four hinged flaps that could be left open or closed, allowing Barius to shutter the lantern completely when necessary. Or, by leaving only one flap open, the lantern could send a beam of light into the tunnels without being as obvious as a torch.

"I shall go first, accompanied by our goblin

guide. Darnak will follow behind me, that he may continue to draw his map by the light of the lantern. Brother, I trust you are able to guard the rear? As well as keep an eye on our young elf, of course."

A few scrapes of flint against steel sent sparks into the lantern to light the wick, and a yellow glow spread throughout the room. Darnak stomped out the few smoldering torches the goblins had brought with them.

"Be wary, my friends." Barius's brown eyes gleamed with imagined glory as he stared into the tunnel. "We have beaten the enemy's first attack, but their resistance will only grow as we venture deeper into their nests. No doubt we will need every bit of courage, every ounce of strength, to survive."

Jig guessed he would have gone on that way for the rest of the day if Ryslind hadn't interrupted. "Either lead the way or hand the lantern to someone who will."

Barius blinked. With an offended sniff, he tugged Jig along and set off into the tunnel.

Progress was much slower than Jig had expected. After an hour, they still hadn't reached the junction of the three tunnels. Goblins in a hurry could run the distance in under ten minutes.

But goblins weren't accompanied by a dwarven scribe, one who insisted on mapping every twist and turn, often retracing his steps so he could get a more accurate sense of the distance. By the time they finally reached the junction point, Jig wanted to scream. Bad enough to be a prisoner whose only hope at this point was to die quickly before they reached the lake. Listening to Darnak mumble to himself, "Twenty-four, twenty-five, twenty-six . . .

no wait, there's a turn here, better pace off the inside and outside walls . . . wonder if the tunnel narrows at all . . . nope, still six paces wide . . ." was pure torture.

Worse, as a dwarf and a teacher, Darnak apparently thought it his duty to critique the stonework as they went, and he was eager to share his observations with the others. "Mahogany obsidian, definitely magic. Someone sent enough heat through this place to melt the rock itself. Even the ceilings have a layer of the stuff. Molten rock is denser, see, so Ellnorein basically burned this place into the mountain. The dark red color comes from impurities in the rock, iron and other elements."

He stopped to hit a small hammer against the wall. Jig jumped.

"Look there, not even a scratch. Normal obsidian flakes away and leaves a nasty edge. I'm guessing that's magic at work again. Good thing, too. If the floor were chipped and rough like normal obsidian, it would shred your feet right through those boots."

"Wait," Ryslind said suddenly. He held up a hand, cutting off Darnak's insights on the buildup of dirt and dust by generations of goblins. Taking the lantern, he shone a light back down the tunnel. "There should be bodies here. I shot at least six goblins before joining you."

"You only now noticed their absence, brother?" Barius grabbed his sword. "Your powers of observation continue to astound me."

Darnak knelt to study the ground. No trace of blood showed on the floor.

"Could we have passed the corpses without noticing?" Barius asked skeptically.

"Nah. I'd have drawn them on the map."

"I can understand coming back to collect the bodies," Ryslind said, looking at Jig. "But would your people have cleaned the blood from the floors?"

"Why would we return for goblin dead?" Jig asked. "We've eaten well these past days."

Only Riana seemed to catch the implications of Jig's words. She turned slightly green and clutched her hands tightly to her stomach.

"To give them a proper burial," Barius said.

"You bury your dead?" Jig stared, trying to understand. Well, the surface was probably easier to dig than the impenetrable rock of the mountain. Still that sounded like so much more work than leaving the bodies for the carrion-worms.

"Not always," Darnak said. "At times they're burned on a funeral pyre so their sparks can rise to the heavens."

"That's disgusting," Jig said without thinking.

Darnak stiffened, and the humans wore matching expressions of anger, their eyes narrowed and their lips tight.

"Those who want to keep breathing know it's not a wise thing to be mocking dwarven rituals, goblin."

Jig swallowed. "I only meant . . . well, the *smell*. Burning hair and skin." His own hair had been bad enough when Smudge vaporized it. The idea of burning an entire body was enough to turn his stomach.

The dwarf's eyes were wide with shock. "And how do goblins honor the dead? What, did your friends throw the bodies into a pit somewhere to rot?"

"They're only bodies," Jig said quietly. He wanted to shrink into the shadows, like Riana was doing. With everyone's attention squarely on him, that was impossible. He didn't know what he had said to anger everyone, but he knew he had better calm them down quickly. "We leave them for the carrion-worms."

"For the worms," Darnak repeated quietly. " 'Tis an offense against the gods, even for goblins."

Jig wanted to argue, but that would only fuel their anger. Better to stare at the floor and hope they didn't decide to punish him for whatever offense it was that goblins had committed. The gods had never complained, so why should these adventurers? It wasn't like goblins left human and dwarven bodies for the worms. Dead adventurers were things to be valued and treasured. Especially warriors, who often carried enough muscle to make an entire meal by themselves.

He started to explain, then noticed Riana, who still looked a bit nauseated. Maybe they wouldn't take kindly to hearing that, if they died, they would end up in Golaka's cauldron. But if they didn't want to be left for the worms and they didn't want to fill goblin bellies, they should go somewhere else to die.

The thought of Golaka reminded him of the smells of the kitchen, and in that instant he felt a wash of homesickness stronger than anything he had ever experienced. He would have given anything to be back in the lair, stealing just one sip from Golaka's huge stirring spoon, tasting the tender meat and tangy broth. He eyed Darnak and tried not to think about the last time he had tasted fresh dwarf.

"The tunnel splits," Barius said, raising his lantern so they could see the dark openings up ahead. "Which way, guide?"

Thankful for the change of subject, Jig hurried to the front and stared at the two tunnels. The right branch was one he knew well. Depending on the turns they took, that tunnel would take them back to goblin territory. Other branchings led to the hobgoblins, an abandoned storeroom now infested with giant rats, and eventually to the lake. The left path could go anywhere.

Older goblins had a saying: *Go with the danger you know, for that's easier to run away from.*

"To the right," Jig said, hoping he sounded confident. That tunnel wasn't exactly safe, either. If the other survivor of Porak's patrol had made it back, the goblins might have sent another patrol into the tunnels. That wouldn't cause much trouble for the adventurers, since the second patrol would likely follow the same thick-headed tactics as Captain Porak. If Jig were lucky, he wouldn't survive their suicidal attack. If not, the adventurers would probably believe that he had led them into a trap. Barius in particular would love an excuse to cut Jig's throat.

But goblins were a practical bunch. If the adventurers had killed one patrol, they might decide not to waste a second. Let the hobgoblins finish 'em off.

Which led him to the other danger. Hobgoblins were an angry, vicious, territorial lot. They wouldn't let anyone pass without a fight. Still better to go with the danger you know. . . .

Ahead, Darnak jumped. "By Earthmaker's hammer, what manner of beast is that?"

Jig looked where Darnak was pointing. "Oh. Carrion-worm. Old one, from the looks of it."

"You permit *that* to consume your dead?" Barius said.

Jig shrugged, not wanting to continue that discussion. Carrion-worms resembled oversize white caterpillars. This one was about five feet long, and most of its round segments were bloated, probably with the remains of Porak's patrol. Each segment had a circular mouth on the underside and four black feet, two of which the worm used to shovel food into its mouth while keeping the other two on the floor for balance. When they grew too long, the worms would reproduce by breaking apart, sometimes into as many as six or seven shorter worms. At other times, when food was scarce, they turned on each other, and many starving worms became a single, well-fed carrion-worm. An elegant cycle, and one which kept the tunnels clean.

Carrion-worms were blind, but their senses of smell and hearing were uncanny. They could sense a battle from the other side of the mountain, and they never left so much as a drop of blood.

This one had been munching on a splinter of bone, probably a bit of goblin it had dragged here to enjoy. At the sound of the adventurers' voices, it clutched the bone with the feet of its middle segments and ran into the darkness, moving like an overgrown inchworm.

"It eats even the weapons and clothing?" Barius asked.

"The clothing, yes," Jig said. "Weapons they take back to their nests. They like the feel of metal."

"What's that?" Riana pointed to a thin trail of liquid on the floor.

"Worm piss," Jig said. Her nose wrinkled. "They use it to mark their path. They can find their way back by following the smell, even in the dark."

Ryslind was the only one not disgusted by the worm. His eyes glowed red with excitement and he licked his thin lips as he stared after it. "That was a created creature. Like dragons were born of common lizards, that worm originated from its simpler cousins in the earth. The rod *is* here."

Jig's shoulders ached, and the rope had already scraped his wrists raw. He didn't care about created creatures or Ellnorein's rod. He was hungry and frustrated, and his fear had begun to wear off. There was only so long he could sustain that level of terror. After a while impatience took the place of fear. Sure, Death was going to find him sooner or later, but it seemed as though Death were taking the scenic route to get there.

Darnak dipped his quill in ink. He had secured the inkpot to the strap of his backpack in a tiny harness. A leather thong around the neck of the pot kept it from falling free.

Darnak scratched a few new lines on his parchment, presumably marking the spot they had found the worms. Though why that information was useful, Jig had no idea.

Perhaps Death delayed because he had decided to make a map along the way. If that were the case, Jig might live as long as an elf.

"Let us be on our way." Barius tugged Jig's rope, forcing him forward and wrenching his shoulder.

Fortunately, they encountered no goblins. Perhaps the other survivor of Porak's patrol hadn't made it back to the lair. More likely they waited safe in goblin territory, listening for the sounds of battle. They might even be wagering on how long the adventurers would last against the hobgoblins. Jig wondered who would be sent out at the end of the fight to count corpses. Often he got chosen for that thankless duty, earning a few coins from the goblins who won their bets and a few bruises from the losers. As a change of pace, this time Jig would be one of the corpses instead.

They passed the tall crack that led back to the goblin lair. A slight draft carried the smell of sizzling meat into the tunnel.

"What's up that way?" Darnak asked. "What's that awful stench?"

Jig looked longingly at the ragged crack. His mouth had watered so much that a trickle of drool ran down his chin. To think he had complained about muck duty. He would cheerfully keep the fire bowls lit for the rest of his days if it meant he could go home. He would do anything to be safe again. As Barius tugged at his rope, he added to that thought. He would also do anything if he could just free his hands and scratch the tip of his left ear.

"There's nothing down there," Jig said. "It's a crack in the rock, a hundred-foot chimney to the hobgoblin kitchens below."

After waiting for Darnak to sketch the dark crack and label it HUNDRED-FOOT CHIMNEY TO HOB-GOBLIN KITCHENS, they moved on. The tunnels slanted upward here, and Jig instinctively leaned forward to compensate. After a while the muscles in the back of his legs began to complain. He wasn't used to hiking for so long, and even the slight incline was enough to tire him. Sweat dripped down his face and into his eyes, blurring his already poor vision. He stopped trying to watch where they were going and concentrated on walking. One foot in front of the next, careful not to stumble. He had already fallen once, and with his hands bound, that fall had given him a nasty bruise on the side of his face.

"Halt," Barius said suddenly. "What manner of statue is this?"

To the right, an archway of dark red stone led down another tunnel, this one narrow and low. The humans would have to duck to keep from scraping their heads.

Barius aimed the lantern beam at the wall of the side tunnel, lighting up a detailed statue of a hobgoblin whose glass head nearly touched the ceiling.

Jig blinked to clear his eyes. He could see a wicked double-headed axe in the hobgoblin's hand. A pointed helmet covered most of the head. Muscles bulged along the bare arms and legs, and a round, spiked shield hid most of the hobgoblin's torso.

"Nasty-looking fellow," Darnak commented.

"We should keep going," Jig said. "That's hobgoblin territory. We shouldn't pass the marker."

"Hobgoblin, is it?" Darnak squinted at the statue. "Looks like an oversized goblin, to me."

Jig bit his tongue. Of all the blind, ignorant, stupid things to say. Comparing a hobgoblin to a real goblin. Hobgoblins were big, clumsy, ugly brutes, and goblins were, well, smaller. And weaker. But anyone who had ever tasted hobgoblin cooking knew goblins were the superior species. The differences were endless. If they lingered here for too long, the worst of those differences might quickly become apparent.

Among other things, hobgoblins liked to use nasty traps and ambushes. When they caught a goblin alone in their territory, they had been known to torture it for hours, then send the crippled wretch back to the goblins as a warning.

True, goblins did the same thing if they managed to catch a hobgoblin, but that was simple justice.

"Come," Jig said. In his nervousness, he actually tugged the rope that tied him to Barius.

Barius pulled him back, but with far more force. Jig stumbled closer to the archway, barely managing not to crash into the human.

"Why so afraid? Have you never explored the depths of this tunnel?"

Jig shook his head. "I'm still alive, aren't I?"

Barius grinned and looked at the others. "Then how do we know there isn't some faster way to our goal? Our vaunted guide tells us we cannot go a certain way. But what path should we explore, if not those forbidden even to the monsters? Does it not follow that those forbidden paths should be the ones to lead to the greatest treasures?"

Ryslind frowned. "As a boy, we were forbidden to explore the torture chamber. I seem to remember you following similar logic when you snuck down after father."

"Aye," Darnak said. "You had nightmares for months and kept your brothers awake with your screaming until they moved you to *my* chambers. As much to keep them from killing you in your sleep as to comfort you. Not that I wasn't tempted to shut you up a time or two myself."

Barius flushed so darkly that even Jig could see it. "May I remind you that this is my quest, and the two of you are here at my sufferance? I will be the one to decide our path, and I choose to explore a bit of this hobgoblin lair. Worry not. What is terrible to a goblin is hardly an annoyance to a true warrior."

"You can't," Jig whispered. It was the wrong thing to say.

"Can't, is it?" Barius tightened his grip on the rope and pulled Jig forward. "Come, and we shall teach this goblin what a prince can and cannot do."

The others looked reluctant, but they followed. Darnak had just begun to draw the hobgoblin statue onto his map when a quiet click sounded beneath Barius's boot.

Jig swore in Goblin as the floor fell away and they plummeted into darkness.

CHAPTER 4

❧❦❧

Jig's Bright Idea

The lantern died as it hit the ground, and Jig counted himself lucky to avoid the same fate. He couldn't tell how far they dropped, but he landed on his heels with a jolt that threatened to crack everything from his ankles up to his shoulders and sent him tumbling onto the rock-littered ground. With his arms still tied, he kicked like an upended spider before getting back to his feet.

Still, he couldn't complain. Darnak, yanked backward by the weight of his pack, had landed hard on his backside. If that weren't enough, he wound up with Ryslind's knee square in his gut. At least that was how Jig interpreted the grunting and swearing from that side of the pit.

"Where are we? What happened?" Barius sounded close to panic. So much for the fearless prince. Even children knew better than to openly barge into hobgoblin territory. Barius was beginning to remind Jig of a very young goblin he had once known. Upon being told not to touch the fire in the fire bowls, this goblin had not only raced to the nearest flame, she had attempted to *taste* it. She hadn't survived childhood, and Jig wondered how Barius had managed to do so. *Darnak probably had to follow him everywhere, telling him not to eat the pretty fire.*

"What happened is we fell into a damned trap," Darnak snapped.

"How was I to know?"

"The goblin tried to warn you," Riana said angrily.

"The goblin wanted nothing more than to flee," Barius argued. "He said nothing of any trap."

I didn't tell you not to hold your sword by the pointy end, either. Jig held his tongue and scooted away from the others. Barius had let go of Jig's rope in the fall, and right now the last thing Jig wanted was to let the prince get his hands on Jig's throat.

Ryslind ignored the others. "If this rock is magically strong, Ellnorein himself must have created this pit five thousand years ago," he said reverently.

Riana spat. "Smells like piss and mud down here."

Jig's fingers touched metal, and he froze. Slowly he traced the outline of a pitted, broken sword. If it still had any edge to it, he might be able to free himself from this rope. A quick rub of the blade told Jig luck was with him. Ignoring his now-bleeding finger, he began to saw the knot against the sword's edge.

The awkward angle sent new cramps through his arms, and twice the sword slipped away. The others were arguing too loudly to notice the noise. Another accidental cut told him the edge was sharper near the hilt. With that knowledge, Jig eventually managed to free himself.

He had to clamp both hands over his mouth to

keep from screaming. Blood pounded into his limbs like hot acid. He gripped his fangs and rocked back and forth, trying not to cry. The pain was so great he didn't immediately notice when Smudge found him and crawled up his leg. The fire-spider made it to Jig's thigh before he felt the tiny, burning footsteps.

What was Smudge afraid of? He couldn't see, but he looked in the direction of the broken sword. As the pain receded, his brain started to work again. What had happened to the owner of that sword? The fall wasn't enough to kill. Even Jig had survived the drop. Surely a hobgoblin trap would be more than a simple pit.

"Where's the lantern?" he asked softly.

Barius and the dwarf were still arguing. He didn't want to interrupt and draw their anger toward him, but. . . .

"Shut up," Riana yelled.

Their voices stopped, and for a moment the pit was so quiet Jig could hear them all breathing. His ears swiveled, searching. There was something else. A clicking, scraping sound.

"The lantern?" Riana asked.

"It slipped free in the fall," Barius said.

At the same instant, Jig whispered, "Something else is down here."

This time everyone heard him.

"And here we sit, arguing like children. Earthmaker help us, we've been waiting like lambs at slaughter."

On their hands and knees, they began to scour the dirt. Jig's cut fingers stung, and he jabbed himself in the palm with what felt like a splinter of bone. The owner of the sword? It did nothing to help his fear. Smudge had grown so hot Jig had to set him on the ground.

"Stay close," Jig whispered. The waves of heat beside his leg told him the spider had obeyed.

"I have the lantern," Barius said triumphantly. Jig could hear him scrounging for something. Sparks flew, surprisingly bright, as the prince scraped flint against the steel guard of his dagger.

The sounds Jig heard were growing louder. There were dozens of them, whatever they were.

"I hear it too," Riana said.

Barius paused. "I hear nothing."

Jig wasn't surprised. The monsters would be cracking Barius's bones for marrow by the time those puny human ears heard anything unusual.

"Light the lantern, boy," Darnak snapped.

"I'm trying." The sparks continued, but with no effect.

In those brief flashes, Jig thought he saw movement at the far side of the pit, but he couldn't be sure. He moved toward the others. The creatures were closing in from both sides. In the blackness, his imagination conjured up one horror after another. How soon before huge insects closed their pincers around Jig's throat or giant lizards dripping with black goo sank their fangs into his exposed skin?

He pulled his legs to his chest and wrapped his arms around his knees, trying to present as small a target as possible. They were so close. A squeak of fear slipped past his throat. What was taking so long? Lighting fires was a child's duty, so why couldn't a full-grown human manage it? Panic ripped away common sense, and he lunged at the prince.

"Give me that!" He kicked someone in the process, but by following the source of the sparks, he managed to snatch the lantern into his own lap.

One of the shutters was open, and the glass pane was slid to one side. Jig squeezed his fingers through the opening and felt the wick. It had slipped down through the crack into the oil supply, and only one corner still protruded. No wonder Barius hadn't been able to light the thing. He could shoot sparks all day without hitting that slim corner of wick, and Jig's fingers weren't small enough to pull the wick back out.

Something touched his leg. Jig screamed and barely stopped himself from squashing Smudge. He stroked Smudge for reassurance, and the fire-spider's head immediately set fire to the film of oil on Jig's fingers. He jammed his fingers into his mouth. The fire died, though Jig would have a blister on his tongue. Not to mention the awful taste of lantern oil.

What if he deliberately set his fingers on fire and used them to light the lantern? If it weren't for the intense pain, it would have been a perfect plan. Having had more than his share of pain lately, Jig doubted he could do it. But his smarting fingers had given him another idea.

"Sorry about this," he muttered, scooping Smudge up with his uninjured hand. He stuffed the fire-spider into the lantern and snapped the glass pane back into place.

The wick blazed to life, and Jig got one glimpse of Smudge tapping indignantly at the glass before he was forced to look away. The afterimage of the lantern obscured the center of his vision. They had light, and he *still* couldn't see.

"What are they?" he yelled.

"By Earthmaker's Black Anvil," Darnak swore. Behind him, Jig heard Ryslind muttering a spell.

Jig set the lantern on the ground and rubbed

his eyes. When he looked again, he saw what had frightened the others. "I didn't know they grew that big," he said.

Two carrion-worms circled the party. They could be nothing else, but Jig had never seen worms of such length. Their bodies were at least twenty feet long, and each segment was the size of a goblin's head. The mouths were big enough to take a chunk of flesh large as Jig's two fists together, and black, curved teeth surrounded each mouth. If these were normal worms, they would have a second, sharper row tucked inside and out of sight.

Strangely, Jig seemed the least afraid. This was something familiar, albeit much larger than he was used to. "They're only carrion-worms," he said. "They don't attack living things."

Almost before he had finished speaking, one of the worms lunged toward Darnak, who scrambled backward. "And mighty glad I am to be knowing that," he shouted angrily. He backed himself against a wall and stood with his war club ready. Barius joined him there, guarding his left side.

The worm that had attacked began to circle, long antennae flicking at the dwarf. The other hesitated, then turned toward Riana, who backed away as quickly as she could.

The second worm reared, displaying six mouths in its bellies. The undulating teeth pointed outward, ready to rip the elf apart. Jig couldn't understand it. These were carrion-worms. They wouldn't eat anything live unless they were starving, and even then they limited themselves to rats and bugs.

Normal worms limited themselves, Jig corrected. A twenty-foot worm with about a thousand teeth didn't qualify as normal. Jig and the others might be nothing but rats to these beasts. It was not a comforting thought.

As Jig watched, the worm facing Riana went still. The teeth around one mouth folded inward.

"Look out!" Jig lunged across the floor and knocked Riana down. A thin black tongue shot over their heads. With a loud snap, it returned to the worm's mouth, and the worm lowered itself to the ground.

Ryslind finished his spell. Glowing yellow fire floated from the tips of his fingers to the first segment of the worm menacing Jig and Riana. The fire clung to the worm's pale flesh, and it reared up again, waving back and forth in pain. Slowly the fire spread to the second segment.

The worm lashed more frantically, smashing into the walls of the pit and bloodying the burning segments. The smell was horrid, like charred meat. The worm began to scream, a high-pitched whistle of agony. Jig hadn't known they were capable of sound.

"Get off of me," Riana snapped.

Without taking his eyes away from the dying carrion-worm, Jig rolled off the elf and slowly stood. Ryslind had already turned his attention to the other worm. Darnak and Barius had managed to keep it at bay with their weapons, but neither had done any real damage. The wizard raised his hands again and began another spell.

He didn't finish. There was no warning as the second worm convulsed with such force that it left the ground. The burned, dead half of its body flopped back to the earth, but the less damaged part crashed against Ryslind's back and knocked him into the wall. The wizard fell like a stone.

"Ryslind!" Darnak knocked his worm aside with a powerful two-handed blow, then rushed to the fallen human's side.

The worm turned to track his movement, giving

Barius the opening he needed. Even as Jig shouted, "No," Barius raised his sword and sliced down, cutting the worm in two. Both ends fell still.

"No?" Barius asked, one eyebrow raised as he wiped gore from his sword. "You'll forgive me, I hope, if I fail to heed the advice of a goblin on matters of battle."

Jig didn't bother to answer. Already the split worm was beginning to heal. Each piece ended with an oozing half-segment where Barius's sword had struck. As Jig watched, those damaged segments dropped off, leaving two healthy, hungry carrion-worms. Each was half the size of the original, but that just made them faster. And hungrier. Carrion-worms were always hungry after they reproduced.

Jig needed a distraction. Something to keep the worms busy while Darnak revived the wizard. His eyes lingered wistfully on Barius. No, the others probably wouldn't like it if Jig fed their prince to the carrion-worms. He snatched up the broken sword he had used to cut his ropes and tried to think.

"To me," Darnak shouted. Riana and Barius raced toward the dwarf. Jig started to follow. He didn't know if Darnak's rallying cry had been intended to include him, but he wasn't about to face those monsters alone. Halfway there, he stopped.

Carrion-worms preferred dead flesh. At least, normal ones did. He stared at the dying worm, now almost completely charred. That definitely qualified as dead, and the worms had no qualms about cannibalism. The only question was whether or not they would eat their meat cooked.

He used his rusty blade to hack and tear a chunk of the worm free. The meat was tough, and Jig had to cut through several stubborn, stringlike bits before he had a piece he could throw. He flung the meat at the nearest of the two living worms, which reared to catch it in midair. Meat clutched in its teeth, the worm dropped to the ground to feed.

"This is *the* most disgusting thing I've ever done," Jig muttered as he renewed his attack on the dead worm. Something wet splashed onto his forearms. "Even worse than privy duty after one of Porak's drinking binges."

A second chunk of flesh distracted the other worm.

As it turned out, the giant carrion-worms were not only large and deadly, they were also stupid. Fatally so. As long as Jig kept them fed, they were perfectly content to sit and eat. Even as Darnak ran around smashing one worm-segment after another with his war club, the worms continued to feed on bits of their fellow. At last the dwarf called out, "S'okay, you can stop. The beasts are dead."

The blood-slick blade fell from Jig's numb fingers, and he tried very hard not to look at the carnage in front of him. "This is *not* the kind of battle they sing songs about," he grumbled. He hadn't expected anyone to hear, but Darnak laughed.

"I don't know. I could imagine a nice little ditty about it." He raised his voice. "First verse should explain how we got stuck down here. Help me out, your highness. What rhymes with 'mule-headed stubbornness'?"

Barius scowled. "The goblin probably did this deliberately, hoping the worms would finish us off."

"Right," Riana said. "Except that the worms would have eaten him as fast as the rest of us."

"Silence." Barius's hand went to his sword. "He hasn't the foresight to consider such an end. And I warn you to keep that tone from your voice when addressing your betters."

Riana started to reply, but Darnak interrupted, which was probably all that saved the girl from a beating. Barius looked angry enough to loose his temper on anyone who got in his way.

"So how are we to be getting out of this little hole?" Darnak asked. He took the lantern and unshuttered all four sides. He couldn't aim the light upward without spilling the oil, but this was enough for them to see the dark shadow of the ceiling. "Looks a good fifteen feet to me. Lucky the ground is softer here."

"Lucky I landed on your belly and not your hard head, Darnak." Ryslind grimaced. "I'd have broken bones for certain."

Darnak grinned. "Aye. Though there's something to be said for the thickness of human skulls as well. They say it's the only substance harder than diamond."

"Enough of your banter," Barius said. "Brother, can your arts release us from this prison?"

Ryslind took a deep breath. "Give me a moment. Magic requires a clear head, and mine still spins."

While they waited, Riana walked over to Jig. She studied him with obvious distaste, but when she spoke, her voice was quiet, even respectful. "Thanks."

"Eh?" Jig blinked, unsure what she meant. He was still a bit dazed by everything that had happened. Worse yet, he had the nagging sense he had forgotten something. The worms were all dead, but still. . . .

"For knocking me out of the way back there."

"Oh. I saw a carrion-worm catch a rat like that once." He sighed. Giblet the rat had been a good pet. To this day, he suspected that Porak had deliberately turned Giblet loose by the worm's nest.

He scowled. Something about pets . . . oh no.

"Smudge!"

He ran at Darnak and tried to pull the lantern away. The dwarf swatted him with his free hand. "Here now, what's this?"

"My fire-spider's in there."

"What?" Darnak held the lantern higher and peered inside. "Ha. So he is. So that's how you were lighting this thing."

Very gently, he set the lantern on the ground and slid the glass back. Smudge scurried out, apparently unharmed. He raced away from the lantern like he was fleeing Straum himself. Halfway to the far wall, he stopped and rubbed his legs together, one pair at a time.

"Probably trying to clean off the lantern oil," Jig said. He knelt and held out one hand for the spider.

Smudge glanced at him. Then, very deliberately, he turned away and continued to groom himself.

"I am ready," Ryslind announced. He had taken another coil of rope from Darnak's pack. As the others watched, he sprinkled a bit of blue powder on the rope and began to chant. One end of the rope rose, reminding Jig of the way the carrion-worms had reared up to attack. The rope climbed steadily higher until it reached the ceiling.

"I don't suppose that magic rope of yours can punch through the trapdoor?" Darnak asked.

Ryslind frowned. "Do not disturb my focus. I need to channel more power." His voice was deeper than usual. His brow wrinkled, and the end of the rope curled into a tight ball. Ryslind's eyes flashed red, and the rope slammed against the trapdoor.

A shower of dust fell from the ceiling, making Jig's eyes water. Ryslind said the word again, this time with a wave of his hand for emphasis.

On the third try, a large square of rock swung

down. Jig leaped back, afraid the stone would crash onto their heads. But it scraped to a halt, spraying them all with another layer of dirt and grit.

"Quickly," Ryslind ordered. "The longer I hold it open, the more it drains me."

Barius was already climbing. Darnak sent Riana up next, then looked back at Jig. "Your turn, goblin."

"My name is Jig," he grumbled. Climbing out of the pit was difficult. Jig had never been strong, and his hands and arms weren't used to this sort of work. But he eventually reached the top. Barius, who had reached down to help Riana out of the pit, didn't even look at Jig as he struggled to hook his ankle over the edge. Darnak followed a minute later, and then Ryslind, pulling the rope up behind him.

Stone grated loudly as the trapdoor sealed itself. Jig sat on the floor, trying to catch his breath, when he noticed Smudge clinging to his leg.

"Decided to forgive me after all, then?" Or maybe the spider had simply decided that coming with Jig was better than being left alone in the pit. It didn't matter. Jig felt better for Smudge's company. At least, he felt better until he spotted the hobgoblins coming down the corridor.

This was the first time Jig had really seen the adventurers in battle. During that first attack, he had been too busy hiding to watch much of the fight. He only saw the end, when Darnak and Barius beat the last few goblins. And the fight in the pit would have been too chaotic to follow even if he hadn't been elbow-deep in worm guts at the time.

But now, watching the others draw weapons and prepare for the hobgoblins' attack, Jig began to understand why surface-dwellers slaughtered goblins time after time.

Ryslind slipped his bow from his shoulder and nocked an arrow in one smooth motion. Barius and Darnak each took a step forward, leaving room for Ryslind to fire while at the same time shielding him from attack. Two hobgoblins fell before they even reached the adventurers. A third stumbled over the bodies of his fellows, and Barius's sword licked out to slice deep into the side of his neck.

Three hobgoblins down before the fight had even begun. Jig stared in disbelief.

All the hobgoblins wore armor they had cobbled together. Bits of plate mail strapped over leather and chain, and several had shields of varying designs as well. All used swords or axes. No kitchen knives here. This was a force that could overrun a goblin patrol in a matter of minutes.

Despite their strength and numbers, the hobgoblins didn't stand a chance. Jig wouldn't have recognized the adventurers as the same people who had, minutes before, shouted and snapped at one another like children. They were a team, working *with* one another, whereas the hobgoblins struggled as much among themselves as with the enemy.

That was the key, Jig realized. That ability to trust and work together in battle. Barius didn't bother to protect his vulnerable left side, trusting Darnak to smash anyone who tried to attack him there. Neither faltered at all when Ryslind fired his arrows between them, and each of those arrows took a hobgoblin in the throat or chest. Were these goblins, they never would have trusted one of their number to stay behind with a bow. The temptation to "accidentally" shoot someone who might have stolen your rations, insulted your family, or stepped on your foot at last night's dinner was too great.

The hobgoblins suffered from the same lack of trust. They tripped over one another, yelled and fought their way to the front, and seemed to have no plan beyond this straight charge. Jig watched as one hobgoblin pushed another out of the way. The one being pushed stumbled forward, and Darnak smashed his skull with a twirl of his club. The adventurers hardly needed to work at all. The hobgoblins were killing *themselves*.

And then it was over. Jig heard the survivors retreat back up the tunnel. Bodies covered the ground in front of the three adventurers. The carrion-worms would eat well tonight.

As he watched them clean their weapons and armor, Jig began to think he had been lucky when Porak sent him ahead as a scout. Had he remained with the patrol, he would have been cut down as easily as these hobgoblins. Easier, since he had been unarmored and practically unarmed. It made him embarrassed to be a goblin.

One unexpected blessing was that victory had improved Barius's temper. He didn't even insist on retying Jig's bonds. Instead he seemed to glow with pride as he checked to be sure the others were uninjured.

"Three victories in a single night," he gloated. "Surely the gods smile upon my quest. We shall find the rod, for nothing beneath this mountain has the strength to stop us." He didn't wait for an answer. "Come, let us find the entrance to the lower tunnels. We will rest there before descending, to give my brother time to renew his strength. Lead on, goblin."

Lead he did, guiding them away from the hobgoblins and through the slowly descending tunnel that led to the lake. He didn't even worry about what they faced there. Jig was too confused by what he had just seen and by what it meant.

All his life Jig had believed surface-dwellers

killed goblins through trickery. They used enchanted weapons, spells to call fire and death, and fine armor the likes of which no goblin could make. Certainly some of that was true. That spell Ryslind had used to sneak up on their patrol, the one that made him appear to be a part of the rock, was magic no goblin could hope to fight. Nor was Jig's knife a match for Barius's sword or Darnak's club.

But there was more. In their fight with the hobgoblins, the adventurers had used no magic. Their weapons, while of good quality, were no more magical than those of their foe. There had been no time for trickery or ruses. And still *they had wiped out three times their number without losing a single one of their party.* Barius struck like a serpent, fast and deadly. He knocked hobgoblin swords aside with ease, because he *knew how to fight.* His sword was a part of him, and it twisted and dodged past his enemy's guard like a living thing. How many hours had he trained to be able to do that?

Jig flushed when he thought back to his poor kitchen knife, and how much he had secretly longed for a sword, thinking that all it took was a bit of steel to make him the equal of these adventurers.

The dwarven follower of Silas Earthmaker had stood like a god himself, unmovable and untouchable as his club lashed out to break swords and bones alike. He too must have worked hard to develop such strength of arm. Sure, dwarves were tougher than most races, but Darnak had taken that toughness and strengthened it further. Jig looked again at the dwarf's pack, remembering how much equipment had been stuffed into that bulging leather pack. Jig would be hard-pressed just to lift what Darnak carried around as though it were nothing.

Ryslind was the worst of them all. As a wizard, he was the one enemy no goblin would expect to defeat. But he had used no magic just now. Instead, he had sent one arrow after another safely past his companions. Jig had watched him more closely than the others, and the wizard had not missed a single shot. That cold precision terrified Jig.

Could it be that what the surface-dwellers said about goblins was true? Could goblins be the clumsy, stupid creatures Barius and the others assumed them to be? If so, what did that mean for the fate of Jig's people? They would never accomplish anything, not if the smallest group of surface-dwellers could slaughter them with such ease. It meant goblins were nothing but a nuisance, existing only to die at the hands of adventurers like this.

No, that wasn't it. The problem wasn't the adventurers, but the goblins themselves. They were incapable of working together, of planning or growing. All they could do was charge into battle and get themselves killed. Or in Jig's case, they could hide and watch from the shadows while the others died.

His people, his entire race, were no more than a joke. Jig had betrayed his captain, letting Porak die for an insult Jig had committed. He was nothing but a worthless coward, the same as every other goblin.

Jig perked his left ear as he heard the faint sound of water lapping the stone shore. His right ear continued to listen for sounds of pursuit. Despite all he had seen, a part of him still couldn't believe the dreaded hobgoblins wouldn't come back to finish them off. Depressed or not, he had no desire to let the hobgoblins get their claws on him.

The air was cooler here. A thin green film of moss covered the walls and ceiling, even the edges of the floor. The air smelled like dead fish as they neared the lake.

"How far to this lake?" Barius asked. "I feel as though we've passed through half the mountain. 'Twouldn't surprise me if we found ourselves emerging from the far side."

"Up ahead," Jig said, reminding himself that they couldn't yet hear the water. "Not far."

"Excellent. Then let us rest here for the night. Assuming it is still night, that is. Who can tell this far underground?"

"It's nigh about an hour past midnight," Darnak said without looking up from his map.

"Who but a dwarf, that is?" Barius said, still in high spirits. "We will take turns watching for danger. I shall watch first. Each man takes a shift of one hour. No longer, or you will begin to lose your focus. Darnak, I will awaken you when my shift is up."

Jig knew without being told that he would not be asked to take a watch. Trust a goblin to protect them in their sleep? Ridiculous. Might as well ask a carrion-worm to stand guard.

He curled into a tight knot, back against the wall, and tried to pretend he was back in his lair. Safe and well-fed, with nothing more to worry about than the jibes of the other goblins. But the waves in the distance slipped into his weary thoughts. In his dreams he found himself in the water, trying to swim away but unable to move his arms while the lizard-fish surrounded him, coming closer and closer with those poisonous spines. . . .

CHAPTER 5

A Day at the Beach

Slender hands shook Jig awake. His vision was always worst when he woke up, and at first he could only stare dumbly at the red-haired blur above his face. Darnak had shuttered the lantern for the night, and the cracks of light that escaped were barely enough to let him make out slender, pointed ears and a narrow nose.

"You sleep *hard*," Riana whispered when she saw he was awake. "Don't speak." She held a hand over his mouth, ignoring the fangs that could have torn through her palm.

"The others are asleep. If you go quietly, they won't be able to catch you."

Jig blinked, trying to clear his head of a dream in which he had been flung into a flaming pit while a huge, eight-eyed face watched from above. Who wouldn't be able to catch him? Where was he supposed to go? How had Riana taken the place of the giant fire-spider of his dreams?

He looked at the others, but saw only three mounded bedrolls, like giant cocoons. The dwarf snored like an earthquake, but Jig could hear the others as well, both drawing the slow breaths of sleep. Riana wasn't lying about that.

Could this be a trap? Maybe once he started to run, she planned to awaken the others and accuse him of trying to escape. That would give Barius all the excuse he needed to finish off the lowly goblin. But why would she go to such trouble to finish off a single goblin?

"Why?" he asked hoarsely. His mouth was dry, as it always was after sleeping. For a goblin, with teeth like miniature stalagmites, it was impossible to sleep with his mouth closed as the other party members did.

"They know I won't run off," she said bitterly. "I wouldn't make it past the hobgoblins, let alone survive long enough to see the surface. But you could escape."

"You're a prisoner?" He stared stupidly, trying to understand. "But you're an elf."

She laughed at him. "So?"

Jig didn't know how to explain. He only knew that elves were supposed to be graceful and powerful. Elven warriors slipped past their enemies like the wind, but when they fought, their slender arms lashed out with the strength of multitudes. Elven wizards were masters of the elements, forcing fire, lightning, water, and wind to obey their will with the flick of their fingers. He couldn't reconcile those images with this helpless girl who claimed to be a prisoner.

"I thought all elves were strong and powerful," he said at last.

"Yeah, and I thought all goblins were selfish, backstabbing cowards."

"But we are."

Riana rolled her eyes. "Never mind. Before they

came here, they stopped at an inn to rest. Ryslind caught me trying to pick his pocket. I thought I could earn a coin or two off those pretty pouches he carries. Instead he dragged me to his room and offered me a choice. I could either come along and help them on their stupid quest, or he could kill me on the spot. He said he would prefer not to kill me, since a dead elf might cause diplomatic problems for his father."

She turned away, hiding her face. "I didn't believe him. I think he *wanted* to kill me. He's as bad as his brother. Those eyes . . . I felt like I was staring into my own funeral fire."

"Why would Ryslind want to kill you?" Barius was the bloodthirsty one. Ryslind was merely cold and distant. He didn't take pleasure out of fighting the way his brother did. He was cold and efficient when he killed, and he didn't strut about for hours afterward like a goblin fresh from the mating bed.

"He's a wizard," Riana whispered. "Remember that powder he used to enchant the rope? What do you think that was made from? I heard them talking earlier tonight. He got that powder by grinding up the skeletons of two unhatched griffons. What sort of ingredients do you think he'd get from an elf? We're magical creatures too. Not as strongly magical as griffons, but I'm sure he could find uses for an elf girl."

"Are goblins magical?" he asked. He didn't want to end up in one of Ryslind's pouches.

"Of course not."

She needn't have answered quite so quickly, Jig thought. "Do all wizards use that sort of thing for their spells?"

"How should I know? Everyone does magic differently, I think. Even the dwarf can do a little when he prays hard enough. I saw him do it before we came here. He prayed over the two humans to make them stronger and faster. After that, they both looked larger, more dangerous." She laughed again, and this time Jig heard the deep bitterness behind it. "They didn't bother to give *me* Earth-maker's blessing, of course."

"I still don't understand why they brought you along. Isn't it dangerous for them to kidnap an elf? Won't the other elves be angry?" Even as he asked, his thoughts wandered back to the goblin lair. Goblins vanished all the time, and nobody thought twice about it. To mount a rescue for a lost goblin would be ridiculous. But he had believed that elves and the other surface-dwellers were different. Maybe he was wrong.

Riana shook her head. "My parents died in a border war when I was a child. A human family brought me up and set me to work as a kitchen drudge. They had a large family: aunts, uncles, grandparents, and a herd of kids. I scrubbed pots and cooked for them for ten years before I ran away.

"I thought I could go back and be with my real family. Even if my parents were dead, at least I could live with other elves. But I couldn't even speak the language. They were terribly kind, of course. They fed and sheltered me, all the while treating me like I was slow in the head. I was more of a pet than anything. So I ran away from them, too."

She was crying, Jig realized. Her shoulders shook, but her voice remained steady. "They were so proud and confident and graceful. Even a crip-pled elf could make me feel like a clumsy fool. Their attitude didn't help matters, either. They talked about me behind my back, called me a half-breed even though I was as elven as they were. But I wasn't. I didn't *feel* like an elf. I hadn't grown up with elves. The simplest rituals of daily life left me confused and angry. Soon I was stealing from the other elves. I didn't *need* to steal. I did it because I was so angry.

"I think everyone was happy when I left. Being on my own was no better, though. I robbed travelers so I would have enough money to eat. I slept in the streets. I thought about buying passage on a ship. Didn't know where I'd go, but anywhere had to be an improvement. Only it wouldn't have been. I think that's why I never really tried. I could have stowed away, but I knew there was no place I belonged."

Her voice trailed into silence. Jig waited, confused. Why was she telling him all of this? He felt like he should say something.

"You don't belong here, either." He ignored her disgusted glare and went on to ask his real question. "What did Ryslind want you to do for them? Down here, I mean."

She wiped her nose and eyes. "I've picked a lock or two in my time. They thought that might be useful. They wanted me to look for traps as well, but I've no more chance of spotting a trap than you would. Barius is furious that I didn't warn him about the hobgoblins' pit. They think that because I'm a thief, I'm a good hand at traps and knives and sneaking around in the darkness. Maybe some thieves do all of that, but I just cut purses and break into the occasional inn room. And it's a rare merchant who plants a trap on his purse."

Darnak's steady snores broke suddenly as the dwarf rolled over. He mumbled, "Earthmaker take you all, villains," kicked his leg twice, and began to snore again.

"Go," Riana said. "You saved my life. I owe you. And it will be good to thwart them in this one small thing."

Jig wondered if he was still dreaming. Before

tonight, Riana had spoken only a handful of words. He understood how those elves in her homeland might have assumed something was wrong with her. He had begun to think the same thing. Could that quiet, withdrawn, angry girl be the same Riana who sat here telling him about her past and offering him his freedom all in the same sitting?

Freedom. The word had a bittersweet taste as he thought about what his freedom could mean. Only hours before, he had wanted nothing but to return to his lair. Riana had handed him his chance. All he had to do was take it. Grab Smudge and run. His bare feet would make no noise to wake the others, and if he was careful, he could probably make it past the hobgoblins.

He could go home. But to what end? To live as a coward among cowards? To watch his people die time and again, and for nothing?

Worse, one goblin from Porak's patrol had escaped. If he made it back to the lair, he would have spread the tale of Jig's cowardice. He might even have blamed Jig for Porak's death. If so, they would kill him as soon as he returned to goblin territory. Because killing Porak made Jig a goblin to be reckoned with. Others would want to prove themselves by killing Jig, preferably as painfully as they could.

A hollowness came over him as he realized he had no place to return to. His home was no longer safe. He was as lost as Riana.

"I can't go back," he whispered, more to himself than to the elf.

"You can." She looked about frantically. "They only let me stand watch because elves need less sleep than dwarves or humans, and they were exhausted from all the fighting. You won't have another chance to get away."

Jig shook his head.

"You goblins are as stubborn as . . . as that dwarf." With that pronouncement, she turned her back on him and stared into the tunnel.

Jig sat there confused, and eventually decided goblins simply weren't meant to understand the minds of surface-dwellers. He had almost fallen back to sleep when he heard her ask, "Do you think we'll make it?"

"Not really," Jig mumbled, and then he was asleep.

When Jig next awoke, he found Darnak's face hovering over him.

"Argh," Jig muttered, trying not to cringe. Waking from a dream to see Riana had been startling. Darnak was a nightmare all by himself. The dwarf had pulled his hair and beard into numerous rope-like braids, and Jig felt like he was under attack by a floating monster with black tentacles and a crooked nose.

"Get up. You've had yourself a better night's sleep than the rest of us, and it's time we were moving." He tossed a chunk of something round and brown onto Jig's lap, followed by a few strips of dried meat. "You're lucky to be getting any meat at all. His majesty wanted you to have nothing but bread. He said you'd be sharing Riana's waterskin. Don't get greedy—I don't know when we'll find fresh water, and Earthmaker's a busy god who doesn't like to waste time on water purification magic."

Jig nodded. He tore the meat with his teeth, and his mouth watered instantly. How long had it been since he last ate? His stomach protested that it had been weeks. Could it have been only yesterday that he was back in the lair, suffering through muck duty?

A few seconds later, the meat was gone, and Jig stared warily at the bread. He had heard of this crusted stuff from Golaka, but had never encountered it himself. Golaka said adventurers often carried it as a part of their rations, but that it was unsuitable for goblin palates. Studying the bread, Jig was inclined to agree with her. A dark brown shell covered a lighter interior of dry foam, visible where Darnak had torn the chunk from a larger loaf. He touched it to the tip of his tongue, but the bread had no taste. Like licking a rock.

He tried a nibble. Like chewing a rock, too. But the others were eating it, and those two strips of meat weren't going to keep his stomach happy. Jig shrugged to himself and smashed the crusted side of the bread onto one of his fangs. He swiftly tore it into manageable chunks, and soon the bread joined the meat in his belly.

Bread didn't taste like rock after all, Jig decided. Didn't taste like much of anything, really. He noticed that the humans had spread some sort of yellow grease over theirs. Though whether that was to improve the flavor or to make it easier to swallow, Jig didn't know.

"Water?" Riana handed him a bloated skin, then walked away without ever meeting his eyes. Was she angry with him for not running away last night? Or had she simply reverted to her usual cold self?

Not that it mattered. Jig was more comfortable when they treated him like a prisoner, or at best an untrustworthy guide. He wasn't used to kindness or consideration from anyone, let alone his captors.

So he didn't know what to say when Riana returned a few minutes later and handed him a long sheathed dagger. Jig stared in disbelief. "Where did this come from?"

She pointed. Down the tunnel, two hobgoblins lay facing the ceiling, one atop the other. Each had a black-fletched arrow jutting from his neck. He looked at Ryslind. "Oh."

He started to draw the knife. More of a short sword, really. The blade stretched the length of his elbow to fingertip, and it was heavy. The pommel and crossguard were simple brass, and the hilt was bare wood, but this was still the grandest weapon Jig had ever held. He shoved the blade back into its sheath, then drew it completely free.

"Are you mad?" Barius loomed over them both, his sword ready. "Let this creature have a blade of his own, and you'll soon find that blade plunged into your back."

"What if we're attacked again?" Riana countered. "Where would we be if Jig hadn't found that old sword when we were in the hobgoblin pit?"

"You'd trust a goblin to defend your person?" Barius shook his head in disbelief, but his sword remained level with Jig's throat. "I could understand if you secured a knife for your own safety, but to hand it over to this blue-skinned monster is absurd."

Riana spat on the floor by Barius's feet. He looked down, momentarily speechless, and when he looked back up Riana had a knife in her hand. "What made you think I didn't secure one for myself?"

"Enough," Darnak snapped loudly. "Put them away before I crack all your skulls. Barius, let them have their pig-stickers. They know well enough what will happen if they cause trouble."

The prince's sword hissed back into its scabbard. In a low voice, so Darnak wouldn't hear, he said, "Do not cross me again, elf."

As Jig tucked his new sword through his belt, he glanced at Riana. Whereas his sword was plain and well-used, hers was trimmed in gold, and even sported a blue gem in the pommel. She grinned at him as she slid it back up her sleeve.

"That blade looks as fine as Barius's sword."

"It should." She glared at the prince's back. "It's his."

Feeling bolder now that he was armed, Jig walked back to the corpses and took a large belt pouch for himself. Dumping a few corroded coins on the floor, he tied the pouch at his waist, then dropped Smudge inside. "Only until my shoulders have a chance to heal," he promised.

Once everything was repacked, new oil poured into the lantern, a few last touches made to Darnak's map, and everyone had eaten enough to take the edge off their hunger, they proceeded to sit around for another hour while Ryslind meditated. The life of an adventurer appeared to consist of roughly six parts boredom to one part stark terror, or so it seemed to Jig.

"What are we waiting for?" he asked.

"Silence," Barius hissed.

"He's needing to clear his mind and renew his focus," Darnak said softly. "Those tattoos on his arms are a spell, one that keeps him ever open to the power he uses for magic. Far better than books or scrolls, but a permanent spell is a permanent burden, and if he doesn't stop to rest, the spell could snap, leaving him powerless when he needs it most."

"What about his eyes?" Jig asked. "Is that a part of his magic?"

Darnak grinned. "Nah. He did that to himself a year or so back. Thought it would make him look scarier or some nonsense like that. Turns out he got the spell wrong, and he hasn't figured out how to make it go away. The glow gets worse when he's pushed himself."

When Ryslind's eyes shot open, they looked almost human, with only the faintest trace of red. "I am ready."

Barius and Jig again took the lead as they neared the lake. They passed several side passageways, but Jig was out of his territory now, and when asked where the tunnels led, could only shrug and say, "The lake is this way."

He didn't like leaving unexplored tunnels behind them, but better to hurry past than to go sticking his nose in places where a large paw might rip it from his face.

The rush of water grew louder. Their cautious whispers became shouts, as anything less was drowned out by the noise from the lake. A fine mist coated Jig's face and tickled his ears. Soon he was constantly flicking his ears in protest.

The tunnel widened, and then the walls peeled back completely to reveal an enormous cavern. Dark red obsidian gleamed as if polished, the water having renewed the rock's shine. The walls stretched out of sight to either side.

"What are those?" Riana pointed to the ceiling.

Jig could barely make out the clumps of green, but he knew what they were. "They're just rocks."

A long time ago, malachite formations had striped the walls and ceiling near the entrance as well, but hobgoblins and goblins had taken the green needles of rock for jewelry and decoration. They still existed over the lake, beyond easy reach. Some were as long as Jig's sword, though malachite made a poor weapon.

"They look like green porcupines."

Jig nodded rather than admit he didn't know what a porcupine might be.

The lake itself was black, with white foam cresting the waves that crashed against the shore. In the distance, toward the center of the lake, the water rushed with even greater violence. To Jig, it was no more than a blur of waves and whitecaps, but the others stared worriedly at whatever it was they saw.

"That's a bloody whirlpool," Darnak shouted.

"The way to the lower tunnels is through *that*?" Barius yelled at Jig.

Jig nodded, trying to project confidence and calm. In truth, he hadn't a clue how to get to the lower tunnels. *They* were the ones who had mentioned going through the lake. A sense of self-preservation kept goblins from even trying to venture into the water.

"I sense power here," Ryslind said. Though he alone didn't shout, somehow his voice pierced the roar of the water. "No natural lake could sustain a whirlpool for long. If the lake bed itself were cracked, the water would soon drain into the tunnels beneath."

"Wager the way through is at the bottom of that twister?" Darnak asked.

Jig wanted to laugh. All this way, past goblins, hobgoblins, and carrion-worms, to face a dead end. But would the adventurers face reality and turn back the way they had come? He doubted it. More likely they would continue on, stubbornness pushing them all to their deaths. The only question was whether they would drown first, or if the whirlpool would batter them to a bloody pulp.

Something slipped out of the water and began to crawl toward them. Oh yes, that was the third possibility. They could all die from lizard-fish poison before they even made it to the lake.

"Lizard-fish," Jig yelled, hopping and pointing and scanning the shore for others.

"Ugly things, aren't they?" Darnak drew his club and calmly waited while the lizard-fish crawled closer.

Jig had never seen a living lizard-fish before. This one was as long as his arm, with clawed front feet and webbed rear feet that dragged behind in the sand. The round head had slits for a nose and a wide mouth filled with needle-sharp teeth that could rip flesh from the body so cleanly you wouldn't even notice. The eyes bulged like white bubbles that had been stuck to the skull as an afterthought. Most dangerous, Jig knew, was the line of two-inch spines that started at the back of the skull and ran all the way to the tip of the lizard-fish's long tail.

"The spines are poison!"

Darnak ignored him. The dwarf watched as the lizard-fish drew nearer. When it was only a few feet away from the dwarf, it raised its head and hissed. The blue tongue flicked out, and the spines lifted threateningly.

Threatening or not, Darnak didn't appear to care. He waited for the lizard-fish to finish hissing, then calmly stomped its skull into the rock. "Stupid little beasts, too."

Stupid they might be, Jig thought, but there were a lot more lizard-fish than there were adventurers. Even as he watched, several more emerged from the water and crawled toward the dwarf. Barius stepped forward to join him. His sword impaled one of the creatures and flipped it back into the water. Another attacked with a sudden burst of speed, only to die beneath Darnak's heavy boot.

Even as Darnak wiped lizard-fish guts from his boot, however, more were racing forward to attack.

"Back," Barius shouted. Jig rolled his eyes. He and Riana had already retreated to safety.

The others joined them farther up the tunnel. Nothing followed. The lizard-fish wouldn't come this far from the water, it appeared.

"We could stand there until we were hip-deep in the things," Darnak grumbled. "They'd still keep coming. Not a brain in the lot of 'em."

Like goblins, Jig thought suddenly. Swarming to their death and hoping to overwhelm the enemy with sheer numbers. But he said nothing.

"All it takes is one slip, one moment of carelessness, and those spines would be the end of us," said Barius.

"Then I guess we'd better stay on our toes, eh boys?" Darnak grinned.

I was right, Jig realized. *They won't turn back. They probably don't know* how *to retreat.* As they continued to discuss how to get past the lizard-fish, Jig walked to the end of the tunnel and stared at the beach. The lizard-fish had returned to the water, leaving the dead bodies behind to rot. Something else would no doubt come along to feast on the remains. Carrion-worms, perhaps. Or maybe some other creature scavenged the lakeshore. That was how the cycle worked.

At least that was the way things were back home. Who knew what life might be like lower down? No goblins had ever explored much beyond their own territory. Nor had anything from the lower depths ever emerged into Jig's world. Which was probably a good thing. In fact, for all Jig knew, the lizard-fish might be there as much to keep the monsters of the lower caverns trapped below as to keep those from the surface out.

Still, he wondered if things would be different there. Jig's world was a constant battle for territory between goblins, hobgoblins, and the other creatures. But the world below belonged to the Necromancer. Maybe he would keep the creatures under his control from charging off to be senselessly slaughtered every time something came through the entrance. The monsters there might actually win battles from time to time. Jig's imagination conjured an image of a patrol all his own, returning to the lair with the bodies of the adventurers dragging behind them. There was cheering and shouting and singing. Songs that *weren't* about goblins getting themselves killed.

He didn't care if he was the one leading the patrol. Even to be a part of such a group, to work with other goblins to *win* battles, would be a thing worth all the treasure in Straum's lair.

Reality intruded as Jig remembered the sound of Porak's last gurgling breaths, right after Barius's sword poked out of his back. Jig shook his head, angry at himself for his silly fantasies. Goblins were nothing. The natural hierarchy meant the deeper you went, the stronger the monsters. That was why goblins lived here, closer to the entrance than any other monsters. Things had always been that way, probably since the day Ellnorein made this place.

"Goblin, get in here," Darnak yelled.

He joined the others. Ryslind held out five vials of a dark green liquid. "This is an antitoxin," he said. "I had hoped to save it for emergencies, but I see no other way to survive the lizard-fish."

Jig took one of the small vials and stared at it with suspicion. *What had died to create these potions?* he wondered, remembering what Riana had told him about the blue powder. And how had Ryslind known to bring antitoxin? Was this common practice among mages? Maybe so. If Ryslind was a normal mage, Jig could understand why people would try to poison them.

The others drank it down, even Riana. If anyone had reason to doubt the mage, it was her. Jig shrugged and swallowed his own potion in one gulp. After all, it couldn't be worse than bread.

The potion tasted salty, and it was thicker than he expected. A thin, slimy coating clung to the roof of his mouth and the back of his throat. This would save him from the sting of the lizard-fish? He didn't understand how, but what did he know about magic? If Ryslind said this would work, who was he to question? Nobody else seemed to have any doubts.

"We have a half hour. Maybe more for the goblin and the elf, as they're smaller. Come." Ryslind rose and strode back toward the lake. Darnak hurriedly finished drawing a small lizard-fish on the map, marked it DANGEROUS, then rolled the whole thing up and tucked it into a hard leather tube. As they walked, he used a block of sealing wax to waterproof the seams. By the time they reached the shore, Darnak's precious map was safely tucked into his pack.

"Follow," Ryslind commanded. He walked straight toward the water, ignoring the lizard-fish that scurried up the beach. Darnak and Barius killed them as they approached, but Ryslind appeared oblivious.

What was he planning to do, just swim out to the whirlpool? The wizard's hands began to move in small circles, fingers pointed toward the surface of the lake. Jig waited for a flash of lightning to kill the lizard-fish, or a magical bridge to suddenly appear over the water. As he stared, a lizard-fish ran up and jabbed Jig with the spines of its tail.

Cursing, Jig grabbed his knife and stabbed at the lizard-fish, which dodged to the side and ran off. Lizard-fish weren't terribly bright, however, and it ran straight into the path of Darnak's club. *I guess I'll find out whether or not this potion works.*

He looked back toward Ryslind, and his eyes widened. Ryslind had begun to walk across the surface of the lake. As Jig stared, Barius followed his brother. Jig hurried after them, not wanting to be the last target for swarms of angry lizard-fish.

He and Riana reached the edge together, and only then did he see what Ryslind had done. "It's frozen," he whispered. A path of ice several yards wide led straight toward the center of the lake. "Incredible."

"But at what cost?" Riana asked. At Jig's confused look, she said, "Where does he get all that power?"

Jig shrugged. Magic was beyond him. All he knew about wizards was that you were smart to get out of their way, and lucky to do so with your skin intact. He was more interested in knowing how he was supposed to walk along the ice path without slipping.

Several of the lizard-fish started to follow, but Ryslind's spell had an added bonus: lizard-fish didn't like ice. Some of them took a step, then backed onto the shore shaking their claws. Others, apparently more stubborn than the rest, tried to run after the party. Their legs danced like marionettes as they tried to minimize contact with the ice, and eventually they slipped out of control and splashed back into the water.

Halfway to the whirlpool, something cold touched the back of Jig's neck. He turned to protect himself, but saw only Riana. He stared, suspicious, until it happened again. This time the water dripped onto the top of his head and rolled down the side of his face.

He looked up and caught a third drop in his left eye.

"Stupid lake."

As he walked, he wondered if the entire lake was nothing but water droplets that had collected over the years. Had this all begun as a few puddles? How long would it take for a few scattered drops to become a lake this size? Trying to comprehend time on that scale made his head hurt.

At the whirlpool, Ryslind stopped. The water wasn't as violent as before. Jig wondered if the ice went deep enough to blunt the whirlpool's power. He still had no desire to leap into that funnel of death. The water splashed them all as it passed Ryslind's path of ice, and Jig shivered. Whether because of the ice, or because the water itself was colder here, the air carried a bitter chill. Jig longed for something more than his old loincloth.

"There *is* something below," Ryslind said, his voice tight. "I sense a buildup of power beneath us, and none of the creatures have come near this place."

Of course not, Jig thought. Lizard-fish might be stupid, but no monster was *that* stupid. Except, perhaps, for the occasional goblin. And adventurers, naturally.

"Hold your breath. As you pass, I will cast a charm to strengthen your lungs, but you must fight the urge to breathe. Water is a powerful element, and it will throw all its power against you. If you fail, you will die."

With that pronouncement, he rested his fingertips on Darnak's shoulder. The dwarf waited for the wizard to finish. Shooting a dark look toward the roof of the cavern, he shouted, "Earthmaker

watch over me." In a slightly lower tone, he added,
"But if you had told me what I'd have to endure
to keep these two safe, I'd have told you to send
a bloody merman in my place."

He checked to be certain his club was lashed to
his belt, tightened the straps of his pack, and leaped
into the water. Jig tried to follow his progress. Several times, he saw the dwarf bob past, hair flattened
to his head, arms waving madly. Once a pair of
booted feet rushed by. Then the water dragged him
down, and Jig saw nothing.

Barius went next, followed by a reluctant Riana.
When Jig's turn arrived, he couldn't help looking
back at the shore. He wished now that he had
seized the chance to escape last night. Maybe he
could have snuck past the hobgoblins. If he made
it back to the lair, he could have figured something
out to explain Porak's death. There had to be a
way. Why hadn't he run when he had the chance?

His heart was racing, and Jig realized he was
terrified. His heart was pounding, and he was on
the verge of soiling his loincloth. When Ryslind's
fingers brushed his forehead, he yelped in fright.

The wizard's touch was cold, almost skeletal.
Jig's skin crawled, and his head felt stuffy. Between
one breath and the next, it was as though he had
come down with the worst head cold of his life.
His eyes watered.

"Remember to hold your breath," Ryslind said.

Jig stared at the whirlpool. The ice actually extended a few inches past its edge, so he would fall
several feet into the freezing water. All he had to
do was jump. The others had done it.

Another look back told him he had no choice. He
could see unbroken waves behind them. The bridge
of ice had begun to melt. He couldn't go back.

But he couldn't go forward, either. Not into that.

The whirlpool was a giant mouth, waiting to devour him. The lake had swallowed the others in seconds. He had seen Riana's face, white with fear as she flailed about, trying to keep her head above water. None of her struggles had made the slightest difference to the lake. As Ryslind had said, water was a powerful element. Why should Jig be sacrificed to the lake's hunger?

Tears slipped down his cheeks. He wiped them on his shoulder. Jig had expected to die since he first saw the adventurers. But death by sword was one thing. This was fear on an entirely different scale. At least in combat, you didn't have time to watch death approach. The whirlpool watched Jig in return. It taunted him. In the center of the cone, the water's surface was glassy and clear, and only the whitecaps at the edge hinted at the pool's true might.

At that point, Jig's frightened thoughts were interrupted by the foot that kicked him headfirst into the whirlpool. He barely remembered to hold his breath.

The whirlpool jerked him sideways and plunged him deeper into the water. Jig reached out for the surface, but which way was it? He spun faster and faster, and finally he gave up on reaching the surface. He clutched his knees to his chest, closed his eyes, and waited for the lake to decide whether he would live or die.

Without warning, when he was spinning so fast he thought his stomach would explode, the water spat Jig out like a quarrel from a crossbow. He flew through the air and collided with something hard.

As the world flashed white, he had time to realize that Smudge was still tucked into his belt pouch. He hoped the fire-spider had survived.

He hoped that he survived as well.

CHAPTER 6

❧❦❧

More Needling

Jig hurt. His head felt like one enormous bruise, his muscles ached, and his waterlogged loincloth gave him a chill he couldn't ignore. But to squeeze out the excess water would require him to move, which didn't seem like a good idea yet. Not to mention that modesty prevented him from stripping down in front of the adventurers.

While he waited for the throbbing in his head to die down, he cracked his eyes and took his first look at the Necromancer's territory.

As Ryslind had predicted, the whirlpool flowed through a large crack in the ceiling and into this room. The spinning cylinder of water stood like a pillar as wide as Jig's outstretched arms. The surface was smooth as glass, and only the bubbles rushing around in quick circles broke the illusion. Jig wondered how he had passed through the barrier that kept the water in place. Was it a part of Ryslind's spell, or the nature of the pillar itself? Neither answer brought much comfort. Especially given the force of the water trapped behind that invisible barrier.

I fell through *that. As if I didn't have enough fodder for my nightmares.*

Everyone else had made it through more or less intact. Ryslind was checking on the dwarf, who looked as though he was still unconscious. Riana bled from a cut on her head, and her cheek sported an angry bruise. Barius slumped against a far wall, barely awake. All of them, Jig noticed, sat in the center of large puddles. At least he wasn't alone in his discomfort.

Moving slowly so as not to aggravate his headache, Jig fumbled with the wet ties on his belt pouch. Eventually he managed to undo the knot so he could check on Smudge.

A blast of steam caught him in the face like a miniature geyser. Smudge leaped a good foot into the air, trailing steam beneath him. He turned to run away from Jig, spotted the tail of the whirlpool, and raced right back to the goblin's side. Jig searched the room for something to feed the battered fire-spider. A few bugs, an old rat, anything would do. Smudge had been through a lot, and he deserved some reward. But the room was as clean as any he had seen.

The walls were black marble, polished to reflect the lantern light. Someone must have relit the lamp, since Jig doubted the flame could have survived the trip. The floor was the same black marble, and up close, Jig could see that red lines ran jaggedly through the marble like tiny veins. As for the ceiling . . . Jig stared. Before when he glanced at the crack in the ceiling, his mind hadn't registered the glass tiles and swirls of color. This was another mosaic, the same as in the shiny room up above.

The same style, but not identical. The colors were brighter. Perhaps the maker had used different types of glass, or perhaps the Necromancer's minions weren't as dirty as the goblins and hobgoblins. The column of water interrupted the image. Rather, the picture had been created around the pillar. Whorls of color came together around the column, where flecks of blue glass gave the impression of splashing water.

"Ach." Darnak spat weakly into the puddle that surrounded him. "Feels like I took a nap on Earthmaker's anvil and woke up with his hammer pounding my bones." He reached back and pulled off his pack. His movements showed the same stiffness Jig felt. The dwarf grumbled a bit more as he sorted through his belongings, eventually pulling out a large blue wineskin. A few long swallows, and he sat back again.

"Much better," he said contentedly. "Nothing like dwarven ale to take the edge off a bad day." He took another drink before glancing around. "Everyone got a bit banged up, it seems."

He used his club to push himself up. With a nod of thanks to Ryslind, who had cleaned a cut on Darnak's scalp, he hobbled over to check on Barius.

"I'll get him fixed up, and then we can see about paying a visit to this Necromancer of yours."

"Um, Darnak?" Jig searched the room again, hoping his poor eyes had betrayed him.

"What is it?"

"How are we going to find the Necromancer?" When the dwarf didn't appear to understand, Jig said, "There are no doors. How are we supposed to get out of the room?"

Darnak stared at the walls. "Damn me." He took another long drink from his wineskin. "Check around for hidden doors. I won't believe I let my-self be flushed through *that* for nothing. As I'm not looking to go back through anytime soon, there must be another way out."

Leaving Jig to cock his head at the questionable logic, Darnak knelt next to Barius and took the prince's head in his hands. He studied Barius's eyes for several minutes before reaching inside his armor and pulling out a small silver hammer on a chain. He clasped both hands around the hammer, as if to pray.

"Go on then," Darnak snapped. "Get the elf to help search."

Jig pushed himself to his feet. Riana joined him, limping slightly. One hand pressed a large, raw scrape on her elbow.

"I feel like I swallowed half that lake on the way down," she complained.

Jig didn't answer. He studied the walls closely, wondering how he should go about searching for hidden doors. Dwarf logic aside, what made Dar-nak think there was a door here? Wouldn't it make more sense to drop adventurers through the whirl-pool into a room with no way out? Let them starve. That way the intruders died without a struggle. It would be easier and more effective than sending wave after wave of monsters to fight and die each time someone snuck through the lake.

The marble was smooth and cold to the touch. Jig shivered and wished for a fire to dry himself. Even Smudge's warmth would have helped, but for once the fire-spider was uncooperatively cool, hav-ing steamed any trace of water from his small body.

Already he hated this place. He distrusted the magic that kept the lake from pouring in on them. If Jig and the others could pass through that bar-rier, how long before the lake broke free? The room itself was equally disorienting. At home the walls *flowed* into the floor, like liquid rock frozen in place. Which, if he were to believe Darnak's crazy explanation, was exactly the case. The sharp corners of this room were alien, and they emphasized Jig's sense that he didn't belong.

Jig saw Riana rap her knuckles against the wall. She was listening for hollow areas, he realized. Knocking on a door would produce a different sound than knocking on a wall. How clever of her.

Jig followed the wall in the opposite direction, tapping and running his hands over the marble as he walked. He heard nothing unusual, and his knuckles swiftly began to complain. He took out his new sword and used the pommel to tap the wall instead. Still nothing.

By the time he ran into Riana on the opposite side of the room, Barius was up and pacing impatiently. Darnak's prayers had apparently done wonders for the prince. Jig wished he could have seen exactly how this magic healing worked, but the dwarf had already pulled out fresh parchment to begin his new map.

"Have you found nothing?" Barius demanded.

Neither Jig nor Riana bothered to answer. *The least you could do is help us search.* But Jig knew enough to keep that thought to himself.

"The fool goblin has led us to a dead-end." Barius glared at Jig, ignoring the fact that the fool goblin was just as trapped as the rest of them.

He was like Porak in that way. If things went wrong, he searched for a scapegoat. He had to first find someone to blame before he could try to solve the problem. Porak used to beat up the younger goblins every time he lost at Rakachak. Jig wondered if this was something all leaders did.

"Brother, use your art to find a way out of this trap."

Ryslind's face was as cold as the marble walls, but his eyes burned brighter than Jig had ever seen. On Jig's shoulder, Smudge grew warmer, echoing his unease. Jig tried to move Smudge back into the pouch, but the spider would have none of it. He wriggled free and ran back up Jig's arm. After what they had gone through, Jig couldn't really blame him. He simply didn't want to burn his other shoulder. Besides, tucking Smudge into the pouch would put the spider's heat closer to Jig's dripping loincloth, and if he didn't get dry soon, he would start to chafe.

But he couldn't pay attention to Smudge, not without taking his eyes off of Ryslind. Jig knew Smudge well enough to heed his warnings, and at that moment, Smudge thought the wizard was dangerous.

"Yes," Ryslind said softly. "Let me use my art once more. As if it were no more than a tool to be used at your convenience."

Nobody missed the fury in Ryslind's normally calm voice. Even Darnak froze, his quill leaking black ink onto his thumb and fingers.

"Easy lad," Darnak said. "Barius meant nothing by it." Jig wondered if anyone else saw the warning glare the dwarf shot at Barius.

"No need to apologize," Ryslind said. "Indeed, without my power, we could spend the rest of our lives in this room."

"Without your brother, we wouldn't have come after the rod in the first place," Darnak pointed out. "Without the elf, we'd have had a rough time getting through that first gate. And without me, you two would have killed one another before we ever made it to the mountain. We're all needed here, and nobody's questioning your importance."

Jig didn't find that reassuring. Nor did Smudge, if the waves of heat on his shoulder were any indication. He also noted that Darnak's argument had ignored anything the goblin might have done for the group. Not that this came as a surprise.

Jig watched closely as Ryslind strode to one wall and raised his head. He studied the unbroken marble and frowned, as though insulted by its presence. The green tattoos on his hands began to glow. Once Jig thought he saw them move, like luminescent worms crawling beneath white skin.

Hands still at his side, Ryslind began to circle the room. Jig hurriedly got out of the way. So did the others, though Barius tried hard to make the move appear casual.

A few paces past Riana, the wizard stopped. "Here." He raised one hand and pointed. Green light spread out from his finger to form a rectangle on the wall. His hand closed into a fist.

Nothing changed. Ryslind squinted at the door. "Ah." Another beam of light struck the center of the door, revealing a narrow keyhole.

"This is the elf's responsibility, I believe. Will there be anything more, my brother?" The light died as Ryslind walked away, but the door remained visible behind him.

Jig's eyes widened, and his ears flattened against his head as he realized why he was suddenly so afraid of Ryslind. Ever since they came through the whirlpool, the wizard's voice had been different. The difference was so subtle Jig hadn't noticed at first, and he doubted any of the others could hear it at all. But each time Ryslind spoke, it was as though a second voice spoke the same words along with him.

He stroked Smudge's head and body, trying to calm the agitated spider. Was he imagining things? Slamming into the ground on the way out of the whirlpool could have affected his hearing. Yet if that were the case, why wasn't he hearing the same distortion when the others spoke?

Besides, he wasn't the only one afraid of Ryslind. Even Barius regarded his brother with wary eyes, and one hand rested on his belt, close to the hilt of his sword. Whether they heard the change or not, they knew enough to be watchful.

"I will be fine," Ryslind said wearily. "I have simply . . . overexerted myself. By the time you open the lock, I shall be myself again."

Nobody relaxed, but Barius did wave Riana toward the door. She rolled her eyes and pulled several thin metal tools from a pack at her belt. She grabbed the lantern in passing, leaving the rest of them in shadows.

Jig heard her curse as she dried her tools. The scratch of metal against metal told him she had begun to work on the lock. But he didn't watch. He couldn't look away from Ryslind's struggle.

For the human was obviously at war within himself. His fists clenched into knots, and his neck had tightened to the point where the muscles formed raised lines of skin between the neck and shoulders. Each deep, ragged breath sounded like that of a dying man.

Barius had gone to watch Riana work on the lock, but Darnak remained close by the wizard. He kept saying Ryslind's name over and over. One hand went to the small hammer around his neck. His other reached toward Ryslind.

Ryslind's fist shot out, and the dwarf caught it in his free hand. Between the darkness and his own poor vision, Jig couldn't be certain, but he thought he saw the dwarf flinch. *What kind of strength did it take to do that to Darnak?* He decided he would rather not find out.

"I am . . . all right," Ryslind whispered.

"Almost lost it there, did you?"

Ryslind didn't answer. He turned around, and his eyes narrowed when he saw Jig watching.

Jig tried to swallow, but fear stuck in his throat like an oversize chunk of meat. He couldn't apologize for watching. He couldn't even break away from Ryslind's angry gaze. The faint red lights of those eyes seemed to call to him. Even blinking had become difficult, and his eyes began to water. This was something beyond fear. His body was no longer under his control. What was Ryslind doing to him? His eyes grew dry. He could barely breathe. Was this his punishment for daring to see Ryslind's moment of weakness?

Behind him, Riana yelped.

Ryslind looked away, and Jig gasped for breath.

"What happened?" Darnak asked.

"The silly girl triggered a trap," Barius said angrily.

A trap? Jig followed the dwarf to the door. Riana sat on the floor, clutching her index finger with an expression of shock. A tiny bead of blood glistened at her fingertip.

"A needle trap," Barius said. "Probably poisoned."

His words chipped away at Riana's hard facade. She shot a pleading look at Darnak. "It was an accident."

"Wait," Jig said. "What about the potions we took, to protect us from the lizard-fish poison? Will they be enough to protect her?"

Hope and gratitude flashed in Riana's eyes as she looked to Ryslind for the answer.

The wizard shrugged. "The potion was a short-acting one. I don't know if it will still be effective. Nor, without knowing what poison was used, can I be certain that even a full dose would have protected her. Were I to create such a trap, the types of poison I might choose would still kill her."

Jig stepped closer to the door. A tiny needle protruded from the lock. It reminded him of the way the lizard-fish had flicked their tongues as they attacked. "Is this sort of thing common where you come from? Hidden doors, trapped locks . . . how do you people survive from day to day?"

Barius shrugged. "Only a fool would put his faith in a simple lock."

He wondered how many accidents came from trying to build such intricate traps. It was a strange world where the job of the locksmith could be more dangerous than that of a soldier.

Riana whimpered suddenly. Darnak gasped. "Earthmaker help us."

Her finger had begun to shrivel, and the skin turned gray as they watched. The nail yellowed and cracked at the tip. She touched the dying flesh with her other hand. "It's cold."

"The Necromancer's work, no doubt," Barius said.

That much Jig could have figured out without the prince's dramatic pronouncement. What he didn't know was how to stop whatever was happening to Riana. Would this poison spread throughout her body, or would the potion be strong enough to stop it before she died? Worse, if the poison took her, what would happen to her then? The fingertip still moved like living flesh. Would she be truly dead, or would she become something worse, some kind of toy for the Necromancer? If this was a taste of the Necromancer's power, Jig would happily stay up above with the hobgoblins and the lizard-fish.

"Can you heal her?" Jig asked.

But Darnak was already shaking his head. "It's in the gods' hands now."

Jig turned to Ryslind, but words caught in his throat. Could the wizard save Riana? He had made potions to counteract the lizard-fish, after all. Seeing the shadows beneath Ryslind's eyes, and the sweat still shining on his bald scalp, Jig decided against asking. If the overuse of Ryslind's art had caused the fit Jig saw, the last thing he wanted to do was ask the wizard to exert himself further.

The decay spread toward the second knuckle. Riana held her hand away from her, clutching the wrist with her good hand.

"Broken bones, bloody cuts, and other wounds of honest battle, those I can heal with Earthmaker's blessing. Poison and magic, though . . ." Darnak shook his head. "Those are beyond me."

"Your counsel, old teacher," Barius said. He drew the dwarf to the other side of the room and began to speak in a low whisper.

Jig perked his ears. No doubt their voices were too quiet for Ryslind to overhear, and Riana was too distraught to listen. Goblin ears were another matter. With everything he had seen in the past hour, Jig wasn't about to let *anyone* start plotting behind his back.

"How long before the poison slays her?" Barius asked.

"It's not the slaying that worries me. You saw her finger. Dead, but still moving. I fear what she'll become."

Jig nodded. He had seen the same thing. Good to know Darnak agreed with him.

"If the poison takes her, she could turn upon us. That cannot be permitted."

"And what would you have me do about it?" Darnak sounded suspicious.

"I will distract the girl. Make her end quick and painless."

Barius was so calm that it took Jig several heart-beats to understand what he was saying. He wanted to kill Riana! No, that wasn't true. He wanted Darnak to do it.

" 'Tis not in me to murder an innocent girl in cold blood," Darnak said sternly. "Nor is it a worthy thought for a prince. I'd have expected such from the goblin, but not you."

Jig scowled. Why would he have made such a suggestion? They didn't listen to him anyway. Nor would he have proposed murdering Riana even if they did listen. Running away before she finished her transformation, maybe, but not murder.

"She's no innocent," Barius snapped. "She's a thief. By law, she should have been imprisoned the moment she tried to rob us."

"Imprisoned, aye." He took another swig from his wineskin. "But not executed. Your father would have my head if—"

"My father is not here with us. In his absence, my word is as law."

Darnak fell silent. Jig risked a glance back to see what was happening. Both had their arms crossed, and Darnak was shaking his head.

Jig also noticed Ryslind leaning against the wall, looking bored. His lips curled slightly, hinting at amusement. He probably couldn't hear what was being discussed as well as Jig, but that didn't matter. He knew Darnak and his brother, and he must have deduced what Barius wanted to do. He only waited to hear who would win the argument.

"I'll not do it," Darnak said finally. "I'll not kill a girl in cold blood. Not even for you."

Jig nodded with satisfaction. Only an instant passed, though, before he realized what the dwarf had not said. He'd not kill Riana, but he wouldn't stop Barius from doing so, either. Jig looked again, and saw Barius walking toward Riana. His hands were empty, but his face was carefully expressionless. Ryslind fell into step behind his brother.

"Riana, give me your hand," Jig whispered. She obeyed, too scared to argue.

Jig rolled his eyes. "The other one."

Trembling, she held out her poisoned hand. The decay had taken over most of the finger, with only a thin ring of healthy skin above the knuckle. Jig studied it closely, folding her other fingers back so he could see better.

"What's going to happen?" Fresh tears dripped down her cheek, making her look like a young child.

"How old are you?" Jig asked absently.

"Sixteen."

He stared. "But I thought elves lived to be hundreds of years. Even thousands."

That earned a small, brave grin. "You think we're born with centuries already behind us? That'd be hell on the mother."

He shook his head, confused. Of course there were young elves. It was only that none of the songs or stories ever mentioned them, so Jig had never stopped to imagine an elf less than a century old. Elves were ancient beings who had lived through events other races only knew of as distant history. That was what made them so hard to kill. How did you beat someone with that much experience?

"Riana," Barius called. "We must speak of your injury."

"They're going to let me die, aren't they?"

"No," he said. An honest, if misleading answer. They wouldn't *let* her die. All that remained to be seen was whether Barius or his brother would do the actual killing. Jig wagered it would be Ryslind.

When Riana started to move toward the humans, Jig tightened his grip and pulled her off balance. With his other hand, he drew his sword and placed it at the base of her wounded finger. She looked back, eyes wide with fear and betrayal.

Jig didn't have time to explain. Before she could speak, he pulled the blade toward himself as hard as he could.

Which was harder than necessary, as it turned out. The poison must have weakened the bone, or else the blade was sharper than Jig was used to. His sword sliced through the finger, then continued on to slash Jig's own forearm.

Riana stared, shocked, at the blood leaking from the stump of her finger.

Jig watched his own blood drip from the long cut in his arm. All of his strength drained away. His legs threatened to give out, and the sword slipped from his fingers. Pain and shock spread from his arm throughout his body. He looked to Riana, mouth open to speak, but words failed him.

Her eyes narrowed, and with her good hand, she punched him in the nose. As he staggered back into the wall, Jig realized that at least one of the legends was true: Elves were much stronger than they appeared.

Jig probed his throbbing nose. Blood dripped from both nostrils, but the nose itself didn't feel broken. "Gak," he said as blood ran down the back of his throat. "Disgusting." Even worse than Ryslind's potion. He sat down and rested his head between his knees, using one hand to pinch his nose shut.

Hot footsteps on his back brought him back to alertness. What was Smudge running away from?

He looked up, and when his eyes focused, he found himself staring at the tip of Barius's sword. As he had noted earlier, it was a masterful work of weaponscraft. The blade was perfectly straight, and three narrow grooves ran the length of the sword. To make it lighter, Jig guessed. Which no doubt made it easier for Barius to keep it leveled at Jig's heart.

"We should have slain you from the outset, goblin."

"Me?" Jig asked. *Stupid question. How many other goblins do you see down here?*

"I turn my back but for a few brief moments, and you draw steel against your own companions."

The quiet outrage in Barius's voice was so perfect that, for a heartbeat, Jig felt guilty. Only for a heartbeat, though. Then he remembered *why* he had done it.

"Me?" he said again, dumbfounded. "I heard you talking to Darnak. Better to cut off her finger than—"

The prince stepped forward and punched Jig in the jaw, knocking him to the floor. As he lay there staring at the beauty of the ceiling, he wondered if there was any reason to stand again. Not if people were going to keep hitting him, he decided. No, he would stay right here. If the gods were just, Barius would at least chip his sword on the floor when he finished Jig off.

His eyes traced one of the blue whirls toward the center of the ceiling, where it vanished into the water. *Yes, this is much better. As long as I don't move, nothing hurts. I should have thought of this from the beginning. They could have killed me and been done with it. At least I would have died comfortable.*

He wondered what was taking Barius so long. *Maybe he doesn't want to chip his sword.* Jig grinned. The prince would be so offended if he damaged his weapon on a mere goblin. Smiling turned out to be a mistake. The prince's blow had split his upper lip, and his amusement vanished with a hiss of pain.

He closed his eyes and tried to relax as he waited. *This is why goblins make such poor adventurers,* he concluded. A few blows to the head, and Jig was out of commission. Well, to be fair, he had also been flung out of a whirlpool into a stone room. That cut on his arm hadn't helped, either. And he'd be in better shape if he had eaten a real meal in the past day and a half. Still real heroes were the men who shrugged off a half-dozen arrows and continued to fight. Goblins tended to run and scream if they stubbed their toe on a rock.

A strong hand grabbed his injured arm. Until that moment, Jig had thought he was ready to die. He had been expecting it all along, ever since Porak sent him off alone. Death should have been a relief. But as powerful fingers pulled him into a sitting position, Jig realized the waiting wasn't so bad after all. Perhaps he could stand to put things off for a mite longer. He raised his other arm to protect his head and kicked blindly.

"Here now, none of that," Darnak grumbled.

The alcohol on Darnak's breath was enough to knock Jig backward, even with his nostrils half-clogged by blood. His eyes snapped open. "What?" Where was Barius? Why wasn't Jig dead yet?

"I know what you did," Darnak said in a low

voice. "True, she hates you now. And that wouldn't have helped her against normal poison, but you may have saved her life."

"I did?"

"Not a word about it, I warn ye." The dwarf wouldn't meet his gaze. "He's got a temper, Barius does, and he's throwing a right fit about you. I persuaded him to let you keep breathing for a while yet, but you're to lose the sword. And it's back to the rope."

"Riana?" Jig asked.

"I stopped the bleeding. Earthmaker should kick me for not thinking of that myself. A bit of magic, and the skin healed over as smooth as an egg. She's a little put out, mind you, but she should live." He grabbed his hammer on its thong and closed his eyes. "Now let me see what I can do about that arm."

This time, Jig watched closely as Darnak called upon his god to work his healing magic. With the hammer hidden in his thick fist, he began to mumble. Jig listened closely, but the words were foreign. Dwarvish, he guessed. The language sounded like a mixture of coughing, spitting, and gnashing of teeth. A bit like Goblin, really, but not close enough for him to understand.

So intent was Jig on watching the dwarf, he didn't notice when the pain in his arm began to recede. What had been a sharp tearing pain became a dull burn, unpleasant but less intense. He could feel his blood pound with each beat of his heart. The rhythm grew louder, booming in his ears until he expected to see his very skin throb. The heat in his arm grew.

Like a blacksmith, Jig thought suddenly. Each pulse was a hammer blow that forged the flesh whole again. Fitting, coming from a dwarven god.

When Darnak pulled his hand away, a dark blue

scar ran the length of Jig's forearm. Blood still smeared the skin, but it was dark and crusted. He brushed his arm, marveling at the new scar. His battle scar. Not, he admitted, that he had come by it in the normal way. But he doubted any goblin would ever learn he had inflicted the wound with his own hand.

"Best I can do, lad. Dwarven magic doesn't work so well on goblins, it seems."

Jig ignored him. He flexed his arm, watching the way his new scar moved with the muscles beneath. Bits of blood flaked away as he moved. He wondered if the scar would fade with time. If only he had been allowed to keep the short sword as well. But Barius had already taken the weapon and tucked it into his own belt. The exuberance of his scar faded as he realized what it had cost him.

He had lost the first good weapon he had ever owned, and for what? To protect an elf girl's life? These were the people he was supposed to kill. Porak would have taken the sword from Riana and buried it in her back as soon as she turned. Not Jig. No, he had tried to *help*. See where that misguided effort had landed him. Unarmed, and soon to be tied up again like a slave.

Jig tried to tell himself it would have made no difference, that had he used his sword against the adventurers, he would have died instantly. He had seen them fight, and he knew he had no chance. But still the guilt and confusion warred. What was wrong with him?

His only consolation was that the Necromancer would soon make it right. Already one of the party had almost died, and they hadn't even left the first room. What would they face beyond that door, and how many of them would wish they had drowned in the lake above?

CHAPTER 7

The Heat of Battle

Barius was not happy. "We have still accomplished nothing! The door remains sealed both to my brother's art and the elf's tools."

And the party is short by one finger, Jig added silently. He watched as Riana examined the lock. She struggled to grasp her tools with her crippled hand, a task made harder by fear. Her hands trembled as they approached the door, and she had yet to actually touch the lock.

Not that Jig blamed her. If he had been in her place, the last thing he'd want to do is poke around the trap a second time. But the ache in his jaw and the rope around his wrists made it hard to feel any sympathy. As Riana tried again to examine the lock, he commented, "I wonder if the Necromancer was clever enough to put a second trap on the lock."

She leaped away from the door so fast that she tripped and fell. Her tools jingled as they hit the floor. Jig grinned at his mischief. The enemy might be stronger and better armed, but he could still cause trouble.

"Enough," Barius shouted. He stomped toward Jig. "*You* will probe the lock for further traps."

Wordlessly, Jig held up his bound wrists. Barius turned a deeper shade of red, and Jig wondered if he had pushed too far.

The prince grabbed the end of Jig's rope and yanked him upright. He untied the knot and jerked the rope away so quickly Jig lost a layer of skin. Jig started for the door, but Barius caught his ear and held him in place.

Jig stopped, indignant. Didn't he know you only grabbed *children* that way? No adult goblin would allow himself to be dragged about by the ear. He should bite off Barius's hand for this. He should plant a lizard-fish in Barius's bedroll!

Glimpsing the prince's face, he decided that he should do nothing at all. Barius tied a quick loop in the rope and tightened it about Jig's neck. Still, the freedom to use his hands was a victory, if a small one. Jig was a small goblin. Perhaps his triumphs were better taken in small bites.

With an impudent grin, Jig headed for the door. Darnak knelt with Riana to one side, trying to boost her spirits. He had given her a bit of his ale, a kind gesture which may have been a mistake. To judge from the way her head wobbled, elves didn't handle dwarven ale very well.

"Don't worry about a lost finger," Darnak said gently. "Many an adventurer has lost a finger, or worse, and still gone on to accomplish great things. Have you heard the song of . . . I forget his name. The little guy with nine fingers, from the middle continent. The one involved with that ring business a while back."

Jig hovered over them both, clicking his toenails against the floor until Darnak acknowledged him.

"I need a bit of twine." He held his hands a foot apart to indicate how long.

Darnak said nothing. He still seemed a bit uncomfortable with Jig. Did he feel guilty for almost letting Riana die? Jig didn't care. In fact, the more uncomfortable they felt, the happier he would be.

Riana wouldn't look at him at all, but it was harder for Jig to feel pleasure at that. Still, what did Jig care for an elf's goodwill? If they hated him, he would hate them right back. That was his job. He was a monster and they were adventurers.

As he had hoped, among the endless junk the dwarf carried upon his back, Darnak managed to find a ball of twine, tangled up like an abandoned nest. He ripped a piece free and handed it to Jig.

He seized his trophy and moved to the front of the door, humming quietly under his breath. For once he knew exactly what to do. Better still, none of the others had thought of it. He scooped up one of Riana's discarded tools, a thin steel rod as long as his hand with several diamond-shaped ridges near one end. He also grabbed her severed finger.

As he lashed the rod to the end of the finger, he began to sing. In Goblin, of course. The song sounded ridiculous in Human.

Oh, down came the humans into the dark.
Up raced the goblins, ready for a lark.
The humans were weary, much had they drunk
    that day.
The goblins found them sleeping, said, "Come
    on, let's play."

First they stripped the humans bare, then they
    painted 'em all blue,
Said one goblin to his mate, "This one looks
    a bit like you."

*From a fighter's leather shield, they carved ears
  with points so keen,
And moldy old potatoes made noses large
  and green.*

*When the humans all awoke, they were in for
  quite a fright.
The goblin-looking fools instantly began to
  fight.
The wizard who survived called upon his
  magic flame
To slaughter the real goblins, then he killed
  himself from shame.
For if you fall in battle, all your friends and
  family mourn,
But to fall against the goblins is a thing that
  can't be borne.*

As he sang, he jabbed the metal rod into the keyhole and wiggled it around. The finger itself felt strangely stiff, more like leather-wrapped wood than flesh. No trace of blood showed at the severed end, and a bit of bone protruded a half inch past the shrunken skin, giving Jig a convenient handle. The poisoned needle jabbed the fingertip repeatedly as he worked, but nothing else happened. He tried for several more minutes, not knowing what exactly might trigger the traps. He could feel the rod scrape the inner workings of the lock, and he poked those as well. Still nothing.

"I guess there are no more traps," Jig said. He dropped the finger, still tied to the lockpick, and walked back to sit against the wall. If he had built this room, he definitely would have put a second trap there.

Riana stood. Her face was stone as she walked determinedly, if a little unsteadily, to the door. Pale as she was, she didn't flinch when she picked up the finger and tugged her lockpick free. She used her knife to bend the needle aside, then began to work on the lock itself.

While she worked, Jig went over to claim the discarded twine. He returned to his spot by the wall, where he took his belt pouch and chewed at the leather cord, trying to remove it without damaging the pouch itself. After a few minutes, the old cord lost its fight against goblin teeth, and he slipped it free.

He used the cord to tie the pouch over his right shoulder. Bringing the end of the pouch to his mouth, he used his fangs to bore two holes in the bottom. The twine secured that end to his upper arm. Smudge still refused to crawl into the pouch, and Jig couldn't blame him. But this would provide a perch where the fire-spider could sit without burning Jig whenever they walked into danger. Which seemed to happen every time Jig took a breath.

"Prepare yourselves," Barius said. "We've dallied here long enough, and the gods only know what waits behind that door." He grabbed the end of Jig's rope, looped it once around his wrist, and tugged.

Jig gagged and scrambled to his feet. Riana still hadn't picked the lock, but Barius's patience had run out.

Darnak drew his club and moved to stand behind Riana. Ryslind remained where he was, resting against the far wall. His eyes were alert though, Jig noticed. He watched, not the door, but the other adventurers. Jig looked away.

Three bodies peering over Riana's shoulder did nothing to help her concentration. Her pick slipped, and she turned to glare at the dwarf. "Bad enough that my head pounds from your ale. I don't need your breath adding to my drunkenness."

"Your pardon," Darnak said, taking a step back. Only Jig heard her mutter to herself, "This would be easier if I wasn't seeing double. Hard enough to pick one lock, let alone two."

Something clicked. Riana grabbed a second tool, a thicker, angled rod which she jabbed into the keyhole. Keeping the first pick in place, she turned the larger rod, and the door popped inward.

Riana scrambled back to avoid the door and fell with a loud "Oof." Darnak stepped over her body, club held high.

"Nothing," he said.

The others moved toward the doorway as Darnak raised the lantern, shining a beam of light down the corridor.

Where the goblin tunnels had been smooth obsidian, this hall shone with the same black marble as the room behind them. Large panels of marble covered floor, walls, even the ceiling. Only the threads of red in the marble and thin stripes of glittering silver mortar gave the passage any color.

The labor that must have gone into building these tunnels didn't impress Jig as much as the fact that they were so *clean*. Not a trace of dust marred the gleaming tiles. After all these years, he would have expected the floor to lose its polish. Either the Necromancer used magic to maintain his domain, or else nobody ever walked these tunnels. Jig decided to believe the first explanation.

"Nice," Darnak commented.

"Dangerous," said Barius.

Jig looked up, confused.

"Each panel is wide enough to cover a pit, like the one we encountered above," the prince explained. "We must be cautious."

Cautious meant sending the goblin ahead to trigger any traps. As Jig moved to the front of the party, he consoled himself with the fact that Barius kept a firm grip on the rope trailing from his neck. If the floor did fall away, at least the human would be able to haul his choking body back out. Assuming, of course, that Jig didn't break his neck in the fall.

Once again they made slow progress as a result of Darnak's compulsiveness. The dwarf had taken it upon himself to draw each individual tile on his map. "If one of these squares hides a trap," he explained, "we'll be wanting to know which one."

This time, Jig had no complaints. The sluggish pace meant that he could test each tile before putting his full weight on it. He would press his back against the wall for balance and extend his toes to tap the next tile up the hall. If that felt safe, he ran to the opposite wall and did the same on that side. As the corridor was three tiles wide, this procedure eliminated all but one. The middle tile he simply tested with the ball of his foot. If something happened, he would be off-balance, but without a convenient wall to lean against, he had no choice in the matter.

Naturally it was a middle tile that turned out to be trapped. The corner sank a half inch, and Jig leaped back, flailing his arms for balance.

"Which tile?" shouted Darnak. He hurried to Jig's side, counting as he went. "Ten, eleven, twelve . . . the thirteenth tile. Center one, right?"

Jig nodded. That had been too close. He could have easily fallen forward instead of back, and who knows what would have happened had he landed on the loose tile. *But I didn't.* That was the important thing. He glanced to either side, waiting for the trap to spring.

Darnak's quill scratched furiously as he penned a warning about the tile. Barius stepped closer, shoving Jig to one side. With his sword, Barius prodded the corner Jig had stepped on. Another click, but nothing else happened.

He tried again, harder this time. "Perhaps it's stuck," he mused. "The mechanism grown tired from disuse? A clumsy oversight by whomever maintains these tunnels. What could be more useless than a trapdoor that refuses to open when triggered by its prey?"

"Behind us," Riana yelled. At the same instant, Smudge flashed red-hot.

Darnak whirled, blinding Jig as the lantern's beam passed over his eyes. The rope tugged Jig forward, then went slack. Jig crashed into the wall and stayed there, out of the way. Whatever was coming, Barius had decided to keep both hands free to deal with it.

Jig blinked and squinted. Riana had stayed behind, next to him. He could make out the shapes of Darnak and the humans moving back up the tunnel. Beyond, more humanoid figures moved in silence. Jig saw the glint of weapons from the newcomers. What were they? His vision was bad enough without the party blocking his view.

Riana had drawn her stolen knife, and her chest moved rapidly as her breathing quickened. She and Jig both jumped at the first clang of steel against steel.

But what was it they fought? Where had they come from? He suspected it was something to do with the trapped panel, but he didn't understand what.

As if in response, the wall Jig had been leaning against vanished. It didn't slide or fall away, as Jig would have expected. One moment it was there, and the next Jig was falling back into a small alcove. He looked up. A pale, dead face looked down at him. Nothing but an old corpse, Jig thought at first.

The corpse raised a spiked mace to strike.

Jig squealed and rolled aside as the mace cracked into the floor beside him. The thing's decayed arm was little more than bone and a thin layer of dried flesh, but the strength behind that blow was a match for Darnak.

Smudge sprang free and hid behind the creature, out of sight. Lucky spider. Before the thing could attack again, Jig scrambled out of the alcove and collided with Riana.

The panel had disappeared from the opposite wall as well. Unlike the first creature, however, the inhabitant of this alcove was truly dead. The skin had decayed and flaked away, and one skeletal arm lay on the floor. Dust mingled with the smell of preservatives, and Jig had to grab his nose to keep from sneezing.

"There's another behind me," Jig yelled.

Whatever it was, it had begun life as a human, to judge from the rounded ears. Like the rest of its flesh, those ears were white and shrunken, but still recognizable. Rusted chain mail hung loosely from its shoulders, reinforced with metal plates at the knees and elbows. The hair was gone, making the head look like a skull covered in white mud except for the slight bulge of a nose and the clouded eyes that moved to track Jig's movements.

The mace came up again. Riana fled farther up the corridor, and Jig started to follow, only to slip on the smooth marble. He rolled out of the way of another attack, but this moved him into the thing's legs. It kicked Jig in the stomach, knocking him to the other side of the hall.

Jig gasped for breath. Doubled over, he could still see from the corner of his eye as the creature closed in.

But it stopped a few paces away. The skull-head turned to the right, then the left. Jig swore he saw the skin of the forehead wrinkle, as if in confusion. As the creature turned around, he saw why.

Beneath its armor, the creature wore tattered rags that had no doubt been magnificent finery, back when it was alive. Over time, decay had turned them to dry scraps. No color remained, and bits of thread hung down like the roots of a plant. Somehow those scraps had begun to burn, and nothing made better tinder than dry rags. Orange tendrils of flame danced beneath the armor, slowly climbing up the creature's body while the threads blackened and shriveled.

As the fire grew, the creature began to slap the flames, but to no effect. Its own skin began to burn as it tried without success to extinguish itself.

Whether it was truly dead, or if some spark of life remained to guide it, Jig didn't know. But the creature was apparently able to make decisions. Having realized it couldn't stop the fire, it turned again toward Jig. A few more minutes and it would be consumed, but that was plenty of time to dispose of one little goblin.

So instead of the walking dead, Jig found himself facing a warrior of fire. Who still carried a big mace. This was not good. At least there was more light to see by, though. *I guess there's a bright side to every flaming corpse.*

Jig grinned. That would make a good proverb, assuming he survived to tell it to anyone.

He scooted backward until he bumped into the bones that had fallen out of the far alcove. In his desperation, he grabbed the arm bone and flung it at the approaching creature.

It ducked out of the way, and the bone clattered into the far alcove. The far panel reappeared.

Jig stared. The panel was really back. He could see the flames reflected in the polished marble. *That's how they seal the alcoves after they kill off the intruders. That way they can go back and wait for the next adventurers.*

"In here," he shouted. Riana looked confused, so he grabbed her arm and threw her into the open alcove behind him. Even as she collided with the skeleton, her weight triggered the magic, and the marble panel began to shimmer into existence.

The creature swung as Jig leaped. He felt the wind and heat pass his head, and if Smudge hadn't already burned his hair off, the creature probably would have ignited him. Passing through the shadowy panel was like swimming against a strong current. Or struggling against a whirlpool. His head and arms were already inside. He tried to push against the panel to help him through, but his hands sank uselessly into the half-formed marble.

What would happen if the panel finished appearing before he was inside? Would it fling Jig back into the creature's grasp? Would it form around him, leaving his legs sticking out in the hallway?

Probably not, he decided. A better trap would simply cut him in half. Which would at least save him from a slower death by fire and mace.

Jig reached out blindly, caught Riana's arm, and pulled as hard as he could.

He made it through. Old bones snapped as he landed on the now ruined skeleton, and Riana grunted with pain. In the sudden darkness, Jig couldn't tell what part of Riana his knee had landed on, but she swore at him as she wriggled away.

Blackness. Not even a sliver of light passed through the panel. At first, Jig didn't even want to breathe. He could hear sounds of combat in the hall. If he pressed an ear to the panel, he could even make out the cracking and popping of flames. A clatter of bones told him the fire had overcome whatever black art held the creature together.

"I hate this," Riana said.

Jig didn't bother to respond. He wasn't too happy with the situation either, but at this point he didn't know what he could do about it. At least they were safe. So he continued to listen to the fighting, wondering which side would come out alive. So to speak.

Only then did it occur to him that he didn't know how to open the alcove from the inside. The dead warriors probably didn't mind being trapped here for years at a time, but Jig did. Even ignoring the stench, he would quickly starve to death. With Riana here, he might last an extra week or so before hunger killed him.

If the adventurers lost, would the creatures leave him here to die? Or would they be intelligent enough to open the panel and finish him off? Of the two possibilities, Jig didn't know which one frightened him more. A quick death was always better, that was a goblin truism. But whoever made up that truism hadn't been fighting animated corpses. The idea of dying at the hands of those creatures left him queasy.

Riana spoke again, distracting him from what was happening outside. "I would have ended up like that."

Remembering the hard, tight feel of her severed finger, Jig thought she was right. Those things had the same shriveled look to them. Were they adventurers who had fallen prey to the same trap that had caught Riana? Or did the Necromancer have other ways to collect his soldiers? This whole place could be nothing more than a trap, one designed to provide new corpses for the Necromancer.

"I hate this," she said again. "Can't we make a light?"

Jig threw up his hands, forgetting that she couldn't see. "Barius neglected to give me a lantern of my own. And Ryslind hasn't taken the time to teach me magic. So I'm afraid we're stuck in the darkness."

"Don't push me, goblin," she snapped. "I'd wager my knife can find your heart even in the dark." The anger drained from her voice at the end, though. Jig heard her shift position. It sounded like she had backed into the corner.

"I've never known darkness like this. Outside there were always the stars. When I scraped together enough gold for a night indoors, or when some innkeeper took me in out of the snow for a night, I always slept in the common rooms, with a fire blazing."

"I've never seen the stars myself," Jig said. The idea of such openness made him nervous. Worse, he had once heard stories about *snow*. Water and ice falling from the sky, with nothing overhead but a thin wooden roof for protection? How could they live like that?

Jig tried to stretch out, but the end of his rope was still looped around his arm, and the movement tightened the noose.

"What's that?" Riana said loudly.

"Me," Jig said, once he finished choking. He quickly unwound the rope from his arm. The noose was too tight for his fingers to pry loose. He felt around for a thin bone to use as a lever. Barius would be furious if he freed himself, but Barius might also be dead, and Jig was tired of being tied up.

He found two long bones that might work. One

was too thin, but the other had a broken end with a jagged point. This could make a passable weapon. Not as nice as his sword, but better than nothing. As he felt along the other end of the dry, scaly bones, his fingers touched a loop of cold metal.

A bracelet? It was wide enough. The oval ring was as wide as his upper arm, but might fit snugly about a human's wrist. He could feel hammer marks on the metal, and a bit of engraving on the inside. That was odd. Who engraved jewelry on the inside, leaving the outside bare and ugly?

Still maybe he could swap it to Barius for his sword. He slid the bracelet onto his arm, above the elbow, then snorted. Sure, and after Barius returned his sword, Jig would get Ryslind to teach him that fire-shooting spell. Maybe he'd follow it all up by asking Darnak for his wineskin.

He grabbed the bone and shoved it through the noose, close to the knot. The point scratched his neck, and he couldn't pry the knot too hard without choking himself. He tried again, giving up only when blue spots of light began to float across his vision. Had the knot loosened at all? He couldn't tell. Gasping, he fell back against the wall.

"What are you doing?"

Jig felt his neck. The touch stung, and his fingers came away sticky. "Cutting my throat."

"What?"

He ignored her confused question. Tossing the bone away, he went back to searching the floor. Whoever this was, he had died wearing that bracelet. The other creatures still bore weapons and armor. What else might this one have with him? Jig hadn't had time to look at things very closely before flinging himself into the alcove.

"If anyone cuts your throat, it should be me," Riana muttered.

He often brushed against her foot or hand as he searched. Each time she slapped him away. It was too easy to get turned about in here. Time after time, Jig fixed Riana's position in his mind, only to run into her in another corner. Bad as his vision might be, he wished for even that poor sight to return. Worse than his disorientation, Jig was beginning to hallucinate. Movements to either side, colors that vanished when he blinked. But Jig had lived his whole life underground. Darkness was not uncommon. While not a welcome thing, anyone who couldn't cope with the dark tended to die an early death.

Jig closed his eyes and straightened his ears. The most difficult part was letting yourself ignore the lies your eyes told. Eyes were like children. If they had nothing to say, they made things up. Focusing on Riana's breathing, he continued to search through the bones.

His search turned up a few small coins, an old belt, and a pair of boots that came all the way to Jig's knees, but no knife or sword. Nothing he could use to free himself from Barius's noose.

The boots he kept, even though they were a bit too large. Their hard soles would be too loud on the floor, so he tore them off. The threads were loose and broke easily. In the process, he ripped the seams by the toes of one boot, but that didn't matter. They were still better than bare feet, especially down here, where he didn't know what he might be stepping on.

More importantly, they gave him a way to hide his bracelet. Goblins had large feet, but skinny limbs, and with a bit of force, Jig shoved the bracelet around his ankle. It might pinch a bit when he walked, but this way Barius wouldn't take it from him.

The belt tore apart when he tried to use it. The leather had rotted too badly to be worth anything.

"What are you doing, Jig?"

"Trying to find a knife." Failing to find a knife would be more honest. Wasn't it Jig's luck to end up trapped with the only unarmed corpse in the place? If he couldn't find a weapon, he would have to go back to the bone.

"Why? Didn't you already cut your throat?" She snorted. "Or are goblins as clumsy at suicide as with everything else?"

"For this noose. I want it off!" Where was the bone he had used before? There were so many. Could all of these bones really fit into one person? Even a human? And what were all of the tiny ones for? There must be hundreds scattered across the floor.

Before he could find one to use, Jig was jerked sideways by the noose. His head smacked into the wall. His fingers clawed at the rope as he tried to gain himself another breath. He could hear Riana next to him. She had the rope in her hand. What was she doing?

"This noose?"

Jig gagged something close to, "Yes."

Riana stood, pulling Jig with her. "If you had been tied up back there, I'd still have two working hands."

Or you'd have been one of those creatures. Even if he wanted to say it, he couldn't. The noose was too tight, and he couldn't pull it away. He needed air.

Wait, it wasn't the noose he had to fight. It was Riana.

"They were coming back to heal me. Barius told me Darnak had prayed for a spell that would cure the poison."

That made sense. They couldn't have told her

the truth, after all. Not if the prince didn't want to wake up one morning with a knife in his belly. They knew Riana's temper as well as Jig did.

Jig squirmed and reached behind his head. He didn't know if she would really kill him or not, but he couldn't take the chance. His fingers found Riana's wrists. He squeezed, but she was too strong. He couldn't pry her grip loose.

That was okay. He hadn't planned to do this by brute strength.

His hand slipped past her wrist and up her sleeve. She figured out what he was doing and pulled back, but he had already grabbed the hilt of her knife, the one she had stolen from Barius. As she leaped away, the knife stayed with Jig. Seconds later, he was free of the noose and gagging on the floor.

"I can still kill you," Riana warned. "For all you know, I could have a dozen more daggers stashed away."

But she didn't attack. She was afraid, Jig realized. Afraid of him! They had fought, and Jig had won. And he was too tired and sore to give one whit about his victory. He only wanted to curl up and rest.

So he did. He kept one ear aimed at the corridor so he could hear what was happening outside. The other remained pointed at Riana. He thought she was bluffing about the knife, but there were plenty of sharp bones in here. He wouldn't let her surprise him again. Which was why he couldn't allow himself to sleep. Even though he was so tired that the bone-littered floor felt almost comfortable.

The fighting couldn't go on for much longer. If the adventurers won and came back for Jig and Riana, they would be free soon. Otherwise, it didn't matter if Riana killed him or not.

The noise in the corridor stopped a little while later. Despite Jig's vigilance, Riana noticed first. "They've stopped."

Jig had listened as the clash of battle died, but he hadn't really heard it. Dealing with all of these people trying to kill him must have left him more tired than he realized.

"Should we call for help?" Riana asked.

"I don't know. If those corpses won, they might not be too eager to help us. Especially after we burned one of them up like that."

"What happened to him anyway? Where did the fire come from?"

Knowing she couldn't see, Jig grinned at her. "My guess is that Smudge got hungry. I haven't fed him since yesterday." When she didn't say anything, he explained. "Fire-spiders like their meat cooked. Not much meat on those things, but I guess he decided it was better than starving."

He felt bad when he thought about it. Usually Jig took much better care of Smudge. Things had been too hectic lately, that was all. He hoped he'd be able to find something better than ancient human corpses to feed to the spider.

Since he couldn't do that from in here, Jig pounded against the marble panel with his dagger. The noise echoed in the small alcove, and Riana yelped.

"What are you doing? You said yourself that those things might still be out there."

Jig hit the panel again. "Either something lets us out, or else you get to stay in here with me until we both die."

A few seconds later, Riana grabbed a bone and joined him.

CHAPTER 8

Armed to the Teeth

The panel faded to shadow. Jig squinted as light pierced the blackness of the alcove. Outside he saw Darnak's stocky silhouette waiting, club held high.

Before the panel could vanish entirely, Jig moved his stolen knife behind his back, handle toward Riana. Darnak probably wouldn't complain that Jig had, once again, freed himself of the rope. Coming out with knife in hand would be a different thing entirely. Darnak could get a bit club-happy after a fight, and Jig had been abused enough today without adding a whack from the dwarf.

"Take it," Jig whispered as the panel disappeared entirely. He stepped forward, placing himself in front of Riana so she could grab her knife unseen.

Which she did. Jig's relieved grin tightened with pain as she sliced his fingers in the process.

"Thanks," she said sweetly, too low for Darnak to hear. She slipped past Jig and smiled in passing.

Elves. They could be as bad as goblins sometimes. Jig clenched his fist to close the cut and hoped nobody would notice.

"Come on," Darnak said. Sweat streaked his face and plastered curls of hair to his forehead, and he sported a stained red bandage on his arm. "We've regrouped back this way to catch our breath. Undead bastards gave us quite a fight."

Jig could see that for himself. Of the creature Smudge had burned, nothing remained but a skeleton that lay in the middle of a man-shaped pile of ash. Jig felt thankful for his new boots, since he had to walk through those remains to catch up with the others. He tried to ignore the crunch of his footsteps as he followed Darnak.

Smudge scurried over and climbed Jig's leg.

"Good spider," Jig whispered, reaching down to scratch Smudge's head. "*Very* good spider. A warrior-spider." He glanced back at the bones and ash. "And still a hungry spider, I suspect. I doubt you found much meat on that thing. Don't you worry, I'll get something for you to eat."

The remains of the other creatures cluttered the corridor. One had been hacked to pieces, probably by Barius's sword. Another still jerked and twitched, as if trying to continue the attack. It might have succeeded, had its head not been lying upside down farther up the corridor. Darnak gave the body a lazy smack in passing, and the thing fell still.

As for the rest, even Jig could figure out how they had died. Only Ryslind's magic killed with such *finality*. These bodies were the least damaged, but each showed a large, blackened hole where the hearts would have been. Was there any limit to what Ryslind could do? Jig counted four who had fallen to the wizard's fire.

The smell was terrible, and he tried not to breathe through his nose until he had joined Darnak and the others in the room where they had first come through the whirlpool. Even there the charred scent of Ryslind's work followed him.

He braced himself for Barius's outburst as he passed through the door. No doubt the prince would yell and threaten and demand to know how Jig could have been so stupid as to trigger the trap. But Barius was in no shape to yell.

The prince lay in the middle of the room, next to the water pillar. His shirt and armor were piled to one side, and his white skin was pale even for a human. Bandages covered his stomach; another bound his left shoulder. Both were wet with blood.

"Is he dead?" Jig asked, trying to keep his hopefulness from showing.

"Pah." Darnak spat on the pillar. Jig stared, fascinated, as the spittle shrank and vanished, somehow passing through the barrier and into the waters of the whirlpool.

"He's not dead. He just tried a riposte when he should have parried in four."

Jig nodded as though he understood.

"Don't worry, he'll be his charming self soon enough. Earthmaker won't allow us to fail, not from a few scratches like that."

"Earthmaker sounds like a useful person to have around," Jig said.

"Aye. He's one who rewards his followers. Over a hundred years I've offered up my sacrifices and prayed to him for guidance. Far be it from me to guess the mind of a god, but I'm thinking he'll not repay a century of service by letting us all die here."

Ryslind strolled to the dwarf's side. "Yet for all of your devotion, your magic is still limited to those powers your god grants you. To be so dependent on the whim of a deity would be disturbing, to say the least."

"It's called faith," Darnak snapped. "And it's a far cry safer than your wizardry. When's the last time you heard about a priest blowing himself up after trying a new spell and waving three fingers instead of four?"

They glared at each other, the dwarf's tiny eyes not leaving Ryslind's glowing ones. They might have continued for hours had Barius not stirred.

"Forgive my interruption," the prince said, "but could your time not be better spent by aiding one who still bleeds from his wounds?"

"Aye," answered Darnak. He knelt next to Barius and began praying. One hand covered the stomach wound, which looked like the more serious injury. Between his prayers, so low that even Jig could barely hear, Darnak muttered, "I'd love to see your high and mighty wizardry cure this."

After a while, he leaned back and said, "He'll need a few hours of rest. Earthmaker has closed the cuts, but it'll take a bit of Barius's strength to finish the job."

"Perhaps your god is busy with other matters," Ryslind said.

"Aye," Darnak answered agreeably. His easygoing nod contrasted sharply with his earlier grumbling. Perhaps relief at Barius's recovery had put him in a better mood. "A whole world of prayers, and you think he can spend all his time on one dwarf?"

Jig ignored the rest of the discussion. Several times now, Darnak had healed wounds that would have crippled a goblin. What would it be like to have that kind of power available all the time? To know that, no matter how grave the injury, a journey to the closest priest could fix you in a matter of hours?

At first the idea seemed wondrous, and Jig had to fight off a surge of jealousy. The more he thought about it, though, the more he began to question if that sort of power would necessarily be a good thing. What would bullies like Porak do if they knew their victims could recover from almost anything? Instead of tossing rodents into the muck pot, why not set Jig himself on fire? Wouldn't it be far more entertaining to spend the afternoon playing flame-the-goblin? Especially if the victim could come back the next day, good as new and ready to play the game all over again.

But maybe gods were smarter than that. The fact that the gods had always ignored goblinkind might be a sign that they understood how much trouble a magic-wielding goblin could cause.

Darnak dug into his pack for food and came up with a new loaf of bread, which he passed around to the party. He also found several more strips of meat, as well as a small wheel of cheese. This he dusted off and cut into five pieces.

The cheese was good, if a bit strong. As before, Jig received only two pieces of the meat. He would have to endure bread again if he wanted to fill his belly.

Riana, he noticed, had taken some of her bread and tucked it into her shirt, along with a little meat. Saving something for later? That was probably a good idea. He waited until nobody was looking, then slipped one strip of meat into his boot.

The other he tore into with relish, eating half with one bite. As he swallowed, he noticed Smudge. The fire-spider quivered on Jig's knee, and all eight eyes followed the meat in his hand.

"I don't suppose I could interest you in some

bread?" he asked, holding out a piece. Smudge actually heated up a bit as he scooted away, confirming Jig's impression of the so-called food. "Right," he sighed.

Resigning himself to a meal of cheese and bread, he tossed the remaining meat onto the floor. Smudge sprang. His legs landed to either side of the meat like a cage. Seconds later, the smell of burning meat drifted through the air as Smudge cooked his food.

"Enjoy it." Jig brushed a bit of dirt off the cheese and took another bite. By alternating cheese and bread and drinking a fair amount of water, he managed to finish off the meal. But he would have given so much for just one cup of Golaka's stew. Even day-old stew, the kind you had to skin before you ate, would have been heaven-sent.

"If I had the Rod of Creation, I'd use it to make some real food," he decided.

"Another attack like that, and we won't even make it to the dragon's lair," Darnak told him. "Let alone find the rod."

"Will there be more traps?" Riana asked quietly. She tried to sound casual, but Jig could see the way she kept looking at the stump of her finger.

Barius coughed and rolled onto his side. "You're the burglar of this party. What say you?"

She glared at him. "All those dead things couldn't have come from one little trapped lock. The Necromancer could have traps everywhere. He could have armies waiting to pour out of the walls next time. Or maybe he set spells to turn us all into creatures like that. Even if we found every trick panel and poison needle, how are we going to find those traps hidden by magic?"

Her eyes kept going to the whirlpool. Jig knew what she was thinking about. She wanted to escape, to find a way back up to the surface. But she was doing everything she could to hide her fear.

As far as he could tell, nobody else had noticed. None of them showed any sign of fear, so they probably didn't see it in others. They were adventurers, after all. Jig, on the other hand, had enough fear for the entire party.

Maybe that was what made Riana seem smarter than the others. She was no more a hero than Jig was. Of course, she was a young girl, barely more than a baby for her race, whereas Jig was a grown goblin. Why was *he* so afraid?

He didn't bother to answer that question. He could have spent the next three hours listing reasons to be afraid, and all it would do was make him even more frightened.

"Our elven thief has a point," Barius said. "Perhaps she begins to learn wisdom. No doubt the Necromancer's traps litter this place like horse dung on the highway."

"A beautiful image, prince," Ryslind said.

Barius nodded, completely missing the sarcasm. "Brother, I think we must call upon your art once more. Can you guide us through this maze of traps and death?"

"Perhaps we should rest a mite longer," Darnak said quickly.

Remembering the wizard's fit after they came through the whirlpool, Jig was inclined to agree.

"There must be another way to find the Necromancer and the path to Straum's domain. Would anyone be knowing a song, a story, even a rumor about this place?" Darnak looked around hopefully. "Anything at all, no matter how strange or confusing."

Jig spoke up hesitantly. "I know one, but it wouldn't help."

"Let us decide what is helpful," Barius said. "Perhaps we can intuit some vital fact that you never stopped to consider."

He wished he had kept quiet. "I don't think so. It's not much of a song."

"Enough protests. Goblins haven't the intellect to find those kernels of truth hidden within the old songs."

Jig shrugged and began to sing.

Ten little goblins walked off to drink their wine.
Up came the Necromancer, then there were nine.
They screamed and they hid and they ran away,
But those goblins came back the very next day.

Nine little goblins went looking for a mate,
Up came the Necromancer, then there were eight.
They screamed and they hid and they ran away,
But those goblins came back the very next day.

Eight little goblins—

"Enough," Barius shouted.

Jig shifted uncomfortably. "It's more of a children's song, really."

"That is the extent of your knowledge regarding our foe?" Barius had apparently recovered from his injuries, for he pushed himself up and walked over to glare at Jig. "You've lived here your entire life, and the best you can do is 'Ten little goblins'?"

"What about you?" Jig shot back. He had warned the prince it was a stupid song. Why did everyone keep blaming Jig for their stupid mistakes? "You knew what you'd be facing down here. Did you bring anything to help you against the Necromancer?"

The prince's eyes widened. One hand dropped

to his belt, closer to the hilt of his sword than Jig was comfortable with. "I . . . I brought him." Barius pointed to his brother.

"A good thing for us all that you did, too." What was he doing? Jig couldn't believe the words coming out of his own mouth. He had seen the prince's temper. Why was he so eager for Barius to finish him off?

"I saw the bodies in the hall," he continued. "Your brother killed four of those things. If he weren't here, they would have killed you as easily as you killed my patrol. If you ask me, *Ryslind* should start leading this party before you lead us into another trap."

Nobody moved. Over the course of Jig's rant, Barius's face had turned red, then purple. Jig watched him curiously. He hadn't realized humans could change color. Perhaps they were part lizard.

Jig had never seen Barius, or any human for that matter, get this mad. Still angry people all seemed to react in the same way. Jig braced himself. Yes, here it came. Barius's open hand caught Jig on the side of his face and knocked him to the ground. *This is growing old*, he thought as he lay on the floor, staring upward. Still, he would be an expert on ceilings by the time he was through.

"What are you doing, lad?" Darnak asked. "He's unarmed."

"I'm challenging this goblin to a duel," Barius said.

"A what?" Jig turned his head toward the prince. "What's a duel?"

Darnak raised his hands in disgust. "Have your wits deserted you, man? We're in the home of the Necromancer, and you want to stand around fighting duels?"

"A duel," Barius explained, ignoring the dwarf, "is a battle of honor. To the death. As the challenged party, you have the choice of weapons."

Jig blinked. "What? Darnak, is he serious?"

"You've insulted my honor. Choose your weapon. Knives, swords, clubs, even quarterstaves. I saw a pair of spears we could use." His hawkish nose wrinkled in a sneer. "Your presence has plagued this party long enough, goblin."

Jig looked around for help. Him, fight Barius? Why not execute him outright and be done with it?

Ryslind looked bored with it all, and Darnak was shaking his head in disbelief. Riana rolled her eyes. "Men," she muttered disgustedly. Nobody moved to intervene.

"Enough dallying," Barius said. "Choose your weapon." He waved his arms in large circles, presumably some sort of warm-up ritual, then practiced a few lunges against an imaginary foe.

What should he choose? As if it made a difference. The only weapon Jig had ever held more than once was a kitchen knife, and he suspected Barius was as skilled with knives as he was with the sword. Either way, Jig would soon be bleeding his life all over the nice, polished marble.

"Choose."

He can't just kill me. Not with everyone watching. That means he has to play by the rules. Jig glared at him. "If I win, will you let me carry a weapon again? And no more of your stupid ropes, either."

Barius laughed. "Anything you like. Ask for my future barony or my firstborn child, it matters not. But ask and let us done with it."

What would Jig do with a human newborn? Even goblins didn't eat babies. Too little meat. Did humans typically go around swapping their children?

He shook his head and decided he was better off not knowing. "Freedom and my sword. I don't want anything else."

"Very well." Barius appeared close to losing his temper. His cheek twitched, and each word shot out through gritted teeth. "Select your weapon."

"Fangs."

Barius blinked. "What? You can't choose fangs."

"Why not? It's a game goblin children play. We call it Rakachak. You bite one another on the arms and legs, and the winner is the one who goes the longest without crying." He smiled and fingered the three-inch fangs on his lower jaw. "If you want, you can go first."

Jig patted the short sword at his side, reassured by its weight. Not that it would be much use if they were attacked again. Darnak had told him about the fight, how Barius had cut down his first opponent, only to have it rise again and slash Barius's shoulder from behind. Stabbing the creature in the throat hadn't even inconvenienced it. Whatever these things were, they needed to be hacked apart, bludgeoned to a pulp, or dealt with by magic. *Or by a hungry fire-spider,* Jig had added silently.

Ahead, Ryslind raised his hand and brought the party to a halt. He gestured at the right wall. "Another passageway . . . here." He spoke in the same dual-toned voice Jig had heard before.

Jig didn't like it. He didn't like any of it. Well, he had liked watching Barius sputter and curse after Jig named his weapon for the duel. Darnak had to physically stop Barius from slicing Jig's head from his body. Seeing the haughty prince back out of his "duel" and formally ask Jig's forgiveness was worth almost all the pain and indignity he had endured on this quest.

Afterward, they still faced the same problem. Amidst whatever traps and tricks filled this place, how could they find the Necromancer without dying in the process? In the end, they turned again to Ryslind.

The wizard hadn't said a word. He pulled a blue vial from his cloak and drained the contents in one swallow. A coughing fit took him, and the vial shattered on the floor. Jig watched as he doubled over and fell. He wondered if Ryslind had grabbed the wrong potion, taken something deadly instead of the potion he wanted.

Ryslind's eyes glowed brighter than ever when he struggled back to his feet. He blinked and squinted, and finally said, "Too much magic in here. I can't see anything. Someone lead me to the corridor."

Darnak had taken it upon himself to grab the wizard's arm and guide him over the corpses and into the corridor. Once there, Ryslind had begun to walk at a slow, steady pace. He stopped before the trapped tile, gestured at it with one hand, and muttered, "Don't step here."

"I think we're already knowing that much," Darnak said.

Ryslind ignored him. He pointed out two more tiles before reaching the first fork in the corridor. Without hesitation, he took the left turn. Jig wondered if Ryslind even noticed the other hallway, or if he saw anything but the path his magic showed him. He didn't seem to see or hear the rest of the party, much to Darnak's dismay.

"How can I make a good map if you're racing about like a tomcat on the prowl?" He sketched as fast as he could, but Jig could see that his careful map was devolving into a few lines and arrows. "Can't even keep track of which tiles we're to avoid. Probably trigger every one if we have to come back this way in a hurry."

In addition to the traps, there were a number of secret passages, like the one Ryslind had just found. Everything was constructed of the same marble panels, and from time to time Ryslind would point one out at random. Nobody knew how they were *supposed* to open, for the wizard's magic allowed him to bypass the normal mechanism. Even as he pointed, his eyes would flash, and the panel would crash onto the ground, often breaking into thick shards from the impact.

Jig got down and crawled through the hole into the secret passageway. "They could at least make the doors taller," he grumbled.

"You should mention that to the Necromancer when we find him," Riana said as she followed. "I'm sure he'd love to hear architectural suggestions from a goblin."

She hadn't been quite as mean to him since his aborted duel. In fact, she had laughed harder than Jig had ever seen, which only added to Barius's fury. But that didn't mean she had forgiven him, either. She merely flipped back and forth as to whom she hated more, Jig or Barius. With Barius up ahead, following his brother, that left Jig as a target for her frustrations.

At least the corridor beyond opened up to let him walk upright and put a few more feet between himself and her barbs.

"Another trap," Ryslind said. This time it was a thin wire stretched across the floor. Jig's poor vision meant that he couldn't see it at all, and he felt like a fool as Darnak guided his legs in an exaggerated motion over the wire. Better this than another attack, though. He wondered how much power it took for Ryslind to sense the traps and the hidden passages. Even tracking the Necromancer at all must take an enormous effort. Jig knew nothing of magic, but he assumed a powerful wizard would have ways to hide himself.

"Do you think this is what the Necromancer wants?" he wondered.

"What's that?" Darnak snapped. He scowled at his map and drew a quick turn, then made a line to indicate the tripwire. "Do I think what?"

"Well, he has to know we're here. And he probably knows we've got a wizard. So wouldn't it make sense to force the wizard to use up his power before we actually face the Necromancer? That way, when we finally get through this maze, the Necromancer will be able to kill Ryslind like a bug." Not to mention what the search might be doing to Ryslind's already questionable sanity. Those dual voices sent creepy tingles down Jig's back every time the wizard spoke.

"Aye, it's possible." Darnak hurried ahead, forcing Jig and Riana to jog to keep up. When they were closer to the humans and their lantern, he slowed his pace again to draw. As he sketched, he explained. "That's why we all have to be ready to strike. Only two ways for the likes of us to deal with wizards of the Necromancer's caliber. Run away, or hit him with a rock."

"I don't have a rock," Jig said worriedly. There were no rocks down here. Had he known, he would have taken one from the lakeshore above.

Darnak's eyes came up to glare at Jig. "Figure of speech. Your sword there'll do the job. The trick is to take him out before he can use his magic. Hard and fast, and no hesitation. Let him get a spell off, and it's your death. I'm afraid you're right about Ryslind being at the end of his rope, so if you wait for him to save your blue hide, you'll not last long."

Jig had no illusions about his skill with a sword. A day ago, he would have taken the dwarf's advice and thought himself a match for any wizard. Like Porak, he had believed that a good weapon made a good warrior. But Porak now resided in the belly of a carrion-worm. Jig had seen Barius and Darnak in combat, and next to them, he was nothing. Even Ryslind was a more skilled fighter, and he was a wizard. What hope did Jig have, sword or no sword?

"What about your magic?" he asked, searching for another option. "Won't Earthmaker help you beat the Necromancer?"

"Doesn't work that way. Earthmaker wants us to choose our own path. He can guide us and give us strength, but where mortals come into conflict, he'll not interfere." Darnak stopped and cocked his head. His face wrinkled like a raisin. "Something's not right. The tunnel changes up ahead."

"How can you tell?"

"He's a dwarf," Riana answered, as if that explained everything. She hurried up to tell the others.

They soon found that Darnak was right. Barius and his brother stopped, lantern held in front of them. When Jig caught up and saw why they had paused, it was all he could do to keep from throwing up.

Not only did the tunnel change, it ended completely. The walls and ceiling stopped, and the cramped passage opened into a huge cavern. The top was too far to see, and the bottom . . . Jig's stomach knotted just thinking about it. At the far side, he could just see a glimmer of reflected light, presumably from the marble paneling the Necromancer seemed to like so much. All they had to do was cross.

"Bottomless pit, you think?" Darnak asked.

Barius nodded. " 'Twould be my guess."

That was when Jig decided they were both as mad as the wizard. They talked about this chasm as if they crossed bottomless pits every day before breakfast. Worse, as he looked at the others, he had no doubt what they were about to say.

"Let us be on our way," Barius said, right on cue.

"Over *that*?" Riana demanded.

Good to know that Jig wasn't the only one who had problems with this. True, the paneled floor continued across the pit, creating a sort of bridge. The problem was that *only* the panels continued. As far as he could see, they rested on nothing but air. Only thin lines of silver mortar held the panels together. Although Jig knew nothing about bridges, he guessed this wasn't how they were supposed to look.

Each panel was no thicker than Jig's thumb. While the others planned the safest way to cross, Jig dropped to his hands and knees and crawled to the tunnel's edge. Peering over the edge, he saw nothing but blackness beneath the bridge. Wind brushed past his face and pushed his ears back. The walls of the pit were smooth black stone. Not polished like the marble, but still too smooth to climb. *What were you expecting? A nice ladder and a sign saying "Here's the* safe *bridge for goblins only"?*

Something landed on Jig's back. He shouted and rolled away, kicking wildly at his attacker. Smudge slipped off his shoulder and started to fall, and Jig barely managed to grab one of the spider's suddenly hot legs. Once he was back in the tunnel, Smudge scurried a good six feet away from the edge and cowered there.

The attacker turned out to be the end of a rope. Darnak and Riana both laughed at him, while Barius muttered something about "stupid, cowardly creatures." Jig noticed they had each wrapped a loop of rope about their waists.

"Best to be safe when crossing these things," Darnak explained. He helped Jig up and tied the rope around his waist with a sure hand. "Earthmaker willing, we'll not be needing this. But I've not yet seen a bottomless pit that didn't have some nastiness hidden away, waiting to knock you to your doom."

"You've crossed these before?" Jig asked.

"Oh, aye. Back when I was a lad, there wasn't a wizard around who didn't conjure up his own bottomless pit. They're less common these days, but you still find 'em lying about in older labyrinths and lairs. They're useful things. If you can cut a shaft through the entire place, you've got some ventilation. Otherwise the air gets stale and things start to die. Not to mention the stink."

He lowered his voice, as if sharing a secret. "Truth is, they're not really bottomless. You'll fall for a while, no doubt, but sooner or later you find the bottom. A real bottomless pit takes too much magic."

Perhaps that was supposed to reassure him, Jig didn't know. He saw Darnak take another drink of ale, and decided that strong drink would have been far more comforting. Strong drink he could enjoy back in the goblin lair would be even better.

"Onward," said Barius. He walked close behind Ryslind, lantern held high to light up the bridge. Riana followed, then Darnak, still scribbling at his map, and Jig brought up the rear. That meant he would be the last one to step onto those floating tiles.

He watched as each member of the group stepped onto the bridge, and each time he expected the tiles to crumble away at the touch of their feet. The tiles didn't even wiggle.

The rope went taut, tugging Jig closer to the edge. Another three steps and he'd be on the bridge. What if he fell? What if the wind got stronger and blew him over the edge? Would the others try to pull him up? More likely they would cut the rope and let him fall. Why else would they put him last? This way they could cut him loose without sacrificing themselves.

Two more steps. Maybe the bridge only worked for certain races. Would it support a goblin as well as a human? Magic was funny that way, and he had a sudden, vivid memory of the marble panels that had hidden their dead attackers. Those had felt solid enough, up until they vanished. Was there a trigger to make these panels disappear as well?

One step. Of course. The spell must be designed to wait until the last person stepped out of the tunnel. Only *then* would it vanish. He was the last one. As soon as he took that next step, they would all fall to their deaths. He was the only one who could save them. He had to get this knot undone. His fingers clawed at the rope, but the dwarf had tied a good knot, and it wouldn't budge.

"Wait," he whispered. "Please wait."

The rope jerked him forward, and he fell onto the bridge. The solid, unmoving bridge. Jig froze. Ahead the others glanced back impatiently. The tiles hadn't faded. He wasn't falling. *He wasn't falling!* He was trembling so much he couldn't stand up, but he wasn't falling.

"You planning to walk, or were you expecting us to drag you across?" Darnak yelled. His voice echoed in the chasm.

Jig tried to rise. The bridge was wide enough. Three tiles wide, which was more than twice the length of a goblin. He would be okay. All he had to do was stand up and walk after the others.

"I'm coming," he yelled back. He rose to his knees, glanced over the edge, and promptly dropped back to the floor. Crawling would be just fine, he decided. Smudge crawled everywhere, and he never lost his balance. At that moment, Jig would have been happier with eight legs, but he'd be all right with four. He hoped.

About thirty feet ahead, Ryslind pointed to a tile in the center. "Illusion," he said.

What a nasty trick. Jig chewed his lip as he neared the false tile. He would have to go around. The tile looked as solid as the rest. He touched a finger to the marble surface and watched it pass right through, so it looked like his finger had been severed at the knuckle. Like Riana's. If Ryslind hadn't seen the trap, they would have fallen.

"Watch us, not the bottom," Darnak snapped.

Right. *Watch them. Don't look over the edge. Don't even think about it. Don't imagine the wind rushing past your ears or tumbling helplessly out of control.* Would he see the ground rushing up? Would he feel the impact, or would death be too quick? His head began to spin from breathing so fast. *No, don't get dizzy. Not now. Relax. Be calm. Anything to distract yourself.*

He crawled forward a few inches and began to sing in a strained voice. "Ten little goblins walked off to drink their wine. . . ."

He curled his fingers around the edges of the tile for stability, but that only reminded him that a single tile hung between him and the abyss. To his right was the false tile, to his left, nothing. He hoped the magic and the mortar were strong enough. In his imagination, he could see one side of the tile break free, see himself dangling helplessly as the tile dropped away like the hobgoblins' trapdoor.

A few more steps. He could do this. Everyone else had done it. If the bridge could support Darnak's weight, it would surely hold Jig. It would hold a half-dozen goblins. He clenched his teeth and continued to sing.

By the time he reached the third verse, he had passed the false tile and was back in the center of the bridge where it was safe. Relatively speaking, at least.

"Good job," Darnak said. "Now let's be on."

Jig nodded. He could do this. He could make it. They were going to be okay.

That was when the attack started.

CHAPTER 9

Torment of the Gods

At first Jig thought the fluttering was a figment of his frightened imagination. A trick of the wind, perhaps. He certainly couldn't see anything when he looked around.

The first squeal, so loud Jig grabbed his ears and folded them flat to his head, told him this was no trick. Something really was out there in the blackness.

More squeals followed, causing Jig to change his conclusion. Some *things*.

"Don't stop, but keep your eyes open," Darnak yelled. He pointed his dripping quill at the other side of the bridge. "We're halfway there. If we can make it to the other side, we'll be safer."

"Keep your eyes open," Jig mimicked. "As if I'd do this sort of thing blindfolded." He started to crawl, only to stop when the next squeal deafened him. He couldn't crawl and cover his ears at the same time.

"Why do they have to be so loud?" He couldn't

hear his own voice. Clasping his hands to his ears, he stood up and hurried after the others.

They had gone another twenty yards when something large and black swooped toward Darnak. Huge, leathery wings batted the dwarf's head, pushing him backward.

Darnak dropped his quill and struck out with his fist, knocking the thing away and letting Jig see it clearly in the lantern light.

They were bats. Bigger than any bat Jig had seen, but they could be nothing else. Their bodies were almost as big as Darnak himself, and the wings stretched at least ten feet to either side. Another swooped down behind Jig, giving him a close look at their bristled, piglike faces, and a row of needle-sharp teeth. The only redeeming features were their brown ears, even bigger than a goblin's.

Jig grabbed his sword and swung wildly. More by luck than any skill, the tip grazed the bat's wing and sent it spinning out of sight beneath the bridge.

Darnak yelled something else, but Jig couldn't hear. More bats were coming down behind him. He ran to join the others.

Only to drop through another illusionary tile. He didn't have time to panic. One second he was running, the next he was dropping his sword and scrambling for a handhold. His fingers slipped, and then the rope jerked him to a halt. Jig clutched the rope with both hands and hoped Darnak wouldn't follow him through. If the dwarf and all that equipment fell through the hole, Jig doubted the others would be able to support the weight.

The rope tore skin from Jig's armpits as he dangled helplessly. Smudge flattened himself to Jig's shoulder, legs clinging to the leather pad, and Jig could feel the heat on his cheek. "Don't touch the rope," he warned. The last thing he needed was for the stupid fire-spider to crawl around and set the rope on fire. Fortunately, Smudge appeared to be stiff with fear.

Something moved nearby. He couldn't see very well since the bridge blocked most of the light, but the shifting shadows in front of him took on the ugly form of a bat, only a few feet away. Even if his sword weren't lying useless on the bridge above, he wouldn't have dared release his grip on the rope long enough to use it.

So the next time the bat came near, he kicked as hard as he could. His boot caught the bat's snout, and it looped away.

The movement started him twisting. Another bat flew at him and clobbered his head with a wing. The bat's small claws reached out but missed. Now he was spinning the other direction. Much more of this, and he'd lose what little food he had eaten. He imagined the undigested bread dropping endlessly through the darkness and wondered what the bats would make of it.

More squeals ripped at Jig's ears. What he wouldn't have given for another alcove to hide in. He twisted his head, trying to see where the next attack would come from.

Nothing but blackness. Which, between his own poor vision and the fact that he was looking for brown and black bats in the dark, meant very little. Wind buffeted Jig's body as a bat flew up to land on the edge of the bridge. The smell of guano was so strong he could practically taste it.

There was a crunch, and a huge, senseless body plunged past Jig's left side. That would be Darnak, teaching the bats the futility of a ground-based attack.

He wondered if the others would be able to pull

him back. Would they even bother? With so many bats to fend off, why lower their guard long enough to rescue one goblin?

Darnak's head poked through the illusionary tile. To Jig, it looked as if the marble had sprouted a small, hairy face. Darnak's braided tangles hung upside down, like black moss. His mouth moved silently, and he grinned at the goblin.

Jig grinned back. He was too deaf to hear what had been said, but what did it matter? Probably boasting about the bat he had just slain.

The rope jerked up a foot, costing Jig another strip of skin. *Or maybe he was telling me to hold on.* Jig's fingers tightened on the rope as he lurched closer toward the bridge. Another bat came at him from behind, and Jig kicked again. He missed, but it was enough to make the thing change course. Then thick fingers grabbed his wrist and yanked him onto the bridge.

Darnak nodded sharply, said something Jig couldn't hear, and then he was off to whack another bat. Riana stood close behind Barius. The bats had apparently learned to avoid the human's flashing sword. Ryslind waited a little way beyond, arms folded. One bat flew down behind him, only to bounce off an invisible wall. It landed on the bridge, took a few stunned steps, then teetered over the edge.

Another bat gone, but it made little difference. Jig spotted his sword sitting close to the side of the bridge. He grabbed it and turned to join the others, for all the good he could do. Bats were everywhere. The adventurers were doing a good job defending themselves, but the bats could wear them out with sheer numbers. Eventually they would all be knocked into the bottomless pit.

Jig grimaced as he recalled Darnak's assurances.

The pit wasn't truly bottomless. So maybe if they killed enough bats, the bodies would pile up at the bottom and provide a softer landing. Not that being trapped at the bottom of a pit up to his neck in giant bat bodies was much of an improvement.

They were close to the end of the bridge. If they could make it across, they could hide in the tunnels. The bats' wings were too wide for them to follow. The group would be safe. Safe from the bats, at least. If the Necromancer's personal labyrinth could ever be considered *safe*.

Jig began to walk, testing the tiles as he went. He made it about ten feet before the rope grew taut. Darnak was still behind him, merrily crushing bat skulls and breaking bat wings. Jig could no more pull the dwarf along than drag the mountain itself.

"Come on," Jig shouted.

Darnak yelled something back.

Jig rolled his eyes. *He can't hear me any better than I hear him.* He grabbed the rope and pulled. Darnak tilted his head, and Jig pointed toward the tunnel.

Darnak frowned, then shook his head as understanding came. He waved his club at the bats, as if to say he wasn't finished yet. Ignoring Jig's pleas, he spun and leaped into the air after another bat.

Between his own bulk and that of his pack, the dwarf's tremendous leap took him nearly six inches into the air. High enough to break a bat's foot, but no more. As Darnak landed, the bridge vibrated beneath their feet. Jig fought the urge to go back to all fours.

So Darnak wanted to stay until the fighting was done. That could take a while. The bats showed no sign of slowing. Jig was half tempted to cut the rope and cross to the far tunnel himself. Let the adventurers enjoy the battle; *he* would enjoy some peace and quiet. Only two things stopped him. One was the knowledge that, were he to cut the rope, the next illusionary tile would send him to his death below. The other was that he didn't know what waited for them beyond that dark opening in the far wall. With Jig's luck, he would escape the bats but find himself surrounded by more of those fighting corpses.

Jig tugged the rope again. When he had Darnak's attention, he pointed to Ryslind, who still waited motionlessly as bat after bat bounced off his magical shield. The dwarf didn't understand, so Jig did his best to pantomime Ryslind's fit from earlier. He clutched his head and walked in tight circles. One hand fluttered as if he were casting spells. Didn't he understand? How long before Ryslind overexerted himself again? The only thing worse than another of Ryslind's seizures would be another seizure in the middle of a fight.

This approach appeared to work. Darnak glanced at Ryslind. He grabbed a hank of his beard and worriedly twisted it around his index finger. A bat came at him from the side. Darnak knocked it senseless, but this time his heart wasn't in it. Jig had guessed right. No matter how much Darnak enjoyed battle, his loyalty to the humans took precedence.

That was a good thing to remember. A very different attitude than goblins, most of whom would have simply cut the rope and shoved Ryslind over the edge.

Darnak nodded. He kicked the unconscious bat he had just bludgeoned off the side of the bridge and headed toward the others.

Jig glanced over to watch it fall out of sight. He shivered and hurried back to the middle of the bridge. Darnak had his map out again in his off-weapon hand. Had he been able to mark most of the trapped tiles? Jig hoped so, because he was following the dwarf's steps as closely as he could.

They reached Barius and Riana. Darnak went through the same hand-waving that Jig had done, pausing from time to time to help them kill more bats. Barius needed less convincing than Darnak.

Moving slowly, Darnak and Barius escorted the others toward Ryslind. From there, they inched their way to the other side. The bats launched a desperate attack near the end. They flew as a group, no longer bothering with claws as they tried to physically knock the party off the bridge. It might have worked if they hadn't picked Ryslind as their first target.

Bats bounced in all directions, like water splashing from a boulder. Jig saw Ryslind smirk as one bat spun off and crashed into the chasm wall.

A few more steps, and they were through. Once they passed into the tunnel, the bats gave up and returned to whatever they did when they weren't attacking innocent adventurers. Well, maybe "innocent" was too strong a word.

Still, Jig wondered what sort of life there was for giant bats trapped in an endless chasm. Did they spend their days trying to find enough bugs to keep from starving? If so, no wonder they were so desperate to attack the party. This could have been their first real meal in months, or even years. Whose cruel idea had it been to trap bats in the chasm anyway? Was that part of Ellnorein's design when he created this place? Or perhaps Straum the dragon had brought them.

How long had the bats lived here, knowing nothing beyond the walls of their pit? Then again, the same could be said of the goblins. For thousands of years, goblins had lived in their small lair, and those few who left for the outside world tended not to return. He wondered what that kind of isolation had done to them over the centuries.

As he followed the others, Jig decided he was just as happy the bats couldn't escape their pit. He had seen enough of those black-eyed, flat-nosed faces to last a lifetime.

A lifetime, or at least until Jig and the others came back on their way out and had to cross the bridge again. The thought didn't bother him as much as it might have. What were the odds that they would survive to make it past both the Necromancer and the dragon? His chances of seeing the bridge again were slim, so why worry about the bats?

His hearing returned slowly, bringing with it a splitting headache, as if Smudge had crawled into his ear and set his brain afire. Maybe there was an advantage to the humans' tiny ears after all. Neither they nor the dwarf seemed to suffer any after-effects of the deafening shrieks that still occasionally echoed up the tunnel after them. Even Riana's slender ears would have been considered small and malformed by any goblin.

Darnak had healed him before, Jig remembered. Would he and Silas Earthmaker be able to do anything for this headache? More importantly, would they bother? Probably not, he decided. *What kind of god is going to waste his time and power on a goblin?*

Another shriek fanned the fire in Jig's head to a white-hot blaze, and he reconsidered. *What's the worst the gods could do? Strike me down for asking? At least that would make the pain stop.*

Jig hurried up to Darnak. His hand was out to tug the dwarf's sleeve when, up ahead, Ryslind stumbled.

The wizard dropped to his knees and pressed the palms of his hands against his ears. The tattoos on his hands writhed in the light.

A strange pressure filled the air, and Jig's skin tingled.

"Get back and leave me alone," Ryslind yelled.

Barius, who had been hurrying to his brother's side, stopped at once. Riana backed off until she had put Barius between herself and Ryslind.

"Get away!" Ryslind ordered.

Personally, Jig thought that was the wisest suggestion either of the humans had made so far. So naturally Barius began to argue.

"What's that? Abandon my quest? Surely you jest, brother." Barius folded his arms. His foot tapped impatiently on the marble floor. "If this is no more than a feeble ploy to frighten me off and allow *you* to seize the rod, I shall be most incensed."

Ryslind snarled, a sound more animal than human. His red eyes fixed on his brother.

"Not good," Darnak mumbled. His pack slid to the ground, nearly smashing Jig's foot. He noticed the goblin standing there and handed him the lantern. "Hold this and stay out of the way."

"What can we do?" Jig asked, headache forgotten. He didn't know what was going on, but he sensed that it was bad. Darnak looked grim, his mouth tight. As the dwarf had displayed nothing but merriment at an onslaught of giant bats, that was enough to worry Jig a great deal.

"You can shut your flap and let me work," said Darnak. He grabbed his holy amulet and dropped to one knee. "Come on, Earthmaker. I know I've asked a lot lately, but if you'd be giving us a hand again, I'd be mighty grateful."

He was praying, Jig realized. He listened closer. Goblins didn't pray. They had no use for gods, a disinterest matched only by the gods' disdain for goblins. If they cared for us, goblins figured, they'd help us win a fight or two from time to time. Since the only time the goblins won a fight was when they outnumbered the enemy by at least five to one, they assumed that the gods, like everything else, were the enemy.

On those few occasions that goblins got the upper hand, their victims had been known to pray for help or mercy from their gods. Generally this was taken as a weakness, an opportunity to slip in and stab them in the back. But having seen Darnak work his magic before, Jig perked his ears as the dwarf talked to his god. He sounded almost like he was having a normal conversation, albeit a one-sided one. Did the god respond? Jig moved closer, hoping that maybe if he listened hard enough, he might hear Earthmaker answer.

"The idiot boy strained himself again," Darnak said quietly. "If 'twere up to me, I'd say he dug his own tunnel, so let him find his own way out. But you know I can't be doing that. I'm sworn to protect them, and he'd kill us all in his madness."

He sniffed in what could have been amusement. "You wouldn't let your humble servant die of dark magic, would you? Give me an honest fight, at good odds, not this invisible art that slips past an honest blade like smoke."

Jig swallowed. Darnak worried that Ryslind was going to kill them? Maybe he was exaggerating in order to persuade the god. Jig used to say he was starving to try to con a bit more food from Golaka. Somehow, though, he doubted Darnak would do that. And since Golaka had never believed Jig, why would a god be any more gullible?

Darnak stopped breathing. Jig wouldn't have noticed if he hadn't been standing with his ear practically at the dwarf's mouth. What kind of god would suffocate his own followers? Maybe Darnak *had* been trying to deceive the god, and this was his punishment. Jig vowed at that moment that, were he ever in a situation to talk with a god, he would stick to the unadorned truth.

"Darnak?" Dare he touch the immobile dwarf? Would it make any difference? He looked around, but the others were with Ryslind. Darnak's face and lips had taken on a bluish tinge. *How long could dwarves hold their breath?* he wondered.

A terrible thought hit him. If Darnak died, the others would find Jig standing over his body. How was he going to explain *that*?

"Darnak, wake up." He grabbed the dwarf's shoulder and shook him. Rather, he tried to shake him. It was like trying to move a wall. Darnak's muscles were hard as rock.

"Wow," Jig whispered. Growing braver, he poked Darnak's chest and arms. No wonder he hadn't worried about a few bats.

Jig's stomach growled, turning his thoughts down another path. A dwarf like this could keep the entire lair fed for a day and a half.

He shook his head. *I couldn't eat Darnak any more than I could eat Smudge.* Still after a day and a half with nothing but dried meat and bread, the idea was tempting.

"Come on, Darnak. Breathe!"

Darnak gasped. Jig's heart scrambled up into his throat with fright. Even as Jig tried to get his own breathing under control, he turned toward Ryslind. For his ears had noticed something none of the others could possibly have heard. Ryslind had gasped for breath at the exact same moment as Darnak.

What does that mean? What is it that connected them?

"Go see if he's all right," Darnak said. He took a long drink from his wineskin. A line of dark ale trickled from the corner of his mouth and into his beard, a tiny stream through a black forest. "Go on now."

Jig hurried up the hallway. Ryslind stood with one hand on the wall for support. Jig's attention had been on Darnak, so he didn't know what had happened. That was a shame, for he would have loved to know how Barius had ended up on the floor with a puffed lip. Ryslind didn't usually rely on his fists, but maybe in his madness, he had made an exception.

"Brother?" Barius asked.

Ryslind nodded. "I am ready to go on." With that, the mage straightened his robes, used his sleeve to mop his sweaty face, and walked up the corridor as though nothing had happened. Whatever he had done to Barius was enough to stifle the prince's imperious manner, and he fell in next to Ryslind in silence.

Jig slowed until he and Darnak were walking side by side. "Is this a common thing with wizards?" he asked nervously.

Darnak kept his eyes on his map. At first, Jig didn't think he was going to answer. He scribbled another row of tiles, extended the tunnel another few inches, then dipped the quill in his inkpot.

"No, it's not," he said at last. He counted tiles and continued to draw as he spoke. "Never seen anything like it, truth be told. Mind you, Ryslind's always been a queer one. But he never warred with himself like that. Makes me wonder if he hasn't taken on more than he can handle with this quest."

They walked in silence down the right-most of a three-way fork. If Darnak was right, could they trust Ryslind to lead them in the right direction? Without the dwarf's help, would he have even made it this far?

"What did you do back there?" Jig asked.

"Eh?"

"When you prayed. You and Ryslind were connected somehow, and you stopped breathing." At the dwarf's scowl, he quickly said, "I didn't mean to listen in. But you were distracted, so I thought someone should watch for more of those creatures." Jig almost smiled as he thought up the lie. No goblin would have believed it. But Jig didn't want to admit he had been eavesdropping. Fortunately, Darnak didn't know goblins well enough to understand that rather than try to protect the others, the average goblin would have simply cut the dwarf's throat and fled.

"Something's been draining his strength," Darnak said quietly. "Felt it when we first reached the mountain two days ago. Been growing ever since. Earthmaker can't help him directly. Wizards don't get along with gods, never have. But through Earthmaker, I can lend him a bit of power and will."

He shook his head. "There's some who'll be telling you that dwarves have the thickest, hardest heads of any race in this world, and I'll not argue with them. And a good thing for Ryslind, too, for without my help, I've no doubt he'd have lost himself when we came through that whirlpool. My help and that of the god, that is," he amended hastily.

Jig bit off his next question as Darnak stopped

to note another trap Ryslind had pointed out. When he finished, Jig asked, "How long until you can't help him anymore?"

Darnak didn't answer.

Despite Ryslind's magic, they still triggered another trap. At least this time it wasn't Jig's fault. So intent was Darnak on mapping every detail of the tunnel that he stepped squarely on a trapped tile, even as he drew that same tile on the map.

Like before, a panel in the wall flickered and vanished. Another of the corpselike creatures looked up and raised his sword. Darnak dropped his quill and raised his club, screaming a battle cry.

Before he could attack, something flew by and hit the wall of the alcove. This triggered the magic again, and the panel reappeared seconds later. As the marble solidified, Jig imagined he saw a look of annoyance on the creature's sunken face.

Darnak stood there, club still raised, mouth still open, as if he didn't know what to do now that his opponent had been taken away. After a few seconds, he lowered his club and glanced back at Riana. "I guess that'll work too."

Riana had thrown a piece of the bread she kept hidden in her shirt. Hard as stone, the bread had been more than enough to activate the magic of the alcove. She smiled sweetly. "But it cost me the remains of my lunch."

Wordlessly, Darnak dug through his pack and handed her a small loaf. Jig grinned, happy to know that bread did indeed serve *some* useful purpose.

They stopped to rest in a small chamber, empty save for a black crystal fountain in the center. A wide pillar rose to Jig's waist. Atop the pillar sat a wide bowl, guarded by four carved dragons perched on the rim. Each one looked almost lifelike, every scale glistening in the light. Their eyes were smooth blue jewels, and their teeth clear glass.

"Interesting," Darnak said. Riana smirked.

He referred not to the carvings, but to the actual plumbing of the fountain. For each of the dragons stood with a leg cocked, and the water arced from between their legs into the pool at the center.

Jig knelt beneath it, staring through the black crystal to learn if it was pure enough to see light from the other side. He could, though the light was faint and diffused. He had never encountered anything like this. The bowl itself was ridged on the underside, cut so perfectly that Jig sliced his finger on the crystal. The wide rim formed the impression of a dirt trail with rocks and roots and even small plants. "It's beautiful," he whispered.

Barius sniffed. "Created, no doubt, by goblin artisans."

Jig ignored him. The water in the bowl moved in a gentle swirl, propelled by the four streams. But how did the water get from there up into the dragons? It must drain through the pillar, then flow up through the sides of the fountain. He knelt again, trying to find where the water went.

What wonderful magic, to be able to move water about so easily. But why was it wasted here, where nobody could appreciate it? If Jig could build something like this, he would move water from the few pools around the goblin lair into the kitchens, so nobody would have to toil back and forth with the buckets. He could create fountains where goblins could go for drinking water, fountains that constantly replenished themselves. And washing down the privies would become at least a little less disgusting.

"Don't be drinking that, mind you." Darnak

sighed. "A strange day, when I find myself warning a goblin not to drink dragon piss."

"It's only water," Jig said.

"First rule of adventuring," Darnak answered, voice muffled as he chewed his bread. "Never drink from strange fountains. Half the time it'll turn you to stone, or shrink you to the size of a roach, or kill you on the spot."

"I imagine you would more likely suffer the same fate as those wretched corpses," Barius said. "Worry not, goblin. You can rest assured I would strike you dead at the first sign of such a transformation, rather than permit you to suffer such horrors."

He took a small sip from his waterskin. " 'Ware the dragons themselves as well, lest they come to life and tear out your throat when you turn your back."

Darnak laughed. "Getting a mite paranoid, aren't you?"

"Cautious, friend dwarf," Barius corrected. "In a place such as this, who knows what magic lurks in seemingly innocent things."

That did it. Jig was tired of magic. Dead people coming through vanishing walls, giant bats, floating bridges, Ryslind talking with two voices, Darnak talking to his hammer, it was enough to make a goblin mad. How was he, with no more than a short sword and his wits, to deal with all this magic?

He would have to get some magic of his own. That was the goblin way. If your enemy had a knife, you got a sword. If he had two friends, you brought twelve. From what Jig had learned about magic, he had two choices. He could try to be like the wizard or the dwarf. Both of them had magic of a sort. Jig only had to figure out which kind of magic he wanted on his side.

Tough choice. Learn to talk to the gods, or become a freak of a man with tattoos and robes, fighting a losing battle with his own mind. Jig's bald head, courtesy of Smudge, already gave him more in common with the wizard than he liked. He left the fountain and went to sit with Darnak. Better the lesser of two oddities.

"Tell me of the gods," Jig said. A simple enough request, or so he thought. Barius cringed and moved to the other side of the room. Riana followed a few minutes later. Even Ryslind walked away until he had positioned the fountain between himself and the dwarf.

For it turned out that Darnak considered himself a bit of a historian, as well as an expert on the gods. A huge grin split his face. He finished off another wineskin and launched into a detailed saga, starting with the creation of the universe. Jig tried to listen, he truly did. But after a few minutes, he found himself wondering if Ryslind's brand of magic was really as bad as it looked.

"To start with, you had the Two Gods of the beginning. All they did was fight. Spend an eternity with someone, you're bound to get a bit tired of their company. They hurled magic back and forth, trying to get the upper hand, even though they couldn't actually kill each other. The universe was young, and they were dumb as newborns. But powerful. They had all the power in the universe to themselves, you see. But some of it began to leak. And sooner or later this loose magic came together to form the Twenty-One Lower Gods. They were the ones who actually went about making the world and all the creatures on it."

He ticked off their names, one after another, counting on his fingers and toes as he went. That only took him to twenty gods, but Jig didn't bother

to ask about the twenty-first. He didn't try to remember all the names. Not one had fewer than five
syllables, and they all had some sort of fetish about
hyphenation and apostrophes. Really, what kind of
a name was Korama Al-vensk'ak Sitheckt, anyway?
When Darnak first mentioned that one, Jig thought
he was hacking up yesterday's dinner.

"What about Earthmaker?" Jig asked. "If the
Twenty-One made the world, why didn't you mention him?"

He looked embarrassed. "Well, Earthmaker
didn't actually make the world, as such. He came
along a bit later, and he was after helping those
blessed races who lived *in* the earth. Dwarves,
gnomes, and the like. But he didn't appear until
after the Year of Darkness."

"The Year of Darkness?" he asked before he
could think better of it. As Darnak started in again,
Jig looked longingly at the others across the room
who sat safe from this endless storytelling. What
had he started? And how could he steer the dwarf
toward something useful, something that would
help Jig?

Jig tried to understand the difference between
the Lower Gods and the Gods of the Beginning
and the Gods of the Elements, but then Darnak
would mention something new, like the Gods of
Men, and Jig was back to being confused. He began
to wonder if the others would hold it against him
if he stabbed Darnak to shut him up. Or perhaps
it would be easier to turn his sword on himself.

Jig interrupted, desperately trying to break the
endless flow of words. "How many Gods of Men?"
From the other side of the room, his sharp ears
caught a very unprincely groan from Barius.

"Nine hundred fifty-four," Darnak said happily.
"Starting with Abriana the Gray, Goddess of

Storms and Sailors. She was born of a union be-
twixt Taras of the Oak—he's a tree god—and a
human woman named. . . ." Darnak frowned.

"Well, her name's not important. Taras appeared
to her in the form of a three-hundred-pound tortoise and propositioned her. Gods were always
doing strange things back in those days. A right
kinky lot, if you ask me. But like any good lass,
this girl grabbed the nearest hammer and cracked
that tortoise on the back. Split Taras's shell right
in two. Did I mention she was a dwarven girl?"

He hadn't, but Jig wasn't terribly surprised. He
had only met one dwarf in his life, but he could
imagine Darnak doing something like that. As for
the rest of the story, Jig tried not to think about
it. He didn't know much about mating rituals, but
he did know that all this changing into tortoises
and other shapeshifting was a bit peculiar. Though
maybe this explained why surface-dwellers were so
fascinated by religion.

"Anyway, out sprang Abriana the Gray in a flash
of thunder. She was twin to Wodock the Black,
God of the Deep Ocean."

"If they were twins, did he come out of the tortoise too?" Jig asked, trying to keep up.

"Nah. He came later. Had something to do with
a mortal who fell in love with an acorn." Darnak
frowned. "Human, naturally. Wouldn't catch a
dwarf pining over an acorn." He burst into laughter
and punched Jig on the arm. "Pining. Get it?"

Jig got back up and rubbed his arm. He didn't
get the joke, and he didn't want to. His arm hurt,
his head hurt, and he still hadn't learned anything
useful. Over nine hundred gods. How was Jig to
choose which one would be best suited for him?
All he knew was that he didn't want any god who
turned into an acorn or a turtle to have sex, fell in

love with a campfire, trapped mortals with bits of dandelion fluff, or any of this other nonsense. Which seemed to eliminate almost all of those nine hundred gods. "Are there gods for goblins?"

Darnak snorted. "Nah. Gods aren't much for the dark races—goblins, orcs, ogres, kobolds, and the like."

The dark races. Jig liked the sound of that. Intimidating and mysterious. But it didn't help his problem.

He listened with one ear as Darnak droned on and on. The dwarf must have studied for years to memorize all of this information. He knew the stories of origin for almost every god. How he managed to keep the divine family trees straight in his head was beyond Jig. Or perhaps family vines would be a better term for the way the relationships twisted and intertwined and looped back on themselves, as gods mated with their mothers' sisters, and so on. Jig twisted his ears, trying to filter out the worst of it.

There was something Darnak had said before, back when he was healing Barius. Something about Earthmaker being busy with the prayers of an entire world. Too busy to spend all his time on one dwarf.

Jig chewed on his bread without tasting it. Not that there was much to taste. But his mind was elsewhere. He could see two ways to use the power of the gods to his advantage. One would be to become a follower of the most powerful god, one who could hurl thunderbolts and destroy worlds without breaking a sweat. Did gods sweat? It didn't matter.

The problem was that such a god wouldn't have much of a use for a mere goblin. Which brought Jig to the other option. He could follow a god who had grown unpopular. One with few worshipers, who wouldn't be busy answering other prayers. One who could devote his full attention to people like Jig. One who might be grateful even for a goblin follower.

His ears shot up as a phrase caught his attention. "What was that?"

Darnak blinked. "Eh? Oh, the Fifteen Forgotten Gods of the War of Shadows?"

Forgotten Gods. That sounded perfect, if a bit misleading. If they really were forgotten, how would Darnak know about them?

"Who were they?"

The dwarf played with his beard. "Let me think . . . they fell out of favor for going up against the Two. You can't kill a god, of course, but the Two showed them all that you *can* beat one within an inch of his or her life. Take the Shadowstar. They stripped his mind, flayed his body with blades of lightning, and cast him loose in the desert. May have turned him into a lizard for a while, I'm not sure. He wandered there for two hundred years, all but forgotten."

"Tell me about him," Jig said eagerly.

"Well, Tymalous Shadowstar was God of the Autumn Star. When his lady brought the snows of winter, Shadowstar lengthened the nights and danced in the darkness."

There was more, but Jig had heard enough. A forgotten god, one with power over the darkness. He didn't understand this idea of longer nights, and he knew nothing of the seasons, but it didn't matter.

Jig the goblin would be a follower of Tymalous Shadowstar.

CHAPTER 10

~~~◆~~~

Falling Short of Expectations

They might have stayed there forever, listening to Darnak's endless recitation of divine history. He was determined to tell Jig about every wart on the frog-god's back and every copper coin claimed by the god of gamblers. No matter how often Jig cleared his throat or glanced at the others, Darnak kept on talking. Jig could have done without this demonstration of dwarven stamina.

Finally Barius strolled around the fountain and tapped his boot for attention.

Darnak hesitated.

"You have not yet completed your map of this room, friend dwarf?" He waved at the fountain. "Such a creation deserves to be noted, would you not agree?"

"Aye." He looked torn. "But I've not yet told the goblin of the godless years."

The goblin had already taken the opportunity to scoot away, and now hid on the other side of the fountain. He wondered why Barius hadn't intervened an hour ago. *Probably this was one more way to punish me.* If so, Jig hoped the prince would go back to hitting him next time. Still, he felt a strange sense of gratitude to Barius for having rescued him at all.

He remained hidden until Darnak finished his map. They moved on, again following Ryslind as he used his magic to track the Necromancer. While they walked, Jig pondered a new problem. How, precisely, did one go about worshiping a god? Maybe he would need a necklace like Darnak's. Something with the starburst and lightning of Tymalous Shadowstar instead of Earthmaker's hammer. But what else?

In his tale, Darnak had mentioned mortals who made sacrifices to the gods in exchange for divine help. Jig tried to remember the details. There had been something about giving up one's firstborn son, and another who killed "lambs," whatever they were. Jig had no son, no lamb, and he wasn't about to try to sacrifice one of the adventurers. The best he could do was Smudge, and the little fire-spider wouldn't make much of a sacrifice. Not that Jig would have given him up. Except for right after Smudge had burned off Jig's hair, maybe.

That left prayers. What did you say when you prayed? How did you strike up a chat with a god? Jig wasn't even very good at starting a conversation with other goblins. Did you have to say the words out loud, or would the god hear you in your head?

He decided that gods could hear your thoughts. If he had to speak the words, he'd be too embarrassed to try. He could already hear Barius's reaction. "What god would tolerate a follower of your ilk?" he would say. And he might be right. To be honest, Jig didn't expect much. Goblins and gods were like . . . well, like goblins and every other race. There wasn't much in the way of mingling.

Still it couldn't hurt. All things considered, it would be difficult for Jig's situation to be any worse. So he began to talk in his mind as they crept through the corridors.

Tymalous Shadowstar? What a clunky name. He wondered if he could get away with calling a god "Tym." Probably not. *My name is Jig. Can you hear me?*

He paused, but there was no answer. Then again, Darnak's conversations with Earthmaker seemed pretty one-sided as well, so it might not mean anything.

I'm wandering around lost with a dwarf, an elven child, an arrogant prince, and a wizard teetering on the edge of madness. Well, not so much teetering. More bouncing back and forth between mad and really *mad. I wondered if you could help keep me alive long enough to get home in one piece?*

Still nothing. Jig sighed and started to hurry after the others when inspiration hit. No goblin helped another without getting something in return. Why should gods be any different?

I don't know how worship works or anything, but if there's anything you need, I'll try to help out.

That felt better. A fair deal, just like a human would make. Jig would help Tymalous Shadowstar, and the god would help Jig. He wondered what kind of favors a god might need. He hoped it would be nothing like that acorn story Darnak had told.

"Hold," Barius said in a low voice. "A door. Thief, check for traps and locks and such."

Riana grimaced. Remembering what had happened the last time, Jig couldn't blame her. A few more traps, and she would have no fingers left.

"Wait," he called.

He hurried up to the door with her, to Barius's annoyance. There, he reached into his boot and retrieved the strip of meat he had been saving for later. He brushed off the dust and fuzz and tried to ignore the rumbling of his stomach.

"Tie your tools to this." He handed the meat to Riana.

She nodded, apparently remembering how Jig had checked the other door. With a bit of Darnak's twine, she secured her pick to the meat and probed at the keyhole. As before, there was a click, and a silver needle lodged in the meat. Dry and stiff the meat might be, but Jig swore he saw its color fade.

"Why do you delay?" Barius asked. "Disarm the trap and open the door."

Riana muttered, "Disarm it yourself, you over-dressed sheep-lover."

She pulled out her knife and used the blade to bend the needle out of the way. That left only the lock itself. She stared angrily at her hands.

"I wasn't very good at this even before I lost my finger," she snapped. Jig took a step back, hoping she wouldn't decide to punish the one who cost her that finger. She slid the lockpick into the keyhole and probed the mechanism of the lock. Her eyes narrowed with concentration, and her tongue tip stuck out of the corner of her mouth as she worked. "Come on, damn you."

The pick slipped from her fingers. With an icy glare at Jig, she tried again. Then a third time. She tried using the pick in her left hand, but it was no use. "I can't do it."

"You did it before," Barius said.

"That was an easier lock. This has two tumblers instead of one, and I think there's some kind of button in the back that needs to be pressed."

"Try again," Barius said. He shook his head. "We've dragged you through half this accursed place, and on the two occasions we require your help, you fail us."

"I'm sorry to interfere with your great quest. Next time bring a key instead." She punctuated every third word with a vicious jab at the lock. When that still didn't work, she grabbed Jig's wrist. "Hold this."

She pressed the stronger rod into his hand, keeping the slender pick for herself. "Place the bent end into the lock and twist toward me. There are two tumblers in there, and I can't get both of them at once. I'm going to try to rip the lock."

"What?" He had an image of Riana tearing the door loose with her bare hands. Darnak might be able to do it, but he couldn't see Riana succeeding, no matter how strong elves might be.

"It's a thieving trick. I'm going to yank the pick past the tumblers and hope it knocks them both up long enough for you to turn the lock." She adjusted the rod in Jig's hand. "There, like it's a key. I've got the end pressed against the button in the lock. Hold it still, and keep pressing sideways. If this works, the tumblers will bounce up, and you need to turn the lock before they fall."

He squinted, trying to bring the lock into focus in the dim light. The least Barius could do was bring the lantern closer.

"Not that tight," Riana said. "Didn't you see how I held it before?"

"I don't see very well," Jig muttered.

"Oh." She grabbed another lockpick from her kit, this one with a smoother bump on the end. "The elves make lenses that would help. Jewelers use them a lot. Sometimes they sell them to old rich humans whose eyes are starting to fail."

"Sure," Jig said. "I'll remember that the next time I pass through an elven jewelry shop."

Riana ignored him. She slid the pick in past Jig's fingers, took a deep breath, and jerked it free. Nothing happened. "Too hard," she muttered. She tried again, and again.

The fourth time, it worked. The rod in Jig's hand turned, surprising him so much he dropped it. He winced, waiting for Riana's explosion. But that first quarter-turn was enough. She picked up her tools and finished opening the lock.

"Back up," she said. Once Jig was clear, she yanked the door open and shot Barius a look comprised of equal smugness and annoyance. Blinking innocently, she asked, "Will there be anything more, Your Majesty?"

Barius didn't answer. He stared in shock through the door into the room beyond. His lips moved without speaking. This from a man who had faced hobgoblins, lizard-fish, and even the Necromancer's warriors.

Jig peeked around the door, half afraid to see what monster awaited them. But better to see what it was, so as to know if he had any hope of running away. His eyes widened.

The door opened into a large, empty room. The floor and walls were made of the same black marble they had seen all along, but the ceiling was a familiar mosaic of tiled glass. In case Jig had any doubts about where they were, a pillar of whirling water stood at the center of the room.

Of everyone in the party, Darnak appeared the most distraught. He shoved his way into the room and stared at the pillar, as if sheer indignation would make it disappear. He counted the tiles of the floor and walls and compared his figures to the notes on his map. He studied the patterns in the ceiling, trying to persuade himself that they hadn't in fact come back to the very room where they first arrived.

"One forty-seven, one forty-eight, one forty-nine." He spat on the final tile as he finished his second recount. "How could I have been so far off?"

He had spread his map on the floor to better study their path. Jig peered over his shoulder, looking at the winding tunnels that led from the center of the map—this room—through various tunnels and over what must be the bridge, to judge by the small bats Darnak had drawn, and finally to a door in the upper right corner of the map. Jig didn't know much about maps, but he knew that the door in the corner shouldn't have led them into the room in the center.

"There's no way we got turned about that badly." Darnak chewed the tip of one dark braid as he paced tight circles around the map, nearly colliding with Jig. "Even if I were off four or five degrees on those turns. A right rotten trick that would be, using eighty-five-degree turns instead of solid right angles. I'll have to remember that when I get home. I could design a nasty maze that way. But we didn't even pass over the chasm a second time.

"And what happened to get your magic so clogged up?" he demanded of Ryslind. "You said you were taking us to the Necromancer. Unless he's a wee fish swimming about in that column, I'm not seeing any Necromancer here."

"As I said before, this room was blocked to me." Ryslind's eyes were cracks of red light as he studied the walls. "I thought it was the magic of the water that overwhelmed my spell, so I commanded my power to ignore this room and take me to the Necromancer."

Darnak glanced down at his map once more. "Ah, hell." So saying, he grabbed the map, crumpled it into a ball, and tossed it into the corner. "Getting cramps in my fingers anyway."

"Is that all you have to offer me?" Barius threw up his arms. "One hundred and thirty-two years of age, Silas Earthmaker at your side, and all you can do is complain of cramped fingers."

He whirled on Ryslind. "As for you, my brother, what are we to make of your vaunted powers? Where is your otherworldly wisdom, great one? I was wrong to doubt you. How great your art must be, that it led us back to the very spot from which we left."

"What if he's right?" Jig asked. The room felt much colder to him. Colder and darker. "What if the Necromancer *is* here?"

"Ridiculous." Barius waved one hand. "He must be hidden away, down some tunnel we neglected to explore. Only after defeating the minions do we face the master. Else what point to having minions at all?"

Jig frowned. That was a good question. Maybe this was a good time to ask for help again. *Shadowstar, am I right? Why would the Necromancer play with us like that?* He blinked as a thought occurred to him.

"Maybe . . ." It sounded ridiculous now that he started to say it out loud. Too late, though. Everyone waited for him to finish.

"Well the Necromancer isn't a very nice person, right?" Barius rolled his eyes, and Jig hurried to finish. "Maybe he's doing this just to be mean. Teasing us, like animals, before he kills us. He probably doesn't get much company here, you know. He probably gets lonely."

"A master of the dark arts lonely?" Ryslind raised both eyebrows.

Is that the answer? But if so, that would mean the Necromancer was here, watching us even as we argue. He probably laughed when we found ourselves back here, like it was the greatest joke in the world. But where is he watching from?

Jig's gut tightened, and sweat ran down his back as he looked around. The room was empty, as before. Nothing but the water. No place to hide. Even with magic, it would be difficult to hide in here, with the way the light bounced off the marble panels, illuminating every corner of the room.

The panels. Jig stared. Like the panels in the hall that disappeared when those creatures had attacked.

Riana sat by one wall, gnawing on her bread and looking bored. Ryslind looked like he was trying to use his art to find the Necromancer again, but Barius kept interrupting. Darnak had flattened his map and begun again to retrace their path. Aside from a few chuckles and Ryslind's raised brows, they thought Jig's idea was a waste of time. What could a goblin know? But he was right. He knew it.

"He's behind the panels."

Only Riana heard. Her eyes widened, and her cheeks went pale. "Are you sure?"

Before he could answer, a booming laugh came from the walls. Ryslind raised his hands, fingers twisted to hurl a spell, but he could find no target. Barius's sword hissed free, and Darnak grabbed his club. From Jig's shoulder came the smell of singed leather as Smudge branded eight dots onto his shoulder pad.

"Very good, little goblin." The voice came from every part of the room at once. Not even Jig's ears could pinpoint the speaker.

"Show yourself, Necromancer," Barius said calmly. "Face us with honor and die like a man."

Even Darnak sighed at that. Jig didn't know a lot about adventuring or quests, but even he knew that "honor" wasn't a word that went with "necromancy." But if Barius insisted on playing the noble hero, Jig had no complaints. Barius's posturing made him the center of attention, as he no doubt intended. It also meant that he, not Jig, was the obvious target.

"You've all done very well," the voice went on. "I thought my warriors would finish you off in the hallway. But your wizard had more power than I expected. He's a fool, but a powerful one."

Ryslind's eyes burned a deeper red at that; he said nothing.

"Come, wizard. Find me if you can. I'm here, right beyond your grasp. Waiting and laughing."

"Can you find this villain?" Barius demanded. At Ryslind's angry nod, he snapped, "Why then do you delay?"

No, that's what he wants! Jig didn't know where the thought came from, and it was too late anyway. Ryslind's fingers straightened. He turned toward one of the panels, and fire shot from his hands.

Jig cringed and turned away as orange light brightened the room. Black smoke stung his nose, and even from behind the pillar he felt the heat against his skin. How Ryslind could touch that fire, hold it in his fingers, and control it was beyond Jig.

The flames stopped. Ryslind's fingers curved and straightened again, and this time water shot forth, freezing instantly when it touched the wall. Flakes of snow fell from the stream as he shot more water at the icy wall.

Smudge hid behind Jig's neck, making Jig wish he had something more substantial to hide behind.

He had seen evidence of Ryslind's power before,
but never in such a raw display. Those two spells
alone would wipe out a goblin patrol before they
could even grab weapons.

A thick layer of white ice covered the marble
panel. Ryslind sent a second line of fire into its
center. As soon as the flames touched the marble,
a loud crack shot through the room. The panel fell
to the floor in a dozen triangular pieces that shattered upon impact. Behind the steam and smoke,
one of the dead warriors drew a sword and
stepped forward.

Ryslind's lip curled into a sneer, and another
blast of fire incinerated the corpse. Seconds later,
only ashes remained.

"You might try toning it down a little," Darnak
said nervously. "Better to keep a bit of power in
reserve, just in case."

Ryslind either didn't hear or didn't care. The
flames that had destroyed the corpse moved to the
next panel.

How many were there? Jig counted as fast as he
could. Twenty-eight panels. He didn't know much
about magic, but he doubted Ryslind could keep
up this kind of magic long enough to destroy them
all. Darnak appeared to have the same idea, for he
was tugging Ryslind's robe, trying to make him
stop.

The wizard brushed him away with a gesture that
left Darnak angrily patting wisps of flame from his
beard. One hand fell to his club, and Jig watched
as Darnak fought the urge to club the wizard unconscious. Jig didn't know if that would be an improvement or not, but in the end, the dwarf decided
against it. Instead, he grabbed his amulet and began
to pray. *Probably trying to lend Ryslind more
strength,* Jig guessed.

Ryslind made it through two more panels and destroyed two more of the creatures before collapsing in pain. This time, as Ryslind fell, so did Darnak. But where the dwarf remained on the floor clutching his head, Ryslind stood back up as swiftly as he had fallen.

"Excellent," came the Necromancer's voice. The rest of the marble panels vanished, and two dozen dead soldiers stepped into the room. "You proved stronger than I had guessed, wizard."

With the panels gone, the Necromancer's voice no longer echoed from all directions. Nor was it the deep, threatening voice they had heard before.

To Jig's left, guarded by two well armored corpses, stood a throne. Jig had never seen a real throne before, but this could be nothing else. No gold or gems decorated this chair. It had been carved from a single piece of stone, so black that even the marble looked bright by comparison. Light vanished into the throne, sucked into shadow. The legs formed claws, and the arms ended in small animal heads. Jig couldn't see well enough to identify them. The back of the throne rose to the top of the alcove, nearly ten feet. The Necromancer himself sat cross-legged upon purple cushions of velvet. In one hand, he held a long silver wand.

Jig smirked. He couldn't help it. After all his fear, all the legends and songs about the terrible Necromancer, this was not what he had imagined in his nightmares. For starters, Jig had expected him to be, well, taller. For another, a dark wizard shouldn't have large, gossamer wings. And didn't wizards wear robes? Granted, the Necromancer's loose trousers and vest were both black, and his bare arms did have a pale, deathlike pallor, but the effect was spoiled by the mop of brilliant blue hair that topped it all off.

"He's a mere fairy," Barius whispered, an uncharacteristic grin tugging his lips.

That was the wrong thing to say. The Necromancer stood up in the chair, pulling himself to his full height. Had he been on the floor, he would have been at eye-level with the prince's knee. He waved his wand about like a sword. "A mere fairy, eh? And what's to keep this mere fairy from mastering the dark arts? I'll show you what real power is. I killed the old Necromancer, you know."

He hopped down and ran at Barius. His dead bodyguards flanked him, weapons ready. Barius slipped back and raised his sword in a defensive stance, but the Necromancer slid to a halt a few feet out of range.

"This was his domain, but I took it away from him. Me! By myself. The others all died, but I lived long enough to cast a spell of dancing on him." He giggled. "He couldn't stop long enough to cast a spell, and that gave me time to put a knife in his eye. Horrid mess. Eye gook everywhere. Disgusting."

"Ryslind, destroy this pest," Barius said.

"Destroy him yourself, brother."

Jig froze, not even breathing. No longer did Ryslind speak with two voices. The voice that remained was not Ryslind's. Whatever had happened to the wizard when he overexerted himself, he was now as dangerous as the Necromancer. Jig hoped the others realized it, because the last thing he was going to do was face either mage himself.

"Take them," the Necromancer said, pointing absently with his wand. The other creatures stepped out of their alcoves.

Barius's head snapped one way, then another as they closed in. Even human arrogance had limits. With Darnak unconscious and his brother as great a danger as the Necromancer, Barius had no choice. His sword slipped through limp fingers, and he raised his hands in surrender. Two creatures grabbed his arms and forced him to his knees. Others did the same with Riana and Jig. They even grabbed Darnak's limp body and held him in a kneeling position.

"Very good." The Necromancer strutted before them. He still had to look up to meet their eyes. "You see, prince, your brother is . . . well, not himself today." He giggled. "If you're nice, I might even tell you who he *is*."

"What do you want?" Barius sounded tired and beaten. Maybe reality had finally tunneled through his skull, and the prince realized he was going to die. Jig wanted to reassure him that he'd get used to the thought after a while, but decided it would be better to remain silent.

"It's not about what I want. It's what *he* wants." The Necromancer nodded at Ryslind. Then he smirked again. "Still, nobody could complain if I kept one or two, to replace a few of my toy soldiers. The dwarf, I think. He'll make a good warrior. And one other." He rubbed his tiny chin.

His eyes looked from Riana to Jig and back. To Jig's shame, all he could think was, *Take the elf. Elves are stronger than goblins. They're smarter. You don't want me.*

"The elf could be useful for the task ahead of you, but I see no reason for you to take the goblin. Leave him for me."

"Dung!" Jig shouted. "Why me? Why not her? Why does it always have to be the goblin?" His voice trailed off as he realized what he was doing. He had shouted at the Necromancer. "Uh . . . sir," he added quietly.

The Necromancer didn't take offense. "You intrigue me, goblin. You were the one to figure out my little game. You were quite right, you know. Dreadfully lonely down here. Sometimes I summon one of my bats and play with it, but they die so quickly. With the lizard-fish guarding the vortex, I rarely get to talk to anyone from above. I've even snuck into Straum's domain a time or two, just for the company.

"You should be honored, little goblin. You'll be the first of your race to become one of my servants." He gestured toward the corpses. "I've humans and dwarves and even an elf or two." He lowered his voice and looked at the others, as if sharing a deep secret. "Though elves don't take too well to being dead."

"Neither do I," Jig said.

The Necromancer grinned, revealing blackened gums. Seeing Jig's stare, he explained, "Nothing much to eat down here. Had to make do on what I could conjure, and I'm afraid it wasn't all that healthy. Rotted the teeth right out of my head. What I wouldn't give for a crisp, juicy apple. Some days I think I'd trade all my power for one apple."

Jig stared. "But without teeth, how would you eat it?"

"Shut up!" The little fairy flew into the air and shouted. Spit sprayed Jig's face. "You know nothing of the sacrifices I've made. Stupid goblin. Within an hour, I'll give you a few sips from my beautiful fountain, and you'll never worry about anything again. But for me, there's always something to worry about. What if the magic wears off? What if a stronger mage comes after me?" He looked around fearfully. "What if Straum comes to take my beautiful lair?"

"I don't think he'd fit," Jig pointed out. "And doesn't Straum already have a lair of his own?"

The Necromancer blinked. "I suppose so. See, that's why I chose you. You're a smart one." He waved at one of the creatures. "Take the dwarf and the goblin to the fountain and drown them."

He winked at Jig. "That way you'll be sure to swallow some of the potion as you die. I've tried a lot of ways, and trust me, this is the best. Why, once I even changed a man into a fish and dropped him into the fountain. It worked, but I wound up with an undead bass. It's no good, you know. You can't kill an undead bass. I took him out of the water, and he flopped about for hours and hours until I finally had one of my warriors stomp on the poor thing. Laughed for days about that one, I did."

"What are you going to do with me?" Barius asked. "With us?"

The Necromancer's eyes sparkled merrily. "It's a surprise."

Unfair, Jig thought. Barius and the others would probably be taken prisoner, left in a dungeon somewhere until Riana helped them break out. That's what always happened. No matter how secure the dungeon, the heroes always managed to escape. Luck favored adventurers, while goblins got dragged off to be drowned. Why him?

The question burned in Jig's brain. Why was he the one to be kicked around by the prince? Why, when he tried to help Riana, did he get threatened and punched and end up with everyone hating him? How had he ended up with this doomed party, fighting dead warriors and eating *bread*? Bread which, as it turned out, gave him terrible gas in addition to having no taste. He hadn't seen a proper privy in a day and a half, and this pissing in corners was a thing for beasts. Why had he been born a goblin at all? Sure, he was smart for a goblin. Look where it had brought him. Had he died

with Porak and the others, at least it would have
been a fast death. Why in Shadowstar's name
couldn't things go right for him, just this once?

*Why, in my name, don't you quit whining and do
something for yourself, just this once?*

Jig froze. "Who said that?"

The Necromancer frowned. "What?"

*Smart for a goblin. That's what the little blue-
haired one said, right?* The voice in Jig's head
sighed. *I see this is a relative thing.*

Jig's eyes went wide. *Tymalous Shadowstar?*

Well done. Perhaps there's hope after all. Jig got
the sense that the god was shaking his head. *Still,
a goblin follower. Have I really fallen this far? Well,
what are you waiting for, goblin?*

"Jig," he said.

"What are you talking about, little goblin?" the
Necromancer asked.

"My name is Jig." He heard Shadowstar laughing
in his head. "Jig! Why does everyone call me 'goblin'? I'm Jig!"

He squirmed and bit and kicked and tried to
wiggle free, but the dead hands held him fast. His
arms hurt where their fingers dug into his skin, and
his shoulder was beginning to burn even through
Smudge's leather pad.

"Smudge!" Jig turned and pushed Smudge with
his nose. It hurt terribly. He would have a blister
on his nose, and Smudge clung to the pad even
tighter when he realized what Jig was doing.

"Please," Jig said. He pushed again, harder, and
Smudge came free and dropped onto the creature's
arm. The Necromancer didn't notice, and without
orders, it continued to hold Jig even as its skin
blackened and burned.

"What's the problem, goblin?" the Necromancer
snapped. He raised his wand.

"My name is Jig!" he screamed. He bit down on the second corpse's hand and used his fangs to pry the fingers free. By now the muscles of the first creature were on fire, and it was a simple matter to bend the hand back. Jig was loose. He whirled on the Necromancer and drew his sword. "Jig, Jig, Jig!"

The fairy raised his wand. A line of yellow smoke shot out, and Jig's vision sparkled. The smoke smelled fruity and sweet. Jig's ankle flashed in pain, but nothing else happened.

The Necromancer stared at his wand. So did Jig, but only for a second. Then he leaped into the air, screaming incoherently as he flailed about with his sword.

The Necromancer started to take to the air, but Jig's blade slashed through one wing. As he fell, he raised his wand, and fire rushed into Jig's face.

Again Jig's ankle felt like it had exploded, but the fire didn't harm him. No worse than Smudge had done on many occasions, at least. But he couldn't see with all that fire in his face. Where had the Necromancer been?

He lunged blindly, felt his blade sink into something soft, and the flames disappeared.

On the ground in front of him, the Necromancer stared in disbelief at the sword sticking out of his belly. He had dropped his wand, and both hands gingerly touched the blade, as if he couldn't believe it was real. Only Jig was close enough to hear the Necromancer's final tormented words.

"By a goblin?" And then he died.

Jig stepped on the fairy's chest and pulled his sword free. He wondered briefly if fairy would taste as good as elf, but decided he wasn't hungry enough to find out. Not when the fairy had also been a Necromancer. Who knew what potions and preservatives might be mixed in with that flesh? Besides, the fairy was a little thing, scrawny as well as short. Hardly any meat at all.

Jig turned to face the others. The Necromancer was dead. That left only two dozen dead warriors and a possessed wizard.

Jig grinned like a madman and waved his sword. "Who's first?"

CHAPTER 11

Between Death and a Dark Pit

Two dozen dead faces stared at him. Riana's mouth hung open in shock, and Barius looked every which way as he tried to comprehend what had happened. Ryslind's red eyes swept over the Necromancer's body, then locked onto Jig. He did not look happy.

Jig could think of only one thing to do. He prayed. *That worked great! Thank you so much. What next?*

The answer, when it came, sounded a bit put out. *I don't know. I didn't expect you to live through it.*

Oh. Some of Jig's elation drained off at that. Some, but not all. What had Shadowstar said? Quit whining and do something for yourself for once. And he had. He had slain the Necromancer. A deed worthy of song! A song about him, Jig the goblin. Sure, the Necromancer looked harmless now, a dead fairy bleeding a puddle onto the floor. But that fairy had been the Necromancer, a two-foot-tall master of death with hideous blue hair.

The point was, Jig had done it. He had been stronger than the Necromancer's magic. His sword had ended the Necromancer's life. *He* had done it, not Barius or Darnak. It was all he could do not to giggle. He spun to face Ryslind. The dead creatures hadn't moved, which made Ryslind the next threat to be faced.

The wizard smiled, and the ground beneath Jig fell away. No, he was floating! Even as he watched, the room start to spin, his ankle throbbed, and he fell onto his backside. He stood back up with a grimace, rubbing his bruised posterior. *So much for the dramatic hero.*

"What have you done?" Ryslind demanded. He tried another spell, but nothing happened. "Where did you find this protection?"

Protection? Jig remembered the pain that had come as each of the Necromancer's spells failed. He looked down at his ankle. Inside his boot he saw the bracelet he had taken from the skeleton in the hallway. That bracelet must protect him from magic. That was why the Necromancer hadn't been able to stop him.

That must be why the skeleton had stayed dead, while all the others had come back to fight. The bracelet couldn't stop all magic—the stinging burns on Jig's face told him that much. The Necromancer must have turned the bracelet's former owner into another dead guard, and there had been just enough magic for him to walk to his alcove. There the spell had worn off, and he had died for real.

What a marvelous find. Jig was safe from magic. He looked up. Safe from magic, but not from his own foolishness. While he had been figuring out how the bracelet worked, Ryslind had strung his bow. He had an arrow nocked to the string, pointed at Jig's chest. His eyes fell on Jig's boot. "What have you got there, goblin?"

"Jig," he muttered with an echo of his earlier

rage. Ryslind's fingers tightened on the bowstring, and Jig decided against another mad rush. "It's a bracelet I found."

"Let me have it."

Jig saw movement behind Ryslind. If he could keep the wizard distracted, maybe someone would help him. He sat down and pulled at the boot.

"I see you, brother, so please do not try anything foolhardy." Ryslind nodded over his shoulder, and Barius flew through the air and into the wall.

Jig started to go for his sword, but even though Ryslind wasn't looking, the bow followed his movements. "That's a dangerous idea, goblin."

That wasn't Ryslind. His body, yes, but not *him*. Jig could hear the difference, even if nobody else could. "Who are you?"

The wizard's smile widened. "One who searches for the rod, the same as all of you. Now give me that bracelet."

Jig sighed and went back to wrestling with his boot. He could have slipped it off easily, but he wanted time to think, and as long as Ryslind hadn't noticed how overlarge the boots were, Jig could continue to stall. What should he do? Barius was helpless, pinned against the wall. Which wouldn't have bothered Jig in the slightest, except that Barius had been on his way to stop Ryslind. Riana was still free, but as soon as she moved, she'd join Barius.

At least the creatures hadn't attacked. *They had no minds of their own.* He remembered the one who had burned to a crisp rather than take the initiative to push Smudge off of its arm. They would stand there and wait for instructions forever, at least until the magic wore off.

Jig's eyes fell upon the Necromancer's silver wand. Could he use that to fight Ryslind? Sure he could, if he knew anything at all about magic. He wondered how much power remained in the wand. Maybe he could bluff. If he could get his hands on the wand, could he convince Ryslind to let him go?

Probably not. Ryslind hadn't been afraid of the *real* Necromancer. What were the odds he would surrender to a goblin?

"You're delaying," Ryslind said.

"I'm trying!"

"Perhaps you need help." He didn't appear to do anything, but suddenly the Necromancer's guards were closing around him.

Jig's eyes widened. Ryslind wasn't supposed to be able to control them. These were the Necromancer's creatures. How much more unfair could things get?

"I've got it." He hastily ripped off his boot and grabbed the bracelet. The skin of his ankle was a bit blackened. The bracelet had probably burned him when it tried to absorb too much magic. Still, better another burn than to end up like those mindless corpses.

"Throw it here," Ryslind ordered.

Jig obeyed. He threw as hard as he could. And as he dove out of the way, he thought, *Is it my fault Ryslind didn't specify what to throw?*

Ryslind ducked as Jig's boot flew past his face. The creatures walked closer. Jig snatched the Necromancer's wand and scampered back. Something buzzed past his face. Probably an arrow.

Trying not to think about how close that shot had come, he thrust the wand through the center of the bracelet.

The creatures collapsed. Jig tried to smile, but his teeth were clenched too tightly from fear. *Another victory for Jig.*

Ryslind's next arrow slammed into Jig's shoulder

like a fist, spinning him in a complete circle before he fell. His eyes wide, he tried to push himself back up, but his arms wouldn't work. His cheek was wet and sticky. What was that blue stuff on the floor? Oh, right. That was his blood.

He lay there and waited for Ryslind to finish him. Would it be magic? The fire and ice he had used to blast away the walls? Or maybe he would settle for cutting Jig's throat. Either way, Jig hoped it would be quick. The floor was cold, and the longer he waited, the more his shoulder hurt.

A hand rolled him over, and he found himself looking into Darnak's bushy face. He tried to say something, but at that moment the pain increased tenfold. The dwarf had rolled him onto the arrow. Jig felt like someone had twisted a knife in his shoulder. He heard himself mutter something like, "Grargh."

"Hold on, lad," Darnak said. "The arrow was barbed, so I'm needing to break off the end. This is going to hurt."

Going to hurt? Through teary eyes, Jig tried to see what was happening. He saw Darnak's hand close around the back of the arrow. The shaft snapped, and the world went white for an instant. "Aach," he whimpered.

Darnak placed a hand over Jig's shoulder while someone else pulled the broken arrow through his back. Jig felt nauseous as he realized that he had a hole passing all the way through his body. And how much blood did he have left? That warm puddle all over the floor, that was *him!* He needed that stuff to stay inside his skin, not be spreading across the marble and soaking into his loincloth.

"What happened?" He had to ask three times before someone understood his pain-slurred speech.

"Darnak clubbed Ryslind on the head," Riana said. "With all of those creatures falling, he got so angry that he stopped paying attention to the rest of us. He's tied and gagged, so we should be safe when he wakes up."

"Oh. That's good." Jig's head felt tingly. Was this what happened when you lost too much blood? Darnak was praying and working on the wound, but Jig still hurt. Maybe that was a good thing. Maybe he shouldn't worry until the shoulder *stopped* hurting.

"Have him drink this." Darnak handed a water-skin to Riana, who put it to Jig's lips. His mouth felt parched, and he sucked eagerly.

Only to spit and cough a moment later. That wasn't water; Darnak had passed over his wineskin. In other circumstances, Jig would have been stunned by the gesture.

"Here now, don't be wasting it. That's good stuff, and I can't get more until my cousin returns from down south." Darnak grabbed the skin and took a swig for himself. "Care to take another shot at it?"

This time, Jig forced himself to swallow, even though it made his throat burn and his eyes water even harder. He felt vapor rise into his sinuses, making his head light. The pain in his shoulder was still there, but somehow it didn't matter quite as much. He took another few swallows.

Darnak grinned. "Dwarven ale," he said, a note of pride in his voice. "Made in the finest underground breweries in the land."

"Tastes like klak beer," Jig said.

"Watch your tongue," Darnak snapped. "This is fine dwarven drink. No race in the world can match it, least of all goblins. You can't even make this stuff without knowing where to find the best Bluespotted Mushrooms, the oldest Nightblooms. . . ."

"And a lot of Ruffled Lichen root," Jig added. He considered the taste. "This needs to age more, though."

Darnak scowled at him and snatched his wineskin back. "You need to rest."

Jig smiled as the dwarf worked on his shoulder. This was more like it. Riana was watching him with, well not exactly respect, but at least without her usual loathing. Darnak was healing him, just like he had done for Barius. And for the first time in Jig's recollection, probably the first time since the world was born, a dwarf had shared a drink with a goblin.

Riana pressed something into Jig's mouth, and he chewed automatically. "Ptah," he muttered. He should have known it was too good to be true. First they treated him like a friend, then they tried to feed him *bread*.

"Eat it," Darnak said firmly. "You'll need your strength."

What else could he do? He didn't want to offend the one who was closing the hole in his shoulder. So he forced himself to chew and swallow. He took small bites. That way he didn't have to chew as much, and the dusty aftertaste didn't linger as long. He hoped Riana might take the hint, but she kept shoving bread at him until the whole thing was gone. She even seemed to enjoy his disgust there at the end.

"Where's Barius?" Jig asked.

"With his brother." Darnak shook his head. "They hate each other, but neither wants to see the other die. Not unless it's by their own hand, that is. Strange and tragic, but true."

The dwarf sat up. "Best I can do, but a mite better than I'd hoped. You'll have an ugly scar, and a matching one on back. Don't strain that left arm anytime soon, either. But you'll live." He laughed. "At least until the next time you go picking fights with two wizards in one day."

He helped Jig to sit up. Smudge had rejoined him at some point, and now scooted to his normal spot on Jig's shoulder. "Good spider," he muttered.

Jig tried to stand, but his head spun, and he decided maybe it would be better to stay on the floor and not move for a while. Yes, that would be for the best. He perked his ears—even his *ears* hurt— and listened as Darnak joined Barius.

"So how's his wizardness doing?"

"My brother will survive," Barius said angrily. "A fortunate thing for you, Darnak. Even striking a prince is an offense worthy of death. Had you killed him, you would have left me no choice but to execute you."

Darnak grunted. "Aye, and you'd have left me no choice but to box your ears. Would you rather I let him kill us all then?" He didn't give the prince time to answer. "Come on, we've got to be finding a way out of here. Maybe if we get him back home, your father's advisers will have some ideas for restoring his mind."

"What do you mean, leave? Our quest is unfinished, Darnak."

"Aye, and your brother the wizard has lost his mind, or were you forgetting that? He's beyond my power to help, Your Majesty. How were you planning to finish your quest without Ryslind?"

"It is *my* quest," Barius said coldly. "My brother has experienced these fits of weakness before. He shall recover in time."

"Fits of weakness, are they?" Darnak laughed. "This is the first time he's been shooting members of his own party. And he wasn't too weak to toss you about, was he?"

"That goblin is no member of my party."

Darnak's eyes widened. "Oh, is that so? Then I suppose he should have left the Necromancer alive for you to kill."

"Your tone borders dangerously close to treason, Darnak."

The dwarf snorted. He looked ready to speak, but paused when he saw the fury in Barius's bulging eyes and white lips. "Perhaps, Majesty," he said. "I'm only trying to do my job and keep you alive."

Barius smiled at this concession. "You are my tutor no longer. You were brought for your skill at arms, your experience in the bowels of the mountains, and your gift for cartography. If you find yourself unable to restrict yourself to these duties, you may wait here for my return." He turned his back on the dwarf and ran his hands over the arms of the throne.

"Where are you going?" Jig asked. "And what's a cartographer?" He couldn't figure out what carts had to do with anything. Unless they planned to build a cart to carry the treasure out with them. That made sense.

"I am departing this accursed place," Barius said. He tugged the top of the throne. Nothing happened, so he ripped out the cushions and began to poke and prod at the seat. "There may be a concealed passageway by the throne."

"And how would you know that?" Riana asked.

Barius gave her a tolerant smile. "Common sense. At any time a ruler could find himself in need of a quick escape route. That truth is even more common for black-hearted lords such as this Necromancer, whose enemies are many. What better place to make your escape than through the throne itself?"

Jig's brow wrinkled. "Is there a hidden door behind your father's throne?"

"Of course not," Barius said quickly. "My father is beloved by his subjects, and has no need to plan for escape."

Perhaps Barius is adopted. For if the father were anything at all like the son, Jig couldn't understand how he had survived long enough to walk upright, let alone to rule a country.

"Behold," Barius said. His chest swelled with triumph. "The throne itself moves. Darnak, help me to shift it back."

The dwarf lent his bulk to the task. Slowly the great throne scraped back a few inches, screeching like a tortured animal. Jig pinched his ears shut. Apparently Barius had been correct this time. Though if this was meant to be a quick escape route, why was it so hard to move the throne? Jig had a hard time imagining the diminutive Necromancer shoving the throne aside when Darnak and Barius together could barely move it.

The floor around the throne vanished. Darnak and Barius tried to cling to the now-floating throne, but couldn't find handholds. Jig had one glimpse of Riana's face before she fell. She had come over to watch the prince search, and thanks to her curiosity, she now tumbled after the others.

That made more sense, Jig decided as he crawled to the edge of the hole. So it had been a trap, not an escape route. Yes, that was more in keeping with the Necromancer's style.

Darnak had set the lantern on the floor next to the throne. When the floor vanished, the lantern had followed the others into the pit, leaving Jig blind. He moved slowly and tested every inch of the floor as he went. A muted chuckle drew Jig's attention away from the pit. Ryslind was awake and laughing, though the rag Darnak had tied into his mouth muffled the sound. The light from his eyes gave his face a demonic red tinge.

They're going to die down there.

Ryslind's voice spoke in his head. No, not Ryslind, but the second voice, the voice of whatever had taken control of the wizard.

Fools and children. Straum will slaughter you all like insects.

Jig walked over and kicked the wizard in the stomach. Why was everyone suddenly speaking in his mind? Bad enough when Shadowstar did it. Jig had nearly wet himself that time. Was he now to endure Ryslind's babble as well?

Not for much longer, little goblin.

Jig's eyes narrowed. Moving by the faint light from Ryslind's eyes, he grabbed the ropes around the wizard's ankles and dragged him over to the pit. His shoulder ached, but Darnak had done a good job, and his wound remained closed. Jig looked into Ryslind's glowing eyes, and for the first time, he didn't flinch away from that dark red light.

The only escape is to fall on that sword of yours.

Jig shoved him into the pit. Then he sat down with his legs dangling over the edge and tried to figure out what he should do.

"Which tile was it?" Jig slid his sword along the floor until it hit the slight dip that marked the edge of a tile. He tapped the next one with his sword. One of these had opened the walls. They had killed most of the creatures here the first time they triggered the trap, so if Jig set it off again, he should be safe. He hoped. Besides, the Necromancer's wand was destroyed. This was probably the safest place in the whole mountain.

What frightened Jig was knowing that it was also the emptiest place. Aside from the bats and whatever else inhabited that chasm, he and Smudge were the only living things down here. He could survive for a few days if he stayed, but he would eventually go mad from hunger and thirst.

So he had to get out of here. He couldn't go up, not unless he had a way to swim through the whirlpool and avoid the lizard-fish. Even if Tymalous Shadowstar decided to help him again, Jig doubted he could manage that much. Which left down. He would have to follow the others.

He had shouted into the black pit for a while, but nobody answered. The pit absorbed his voice, making him sound small and scared. Which he was, but he didn't like having the fact thrown in his face.

After putting his boots back on, he had felt around for his bracelet, but the metal had melted into the wand. There was no way for Jig to wear it anymore, even if it still had any power, which he doubted. He tucked the glob of metal into his belt as a souvenir, in case he ever got home. The other goblins would never believe it was the Necromancer's wand. But it would be a good keepsake nonetheless.

The other thing he wanted was light. A lantern, a torch, even a candle would be a godsend. Jig held his breath at that thought, thinking Shadowstar might take the hint, but no candle appeared in his hand. He sighed and kept walking. No light, no bracelet, and no food.

The thirteenth tile shifted beneath his sword. The faint whiff of preservative and dust drifting into the air told him the alcoves had opened again. Logically, Jig knew he was safe. Logic, however, had only a single small voice, and was easily overwhelmed by panic. Jig shouted and waved his sword around his head as he waited for the attack to come.

Nothing happened. Jig lowered his weapon slowly. His chest pounded, and his palms were so sweaty he doubted he could have used the sword, even if something had attacked.

He stepped into the alcove where he had hidden with Riana. The noose should be to his right. Jig hoped he would be able to use the rope to lower himself into the pit. He was about to scour the ground when the god spoke to him again.

The panel, dummy.

Jig jerked up indignantly. What did he . . . the panel . . . oh no. Jig leaped for the hallway, hoping he was fast enough. He had only been in the alcove for a second or two. Was it too late? Had the panel already reappeared, trapping him inside? If so, he prayed he would hit it hard enough for the impact to kill him.

He made it through. He felt like he had leaped through an icy waterfall, but he was out. His legs were shaking so badly he had to sit down. That was stupid. Stupid! He could have died. After surviving the Necromancer and everything else, he could have starved to death because of a dumb mistake. Nobody would have come around to let him out of the alcove this time.

Once his hands no longer shook, he opened the panel again. This would be tricky even were he able to see. Snagging the rope and pulling it out in the darkness was next to impossible.

But Jig was in no great hurry. For the first time in several days, he didn't need to worry about anyone sneaking up on him or stabbing him from behind.

He experimented for a while to find out exactly

how long he had before the panel closed. It would remain open for a little more than two breaths after he touched the floor or wall of the alcove. Plenty of time to reach in, holding his sword by the blade, and drag the crossguard across the floor toward him. All he had to do was catch the rope.

After cutting his hand twice, he stripped off his loincloth and wrapped it around the blade for protection. Everyone else was dead or gone, so he wasn't worried about modesty.

He pulled out at least half of the skeleton in assorted bits and pieces before he managed to snag the noose. Once he had rope in hand, he stood up and redid his loincloth. Feeling decently dressed once more, he hurried back to the Necromancer's throne room.

The rope measured seven feet once Jig untied the knot. It would have been longer, but he had sliced off the last few feet when he cut it from his neck. Jig sat down at the edge of the pit and began to work.

The rope consisted of three cords twisted together, and Jig guessed that any one of those cords would hold his weight. He wouldn't have wanted to haul Darnak around with one, but goblins were skinny and light. It took a while to get the cords unraveled. The rope acted almost alive, the way it twined about itself and tried to tangle into knots.

In the end, Jig held a thin rope about twenty feet long. He tugged on the two knots that bound the cords end to end. They didn't give. Satisfied, he tied a loop in one end and tried to toss it over the arm of the throne. Looping the arm of a floating throne in pitch blackness would have challenged even the most coordinated of heroes. Jig took close to an hour before the rope caught.

The plan would have worked, save for his cut

hand. As he lowered himself into the pit, his hand flared with pain. His arms were already tired from throwing the rope so many times. With blood on one hand and sweat slicking the other, his hands slipped free, and Jig followed his companions into the darkness.

He landed on his backside on something springy and damp. The sudden light blinded him. After so long in silence, the noise greeted Jig like a long-lost friend. He heard a breeze blowing. A rustling sound surrounded him, and in the distance, he heard the whistling of birds. Birds, in Straum's lair? He shrugged. Sparrows and other birds flew into the tunnels from time to time. They made great snacks. Perhaps there was a crack leading to the surface, small enough for birds to fly in and out.

"Jig? Is that you? We were wondering if you'd be joining us."

"Darnak?" Jig turned toward the sound. Everything was still too bright, but he could make out the dwarf's stocky form a few feet away. "It was either follow you down or stay there and starve."

"Good choice." Darnak's hand clapped Jig on the shoulder. "Since you're here, mayhaps you can help us with a bit of a dilemma. See, this isn't exactly what we were expecting to find down here."

They waited for Jig's eyes to adjust. When they had, he looked around in amazement. He sat in a field of soft green grass. Trees ringed the field at a distance of roughly a hundred yards. Sunlight warmed his skin, and he could smell the soft sweetness of pollen in the breeze. He scraped at the damp ground, digging up a clump of grass to find, not cold stone, but moist, black soil.

"I'm outside," he whispered, not knowing whether to rejoice or cower at the news. He raised a hand and saw his shadow on the ground. It didn't waver, as it would have done in torchlight. Clear and sharp, his shadow-hand followed his real one perfectly. Slowly Jig looked up at the sky.

"Wow."

He even stopped breathing as he stared. He saw no sign of the rope he had used to climb down. Nothing but blue sky, and clouds like white clumps of fur drifting past. He reached out, but the clouds were too far away to touch. How high were they? They looked to be at least thirty or forty feet up, higher than anything Jig had ever seen.

And the sun! An orange circle that shone with warm, perfect light, like a thousand thousand torches all burning together. He squinted, trying to see if it burned like a normal fire.

"It's not real," Darnak said. "If 'twere, you'd be blind right about now."

Jig ignored him. Real or not, this was the most incredible thing he had ever seen. He didn't know how they had come here or even where "here" was, but none of that mattered. After spending his whole life underground, knowing nothing but the lair and a few dark tunnels, Jig had discovered a completely new world. Still gaping, he managed to tear his eyes away from the sun long enough to say, "It's so *big*."

CHAPTER 12

❦

Big Prints, Mad Prince

"I take it then," Darnak said dryly, "that you wouldn't be knowing how to find the dragon."

Jig shook his head. From time to time, he had fantasized about sneaking down and making off with some piece of Straum's treasure. Every goblin dreamed about it. A few of the older ones told stories about their search for the dragon's lair. Some even claimed to have made it past the Necromancer.

Nobody had ever described anything like this place. Jig had known they were lying, of course. Oh, he believed goblins tried to explore the deeper levels. What he didn't believe was that any of them survived to come back and tell stories about the experience.

Staring again at the world around him, he wondered if he would get the chance to share what he had seen. The grass tickled the backs of his knees when he moved, and he laughed with delight. He lay back and stared into the sky. So open and endless . . . after a lifetime of living beneath solid rock, he felt as though he could fall into that blue sea and float forever. A wave of vertigo made him gulp, and he gripped the grass with both hands.

"It's an illusion," Riana told him. She ripped out a clump of grass and sniffed the roots. "No smell. The sun's too orange, and I can only see one kind of tree."

"How many kinds are there?" Jig asked.

Riana laughed. For a second the anger vanished and she looked like a child. "Hundreds. Thousands. Oaks as proud as the gods, willows that sway and dance in the wind. There are trees with leaves as pointed as rapiers, and trees that need rain but once every six months to survive. I've even seen trees only a foot tall that mimic their larger cousins in every way." She laughed again at Jig's delighted expression.

"Elves and trees," Darnak grumbled. "Something unnatural about their love for plants. Besides, I thought you were a city type. Where'd you learn about trees?"

Riana's face hardened. "I spent a month hiding out in an arboretum, behind the Monastery of Batoth."

Darnak held up a hand. "Don't tell me the details. I'm still the prince's man, and I'd not like to be arresting you the second we leave this mountain." Turning to Jig, he asked, "How is it that you've never seen the outdoors?"

"I just haven't," Jig said. Goblins didn't go outside. They rarely ventured past the shiny room where he had first encountered the adventurers.

There was no reason for them to stay inside. No monster guarded the entrance, as far as he knew. The gate locked itself when closed, but it could be opened easily from within. Goblins simply felt no need to explore the surface. Everything they needed, the mountain provided.

Besides, goblins weren't welcome outside. Throughout history, every surface-dweller who came through that gate saw goblins as vermin to be wiped out. Bad enough that the occasional party came through on a killing rampage every few months. The outside world must be even worse, with thousands of people who would put an arrow into Jig as soon as they saw him. His ears would end up on a trophy necklace before he made it ten feet past the gate.

Still, it might be worth sneaking out some night if I could see all of this. That led to another thought. *I wonder if we'll see* stars *while we're down here.*

From a little way off, Barius stood and shouted, "Darnak, come and see this."

Darnak and the others hurried over to join the prince. On the way, Jig noticed the tied and bruised body of the wizard stretched out in the grass. Ryslind glared at him as he passed, and Jig glanced away quickly. He hoped they wouldn't untie Ryslind anytime soon. A hundred years should be long enough.

Barius stood over the huge body of an ogre. Jig yelped and grabbed for his sword when he saw it. But the ogre wasn't moving. To judge by the deep slashes across its chest and throat, it would never move again.

He noticed that Darnak's hand had also gone to his weapon, which made him feel a little better.

"You did this, lad?" Darnak sounded impressed.

"Not I." Barius knelt and pointed to the cuts on the chest. "Three deep cuts, all in a row. A fourth scraped the skin here."

"Claws. Aye, I see it." Darnak chewed at his thumb. "But what beast could best an ogre?"

A good question, Jig thought as he stared at the body. He had never seen an ogre, and now he prayed he would never see a living example. It must have stood over eight feet high, with muscular arms as long as Jig was tall. Its callused green skin looked tough enough to serve as light armor. Ragged black hair topped a long, oval head. The teeth, while shorter than goblin teeth, still looked sharp enough to do serious damage. The huge mouth meant the ogre had a lot more of them, too.

Something shiny caught Jig's eye. A battle-axe, six feet long and double-headed, lay discarded in the grass to one side. Jig bent down and grabbed the handle to take it back to the others.

The axe didn't budge. Off-balance, Jig stumbled to the ground. *Maybe they should come here instead.* "I found something."

Darnak whistled when he saw the axe. The dwarf could lift it, but he needed both hands to raise it in the air, and Jig doubted even Darnak could swing such an axe in a fight.

"You think he was waiting for whoever fell through?" Darnak asked.

"If so, then whatever slew the beast has my gratitude," Barius said.

"Aye. So long as it's not coming back for dessert, that is."

The dwarf's wary tone made Jig see the distant trees in a different light. What creatures might be hiding in those shadows? This place was so open, with too many places for an enemy to hide. He knew nothing of surface monsters, but anything that could destroy an ogre was, in Jig's opinion, a good argument for staying in the tunnels.

"Strange, though." Barius peered more closely at the wounds. "Whatever killed the ogre wasn't interested in food. A kill such as this would feed an animal for days. Why then did it not at least drag the ogre off for safekeeping? Unless it was a territorial dispute, perhaps."

He pointed to a patch of grass behind Riana. "The tracks lead back to the center of the field."

Jig stared at the grass. It looked green, the same as everything else down here. Had madness now touched Barius, that he could communicate with plants?

"Spread out," Barius ordered. "Search for anything unusual."

As they retraced their path, Jig's sharp ears caught Darnak's grumbling comment. "A hundred feet underground, in a fake field beneath a fake sky, with an ogre slaughtered like no more than a rat to a cat, and he sends us to search for the unusual."

They found two more ogres. Together with the first corpse, the bodies formed a rough triangle around the spot where the adventurers had appeared.

"Ambush?" Darnak asked.

"Most likely. By the time we recovered from the fall and drew our weapons, they would have been upon us." Barius chewed his lip, one of the only times Jig had seen the prince show anxiety.

"Even if you and I could stand against such beasts, they still outnumbered us." He clearly didn't consider Riana or Jig worth counting.

The pit was a trap. Anyone who beat the Necromancer was supposed to die here. Sizing up the two-handed sword one ogre had dropped, Jig tried not to think about how long he would last in a fight against ogres, let alone whatever beast had killed them. Perhaps the party had arrived in the middle of a power struggle. Hobgoblins and goblins occasionally slaughtered each other when food ran short, when one group was caught stealing from the other, or when the younger warriors simply grew bored with bullying their own. Jig prayed that the creatures here would finish each other off before he had the poor luck to meet one.

Barius touched the wounds on the third ogre. "Whatever did this, it killed this one last." He crawled around the grass for a few minutes. "It left for the woods, in this direction. We should follow."

"What?" It came out more as a squeak, but Jig didn't care. He must have misheard.

But Barius only nodded, a determined glint in his eyes. "This way we are the hunters instead of the prey. Better this than to sit and wait for it to creep up on us in the night, wouldn't you say?"

"Maybe it only kills ogres?" Jig suggested weakly.

"It pains me to be saying it," Darnak said, "but his highness could be right. Until we know the dangers of this place, we'll be as children walking blindly into the bear's cave."

If we find those dangers, won't we be walking blindly into the bear's jaws? Jig didn't say anything aloud, however. He knew Barius and the others too well to expect them to change their minds.

"Know thy enemy, eh Darnak?" Barius said cheerfully.

He was enjoying this. Jig's mouth hung open in disbelief. He *wanted* to go chasing after this creature. "What about the rod?"

That made Barius pause, but only for a heartbeat. "We can't pursue the rod with this monster at our heels. Nor do we know in which direction the rod may lie. We could be here for days, so it behooves us to learn as much as we can about this land."

Jig pointed at Ryslind. "And him?" he started to ask. The words died when he saw the wizard's face. Though the gag hid his mouth, the corners of his eyes had wrinkled with amusement as he watched Barius's preparations.

"You know what it is, don't you?" Jig asked softly.

Ryslind heard. The wrinkles deepened. Red eyes beckoned Jig closer.

He crossed the clearing, one hand on his sword. With his other hand, he reached for the gag. He hesitated, hand outstretched. Was this another trick?

Of course it was a trick. Ryslind was a surface-dweller, and a wizard to boot. Smudge remained cool on his shoulder, which should mean it was safe to remove the gag. Still he hesitated.

"I'll kill you if you try any magic," he warned.

Ryslind dipped his head in amused acknowledgment.

"As will I," Darnak said from behind Jig. "I was coming to get him," he explained. "Heard you talking. So go ahead, remove the gag. He knows we'll brain him if it comes to that."

Feeling more confident with the dwarf beside him, Jig tugged the rope down around Ryslind's chin and pulled a balled rag out of his mouth. The wizard opened his mouth and inhaled deeply.

"Water," he said hoarsely. Darnak held a waterskin to his lips, and Ryslind took several deep swallows. When he spoke again, his voice was smoother. "You will die for what you did, goblin." He sounded cheerful about the prospect.

"Enough of that," Darnak said. "You were telling us about the thing that did this. Or was that all a ploy to get free of the gag?"

"No ploy." Ryslind smiled. "And there is no need to hunt for him. He will find you soon enough."

"He?" Jig asked.

Ryslind nodded. "He is one of Straum's . . . servants."

"How would you know this, brother?" Barius had returned. Arms crossed, he glared down at the wizard. "What reason do we have for trusting your word?"

Ryslind chuckled. "Believe me or not, it makes no difference."

The pit in Jig's stomach grew deeper. For despite everything Ryslind had done, Jig believed him.

They untied Ryslind's legs so he could walk with the party. At first, Barius had argued, preferring to build a travois to drag the wizard along.

"And how am I to fight if I'm lugging your brother behind me?" Darnak snapped. "I'm doubting the enemy will want to wait while I unstrap a blasted travois."

For once Jig agreed with the prince. Tie Ryslind up and leave him that way. They all knew the wizard was mad. What was to stop him from killing them all? He had promised to use no magic, but who could trust the mind behind those eyes? As soon as their guard dropped, he would attack. Starting, Jig guessed, with the goblin who had insulted him back in the Necromancer's throne room.

But as they reached the woods, it looked like Ryslind would keep his promise. He had not spoken a word, and his hands remained bound behind his back. Darnak walked at the end of their line, so he would see if Ryslind tried anything. So far, Ryslind had been content to follow along.

He still made Jig nervous. Especially the way he smiled at them. Like this was all a game, and only Ryslind knew the rules.

"The trail goes deeper into the woods," Barius said. He squatted by a patch of bare dirt. "See here, the creature has left a partial print."

Jig stared at the brown, scuffed dirt. He saw nothing, and wondered if Barius was hallucinating. To make his frustration worse, he had already become disoriented. He thought he could find his way back to the clearing if he had to, but he wasn't certain. Being lost made him feel uncomfortably dependent on the others.

"Clawed, as we guessed," Barius muttered. He stretched a hand out over the dirt. "Toes spread for balance. The print is deep, so I would guess we face a beast nearly as massive as the ogres. A lion, perhaps. But longer of toe."

He eventually tired of studying dirt and said, "Come, let us continue."

Jig waited for the others to pass by. He took an extra step back to let Ryslind go by, but the wizard only smiled at him. Falling into step beside Darnak, Jig whispered, "Are both of them mad? They prod one another like children. And the only reason we're chasing this beast is because Barius refuses to back down in front of his brother. What's wrong with them?"

Darnak sighed. "Earthmaker only knows what has happened to Ryslind. As for Barius, I'm afraid he sees the competition as being more important than the rest, even more important than his own life."

He shook his head. He had resumed his duty as mapmaker, and he sketched small, bushy trees as they walked. A jagged line marked their progress into the woods. At the center of the map, Jig saw three bodies labeled BIG, DEAD OGRES.

"Barius has competed all his life, and he's always lost. He's the seventh son of King Wendel. That means he's got no more chance to sit on that throne than you or I do, and he knows it. Even with three of his brothers dead on their manhood quests, he's no more than an extra mouth to feed around the palace. A noble mouth, mind you, but still a burden. Sooner or later they'll marry him off, give him a nice little plot of land somewhere out of the way, and forget he ever existed."

"He grew up with his parents?" Jig asked dubiously.

Darnak stopped to blot a smudge of ink on his map. "Aye. What of it?"

He had known that the surface races often built separate homes for every mated pair and their offspring, but it still seemed like a waste of space. Then again, if these woods were any indication of the size of the surface, maybe they could afford the waste. And only seven brothers? Jig had grown up with dozens of cousins, all raised by the entire lair. Jig didn't even know who his parents were. Nor did he care. That sort of thing simply didn't matter.

"Isn't that inefficient?" Jig asked. "To rely so much on the parents, I mean."

"For a dwarven family, 'twould make no difference. For us, family is everything. Parents, cousins, grandparents, brothers and sisters, all of 'em squeeze together in one home and look after one another. But for Prince Barius, his parents were always busy ruling Adenkar. He grew up surrounded by servants and tutors, none of whom saw him as anything but one more spoiled Wendelson to care for.

"He's quite a lonely boy, really. Most of the sons are. They began very early to compete for their parents' attention. Who would be the best fencer, the swiftest rider, the most accurate shot with a bow? Barius fought in tournaments from the time he was thirteen. Never won, mind you, and once he wrecked his knee so badly it took me a week to straighten everything back out.

"He learned the lute, studied every book he could get a hold of, and once stayed out three nights in a row to catch a wolf that had been stalking the stables. It was never enough."

Sighing, Darnak glanced up to make sure the brothers were too far away to hear. "There was always something more pressing, some treaty to negotiate or some ambassador to dine with. Even when Barius accomplished some grand feat, his older brothers were there to overshadow him. He hunted that wolf right after his oldest brother returned from slaying a rogue griffon to the south. I was proud of them both, but especially Barius. He stayed out in the rain and the cold, and killed that wolf with no more than a child's training bow, whereas his brother had gone out with a full regiment of guards and slept in a sturdy tent. But how could Barius compete with his brother's griffon?

"The quake that finally collapsed his tunnel was Ryslind. Ryslind set out one day and didn't come back for two months. All of Adenkar searched for the lost prince, but he had vanished like shadows at midday. Rumors spread and multiplied faster than fleas on a beggar. 'Ryslind had been abducted by elves, he had drowned in the Serpent River, he had run off to be with his spirit lover.' Everyone had a different tale.

"Barius didn't know what to believe, but he saw his chance for glory. He had always been a skilled

hunter and tracker, and he declared that he would
bring his brother back. Interrupted court to make
his pronouncement, and made sure everyone heard.
He spent a week in preparation, gathering horses
and supplies and men and maps, everything he
thought he would need.

"And then Ryslind returned. Walked into the
throne room just as calm and confident as ever. He
had completed his quest, he told us. To demon-
strate, he sent tiny bolts of blue lightning racing
across the ceiling. Levitated his eldest brother into
the air and left him there, shrieking like a banshee.
Before, he struggled even to learn simple tricks and
sleight of hand. But somehow, in those two months,
he had become a master of his art.

"Barius was devastated. His brother, two years
his junior, had outshone him. His heroic preparations made him look even more the fool."

Darnak took a drink of ale to soothe his throat.
"A year ago, that was. Then some idiot gave him
the idea to go after the Rod of Creation. Wish I
could get my hands on the fellow who suggested
it. Everyone thought it suicide, but for Barius, it
was the only thing that could surpass his brothers."

By this point Jig was listening with only one ear.
Darnak's story simply confirmed his belief that the
prince was mad. Given a place to live, food to eat,
even people to wait on him and make sure his
every wish was taken care of, Barius wanted more.
He had to "prove himself."

What was the point? Admittedly, Jig wasn't sure
he completely understood human motivation, even
after Darnak's explanation. But this whole quest
sounded like nothing more than a search for the
most spectacular death. What good was attention
and recognition if you had to be ripped apart by
an ogre-killing monster to get it? All this for a

magical rod that, as far as Jig knew, Barius didn't even want. He only wanted to be the one who found it. Or at least the one who died trying.

There was a reason "glory" rhymed with "gory," Jig thought. He grinned at his cleverness. Maybe he could make up a song about the prince. He worked out the first stanza as he walked.

> Barius the human prince came down in search of glory.
> Ran into a goblin horde and slew them all but one.
> Dragged poor Jig along to face an end most gory,
> All so Barius could prove himself the bravest son.

He glanced up to make sure nobody had heard his mumbling. He would have to finish his song later. Assuming they lived long enough.

His attention turned to the forest. Riana had complained that the trees weren't real, but Jig didn't care. He had never seen anything like them. Brown trunks, thick as his waist, rose a hundred feet into the air. The roots snaked through the dirt, tripping Jig time and again as his eyes wandered skyward.

This must be why surface-dwellers invented boots, he decided as he picked himself up for the fourth time. Even through the oversize boots, his toes throbbed from their encounters with the roots. Were he barefoot, he would no doubt be unable to walk by now.

Gradually Jig learned that this mock forest was less idyllic than he had assumed. For one thing, he had to walk differently. The ground sank beneath his feet, and he found himself stepping ridiculously high to try to avoid those blasted tree roots. Worse, the ground itself was soft and uneven! Soon the backs of Jig's legs burned from climbing small hills where the dirt constantly shifted.

He needed to rest. Sweat stung his eyes, and every step became a quest in itself. He could feel the blisters, each one the size of a small mountain. On his ankles, heels, toes . . . by now, his feet had a landscape to rival the woods around them. He also found that the boots that protected his toes had grown heavy as stones, and only the knowledge that he would be worse off barefoot kept him from flinging them into the woods.

Despite it all, he kept his mouth shut. If he complained, Barius would only hear it as a sign of weakness. He'd probably even increase their pace. Besides, nobody else was having any trouble. Even Riana, skinny as a snake, matched Barius's march without trouble.

Finally, as the sunlight faded to orange, then red, Barius called a halt. He pointed to a large pair of trees.

"We make camp here. Riana, you and the goblin will gather wood for a fire while Darnak and I discuss a plan for dispatching the dragon Straum."

He made Straum sound like nothing more than a nuisance. A carrion-worm to be chased out of the kitchens, rather than a creature of legend that could kill with a single breath.

Jig kept an ear cocked back as they searched for firewood. He couldn't hear well enough to make out what was being said, but he wanted to make sure he didn't get turned about and lose his way. As long as he could hear their voices, he could get back to the others. How did people get around without walls to guide them? Why, he could go in any direction he chose, turn left or right at random.

The trees looked alike, the ground was the same everywhere, and were it not for the low voices behind him, Jig would have been lost already.

This must be why Darnak spends so much time on his map. If the others were as disoriented underground as Jig was here, no wonder they needed to note the way out.

He glanced into the sky and received another shock. *The sun had moved!* Before, it had been directly overhead, but in the past few hours it had traveled to the very edge of the sky. How could they find their way when even the sky shifted position?

Riana had stopped to watch a bird circle overhead. When she didn't move, Jig looked up as well. Following the wide flight made him dizzy, and he wondered if real birds ever felt nauseous. Did Jig and the others seem as small from up there as the bird did to him? Did the bird feel free, able to go anywhere it chose?

"I wonder what it's like."

He didn't realize he had spoken out loud until Riana spat. "I'm sure it's great. You can fly anywhere, right up until some hunter turns his trained falcon loose to break your back and bring you down."

She stomped off, Jig following close behind to make sure he didn't lose sight of her. So much for birds. When she began to gather wood, he picked a tree at random, drew his sword, and chopped at one of the lower branches. The impact jolted his fingers and forearm. Trees were tougher than he thought. He drew back for another swing.

"What are you doing?"

"Getting wood." He saw her expression and hesitated.

Riana shook her head with exasperation. "A fat

lot of good that will do. You don't use green wood for a fire unless you want to make a smoke-tail."

"A what?"

"A smoke-tail. A signal humans use to let one another know where they're at." Her lips tightened. "I don't think we want to announce ourselves to the dragon quite yet, do you?"

Jig stared at the tree. The leaves were green, but the wood itself was brown and rough. Wood was wood. Jig had never seen green wood, and he had no idea why the sticks Riana was picking off the ground were any better than this branch. Except, maybe, that he didn't know how many trees he could attack before his hand grew numb.

Seeing his indecision, Riana sighed and dropped her small pile of sticks. "Put that away," she said impatiently. When Jig's sword was safely back in its sheath, she pointed to the branch he had cut. "See the sap?"

Jig squinted. By putting his face three inches from the branch, he could make out a few drops of clear liquid oozing out of the cut.

"That's because the branch is still alive. It's wet inside, so it won't burn. Gather the branches that have died and fallen off. The dryer the better." She picked up one branch and broke it in half. "See? No sap. I'm amazed you goblins haven't suffocated yourselves if you don't know enough to use dry wood."

"There aren't many trees in the upper tunnels," Jig snapped. How was he supposed to know that brown wood wasn't always brown, and that clear tree blood turned wood green? He gave the tree a disgusted look and began to grab sticks from the ground.

"What do you burn for fuel?" Riana asked.

"Elves." He didn't want to admit that, for the

most part, goblins couldn't scrounge enough fuel for fires. As for the muck, that was barely enough to keep the lair lit, let alone warm. It was all they could do to fuel a real cookfire, and even that required them to trade with the hobgoblins. Unlike goblins, hobgoblins would venture onto the surface. They took the weapons and coins the goblins had scavenged in exchange for a few bundles of wood. Just one more way to keep the goblins weak and the hobgoblins strong. Jig wondered why he had never seen it before. By taking most of the weapons, the hobgoblins kept the goblins from becoming a real threat.

A rustling from ahead made Jig start. He dropped his sticks and grabbed his sword. "Did you hear that?"

Riana shook her head. She did draw her dagger, though, and Jig saw fear in her eyes as she scanned the woods.

"We could get killed out here," Jig whispered. Why had Barius sent the two weakest people off on their own? He remembered the dead ogres. Was this another ogre, one who had avoided the creature that killed its fellows? Jig shivered. Or perhaps this was the creature itself. Having slain the ogres, was it hunting new prey?

The woods had grown quiet. The ever-present song of distant birds died out, and the occasional rustle of leaves sounded far too loud to Jig's ears.

"Barius probably *wants* us to get killed," Riana said, voice soft. "If we die, that's two problems he doesn't have to deal with anymore." Another noise, this time a grating sound, came from the right. Like someone rubbing two sticks together, only much louder. "It sounds big."

Jig felt naked and exposed with no walls around

him. He backed toward a large tree. The tree was a poor substitute for hard stone, but at least it would guard his back. On his last step, his heel caught on a root. His head smacked the trunk, and his sword flipped end over end and stabbed into the ground.

The noise stopped for a second. Jig held his breath, hoping the thing hadn't heard. Riana didn't speak, but her eyes shot profanity that would have done a patrol captain proud.

The beast charged. Clomping footsteps tore through the dirt and the undergrowth toward them. Jig scrambled for his sword. Before he could find it, the thing leaped over a fallen tree, straight at Riana.

It was enormous. Sharp branched horns topped its narrow head. Rocklike hooves kicked the air with every bound.

"Dragon!" Jig yelled. He curled into a ball and covered his head.

Riana ducked, and the thing sprang right over her and disappeared. Jig tried to listen, to make sure it was really gone, but the pounding of his heart made it impossible to hear anything else.

"Are you okay?" he asked. She wasn't bleeding. Though she trembled with fear, she hadn't been wounded.

Jig looked closer. That wasn't fear after all.

The elf was *laughing* at him. Jig's face grew hot. It wasn't like he had intentionally fallen. "We should get back, in case there are more of those things."

"Jig, it was a deer," she gasped. "Not a dragon. And I hope there *are* more. I haven't eaten venison in years."

Jig blushed harder. He knew it wasn't a dragon.

Dragons had scales, not fur, and he had never heard of a brown dragon. "I didn't see it that well," he said sheepishly. "I panicked."

Riana's eyes widened, and she laughed even harder. "Jig, don't worry. Deer are the biggest cowards out there, and they only eat *plants*. Not goblins."

She stood up and brushed dirt from her clothes. "Come on. He was probably rubbing the velvet off his antlers. I'll show you."

Jig gathered up his wood and followed. He ignored her giggles, as well as her warnings about flying squirrels and other terrible surface monsters. Sure enough, they found a tree whose bark showed long gouges. Other places had been polished smooth by the deer's antlers.

She smirked. "Alchemists sometimes collect deer velvet. They use it for an aphrodisiac."

He didn't bother to ask what an aphrodisiac was. "Riana, are deer stupid?"

"I don't think so," she said. "But I've never lived in the woods. Why?"

Jig frowned as he stared at the tree. "The deer couldn't have heard us at first. Otherwise, if they're as timid as you say, it would have fled. But when I fell, he came *toward* us. Which means something else must have scared it even more."

Riana's face went still. "You're right."

From behind them, a dry voice said, "Indeed you are."

CHAPTER 13

❧◆❧

Pointing Fingers

Jig couldn't flee. He wanted to, but several things kept him rooted in place. He could no longer hear the others back at camp, and since he had completely lost his bearings during the confusion with the deer, any attempt to run would probably lead him deeper into the woods. Also, he knew that voice.

Recognition strengthened his desire to escape, while at the same time making him realize that trying to do so would be pointless. No matter how quickly he moved, Ryslind's magic could strike him down. To run would only provide an easier shot at Jig's unguarded back.

"Ryslind?" he said, searching for the wizard's hiding spot.

"Did I startle you, little ones?" Ryslind asked as he stepped out from behind a large tree.

His bonds were gone, as was his bow. To anyone who hadn't seen the charred corpses left by Ryslind's magic, he looked like a harmless man with odd taste in tattoos. Jig didn't move. He still remembered Ryslind's threats, and whereas Barius's temper always warned Jig when to expect an attack, Ryslind would boil you in your skin without ever losing that thin smirk. Now was a time to remain very polite and nonthreatening.

"How did you escape?" Riana asked.

Ryslind smiled. "My brother ordered my hands and feet tied again after you left. I lay there in silence until their attention wandered." He folded his arms behind his back and began to pace. "Barius and Darnak are naïve. They know nothing of true magic or those who use it, so they believed I was helpless."

Ryslind reached into his robes and flourished a short knife. "All that work to prevent me from spellcasting, and they never searched for weapons."

The single-edged blade curved forward like a sickle, and the handle was black bone. Too short for combat, Jig decided. For humans, at least. It was still a far cry better than the kitchen knife Jig had carried at the beginning of this escapade.

Whatever Ryslind used it for, aside from cutting ropes, Jig didn't want to know. There was a sinister aura about it that made him hope Ryslind wouldn't need goblin parts for any of his spells.

"You killed them?" Riana's gaze didn't leave the knife.

"No," Ryslind said. Regretfully? Jig couldn't tell. "I considered it. But he is still my brother." The knife vanished into the shadows of his robe. "I put them both to sleep. They will rest safely until the spell wears off, sometime tomorrow afternoon, or until someone disturbs the glyphs."

"Safe?" Riana repeated. "What if another ogre comes?"

Ryslind smiled. His eyes searched the trees. "I imagine even the thick-skulled ogres have learned to leave us alone. If not, the lesson will be repeated."

Repeated by whom? Jig shivered, remembering the clawed corpses of the ogres back at the clearing. Did something watch over them even as they spoke? "You know what killed the other ogres."

"I know much more than you or my brother ever realized, little goblin."

Jig realized then why Ryslind hadn't killed him yet. It had nothing to do with Barius being his brother, or with any sort of loyalty. No, Ryslind— or whatever had taken control of Ryslind's mind— wanted an audience. He was like Porak, though stronger than the goblin captain had ever been. Both of them thrived on showing off their power and making others afraid.

Both of which, Jig admitted to himself, *he had accomplished quite nicely.* Ryslind was far better at it than Porak was. Especially the fear part. Ryslind sane was enough to twist Jig's stomach. Ryslind with this second, strange voice, and the glow of his eyes brighter than ever . . . if Jig had been a fire-spider, the entire forest would be aflame by now. Fortunately, Smudge had restrained himself to singeing his leather pad.

"You're going after the rod, aren't you?" Riana crossed her arms and cocked her head.

Ryslind nodded. "Barius would take the rod back to our father. Oh, he would receive everything he had ever hoped for. There would be a celebration, with dancing and musicians and all the glory Barius wanted. Until the next morning, when the people's attention turned elsewhere and left him more bitter and empty than before. In the meantime, the rod would be tucked into some vault and left to gather dust, locked away as if it were naught but a mere trinket.

"My brother is like a crow who steals a gold necklace for its pretty sparkle, with no understanding of its real value. Much as I hate to snatch the necklace from my brother's beak, I think I can find a better use for its power."

He pointed a finger at one of the trees. The tattoos on his hand pulsed once, and a thick branch began to twist like a serpent. Small twigs fell from the main branch, and the bark peeled away like dead skin. With a loud crack, the smooth branch tumbled free and flew to Ryslind's hand.

He brushed a few last flakes of bark off of the pale staff. "If you are wise, you will leave."

"How?" Riana demanded. She jerked her head toward the sky. "Are we supposed to fly out of here?"

Ryslind scowled. He grabbed one of the smaller sticks. "Watch." He threw the stick into the air. It whirled end over end for twenty feet, then shot back to earth. Jig heard nothing, but it appeared as though the stick had collided with something solid. It landed somewhere to their left.

Jig stared.

Seeing that they didn't understand, Ryslind sighed and picked up another stick. He repeated his demonstration. "What you see is the stick hitting the roof of the cavern."

"What cavern?" Jig asked.

"And *you* killed the Necromancer," Ryslind said in wonder. "Did you really believe an entire sky existed beneath the mountain? That those clouds are real? You fell less than thirty feet, yet you accept the existence of those birds soaring hundreds of feet in the air. It's illusion, all of it. A powerful illusion, but no more. Which means the pit we came through is still there, if you have the wit to find it again. If not. . . ." He stabbed the end of his staff into the dirt.

Before Jig could work up the courage to ask more questions, Ryslind walked off into the woods. Jig rubbed his eyes and wished for a set of those elven lenses Riana had mentioned. For it looked like Ryslind's feet passed *through* the roots that had snagged Jig's boots time after time. He wondered if Shadowstar could provide the same magic for Jig.

"We should stop him," Riana said. She had her dagger out, and she glared in the direction Ryslind had gone.

"Why?" Personally, Jig thought that going back home was a lovely idea. He thought about Golaka's famous peppered dwarf roast, finding a corner to himself where he could feed Smudge and where the only bullies were goblins, not wizards and princes and dwarves . . . he could almost smell the smoke of the cookfire. "I say we go find the way out."

Riana rolled her eyes. "So we make our way to the Necromancer's little throne room. What then?"

Jig started to answer, then his mouth clapped shut. Ryslind was the only one who could get them past the lizard-fish . . . which Ryslind knew perfectly well. "Okay, so he's still playing with us," Jig said slowly. "What's your plan for stopping him?"

Now it was Riana's turn to hesitate. "We could sneak up on him," she said. "Like Darnak told us, against a wizard, we just have to be fast enough to kill him before he can cast a spell."

"But this is Ryslind."

"Why are you so frightened of him? Everyone dies sooner or later. If you stab him in the heart, he'll die like everything else."

"Not everyone dies," Jig muttered. "Some of them turn into walking corpses."

"Jig, stop being such a coward. You killed the Necromancer, right?"

"I was lucky."

She grabbed his shoulders and pushed him against a tree. "Lucky or not, you did it. There's two of us. If we don't kill him, who knows what he'll do. He's only human, right?"

"No," Jig said. He wiggled free and sat down. "Haven't you listened to his voice? Whatever he is, he's not like any human I've heard."

He told her how the second voice had taken control back in the Necromancer's chamber. "Even Barius was afraid of him."

Riana's jaw tightened. She took a few steps after Ryslind, then stopped. Slamming her knife into a tree trunk, she swore angrily. "I hate bullies. He and his brother both. They expect you to do everything they want, and if you don't, they threaten you."

Jig shrugged. That was the way it had been with every goblin captain he had ever known. What did she expect? Ryslind was too powerful. For all they knew, he could have turned himself invisible and waited to see if they chased after him.

"Besides, if we kill him, how are we supposed to get through the lake?" He didn't give her time to answer. "We should go back."

He listened to make sure Riana was coming. After a few paces, he heard her follow, kicking sticks and rocks with every third step.

Good. Now if they could find their way back, everything would be just great. He looked around nervously. The sunlight was mostly gone, and the stars had begun to appear in the sky. Jig had never seen stars, but he found them a disappointment.

The songs described them as pretty, but all he saw were weak dots of white light. They provided little light, and in the darkness, the roots had begun to attack his feet with abandon. Stars might be fine for surface-dwellers, he decided, but he'd trade them all to have the sun back.

Riana wasn't having as much trouble. She eventually passed Jig, which was fine with him. If she could find the way back to their camp, he would happily let her lead the way.

"They're going to kill you, you know," she said casually.

Jig stopped. "Who are?" He grabbed his sword and looked around.

"Barius and Darnak. They'll kill you as soon as they don't need you anymore. If I'm lucky, they'll toss me in prison."

When he didn't answer, she said, "What did you expect? You're a goblin. I'm a thief. They're not going to let us go once they find the rod and escape."

He tried to think of a good argument. What reason did they have to kill him? He had helped them through the tunnels above. He had killed the Necromancer. But he suspected Riana was right. After all what reason did they have *not* to kill him?

"Darnak wouldn't," he said weakly. The dwarf wouldn't have bothered to heal Jig only to kill him later. Not that Darnak's help meant much. Barius was the leader, and he would be only too happy to put an end to Jig. Especially after that Rakachak incident.

"Everywhere I go, I meet men like him," Riana muttered. "Follow them into Straum's lair or let them toss me into the dungeons. They offer you a choice between hells and expect you to thank them for it."

"They were going to kill you," Jig blurted out. As long as they were discussing impending death, he thought she should know the truth.

"What?"

"Before, when you set off the Necromancer's trap. They were going to kill you to keep you from turning into one of those dead things."

She didn't say anything, but Jig could see her playing with her knife. The starlight glittered on the twirling blade. "He would have, too," she whispered. "Bastard."

Jig nodded agreement.

"We should let them sleep and hope the ogres *do* find them. Or kill them ourselves. They deserve it."

He wasn't about to argue that point. But as Riana pointed out, they couldn't escape either. Killing the others would only leave them that much more vulnerable to attack.

"Maybe we can kick them around a bit before we break the spell," she said.

"I could use a knife and Darnak's ink to draw some rude tattoos," Jig offered. "What do you think Barius's father would say if he came home with 'Goblin-lover' scrawled across his forehead?"

She grinned. "Or we could steal their clothes. Make them face Straum naked." With a frown, she added, "Except that I don't really want to see that. I'm going to have enough nightmares about this place without those images haunting me."

"If we were back in goblin territory, we could rub their clothes in carrion-worm urine. That way they'd wake up surrounded by worms." He didn't mention that Porak had taught him this trick, nor that he had screamed loud enough to wake Straum himself when he felt the worms crawling over his legs.

Riana giggled. "And if we were on the surface,

I'd boil some tea from poison ivy leaves and slip it into their waterskins."

Jig laughed even harder once she explained what poison ivy was.

A while later, she said, "You should have warned me before you cut off my finger." She didn't sound angry, though. At least not at Jig.

"Sorry. I'll say something next time."

She chuckled. "Next time I'll cut off something of yours in return, and it won't be a finger."

A few hours later, after backtracking twice, they managed to find Barius and Darnak. They lay as if dead, hands folded on their stomachs and their equipment placed to one side. The lantern, lit but shuttered, sat between them. Indeed it was the faint orange lantern light that Riana had spotted to guide them here.

Jig opened the lantern and sighed with relief as it lit up the woods around them. He could see again. As well as he ever did, at least.

"Ryslind's glyphs?" Riana pointed at Barius's face.

Two red lines traced a circular path around his forehead, starting at the eyebrows and merging by the bridge of the nose. Darnak had the same character inked onto his brow, though they had to shove his hair out of the way to see it.

"Ryslind said we could wake them up by breaking the glyph," Riana said. Her eyes narrowed. "I'll do it. You take the lantern and make sure nothing's out there."

"Why me?" Jig asked, looking around at the dark woods. The last thing he wanted was to go wandering alone.

Riana's knife appeared in her hand. "Don't argue, Jig."

Right. He picked up the lantern and walked a

few paces into the woods. "And she was complaining about bullies," he muttered as he shone the light around. Despite the stars, the darkness here felt somehow *bigger* than Jig was used to. Up above, the lantern would have revealed solid walls. Here, darkness engulfed the light like a predator. If anything crept near, it would have to step directly in front of the lantern for Jig to notice.

A loud scream came from behind, and Jig immediately dropped the lantern. He started to run, stopped, ran back, and grabbed the lantern. Seconds later, he shifted it to his other hand and stuck his burned fingers into his mouth.

"Grab the lantern by the *handle,* stupid," he muttered, voice muffled by his fingers.

Had he stopped to think, he might have run the other way, into the darkness. Instead he hurried back to the others, to find Darnak and Barius both awake and staring at something in the prince's hand. No, not *in* his hand.

Riana sat on the ground in front of them both. She sounded deeply forlorn as she explained what had happened. "Ryslind cast a spell on you and escaped. He wants the rod for himself. He said we should leave. We came back as soon as we could."

She shook her head sadly. "He said something about a spell that would let him look like you, Barius, to fool your father. I'm afraid that, for one of the spell ingredients, he had to cut off your finger."

Jig bit his lip and hoped that neither the prince nor the dwarf could hear the satisfaction beneath Riana's words.

"I'll slay him myself," Barius raged. He thrust the newly healed stump of his left ring finger in Darnak's face.

Jig and Riana had stayed out of the way ever

since the prince began his tantrum. Seeing the fury on Barius's face, Jig took another step back, strategically putting a thick tree between himself and the prince.

"Once we're home, I'll take you to one of the healing temples. You've more than enough gold sitting around to buy a simple regeneration. Besides, if he was wanting to finish you off, he'd have slit your throat rather than lay you out with a magic lullaby." Darnak glanced at Riana and twirled a lock of his beard. "If it was your brother who was doing this, that is."

"Of course it was him," Barius snapped. "Fearful of my success, he seeks to steal the rod which is rightfully mine."

Jig didn't say anything. Darnak had so far kept his suspicions to himself, and Jig didn't want to draw any attention he could avoid. At least Riana had the foresight to dispose of the finger. She had flung it far into the woods, then wiped her knife on the prince's white shirt.

He found it peculiar the way these adventurers thought anything they found was "rightfully" theirs. Why couldn't they come out and admit they were stealing from the monsters? Nothing wrong with that. Goblins and hobgoblins did it all the time. True, it was mostly hobgoblins stealing from the goblins, but that was part of life. Why this nonsense about the rod really belonging to Barius? Did he think Straum should rush out and present the rod to him? Should the goblins have given over their meager treasure because it "rightfully" belonged to Barius?

No wonder the prince was so bitter and angry. All that treasure was rightfully his, and none of the current owners were considerate enough to realize it.

"We should be off," Barius snapped. "We've no time for slumber. If we are to catch my treacherous brother, we must leave at once."

Barius had taken four steps before Darnak raised his voice and said, "Before you're running too far, you might want to ask which way your brother was headed."

Jig pointed. Barius straightened his shoulders and, refusing to make eye contact with Jig, turned and walked back the way Jig had indicated.

Darnak grabbed the lantern in one hand, hoisted his pack with the other, and followed. "Come on, then. He'll be setting quite a trot until he burns off the worst of his temper."

"Are you sure we should go after Ryslind in the dark?" Jig asked as he half jogged alongside the dwarf. "If we wait until the sun comes back . . . it does come back, doesn't it?"

"Aye," Darnak said. "And I could do with a long, nonmagical nap myself. But yon hothead won't rest until he gets back at his brother, and if he has to, he'll rip off his own eyelids to keep from sleeping."

"Even though he knows Ryslind isn't right in the head?" Jig grimaced. That had come out a bit more bluntly than he meant. Ryslind was a prince, after all, and Darnak might not take too kindly to hearing him insulted.

But the dwarf only chuckled. "Madmen in the noble line are as common as rat turds in the grain shed. Barius couldn't care less about his brother's sanity. He doesn't care why Ryslind showed him up; he just knows he's been made to look the fool. If it happens again, Barius won't stop until one or the other is dead." In a more serious tone, he added, "I expect it will be Barius who finds himself wearing a funeral shroud. A good fighter, but too impetuous. And Ryslind's power is nothing to sneer at."

He dipped his quill into the inkpot. "Enough talk. How many paces since that forked tree?"

The prince's pace was not a good one for map-making, and Darnak valiantly tried to sketch their progress as he jogged. Ink had smeared his fingers up to the knuckles, and several drops of ink tracked across the map like tiny rivers. Even when the quill pierced the parchment, Darnak didn't give up. "Always map the way in," he said. "For it's a far cry harder to do so on the way out."

Jig didn't bother to point out how useless the map had been so far. He was too busy watching the ground. The lantern made it easier to avoid stumbling, but not by much. The light leaped and twisted with Darnak's every step, so the trees appeared to be moving. More than once, Jig gasped when his imagination turned a low branch into an arm reaching for his throat.

He still couldn't understand this competition between the two princes. If matters were so strained between them, why wouldn't they fight and finish the matter? Goblins would have exchanged insults, pounded one another with clubs or whatever was handy, and been done with it. Whoever walked away was in the right, and the loser, if he or she survived, would then acknowledge the other's superiority. Why drag things out?

Based on Barius's fury back at camp, he suspected things would finally be settled once they caught up with Ryslind. That too made Jig uncomfortable. For they needed Ryslind's help to get out of this place. That would be difficult if Barius killed him. If the fight went the other way, as Darnak predicted, would Ryslind bother with the rest of them? Either outcome seemed to leave Jig stranded in the lower levels.

Maybe they wouldn't fight at all. He hoped not, because he needed them both alive if he were to have any chance of escaping. If they did start to fight, maybe Jig would tell them it was Riana, not Ryslind, who took Barius's finger. He didn't want to betray Riana, but at least that scenario left a chance for Jig to get out alive. Riana would turn on Jig, Barius would turn on Riana, and all Jig would have to do was hope the prince was faster.

He thought Riana would understand. She would still try to kill him, but she would understand.

He hoped it wouldn't come to that. Of everyone in the party, Riana was the only one Jig could even remotely relate to. The prince was too greedy, the dwarf too interested in his maps and his gods, and as for the wizard, Jig could only pray he never understood Ryslind's mind.

"This is where you met the traitor?" Ever since they left camp, Barius had refused to call his brother by name.

Jig looked around. There was his firewood, scattered and forgotten. To the right, a pale round wound on a tree marked where Ryslind had torn his staff free. "Yes."

Barius dropped to one knee and examined the ground. "His sandals are smooth soled, harder to track, but I see that he stood here while talking to you. Darnak, bring the light closer."

Darnak drew a quick X and labeled it RYSLIND, then hurried over to Barius's side.

"There." Barius pointed. "That shallow dimple in the earth. That must be the indentation from his staff. Between his footprints and that staff, we can track him even in this black night." He laughed.

"My poor brother. Strong in art, but weak in flesh. He could never outmarch me in the field, even with a staff to support his weight."

They continued through the woods until Jig lost track of time. His stomach grumbled angrily, and his vision narrowed to the patch of trail just ahead. His thoughts faded until he was aware of nothing more than the need to put one foot forward, then the other. His blisters were worse, and a painful dryness burned his eyes. All he wanted was to lie down. How long did the sun take to return? Surely they had been walking for days. Several days without food or water, and the only time they rested was when Darnak insisted on relieving himself, which he did frequently.

He probably drank too much dwarven ale, Jig thought. He had seen Darnak take several drinks as they hiked along. *It's probably the only thing that keeps him sane, living with humans all the time.*

"Strange," Barius mused as they walked. "The traitor fled in a different direction than the creature I had been tracking. Yet another indication that he knows something he refused to share."

Perhaps he knew that chasing a creature that could kill three ogres was a stupid idea. As usual, Jig kept his thoughts to himself.

"He divined the Necromancer's hiding place," Barius continued. "Could he be strong enough to discover the rod's location as well? The tales say it hides itself from magic, but why else would he go this way, if not to reach the rod before me?"

Wait, who found the Necromancer? No doubt Barius had already rewritten that incident in his memory, erasing Jig's role so he wouldn't have to admit to being upstaged by a goblin.

Near morning the forest began to thin. Jig only noticed because he wasn't stumbling as often. The light had come so gradually he couldn't say when he first began to see the faint gray outlines of the trees. Overhead the stars had faded until only a few faint spots of light still showed.

Barius brought them to a halt at the edge of the woods. "Look."

Jig stumbled forward to see what Barius had pointed to. He tried to rub the sleepiness from his eyes. One part of him knew he wasn't imagining things, but another part knew equally well that he *couldn't* be seeing what he his eyes told him was there.

"Odd lair for a dragon," Darnak said. "And I've seen one or two in my time."

Jig hadn't. Maybe this was something other dragons did. Jig had never heard of such a thing, but his experience in the world was terribly limited. Tugging on Darnak's sleeve, he asked, "Do all dragons own flower gardens?"

"First I've run across."

It was an impressive garden, Jig admitted. He sat down and tried to take it all in.

The cavern ended about a quarter-mile away. The bowl-shaped wall rose about thirty feet to end at a tree-covered cliff. Large birds circled the cliff top, and even though Jig knew the sky, and therefore the birds, were all an illusion, he could still hear their harsh cries. Impressive as that magic was, it paled next to Straum's gardens.

Thin snakes of water flowed down the cavern wall. Midway down, they hit a magical barrier and flowed into the air, where they curved around one another and looped back to form an arched overhang. It was like fine lace, but formed entirely of water. Streams split apart and split again. The patterns changed gradually, a row of intricate diamonds fading into a series of interlinked ovals, all formed by those shifting rays of water.

Accenting the magical overhang were numerous vines that blanketed the wall. Their purple flowers hid the rock so well, Jig wouldn't have been surprised to learn that the cliff itself was nothing more than flower petals. The wind created waves of motion across the flowers, reminding Jig of the lake.

The true work of art was at ground level, where a huge flower mural stretched out for at least a hundred yards from the cliff. Jig couldn't see well enough to discern the finer details, but he could tell the pictures were laid out to tell a story. On the left, a large green dragon flew with wings outstretched. Orange and red flowers created flaming breath. Another area seemed to depict the outside of the mountain. Jig wondered where Straum had found gray and brown flowers for that part of the mural.

A narrow white trail wound through the center of the garden to the cavern wall. There, about ten feet up, a wide hole beckoned. Jig hadn't seen it at first, because some of the vines hung over the entrance like a curtain. That had to be the entrance to Straum's lair.

He took a deep breath, letting the sweet perfume of the flowers fill his nose. Immediately his eyes watered, and he sneezed three times.

"Sorry," he said meekly when Barius glared at him.

"The opening is off the ground, and wide enough for the dragon to fly through unimpeded." Barius thrust out his chest and chin as he faced the rest of them. "We should prepare ourselves."

The only preparation Jig wanted was a good, long nap. And maybe something to eat. Water would be nice, too. He wondered if it was safe to drink from one of those water streams.

"Come. Before the sun finishes rising." Drawing his sword, the prince hurried toward the garden.

Jig waited. He wanted to make sure nothing was waiting to leap out and kill whoever went first. Or if something did kill the prince, Jig wanted to be sure he was nowhere near when it happened. But Barius made it to the edge of the mural without incident, and then Darnak's club prodded Jig in the back, and he followed.

At the garden, Jig saw something he had missed before. A tiny wall of blue fire bordered the entire mural. In the red light of sunrise, the points of flame were almost invisible. The fire also segmented different portions of the mural. Over here, wizards dueled at the gates of a black tower. Another image showed a blue-scaled dragon flying through the clouds. He remembered Ryslind explaining the legend of Ellnorein, and wondered if the mural was supposed to depict a battle from those times.

Jig grinned when he spotted something tucked into one corner. In a tiny triangular panel, a squad of goblins fought a catlike creature. Naturally, the goblins were losing, but Jig didn't care. He felt a surge of pride at seeing his people in Straum's garden. It made him feel like he was a part of history.

Looking closer, Jig saw that there were even tiny dark blue flowers, each one with a ball-like tip, to represent all the goblin blood. He overbalanced and fell into the flowers. One hand crushed a troll's belly while the other flattened the end of a serpent's tail. More pollen floated up to trigger a second sneezing fit.

Darnak grabbed Jig's elbow and pulled him upright. "Come on. Once we reach Straum's hoard, you'll see something worth gawking at."

The path through the garden was actually a sort of white grass, so low and soft it felt like feathers beneath Jig's feet. As they neared the cave, Jig began to wonder why they hadn't been attacked yet. Surely if Straum's magic could create water sculpture and flower art like this, he would have no trouble adding a few spells to discourage intruders. Barius was so obsessed with his brother that he hadn't bothered to look for traps along the path. At least Barius was in the lead, so if anything did happen, Jig would have the satisfaction of seeing it happen to him first.

Despite his worries, they reached the wall of the cavern. There, Darnak took a rope from his pack and handed it to Riana, the lightest in the group. She raised both eyebrows and handed the rope right back.

"Stick my head up there and let Straum burn it off? I think not."

"My brother is up there, girl." Barius pointed to an indentation in the grass, one that could have been made by the end of a staff. "I've defeated every foe and every trap we have encountered, and I'll not be stopped by your stubbornness."

Jig cocked his head. *Barius* had defeated everything? From the sound of his voice, he believed that, too. And he'd likely kill Riana if she pushed him much further.

"I'll do it," Jig said. He grabbed the rope from Darnak. "Boost me up."

As he scrambled onto the dwarf's shoulders, Jig wondered what had possessed him. Goblins were cowards—that was what helped them survive. So what was he doing poking his head into a drag-on's cave?

It's simple—I'm hungry, I'm tired, and I don't feel like waiting while they argue for the next hour.

Perhaps courage was nothing more than impatience. Besides, the sooner he got away from the flowers, the quicker his eyes would stop watering.

His fingers caught the edge, and with some pushing from Darnak and Barius, he managed to swing one leg up. That, he decided, was a mistake. Pain tore through a very sensitive part of his anatomy. He pulled the other leg up quickly and rolled into the cave.

He tumbled over several of the flower vines, and spent the next minute untangling himself from a vine that had torn free and wrapped around his legs. Silence followed. The others waited below to see if he would die a hideous death. Looking around, Jig wondered the same thing.

Two trolls lay dead on the tunnel floor. Wisps of smoke rose from the holes in their chests. Barius was right. His brother *had* been here.

CHAPTER 14

❧❦❧

Straum Heads off a Possible Rebellion

If anything, trolls were even bigger than the ogres had been. Uglier, too. They looked like a cross between giant humans and spoiled apples. Their bald skin was wrinkled and rubbery, and they smelled like old eggs. They also smelled of charred flesh, but that was a result of Ryslind's magic.

Jig kicked them both to be sure they were dead. Not that most things could get back up with a hole in the chest big enough to crawl through, but Jig wanted to be safe. The trolls didn't respond, though a few flies buzzed up from the eyes of the closest one.

Smudge leaped off Jig's shoulder. His legs snapped out in midair, and when he landed on the troll's forehead, he held a buzzing fly between his forelegs.

Jig watched jealously as Smudge cooked his breakfast. Even flies were starting to sound good. His eyes went to the trolls. Traditionally, the first bite went to the victor, but Ryslind wasn't around to enjoy the rewards of his kill. His mouth began to water. He had no way to cook the bodies, and raw troll meat probably wasn't the healthiest thing in the world. Though the wounded area was nicely blackened, and the smell no worse than overcooked carrion-worm. . . .

"What's taking you so long up there?"

Jig perked his ears at the dwarf's whisper. Swallowing hastily, he called back, "I was looking for something to tie the rope to. I'm not big enough to pull you up by myself."

He wiped his mouth and scanned the entrance. No stalagmites, no rocks, nothing that would hold the rope. His gaze returned to the trolls. They *were* pretty big.

He wound the rope around both trolls' waists, thinking that dead trolls had turned out to be pretty useful things. He wondered if Golaka had ever cooked troll meat. He'd have to see about bringing some back for her cauldron. If he survived long enough.

Jig poked his head through the vine curtain. "Ready," he said. Pulling back, he braced himself against the trolls, adding his meager weight to theirs.

Barius came up first, then Riana, and finally Darnak. The dwarf in his armor was heavy enough that the trolls started to slide across the ground. If the others hadn't heard Jig squawk and grabbed the rope, Darnak would have pulled Jig over the edge and buried him beneath a pair of dead trolls.

"Now this is a proper dragon's lair," Darnak said. "Much more to my liking." He quickly lit the lantern and retrieved his mapmaking tools. As Jig retrieved the rope, Darnak was happily pacing off the width of the tunnel.

"Twenty-five paces exactly. Figure three or four

paces for clearance, but that still means a pretty good wingspan on the beast."

The tunnel was wide, but the roof was only a few feet higher than Barius's head. If Straum decided to come out for an early-morning flight, there was no place for the group to hide. Indeed, they'd be lucky if the dragon didn't smash them on his way out.

"Quickly," Barius said. "My brother cannot be far. We've outmarched him, and soon he will be back within our grasp." With a tight smile, he added, "And he has kindly led me to Straum's hoard. For that boon, perhaps I shall be lenient."

Perhaps Straum would welcome them with open arms and present Barius with the Rod of Creation as a birthday gift, too, but Jig doubted it. He wondered if death by dragonfire would be quick. Fire was a painful way to go, but the stories said dragon breath was so hot the victim burned to ash in seconds.

"Should I stay here to watch the entrance?" Jig asked nervously. "To make sure nothing follows." *And to run like a frightened mouse once Straum kills the rest of you.* "It's not as though I'd be much use against the dragon," he added, trying to sound helpful.

"You will remain with us." The decisive tone of Barius's voice squished Jig's hope of survival. "If nothing else, perhaps the dragon will waste valuable seconds on you, giving us time to execute our attack. Therein lies your usefulness, goblin."

"Oh." After that he was too depressed to say anything else.

The tunnels grew warmer as they walked. What did a dragon's lair look like? A creature that breathed fire would probably want to keep its home as warm as possible. Would there be bonfires and torches? Dragons were supposed to have great piles of treasure that they used as nests. Uncomfortable as it sounded, it did make a kind of sense. Perhaps dragons followed the same logic Jig used when he slept with his few belongings clutched to his stomach. People had a harder time stealing something in your sleep if they had to roll you over to get it.

Not that this technique had ever made much difference for Jig. True, no goblin had taken Jig's possessions while he slept. They woke him up first. Being awakened and kicked out of the way by larger goblins wasn't much of an improvement, but it did mean he knew who to get back at later.

At least they were back on good, solid rock. Far easier to run away when the ground didn't shift beneath your feet and the roots weren't reaching out to catch your toes.

Jig's ears twitched. He heard something up ahead, too faint to identify. A whispery sort of sound. Too smooth and rhythmic to be voices. It was familiar, though. He fingered a fang nervously as he walked.

"I see something," Darnak said. He raised the lantern and aimed the beam forward.

Soon Jig could see it too, a faint blue glow from farther up the tunnel. At a nod from Barius, Darnak shuttered the lantern.

Jig's eyes were slow to adjust, but his ears made up for that. Over the past few days, he had learned to recognize every sound the group made. From the clop of Barius's boots to the quiet flap of Riana's soles to the ring of Darnak's studded boots against the stone, Jig knew them all. He knew exactly where Barius was simply by listening for the prince's nasal breath, whereas Darnak tended to grunt with every third or fourth exhalation. As they neared the source of the light, his vision improved as well.

A wide portcullis blocked the end of the tunnel. Black bars as thick as his wrist extended from the ceiling into holes in the floor. Flat iron bands ran across the bars, riveted to hold each bar in place. The bars ended in nasty-looking points, like over-size spearheads lodged several inches in the rock. Jig could envision being trapped beneath those points as the portcullis came crashing down. He winced.

"Behold," whispered Barius. "The very resting place of the beast."

Jig moved closer to peer through the bars. Beyond the portcullis, the tunnel opened into a large cavern, and he could see the source of the whispering noise he had heard. A glassy lake filled the far half of the cavern, and the water moved just enough to make small waves on the shore. The lake was small, more of a pond, especially compared to the lake of the lizard-fish. The waves were likewise softer, which was why Jig hadn't recognized the sound at first.

The shore itself was black sand that stretched almost to the tunnel. The sand sparkled like the night sky, illuminated by blue flames around the edge of the cavern, similar to the fire that had bor-dered the flower mosaic. Turning his attention to the cavern walls, Jig felt his mouth open in awe.

Shelves had been carved into every square inch of wall, and every shelf overflowed with . . . stuff. Jig had a hard time calling it treasure. True, many shelves glittered with gold and silver coins of all shapes and sizes, stacked into perfect cylinders. But there was far more to Straum's hoard than mere money.

Weapons played a prominent role in the décor. Swords hung between every shelf, some taller than Jig, others slender as a blade of grass. Jig saw jeweled swords, plain swords, swords with polished steel blades, and swords of hammered bronze. He even saw one that looked like it was made of glass. *No surprise that the owner of that sword didn't last long.*

Another shelf was devoted to footwear. Most came in pairs, but here and there Jig saw a lone boot or sandal. For the first time he understood a little of Barius's greed. If not for the portcullis, he would have run to the shelves and grabbed every pair he could find. Never again would he have to suffer bruised toes, blistered heels, or cracked toenails. Finding his current pair had been fortunate, but this was treasure indeed. He wondered if he would have time to search for at least one pair that fit better. Maybe those blue ones, with the furry white fringe at the top and red flames painted down the sides. That was the kind of dramatic style any goblin would kill for.

There were helmets and bows, books and gemstones, even a long shelf devoted to what Jig took to be feathers, but Darnak quickly recognized as writing quills.

"What a load of junk," Darnak muttered. "Aside from the gold, that is. And I could take a liking to that peacock quill there. Could make some fine maps with such a pen. Wonder what kind of nib she's got on her?"

"Find the rod," Barius said. "Once the rod is safely in our possession, you may help yourself to any booty you wish. But first, find the rod."

Riana cleared her throat. "What does it look like?"

Nobody answered.

Jig fought a sudden attack of giggles. He looked at Riana, whose incredulity was plain in her wide eyes.

"You don't know?" she asked.

"The rod was hidden here thousands of years ago. No man has seen it since, and the bards of old did not see fit to describe it in song." Was it Jig's imagination, or was Barius blushing? "I presumed my brother would be able to identify it through his art."

"I've spotted a mess of quarterstaves there, by the waterline." Darnak pointed. "Could your rod be mixed in with that bunch for camouflage?"

Barius rubbed his hands together like a man preparing for a feast. "Our course is simple. We must search the dragon's lair before it returns." He looked up and down at the portcullis, clearly offended that someone had dared impede his quest with such a mundane obstacle. As they waited for him to speak again, it became equally clear that he had no idea how to get past it.

Darnak grabbed one of the bars and gave it a tug. Pressing the side of his face to the gate, he stared up into the ceiling, where presumably the portcullis went when raised. "I'm not seeing any chains or gears up there. Mechanism must be on the other side."

Jig frowned. If the mechanism was on the other side, and the cavern was empty, who had closed the gate? Riana was apparently thinking the same thing, because she asked, "Are we sure there's nobody in there?" She and Jig glanced at each other and stepped backward.

"I will not be stopped by iron bars. Not when I am so close." Barius crossed his arms in princely determination. "Darnak, open the gate."

Darnak responded by grabbing his wineskin. He

sized up the gate, but didn't appear willing to respond without a drink to bolster his courage. As he pulled the stopper free with his teeth, another voice came from beyond the portcullis.

"Perhaps I can assist you, brother."

"Traitor." Barius lunged at the gate as his brother stepped into view. "Not even Father will raise a hand against me for taking your life. Not after *this*." He shoved his crippled left hand through the bars.

Ryslind frowned. Mind-damaged or not, he had to know he wasn't responsible for his brother's injury. Jig tried to think of something to say, some way to distract them both.

Riana beat him to it. "He's *inside* the lair," she pointed out. "Ryslind must have been the one to lower the bars."

"Indeed, that makes sense." Barius withdrew his hand. "You may have beaten us to the treasure, but you'll not leave this place without defeating us. Hide behind this gate for as long as you want. You cannot wait forever."

"Such an abrasive manner, brother." Ryslind grabbed two of the bars. "In truth, I did not close the gate. But I believe I can assist you nonetheless."

He closed his eyes and took several deep breaths. Jig could see the red glow of his eyes even through the lids. As though Ryslind's magic was a kind of polishing agent, the iron bars began to gleam. Small ripples spread along the two bars he held.

Ryslind released his grip. Smiling at the group, he reached between the center bars and tapped each one lightly. Like the streams of water outside, the bars turned fluid and moved toward the edge of the tunnel. The flat iron crossbeams trickled to the floor. Soon, instead of an impassible gate, only a ring of black liquid ran around the end of the tunnel.

"Illusion." He tucked his hands back into the sleeves of his robe. "To stop the weak-minded."

Barius's sword hissed free of its scabbard. "Steel, to stop the craven of heart."

"Oh, my brother." Ryslind shook his head in dismay. "So bold, yet so predictable." His eyes flashed, and the blade of Barius's sword vanished at the crossguard.

Barius dropped the useless hilt. "You've always been a coward."

"And you've never learned to compromise. It's why even the goblin beat you at your duel. Your 'honor' and 'nobility' are chains holding you back. Had the goblin offended me, I would have crushed him."

He smiled at Jig, a reminder that the goblin *had* offended him, and that Jig could look forward to a painful death at Ryslind's convenience. "The poor wretch would die as quickly as I would, were I to meet your challenge 'honorably,' sword against sword."

With a twisted sneer, he added, "But you seem to lack a sword, brother. Here, take this instead." He tossed a knife to Barius. Halfway between them, it twisted into a hissing snake.

Darnak's war club knocked it aside before it could strike. The snake bounced off the tunnel wall and fell to the ground, where it became a dagger again.

Barius grabbed for the dagger. "Darnak, help me fight his foul magic."

The dwarf looked at them both. The humans wore mirroring expressions, jaws tight and eyes narrow with determination. "No, I can't be doing that, Barius."

To the prince's outraged expression, he said, "I've served your father for longer than you've been alive. I'll not tell him how I was after killing one of his sons. And if you've any brains at all between the two of you, you'll stop this nonsense. We may have found the ore, but we've yet to haul it from the mine, as the saying goes."

Behind them, the sound of the waves changed. Something had disturbed their rhythm. Jig stared at the lake, noting the low shadow that broke up the reflections on the surface. It moved toward the shore, growing more distinct as it neared the sand. Ripples spread out from the disturbance. A head rose out of the water, and Jig felt a surge of fear streak from the tips of his ears down to his toes.

"Dragon," he said. Tried to, rather. His mouth was too dry to speak.

Barius, still searching for an opening against his brother, hadn't noticed yet. But Darnak did, and his head jerked up as he spotted the dragon sliding out of the water.

"Now there's something I can be pummeling on," he said. "Solve your problems quickly, boys. I'm off to tenderize myself some dragon steak."

Barius finally saw the dragon. "We shall resolve this at a later time. For now, there is a common foe to slay."

Twirling his club over his head, Darnak charged into the room toward the dripping dragon. Barius followed close behind, his knife looking like a joke before the dragon's bulk.

Jig glanced at Riana. Their eyes met, and they nodded in silent agreement. Leaving the humans and dwarf to meet their respective painful deaths, they ran back down the tunnel as fast as their feet could move.

"A common foe to slay," Riana gasped, mimicking the prince's crystalline enunciation. "Though maybe Straum will laugh himself to death when he sees Barius's weapon. I swear, it's a wonder there are any humans left."

Jig saved his energy for running, not talking. The tunnel was wide enough; he only bumped the walls twice in the darkness, neither time losing more than a bit of skin against the rock. Riana had a harder time, being less accustomed to darkness. She fell several times, cursing like a dwarf every time she scrambled back to her feet.

I should help her. But another part of Jig's brain overruled that idea, the part that argued, *If she's behind me, that's one more thing between me and the dragon.* Not terribly noble, but he and Ryslind were in agreement on the usefulness of nobility. As Barius had so aptly demonstrated time after time, nobility was the first step toward suicide.

In this case, however, he might have been better off to wait for Riana after all, or even to let her go first. Yes, far better for *him* to have followed *her* out of the tunnel. That way she would be the one to face the large figure silhouetted against the mouth of the tunnel.

Jig clenched his teeth and ran faster, ignoring the cramps in his legs. He was short and skinny. Big creatures tended to be slow. If Jig was quick enough, maybe he could slip past the thing, whatever it was.

He wasn't quick enough. Nor was this big thing at all slow. A long arm snapped out and caught the back of his loincloth so fast that Jig never saw the movement. He grunted as his rope belt bent him double and took his breath away. The arm lifted him effortlessly into the air. Jig grabbed at the creature, but it was awfully hard to get a good grip on something behind his back. He scraped the thing's wrist and felt scales, but he couldn't break free.

Slowly he found himself turned around to face the creature. When he saw what held him, he stopped struggling and concentrated on looking small and harmless. For now he knew what had killed the ogres.

The thing stood a head shorter than an ogre, but Jig would have happily faced all three ogres by himself rather than fight this beast. Dark bronze scales the size of large coins covered most of its body, with lighter scales along the belly and chest. Its legs were jointed like an animal's, so it stood with its thighs hinged up close to the stomach. A long tail helped it balance. As Jig watched, the tail twitched back and forth, causing the barbs at the end to smash against the wall. The creature didn't seem to feel any pain from the impact.

The head was a miniature version of the dragon's that Jig had seen coming out of the water, and he would have been happier had he never gotten the chance to examine it so closely. Curved white teeth lined its long, flat jaws. The eyes were golden, with slitted pupils. Twin horns spiraled back from behind its small tufted ears.

Jig glanced at the nostrils, watching them widen and close as the thing breathed. *Could it breathe fire?* he wondered. Then he banished that thought, afraid one of the gods might hear him and decide to satisfy his curiosity.

Something tickled his back. Jig craned his head and saw Smudge hastening toward his belt pouch. Before, Smudge had fought like a cornered tunnel cat to avoid the pouch. Faced with this thing that had snagged Jig so easily, the fire-spider had obviously decided that maybe the pouch wasn't as bad as he thought.

"Don't struggle, little one," the dragon-thing said. The voice sounded male, though Jig saw no evidence either way on its naked body. But dragons were probably built differently than goblins, and Jig wasn't about to ask. "Once I have your friend, we'll be on our way back to Straum."

His breath smelled like rotting meat. Jig wondered what he ate, and again decided he was better off not knowing.

Riana's footsteps came closer, then faltered as she fell yet again. Jig could hear her saying, ". . . going to kill you, Jig. Leave me behind, will you? I'll take a strip of your skin for every one of these bruises. You owe me a finger anyway."

He almost wished she'd have the chance to take her revenge. Without thinking, he cupped his hands to his mouth and screamed, "Riana, run!"

One golden eye swiveled at Jig, and he wisely shut his mouth. "Very well," the thing said. "The hard way."

He pulled Jig close against his body, and Jig felt the spring of powerful muscles as his captor leaped into the air. Clawed feet scraped against the wall and launched them another twenty feet down the tunnel, where he bounced onto the opposite wall. Three more bounds took them to where Riana stood, torn as to which way to run.

Even had she fled as soon as she heard Jig's warning, it would have gained her only a few seconds. As easily as Smudge had caught the fly, the creature pounced and snagged Riana's tunic in his claws. He tucked Riana under his other arm and continued at a slower pace toward Straum's lair. As Jig fought to keep from throwing up and waited

for the tunnels to stop spinning, he heard Riana
mutter, "I *hate* this place."

The creature dropped Jig and Riana in the sand.
He was so confident, he hadn't even bothered to
take Jig's sword or Riana's knife. Not that it mattered. Riana had managed to squirm enough to
slash at the creature's arm. Against those scales,
she might as well have attacked the stone walls.

"Ah, your friends have returned." Straum's
bronze body rested half-submerged in the lake. His
front legs sank into the sand, and his long neck
stretched just high enough to let him look down at
his newest captives. "I was telling your friends
about my collection of chamber pots. So many adventurers bring their own. That way they don't
leave as much of a trail to follow. I have one hundred and thirteen. Fourteen, now that I've claimed
Barius's pot as well. Ingenious, the way the lid
twists into place so perfectly. I'd guess that elven
craftsmanship went into this beauty."

Straum picked up the gold-trimmed chamber pot,
which looked like a porcelain bead in his claws.
"I'll have one of my children clean it out. The
flowers can always use an extra bit of fertilizer."
He tilted the pot. "Not terribly decorative, though.
No artistic style. See that blue pot on the third
shelf? That belonged to a barbarian lord named
Terinor."

The indicated pot was covered in cloisonné images of huge muscular men and women, their hands
raised high as if they were trying to raise the sky.
The wide-rimmed top appeared to be cushioned in
leather and trimmed with red jewels. It suddenly
occurred to Jig that, were the owner to sit on the
leather, the men and women would appear to hold
him up.

The chamber pot was easily one of the tackiest things he had ever seen, and he felt a wash of pity for those poor bearers of barbarian buttocks.

"Very nice," Barius said sharply. "And now that our companion has been returned, perhaps you can get on with the matter of our deaths." He stood with Darnak on the other side of the dragon. Behind them, Ryslind had taken their weapons and watched the proceedings with a smile. Even Jig could see that, unlike the others, Ryslind was no prisoner.

"Oh, but I so rarely have company," Straum protested. His voice was like an earthquake, though his serpentine tongue gave him a bit of a lisp when he spoke Human. "Most people never make it past the Necromancer. If they even find him. I had such a good time watching you figure that out."

He tilted his head toward two small pools that Jig hadn't seen before. No more than puddles a little way from shore, a short wall of clear glass bricks surrounded and protected each one. The surfaces were so still it was like looking at a pair of mirrors. Instead of reflecting Straum's muscular bulk, Jig saw a whirling pillar of water at the center of an empty room when he studied the nearest pool. A small corpse lay to one side, next to an enormous throne. *The Necromancer's room.* He wondered how the magic could show so much detail when the throne room itself was dark.

Flecks of color sparkled across the both pools, and finally Jig understood the purpose for those two decorative ceilings in the shiny room and the Necromancer's throne room. Straum had been watching them, probably since that first confrontation where Jig betrayed his captain.

While Jig wrestled with a new wave of fear, Straum gestured to a wall full of lanterns. "See that one, with the handle shaped like a naked eight-armed woman? That belonged to Erik the Eunuch. Used to be a slave of some eastern emperor. Once he built a name for himself, he had everything he owned redesigned with a kind of 'melon-breasted naked woman motif.' Personally, I think it's a blatant example of overcompensating."

Lowering his head toward Barius, he asked, "Tell me, do women of such proportions truly exist among your people? If so, are they able to walk upright like the rest of your species?"

"And where in your fine collection do you keep the Rod of Creation, oh great worm?" Barius asked, ignoring the question.

Straum began to laugh. Whitecapped waves crossed the lake as the dragon's chest heaved, and Jig flattened his ears to block the worst of the sound. It was a terrible laugh, one that combined fury and bitterness with genuine mirth. Straum's head and neck slid through the sand until his mouth rested mere feet from the prince.

"Therein lies Ellnorein's greatest joke. 'Twas a joke played as much on you as on me." His voice dropped to a whisper, though a whisper from Straum's mouth still blew Barius's black hair backward. "I don't have it."

"No! You're the guardian," Barius protested. "You must have it. This is a trick! You seek to gull me." His head whipped around as he scanned the shelves.

"No trick, brother," Ryslind said. "Ellnorein had no choice, you see. The rod needed to be safe from even the most powerful adventurers, so his first step was to trap the most powerful creature he could find and imprison him here, at the heart of the mountain. In thousands of years, no party has survived an encounter with Straum.

"Ellnorein knew this would happen. He predicted the tales of wealth, the fame that would draw adventurers from around the world in search of the rod, all of them intent on battling their way here. Many die before they reach this point. Others flee after a few encounters. A fortunate few live long enough to again see the light of the sun."

Straum growled at that. "*They* see sunlight." His claws began to flex in the sand, and Jig could imagine those claws tearing thousands of years' worth of adventurers into scraps of meat. "*I* have been trapped here, alone, for so long that I cannot remember what it feels like to be free."

Clouds of hot smoke formed around his nostrils. "I can create an entire world of illusion, but I can't break these walls. All the illusion in the world cannot change the fact that I am a prisoner. I could grind an ordinary mountain to dust and scatter it on the wind, but Ellnorein, damn him to the lowest pit in the Shadow-elves' icy hell, used the rod to form these caverns and tunnels. Rod-created rock resists lesser magic, including my own. Only the rod can free me."

Ryslind ducked past Straum's mouth, probably afraid that the dragon might loose a jet of fire in his fury. "That is why Ellnorein couldn't leave the rod here," he explained. "Straum, being a created creature, could not use it himself. But like all dragons, Straum collects followers. Ogres, trolls, and other creatures you haven't yet seen. One of them could have used the rod, either to free the dragon, or for their own use. It had to be hidden, but hidden so well that nobody would ever be able to use it."

"Why not encase it in the mountain?" Darnak asked. "Why all this nonsense with the tunnels and the monsters? He had to know that would bring adventurers like beggars converging on a feast."

"The rod's magic is like a living thing," Ryslind said. "Left alone, its magic would have seeped into the mountain itself, the effects could be . . . unfortunate. It had to be left somewhere those effects would go unnoticed."

Straum sighed, and smoke shot across the room. "If I had the rod, I would give it to you with my blessing and send you on your way. I would give you all of my gold, every treasure I own, if you only used the rod to release me. Do you know how bloody *bored* I've been? I tried talking to the other creatures for a while. But the ogres talk about nothing but fighting and food, and as for the trolls, they're a bit too clever. They kept trying to steal from me, and I grew tired of disintegrating them. The smell of burned troll is, by far, one of the most nauseating scents in the world."

Jig thought of privy duty and disagreed. The corpses at the mouth of the tunnel had been almost pleasant by comparison. But he kept his argument to himself.

"I taught myself magic from the spellbooks I collected. The trick was to kill the wizards without damaging their books. A difficult trick, since your races use such flammable materials for books. Though there was one fellow, a bright young lad, who had his spells engraved on brass plates. Heavy book, but it survived just fine."

Another tuft of smoke floated from Straum's nostrils, and Jig tried not to wonder what had happened to the owner of that book.

"That killed a century or two. But all too soon, I was better at magic than the wizards who approached me, and the fun began to wane. And then I created my children."

The dragonlike creature that had captured Jig

and Riana stepped forward. Head raised, it seemed
to preen before Straum's proud gaze.

"Your children?" Darnak asked. "Don't tell me
you've got a lady dragon hidden away in that lake."

"If only there were." Straum's eyes glazed. "I
haven't flown a mating dance in five thousand two
hundred and twelve years. While I may have forgotten most of the surface world, I still remember
the scrape of scales against scales, the lashing of
tails, the twining of necks."

He shivered, and his scales puffed out, turning
him a darker bronze. Jig was thankful that the lake
concealed the dragon's lower body. This adventure
had given him nightmares enough already without
the extra fuel of an aroused dragon.

"No, I used magic to create them. They're fairly
intelligent, stronger than anything else down here,
and excellent company. Their only flaws are arrogance and a powerful loyalty to one another that
tends to override their common sense. You were
tracking this one back to his lair, Barius. Had your
brother not diverted your party, you would have
been slaughtered the moment you threatened his
offspring."

Which meant that by diverting them here, Ryslind had saved their lives. Jig glanced at Barius.

Taken aback, the prince said nothing. The stoni-
ness of his face as he studied Ryslind was an expression Jig had come to recognize. It was the
expression Barius wore when he had made a mistake, but wasn't yet willing to admit it.

"Yes, my children are a clear improvement over
the low creatures Ellnorein abandoned me with,"
Straum said. He gave Jig a dismissive nod. "Goblins. Ogres. Trolls. Worthless creatures. But I'm
afraid that even my children have their flaws."

Jig wasn't sure, but he thought he saw *this* dragon-child's eyes narrow with suspicion.

"See, in order to keep them interesting, I had to give them a bit of independence. Sadly, it goes to their heads from time to time. This one plans to bring me a poisoned deer and take my place as ruler."

Before anyone could move, his head shot toward the dragonchild, who had time for one shrill scream before Straum's jaws closed over its head with a loud crack. The headless body crumpled.

Jig began to shake. For all Straum's bulk, he had moved faster than any creature Jig had ever seen. He watched as Straum's tongue flicked out to clean dark blood from his teeth.

"He'll not get any more ideas into his head," Straum said. When nobody spoke, he added, "That was a joke."

Jig forced himself to smile. *Yes, that was a good joke. Please don't eat me.*

"I can read their minds, you see. I never mention that detail to them. I fear they might react badly."

"How did my brother know where that thing was going?" Barius asked. His toe nudged the headless body.

"There are many ways to grow in the magical arts," Ryslind said. He stepped forward to stand next to Straum's head. The dragon closed his eyes and pulled his lips back. Ryslind drew a dagger and began to clean between the huge teeth. Thankfully Jig couldn't see well enough to identify what that stringy bit used to be.

Ryslind continued to explain as he worked. "I went off alone to seek a teacher, someone who could show me *real* power. I sent my spirit questing for the most powerful wizard around. I found Straum."

"Thank you," Straum said. Ryslind nodded respectfully and retreated. "Novices do that from time to time. Foolish, really. There's a shock when two spirits touch. I understand they seek quick power, but to seek that power from me is like a small child who stands in front of a charging stallion hoping for a ride. Fortunately, this stallion decided not to trample your brother."

"My master had grown bored once again." Ryslind smiled. "He offered me a deal. He would give me magic that the most powerful warlock might envy."

"Magic, yes," Straum said. "But power was another matter. No matter how stubborn he might be, Ryslind's power was limited. Every time he overexerted himself, he drew on my strength to help him. I'm afraid it was too much for his poor mind. Like a weak branch beneath winter snow, it snapped. What could I do but replace it with my own? I locked him away in his own mind so he wouldn't cause any more harm. Otherwise he could have injured himself in his greed."

"You used him, you bloody oversized snake." Darnak kicked the corpse out of the way as he stormed toward Straum. "You killed him. Where's my club? Earthmaker help me, I'll crack you open like a walnut, you damned dragon."

"I warned him," Straum shrugged. His tongue flicked out and slapped Darnak in the face, knocking him to the sand. "But he accepted both the terms of my agreement and the risk it would involve."

Barius grabbed Darnak's arm before the dwarf could resume his charge. Darnak actually dragged him several yards before coming to a grudging halt.

"What were the terms?" Barius asked.

"I can't send anyone in search of the rod. Most are too stupid, and my own children might attempt to betray me. I've attempted to create mindless creatures I could use as puppets, but they lack the wit to find the rod. That was why I created the Necromancer's fountain. A simple warlock used to control those tunnels. I thought I could animate his corpse and use that in my search. I failed. The upper levels are too alien to me, and I could not find what I needed.

"I required someone who would give me control, but who retained a spark of intelligence. Someone who might discover where Ellnorein hid the rod. I found Ryslind. In exchange for my power, he offered to bring me a group of adventurers who could retrieve the Rod of Creation and set me free."

CHAPTER 15

Stirring Up Trouble

Jig had never noticed the smell of home before. Like the smell of his own sweat, it was simply *there*. But as he crouched low against a wall, listening to the growls and curses up the tunnel, he found himself smiling at the familiar odors. The earthiness of the carrion-worm trails, the distant smoke of cooking meat, the moist, fishy smell of the lake . . . it all blended together to create *home*.

"Watch yourself, lads!" Darnak's shout was followed by the crack of wood against flesh. A tunnel cat yowled in pain.

"That's another one down," Riana commented. She sat opposite Jig, her back against the wall in an almost identical position of boredom.

"How long do you think it will take?" Jig asked.

She peeked around the bend. "Looks like at least five or six more cats. How many do the hobgoblins have?"

"I've never tried to count them." Jig leaned his head against the rock and closed his eyes. The tunnel split off past the tunnel cats, but there was no

way to get to it until the adventurers took care of
the cats. Or until the cats took care of the adventurers, he supposed. Funny, but after standing before Straum in the dragon's lair, the huge albino
cats just weren't as frightening.

Jig crawled over to see the battle for himself.
Another cat pounced, only to die on Barius's
sword. Over the generations, the cats' eyes had
grown to the size of Jig's palm, letting them see
perfectly in the faintest light. Their ears were better
than his, and their noses were equally keen. Fortunately, the same inbreeding that left them mean-
tempered and rapier-swift had given them weak
hips. If you could avoid that first leap, as Barius
had done, they tended to stumble.

Not that it mattered. The cats were silent as
shadows, and few goblins ever noticed their presence before being seized by the neck, shaken, and
dragged back to the cats' nest.

Still, tunnel cats or no, Jig would much rather
be here, under siege by the hobgoblins' pets, than
wandering the empty tunnels of the Necromancer's
lair. For the past two days they had searched every
alcove, room, and corridor. Darnak came up with
the idea that the rod might be hidden within the
fountain, so the group had smashed those beautiful
crystalline dragons to dust. The Necromancer's
throne had been similarly pulverized, thanks to a
bit of Ryslind's magic. But the rod was nowhere to
be found.

Claws scrabbled against stone. Barius yelled. A
rushing sound and a squeal of pain signaled another
of Ryslind's spells. Without a word, Jig and Riana
moved a bit farther down the tunnel, trying to get
away from the scent of burned fur and flesh.

"I almost feel sorry for them," Riana said.

"Why?" The more tunnel cats that died, the

fewer there would be left to pounce on Jig in the darkness.

"Ryslind."

"Oh." The wizard hadn't spoken since they left Straum's lair, except to cast the occasional spell. He had used a bit of magic to help them find their way through the sky, into the Necromancer's throne room. A few bolts of fire had scared away the giant bats on the bridge. He had also incinerated a swarm of rats they found in one of the alcoves in the hallway. Jig didn't know how much power Ryslind had at his disposal, but if he could draw energy from a five-thousand-year-old dragon, he probably wouldn't dry up anytime soon.

"I say we charge," Darnak shouted, sounding winded but eager. "If we can scare 'em good enough, they'll turn tail and head straight back to their masters. We can follow them in and use the confusion to start bashing hobgoblins."

Jig crawled back to take another look. Four cats lay dead, two from Ryslind's magic, and the others from more mundane wounds. The corpses didn't seem to deter the other cats, which were as stubborn as they were dangerous. Several more of the snarling beasts had joined their fellows and now waited for the chance to attack. Only a narrow bottleneck in the tunnel kept them from charging as a pack.

Riana scooted close to Jig's side. The instant she started to whisper, Jig knew what she was going to ask.

"Do you know where the rod is?"

Jig bit his lip to keep from sighing. In the past few days, everyone had pulled him aside to ask if he knew the rod's hiding place. Barius had threatened to torture him. Darnak hinted that helping to find the rod might be Jig's only hope of getting

through this alive. As for Ryslind, when he asked
about the rod, Jig had sensed Straum watching him
from behind that glowing gaze. Jig hadn't been able
to think of anything except Straum's terrible jaws
closing over the helpless dragonchild.

"No," Jig answered. Didn't they realize he would
happily give them the rod if he could only go
home?

He watched as Darnak and Barius charged up
the tunnel, the former shouting a dwarven battle
cry. They returned a few seconds later, Darnak
swatting furiously at the cat that had locked its jaws
onto the dwarf's forearm. If not for his thick bra-
cers, Darnak's arm would have been nothing but
shredded meat. He managed to hurl the cat against
the wall. It whined and crawled away, dragging its
paralyzed hindquarters along the ground.

Jig closed his eyes and breathed deeply. He
wasn't worried about the cats. The adventurers
would win or else they wouldn't. Either way, there
wasn't much Jig could do about it. He just wanted
to be done with it.

Was he imagining things, or could he smell the
faint spice of Golaka's ever-simmering cauldron?
Thinking about food made his mouth water painfully. He reached up to his shoulder and stroked
Smudge's head. The fire-spider evidently recognized home as well, for his head was high, and he
kept turning around, as if searching for familiar
landmarks.

Although it felt good to be home, everything
seemed strange as well. Knowing his fellow goblins
would likely kill him didn't help his comfort, but
there was more. Like the smells. He never would
have noticed them before. The tunnels themselves
felt smaller, too. Was it only because he had been

beyond them, because he knew how much more there was past goblin territory?

Yet he still knew so little. He hadn't seen all of Straum's lair, nor had he explored much of those woods. He didn't know where else the Necromancer's not-really-bottomless pit might lead. He didn't even know where the rod was. If Barius and the others were right and it was here, then Jig had lived his entire life within walking distance of one of the most powerful magical artifacts in history.

He inhaled again and remembered Straum's description of the rod. *A seemingly innocent wooden rod, wide as a human's thumb and a little over three feet long.* In other words, a stick. It could be anything from a piece of a door to the chief hobgoblin's favorite tool for scratching between his toes. Magic wouldn't detect it, and the emanations of power would appear natural to those around it, since their wills would shape the way that power manifested. Basically, the thing was next to invisible.

Barius and Darnak charged again. This time, Ryslind helped by sending several arrows past them and into the pack. Perhaps he used magic to augment his skill, for two cats whined in pain and fled. A huge male leaped at Darnak, only to fall as Barius lodged his sword between the cat's ribs. Its spasms wrenched the sword out of Barius's hands, and it wound up trapped beneath the cat's dying body. Fortunately, the rest of the pack had finally seen enough. As one, they turned and fled.

"Come on, then," Darnak yelled. "We'll rout the mangy furballs all the way back to their masters."

Barius had one foot on the dead tunnel cat and was trying to free his sword. His sword wouldn't budge, so he ended up on the floor, both feet against the cat, tugging with all his might. When the sword finally did come free, Jig shook his head at the prince's luck. At that angle, the blade had come within inches of turning the prince into a princess.

Barius didn't notice. He scrambled to his feet and raced after Darnak, his long stride helping him close the distance.

"Come on," Riana said wearily.

Jig hesitated as he thought about the plan Barius had shared as they left the Necromancer's lair. It was both simple and terrible. They intended to use Ryslind's magic and their own considerable fighting skill until every last hobgoblin died or surrendered. Which sounded fine to Jig. If the hobgoblins were out of the picture, that was one less thing for him to worry about. The only question was how long it would take. Hundreds of hobgoblins lived down that tunnel, and they wouldn't simply line up in a neat single-file line to die. In true hobgoblin style, they would set traps, attempt ambushes, and terrorize the tunnel cats into another attack. But in the end, whether by Barius's sword or Ryslind's mystic fire, they *would* die.

Like goblins, the hobgoblins always lost to the heroes. Unfair as it seemed to Jig, Barius and the others were the heroes.

Jig stopped. If the hobgoblins didn't have the rod, what would happen next?

Lantern light faded behind him as he moved toward the right branch of the tunnel, slipping into a jog, then an all-out run as he abandoned the others.

"Where are you going?" Riana yelled.

He ignored her. He knew what would happen if the adventurers didn't find the rod. Once they slaughtered the hobgoblins, the only place left to search would be the goblin lair.

Jig stopped to catch his breath. He heard Riana coming up behind him. She must have followed the sound of his footsteps. Was this the same girl who had cowered in darkness a few days ago? She had changed too, apparently.

He could see the red flicker of torches up ahead. A part of Jig wanted to run past the guards and into the main cavern, to curl up in his corner and forget about everything. He could lie about what had happened, say the surface-dwellers had used magic to make him betray his captain. The next time they chose him for patrol, he would think of some excuse to stay at home. So what if they branded him a coward. At least he could live the rest of his life without having to see another dragon or adventurer.

Except that he knew it wouldn't work that way. If he was lucky, one day might go by before Barius brought the others here.

Maybe Jig could convince the goblins to negotiate. If the goblins gave Barius permission to search for the rod, there would be no cause for bloodshed. But even as he tried to figure out a way to persuade the other goblins, he knew it wouldn't work. Barius *wanted* bloodshed as much as any goblin. He lived for combat and glory and victory, and every time he cut down an enemy, it made him feel stronger.

Nor would the goblins take kindly to surface-dwellers scrounging through their homes. Sooner or later, and Jig would wager on sooner, one of them would try to put a knife in someone's back.

On Jig's shoulder, Smudge waved his forelegs in excitement. He recognized these tunnels and knew they had come home. He couldn't understand that Jig might be killed as soon as one of the guards spotted him. Nor could he know that, even if they survived, it would only be to die as soon as the adventurers arrived.

So why had he come back? Why not stay with the others? At least that way, when they killed the goblins, they might have let Jig live. If Jig was here when Barius arrived, they would kill him without a second thought. They probably wouldn't even know it was him. All goblins looked alike, after all.

Shadowstar, I could use a little help down here. How am I supposed to survive what's coming?

The god's answer was brief and discouraging. *If I think of something, I'll let you know.*

Jig started to laugh. Not even a god could think up a way out of this. In the past few days, Jig had come within inches of being eaten, drowned, poisoned, zombiefied, ripped apart, and if you included having to live on bread, starving to death. He could be an entire song all by himself. "The Hundred Deaths of Jig the Goblin." If he was going to die anyway, why not add a few more deaths to the song by storming back into the clan and trying to prepare for the inevitable battle?

"Keep going," Jig said when Riana caught up. He pointed down the tunnel. "You should reach the way out in a little under an hour."

"I can't." When Jig cocked his head in confusion, Riana explained, "I'd have to go through that room with the glass ceiling. Straum would see me. If he realized I was trying to escape, he might think I had the rod. And he can talk to Ryslind."

Jig nodded. She was right. Ryslind would be after her in a heartbeat. *They might already be after us. They probably think we know where the rod is, which means they won't bother with the hobgoblins.*

We don't have a day after all. They'll come as soon as they realize we're missing.

"Come on." Straightening his shoulders, Jig walked past the goblin marker and into the tunnel. Riana followed, knife in hand.

"What are we doing?" Riana asked.

Jig didn't get to answer. Up ahead, he spotted the two guards. One carried an old spear, the other a club. After spending so much time with Darnak, Jig wasn't impressed with the club. It looked like an old table leg. Darnak would have knocked it into splinters, right before doing the same to the goblin's skull.

"What are you doing out there?" the one with the spear asked. Getting a better look, he said, "Jig? Is that you?"

"You're in trouble," said the other. "We hear you killed Porak."

Jig didn't break stride. They thought *he* had killed Porak? How marvelous! He wondered how much the story had grown in the past few days. Never mind . . . so long as they thought he was dangerous, maybe he had a chance.

The guards pointed their weapons at him. "Who's the elf?" one asked. "Did you bring her back as a gift for Porak's friends?"

"Wait," Jig said, more for Riana than the guards. Another comment like that, and the guard would find himself eating Riana's knife for a snack. "She was with the surface-dwellers. We're going to see the chief."

"Uh . . ." The guards looked at each other uncertainly. "You can't."

Jig walked right past them, motioning for Riana to follow. He had counted on this. Goblins didn't go in for sneakiness. If Jig was the enemy, he should have attacked immediately. Instead Jig acted like nothing was wrong. Like he *belonged* here. He could imagine their confusion.

"Wait," one said. Jig glanced back to see the guard's spear leveled at his back. "I don't know if we should let her in there with you. She's got a knife, you know."

Jig spoke quickly. "She's with me. The other adventurers will be here soon. You should worry about them instead."

The one with the club looked nervous, but the other shook his head. "Porak's friends are mean, and they'll have my head if they find out I let you live. Besides we haven't had elf meat in months." He jabbed his spear in Riana's direction, forcing her to hop back.

Jig nodded. He should have known it wouldn't work. Maybe heroes and adventurers could get away with this sort of trick, but Jig obviously wasn't good enough to make it work. So he would have to do this the hard way.

He stepped closer to the guard, who frowned. Jig had again done something unexpected. *He's wondering why I don't run away,* Jig guessed. If goblins were better trained with their weapons, would this one have realized that the last thing he should do was allow Jig to get inside his guard? If Jig hadn't watched the way the others used their different weapons, would it even have occurred to him to try?

Probably not, he decided. He drew his sword and attacked. The guard snarled and tried to swing his spear, but Jig was too close. The shaft bounced off his shoulder, hard enough to hurt, but nothing more.

Remembering one of Barius's moves, Jig took a quick half-step and lunged. He overbalanced and almost fell, but his sword bit into the guard's stomach. Jig caught himself, pulled the sword free, and spun around before the other guard had figured out what was happening.

Jig pointed his sword at the other guard, ignoring the groaning goblin on the floor. Doing his best to mimic Barius in voice and posture, he said, "I told you we need to see the chief."

"But . . ." The guard glanced at his bleeding companion. He stared at the sword in Jig's hand, his eyes focusing on the blue smear of blood. He took a step back, and the tip of Jig's sword followed him.

"Right," he said meekly. "Sorry about that."

Jig nodded. He lowered his sword, hoping the guard hadn't noticed how his arm shook. Dramatic poses were *hard*! Even a short sword got heavy if you held it outstretched for very long.

"Come on," he said to Riana. He led them down the tunnel toward the main cavern. He hoped he hadn't killed the guard. He had come here to *help* the goblins. Though eliminating some of the stupider guards might be construed as helping. He would have to think about that later. For now, getting past the guards had been the easy part. Getting past the hundreds of goblins they were sure to encounter next would be a much larger challenge.

Apparently Riana was having similar thoughts. As they neared the jagged entrance, she whispered, "Do you have a plan, or was this just another way to commit suicide?"

"Suicide," Jig answered. Plans were for adventurers. He preferred the goblin approach. Blind panic might not work all the time, but at least it saved you the stress of planning.

He blinked. Panic might be exactly what he needed. His jaw jutted into a wide grin. "Come on," he said, grabbing Riana's arm.

"If this doesn't work, I'm going to make sure you die with me." But she sounded resigned, not angry.

"If this doesn't work, I'm sure I will."

A hundred goblin voices washed together in a low roar as they walked into the room. The noise died within seconds as the goblins stared at Jig and Riana, trying to understand what they were doing here, so obviously out of place. At any moment, someone would cry out and send the cavern into total chaos. Jig wanted to make sure that someone was him.

"Adventurers!" he screamed at top volume. He waved his bloody sword in the air, hoping nobody would remember that adventurers tended to bleed red, not blue. "They're attacking the guards! Where's the chief? I have a deserter from their party who can help."

Whispers spread like lice, and Jig heard his name mentioned a number of times. Nobody moved. Didn't they believe him? He waved his sword again. Riana swore at him and wiped off the dots of blood which had sprayed from his sword onto her sleeve.

"What did you say?" she asked.

He had forgotten she didn't speak Goblin. "I told them the adventurers were coming, and you were going to help us."

"Oh." She chewed her lip for a second, then shouted, "They've rallied the hobgoblins and their tunnel cats. They're coming to steal your women and children."

"And our food!" Jig added.

That earned a much stronger response, at least from those who understood Human. Goblins everywhere scrambled for weapons or ran deeper into the warrens to hide. More the latter than the former, but at least they were moving. More importantly, nobody had tried to kill him.

The chief had a large room behind the kitchen, so that he could eat whenever he felt like it. Jig's stomach grumbled at the thought.

"Come on." He struggled through the crowd of goblins, toward the far side of the cavern. Riana followed close behind.

Strong fingers grabbed Jig's wrist. The goblin's grip was weak compared to the dragonchild's, but it was still too powerful for Jig to break. "How do we know this isn't a trick?" the goblin demanded.

Jig felt a moment of bizarre relief. *At least we aren't* all *gullible*. The fact that it could cost him his life took some of the satisfaction away, though. The other goblin had Jig's sword arm, and his fangs were almost an inch longer than Jig's.

The goblin's eyes widened. He looked down. Following his gaze, Jig saw a dagger sticking out of his side. Silently the goblin fell.

"You blindsided him," Jig said, impressed.

"I'm a thief. We're sneaky that way."

A few other goblins had seen what happened, and Jig's stomach tightened as a crowd began to form around him and Riana. They were close to the kitchen. All he needed was a few minutes with the chief. After that Jig would probably die, and Riana would go into the pot, but at least he would have warned them about Barius and the others.

He pulled out his sword and screamed. Compared to Darnak's battle cry, Jig sounded more like a frightened rat than a warrior, but it worked. Goblins fell back, startled and uncertain. Jig dashed through the gap and into the kitchen, Riana stepping on his heels as she ran.

Golaka scowled at him as he entered. "What are

you doing, barging in like that? It's another hour before dinner."

The noise dropped as he entered the kitchen. Nobody followed. Few goblins dared intrude when Golaka was cooking, which was most of the time.

Golaka the chef was the largest goblin Jig had ever known. While not quite as tall as the average hobgoblin, she easily surpassed them in terms of bulk. The goblins liked to joke that you wouldn't be able to tell Golaka from her cauldron if it weren't for the fact that she never stopped complaining.

Jig figured her size was an occupational hazard. How could you spend day after day manning the kitchen without snacking a bit? But Golaka was as much muscle as fat, and she pulled out her stirring spoon and shook it at Jig like a broadsword. "Jig, isn't it? Are you the one causing all that commotion? And what's this morsel here? She's a skinny one, isn't she? Couldn't find anyone with more meat on her bones, I suppose."

Jig gave quick thanks to Tymalous Shadowstar that Riana couldn't understand Goblin. "Golaka, where's the chief?"

"Dead. He went looking for those adventurers and ran into a hobgoblin ambush. Seems there's been all sorts of excitement these past few days. Means everyone will be all stirred up, no doubt. Fighting over who gets to be the new chief and all that nonsense."

Jig's body went numb. He dropped his sword. Dead? He had fought through the entire goblin lair, only to learn that the chief was dead?

"Long as I can remember, it's always the same. Adventurers come in and cause trouble. Bunch of young goblins run out and get themselves killed. Another patrol goes out and ambushes the adventurers. I end up with a few more bodies for the pot and a dozen less mouths to feed.

"At least they'll bring in some wood for the fire. A few arrows, maybe an axe handle or something. Haven't had any new wood in almost a month, since that hobgoblin trader slipped and fell on my carving knife."

Jig ignored her. The shock was so great that his entire body tingled. He stared at the scraps of wood burning merrily beneath her pot. If Golaka was telling the truth, they had continued to burn for *an entire month* without any new fuel.

She snorted. "That'll teach those hobgoblins to get fresh with *me*. Of all the raw nerve. He's lucky I didn't make sausages out of his worthless guts. All for the best, though. Hobgoblin causes indigestion something fierce."

The emanations of the rod would appear natural, shaped by the wills of those around it. "Golaka," he said, voice hoarse. "Have you ever run out of wood for the fire or food for the cauldron?"

"Course not," she snapped. "Though why you young know-it-alls can't bring me a fresh human from time to time is beyond me."

Golaka had run the kitchen for as long as Jig could remember. Older goblins would sometimes tell stories about meals she had made when *they* were children. How long had she been alive? Could *anyone* remember a time when someone else cooked here?

Goblins rarely died of old age, a sad fact Jig had never before stopped to consider. So nobody really knew how long a goblin could expect to live. But surely Golaka had long ago exceeded her life span.

Jig stared at her with such intensity that she actually stopped in midrant, an occurrence unheard of in goblin history.

"What's the matter? I suddenly turn beautiful or something?" She laughed loudly. "Not nice to stare, Jig. And I'm afraid you're a bit too young for me." She took her stirring spoon and smacked him on the arm, splashing broth onto his stomach.

Jig ignored the burning broth as he stared at the spoon. The brass head topped a wooden handle. A simple, unadorned wooden handle, about a yard long.

"What is it, Jig?" Riana followed his stare, and her sudden gasp told him that she had reached the same conclusion.

They had found the Rod of Creation.

CHAPTER 16

Fetching the Rod

Jig snatched for the rod. Golaka stepped back, and the heavy spoon crashed onto Jig's head as he stumbled past. He staggered, white spots floating across his vision.

"Stupid kid," Golaka said. "Get out of here and let me work. Nobody samples the food before mealtime, not even the chief."

"You said the chief was dead."

"That's right, and unless you want to join him, you'll keep your grimy claws to yourself."

Jig leaned against a wall. Maybe he didn't have to do anything more. Darnak had thought a dragon made a fearsome guardian. That was because he had never encountered an angry goblin cook.

Jig could leave Golaka and the rod in peace. When Barius and the others got here, she would pummel them with the rod, throw in a tongue-lashing to make them sorry they ever saw a goblin, and send them on their way. If they protested, well, Golaka could always use more meat for the pot. Yes, that would be much easier.

Riana slipped close to his side and whispered, "Jig, are you okay?"

What a stupid question. But he nodded anyway.

"Good." In a louder voice, she added, "Then let's kill her and get out of here." She leaped toward Golaka, sword flashing in the torchlight.

Jig slapped at his waist. That was *his* sword! Riana had stolen it.

His annoyance was nothing next to Golaka's reaction. Her eyes bulged like a lizard-fish's. Her ears flattened, and her broken fangs scraped against her upper teeth. "Pull a knife on *me*? Not in my kitchen, little elfling. You won't kill Golaka that easily."

She dodged backward and rushed for her butchering table. For all her bulk, she moved as fast as any adventurer. Grabbing a knife in each hand, she spun to face Riana. "You're too small for a meal, but I can make a mean dessert with elf liver and Sweetroot."

Dried blood and other things crusted the blades of her knives. Golaka didn't believe in cleaning her tools, claiming that the remnants of previous meals added flavor. They were still sharp enough to slice Riana into bite-size chunks, though. As a child, Jig used to come watch Golaka cook, so he knew those knives were a far cry from the discarded blades he and the others took to carry on patrol. These could fillet a dwarf in minutes, armor and all.

He didn't know what to do. For the first time, he understood Darnak's struggle when he watched Barius and Ryslind try to kill one another. Like Darnak, Jig didn't want either one of the combatants to die. He could probably grab another weapon and join the fight, but on which side? Stabbing Riana in the back didn't feel right somehow.

Even if she *had* swiped his sword. And he certainly couldn't kill Golaka. Who would run the kitchen?

Riana scurried away from a vicious combination of thrusts and swipes. Having watched the others fight, Jig realized she wasn't a much better warrior than he was.

"Hurry, Jig."

Huh? She pointed past him, at the cauldron. That almost cost her a hand as Golaka chopped at her sword wrist. But Jig understood.

Sticking out at an angle from the top of the pot, the Rod of Creation was unguarded. Jig grabbed the rod and pulled it out of the cauldron. The metal bowl on the end was heavier than he expected, but the rod itself felt like any other stick. Years of handling had smoothed and darkened the wood, turning it deep brown.

"Got it," he shouted. While Riana tried to retreat without taking a knife in the back, he traced a finger through the residue on the bowl and stuck it in his mouth. Delicious. After days of bread, cheese, and smoked meat, Jig was in heaven.

"My spoon!"

Seeing Golaka's rage, Jig changed his mind. He wasn't in heaven after all. Though if Golaka got her hands on him, she would no doubt send him there.

He ran back into the main cave, hoping Riana was behind him but not stopping to check. Not with Golaka swinging knives as if she were the goddess of cutlery. His panicked retreat took him halfway through the cavern before he noticed he was in more trouble than he thought.

"Oops." He should have expected this. He should have wondered why none of the other goblins had followed him into the kitchen. Thinking back, he had heard the tone of the cavern change from confusion and anger to pain and fear. He had simply been too busy to understand what that change meant. "Hello, Barius."

They stood at the entrance of the cavern, looking as though they had come straight out of a goblin's nightmares. Jig remembered the first time he had seen the adventurers and compared their appearance then to the worn, dirty apparitions who now blocked his escape.

Darnak's hair and beard were brown with dirt, and the tangles made him look like a walking nest for mice and other rodents. The fighting had cost him several scales from his armor, leaving bare patches of leather on his stomach, chest, and shoulder.

Prince Barius was even worse. His torn, bloodstained shirt, once immaculate, was little more than a rag. Black stubble covered his face, almost invisible under a layer of sweat-streaked dust. His boots were scuffed, his tights torn and dark with his own blood, and he favored his left leg when he moved. One of his eyes had puffed up with the beginning of a dark bruise.

The wizard showed the least wear. His robes were dirty but otherwise unscathed. His pouches were all in order, and his quiver, now almost empty of arrows, still hung at his side. Where the others looked worn and tired, Ryslind had only grown more dangerous. The emberlike glow of his eyes had intensified until they burned like angry flames, leaving Jig to wonder why the party bothered with the lantern anymore. They could send Ryslind ahead and light up entire tunnels. When Ryslind spoke, Jig could hear the overtones of Straum in his words.

"You found it."

Before Jig could answer, an enraged voice behind him called out, "No, it's mine!"

Golaka managed three steps before a wave of Ryslind's hand flattened her against the wall. Pinned like a child, she could still rail against Jig and Riana and everyone else who had conspired to steal her spoon.

"Wizard, is it? Golaka's not afraid of magic. Haven't seen a wizard yet who could cast a spell with a knife in his gullet. Soon as I get down from here, I'll give you a whipping to make you wish you died before you met me. As for you, little Jig, how funny do you think your little prank is now? You'd better hope the wizard and his friends kill you before I can get my hands on you. I'll twist those ears right off your head and feed them to you."

Darnak gave Jig a strange look that mixed weariness and sadness. "Ryslind saw you run off with the girl. He was thinking you had betrayed us. I told him, goblin or no, you wouldn't do such a thing. But perhaps I was mistaken."

Four dead goblins lay at their feet. The rest stood at a distance, weapons ready. Clearly nobody knew what to do. No, that wasn't right. Like Jig, everyone knew what they *should* do. But without someone to bully them, they simply couldn't work up the courage to do it. Nobody wanted to fling themselves onto Barius's sword or face Ryslind's magic. Who said goblins were entirely stupid?

"I didn't know for sure," Jig said quietly. In the large, silent cavern, his voice sounded tiny. Hearing Darnak's disappointment hurt more than he wanted to admit.

"It matters not." Barius sheathed his sword and stepped forward, hand outstretched. "Give me the rod, goblin."

Jig hesitated. "Will you leave once you have it?"

"Naturally," Barius said. "What more could we possibly desire from goblins?"

"Don't trust him." Riana spoke so softly that only Jig heard.

He glanced back, saw her young, thin face wrinkle with anger. *She's probably right, but what else can I do?* His gaze lowered, and he saw that the spoon had come loose. *Probably when Golaka whacked me on the head.*

Instead of a rivet to hold the spoon in place, a hammered cuff covered the last few inches of the rod. This had been pinched inward, with wire lashed around the upper part of the cuff for additional security. Placing the end on the ground, Jig stepped on the spoon and tugged the rod free.

Barius took another step. He moved like a hunter trying to close in on his prey without frightening it off. What would he do once he had the rod? Would he really depart in peace, leaving hundreds of angry goblins at his back? His honor might require him to wait until the first goblin came after him. But he would use that first attack as an excuse to kill every goblin without a second thought, since after all, the goblins would have been the ones who broke the peace.

Jig was starting to understand how this honor stuff worked. If the prince was allowed to leave in peace, his honor would force him to respect that peace. The problem was that goblins had no use for honor. Turning your back on an enemy was both an insult and an invitation for that enemy to stab you in the back. As soon as Barius appeared to retreat, the goblins would rediscover their courage and attack.

As far as he could see, there was only one way out. Jig would have to do something dumb again.

"Wait," Jig said. Barius hesitated. Speaking Goblin as fast as he could, Jig shouted, "Why are you all wasting your time with these so-called adventurers? They're nothing!"

All around him, goblins protested. Some pointed to Golaka as evidence of the intruders' powerful magic. Others shouted about how the dwarf had slain two goblins before they could even draw weapons. How could Jig say they were nothing? They had come into the lair and killed half a dozen without any apparent effort.

Jig waved the rod in the air and tried to be heard. "I've traveled with this lot for days, and I say they're nothing. Their leader is a frightened child, the dwarf a spineless lackey. The wizard is mindless."

The last point was true, if misleading.

The goblins were still talking. They hadn't made up their minds yet. They hadn't attacked, either, which was good, but Jig knew he still hadn't convinced them. What else could he say?

Barius's hand rested on his sword. He studied Jig, as if trying to determine what the goblin was up to. "What are you telling them?"

"I'm trying to convince them you're too strong," Jig answered, straight-faced. "I'm telling them of all your battles."

That was it. Jig turned back to the goblins. "They cowered in fear at the sight of a mere carrion-worm. They tumbled into the hobgoblins' most obvious traps. When they stood helplessly in the lower tunnels, who do you think was forced to save their worthless lives?"

"Who?" called a handful of goblins, starting to get caught up in Jig's taunts.

"Me," he yelled. "A goblin rescued the brave adventurers."

Sensing Barius's glare, Jig spun around.

"Why do they laugh?"

Jig shrugged. "I told them how you outwitted the hobgoblins. Give me a few more minutes. They're almost convinced."

He continued in Goblin. "Look at them! They dress like beggars, they smell worse than hobgoblin piss, and they eat food even a dog would ignore. That's all your so-called adventurers are, dogs running around in the darkness, searching for bones."

Raising the rod, he said, "I'll prove it. Watch them fetch."

Hard as he could, he hurled the rod over Barius's head and past the others. It whirled end over end through the cavern and into the tunnel beyond to clatter against the rock.

The laughter grew as Barius raced after it, followed closely by Darnak and Ryslind. Jig grinned at the jibes and jeers, for once aimed at someone other than him. It felt good.

"I'll kill them myself," Jig said as he hurried toward the tunnel. He took his sword back from Riana and waved it overhead. Trying to make his voice sound commanding, he said, "Wait here for my return. We'll have a feast tonight."

That reminded him of Golaka. Ryslind's spell had faded, and even as Jig watched, the huge chef slipped free from the magic's grip and fell to the ground.

Jig grabbed Riana's wrist. "Time to go," he said. Hopefully the goblins wouldn't follow, and he doubted Barius would bother to return now that he had the rod. Not for a few worthless goblins, at least.

So why am I going toward *him?* The answer came almost immediately. *Because I'm an idiot.*

Jig collided with Darnak. The impact bought a huff of breath from the dwarf, and sent Jig crashing into the wall.

"I think I convinced them to let us go," Jig said once he had recovered.

"Did you, now?" Darnak's thick brows lifted. "You know, it happens that I speak a smattering of Goblin myself. I couldn't make out everything, but I picked up a few words here and there."

Jig swallowed, but his mouth had gone dry. He had forgotten that detail.

"Spineless lackey, was it?" His fingers drummed the shaft of his club. "One of these days, I'll repay you for that. We dwarves hold a grudge for a long time, you know."

Fortunately, the two humans hadn't heard any of it. Barius stood to one side, clasping the rod to his chest as if it were a long-lost lover, while Ryslind caressed it with his eyes. It was a little disturbing to watch, truth be told. Jig cleared his throat.

"You have the rod. Shouldn't you be on your way? Back to the castle and the king and all that?" *Please,* he added silently.

Barius nodded slowly, but before he could speak, Ryslind's voice cracked like thunder. "No! We must free Straum from his prison."

"You dare to give me commands, brother?" Barius asked softly.

Jig pressed his back to the wall. He had hoped they would simply leave, but if they decided to kill one another, that would work too.

Sadly, things weren't going to be that simple. Ryslind's eyes flashed, but when he spoke again, he sounded calm and reasonable. "Think of the reward, brother. Five thousand years of gold and plunder. Straum will have no need of such things once he is free. You could have your pick of his hoard. Enough wealth to buy a kingdom of your own."

Barius's lips twitched into an involuntary grin as Ryslind went on. By the end, he was practically drooling. "A good point, brother. But why not use the rod to create whatever treasure I need?"

"The rod can only affect what already exists. Rock can be shifted, animals changed to other forms. You could turn a gold crown into a pile of coins, but you couldn't make a diamond out of nothing." Ryslind clasped his hands together. "Imagine our brothers' reactions when you return with wealth enough to make them look like paupers on the street."

"We did make a bargain with Straum," Barius said thoughtfully. "For the sake of our family's honor, we should fulfill that agreement and set him free."

Jig and Riana exchanged tired glances. She looked ready to strangle Barius, and Jig wanted to sit down and cry. Home was only a hundred feet away. He was so close. If only they had left, he could have returned to the cavern and joined the others for evening meal. He imagined the laughter as he told them all how he had driven the half-witted adventurers out of goblin territory. Would he ever be able to go home?

An angry shout echoed down the tunnel. "I'll have your head on my cutting board, you runt," Golaka yelled.

Jig hopped to his feet. "Right. Let's go free Straum then."

Ryslind led them back to the lake, walking like a man in a trance. Several times he had asked to carry the rod. "As a wizard, I know more of its powers than anyone."

Barius had refused, insisting that this was *his* quest, and he would not let the rod out of his hands until he was back at the palace. For once Jig agreed completely. Bad as Barius was, the idea of Ryslind carrying that kind of power was even worse.

But Barius had his own reasons. Jig had to strain his ears to hear the prince's whispered conversation with Darnak.

"He is not my brother," Barius was saying. "Straum controls him."

"If Straum truly controlled him, we'd all be dead, and he'd be taking the rod down himself. He's still struggling, though there's little enough he can do against the dragon. He surrendered to Straum's control all by himself. It was his own greed that did him in." In an angrier tone, Darnak went on. "It's greed that will be your end, too. You don't want to be turning a dragon loose on the country-side, lad, no matter how much treasure you carry away as a reward. You're too young to remember, but I was around the last time one of those beasts came around this way. That was a small one, and he gutted half the kingdom."

"I do not plan to release him," Barius said. "The dragon enslaved my brother, Darnak. Any deal they made is worthless. I will not let this go unavenged."

"You'll be the death of me yet." Darnak stopped for a moment to check his map. "Take the left tunnel up ahead," he said in a normal voice. Handing the lantern to Barius, he grabbed for his wineskin.

"So you're planning to use the rod, I take it?"

Jig thought he heard approval in the dwarf's question.

Barius nodded. "Dragons came from the Rod of Creation, all those years ago. Is it not fitting that the same rod be used to end Straum's existence?"

"Fitting, aye." Darnak took another drink. "I just hope you're not trying to mine more than you can haul. Dragons are a tricky lot, and a dragon with magic at his command is doubly dangerous."

"He must pay," he snapped. "You told me once that Earthmaker requires his followers to avenge themselves upon their enemies."

"Not precisely." Darnak picked his next words carefully. "Earthmaker teaches us to maintain balance and justice. In a case like this, where your brother went off in search of his own doom, I'd be hard pressed to lay the blame entirely at Straum's feet."

"My brother was a greedy, shortsighted fool." Jig shook his head at the blind irony as Barius continued. "But Straum will still pay for what he did."

Ryslind led them to the shore of the lake, where he killed several lizard-fish with bolts of fire. "Perhaps you will change your mind, brother? As a mage, I can use the rod far more easily than you, and its power will make our path easier."

Barius tightened his fingers until the knuckles went white. "I think not. Tell me what I must do to use it."

Ryslind absently sent another lizard-fish to a crispy, smoldering death, and said, "The user must impose his will on that of the rod. You must imagine precisely what you want, in perfect detail. If the rod works like most magical artifacts, you will feel a strong tug. The rod will seem to pull you forward as it tries to draw power from you. You must resist. Brace yourself and force the rod to draw on its own stored energy. Do not lose control, no matter how much it pains you."

"Very well." Barius stepped closer to the shore and raised the rod. "Be sure these creatures do not endanger me while I work."

Darnak and Ryslind took positions on either side, guarding him from the lizard-fish.

"I suggest a tunnel," Ryslind said. "The lake bed is obsidian. Envision the tunnel as a long bubble rising from that stone. Be certain it is waterproof, and large enough for us to move about."

Jig stood behind the prince and watched as he pointed the end of the rod at the ground. It was hard to split his concentration between the lizard-fish and Barius, but he wanted to see the rod work. They had all nearly died many times over to find this stick, after all. At last Jig would see Ellnorein's legendary artifact in action.

Compared to the other things he had seen in the past week, the rod was spectacularly boring. There was no burst of light, no sparks or smoke, nothing but a slight humming sound that any tone-deaf child could have duplicated.

"Be careful," Ryslind said. "Work slowly."

A tiny bulge appeared in the rock by the shore. As Jig watched, it grew taller and wider. A dark hole formed at the center.

"Jig," Riana snapped.

He glanced down to see a lizard-fish climbing over the toe of his boot. With a squawk of alarm, Jig kicked it back into the water. A few more steps, and it could have killed him. From then on he ignored the growing tunnel and worked on staying alive and poison-free.

The humming of the rod grew painfully shrill, then cut off. The instant the noise stopped, Barius gasped and clutched his head. "What did it do to me?"

Ryslind gazed into the newly formed tunnel. He

tapped the stone, as if to insure its solidity. "I suspect your tunnel intersected the magic that held the whirlpool in place. The backlash will leave you with quite a headache for the next day or so."

"You should have warned me."

Ryslind smiled, a picture of innocence. "Magic comes with a cost, dear prince." Before Barius could answer, he ducked his head and entered the tunnel, vanishing in the darkness.

The tunnel was barely taller than Jig, and he hunched over as he walked. The walls and ceiling were damp and cool, but they didn't appear to leak. The cold air was eerily still, and their footsteps echoed down the tunnel. He almost refused to follow. The tunnel walls were only a few inches thick, and Jig didn't see how that could be strong enough to support the weight of an entire lake.

That was another facet of the rod's magic, of course. Those stone walls were probably stronger than the rest of the mountain. Still, Jig expected the tunnel to collapse at any second. He wondered if the water and rock would crush him before he drowned.

They reached the end. A perfectly round hole two feet across opened into blackness. The sides were smooth and damp. Darnak passed the lantern up to Ryslind, who slanted a beam of light into the room below.

The Necromancer's throne room was the same as when they had left, empty and foreboding. The corpses were gone. Darnak had insisted on disposing of them when they came back from Straum's lair, saying it was disrespectful to leave bodies sprawled about like that. They had spent several hours dragging the corpses to what Jig had dubbed the "Pit of Big Bats" and tossing them over the edge. How that was more respectful than leaving the bodies to decay, Jig hadn't bothered to ask.

"Perhaps a ladder?" Ryslind suggested.

Barius frowned, but didn't argue. He pointed the rod at the hole, and a bit of stone dripped into the room to form a thin ladder. From the lines on his forehead and by his eyes, Jig guessed he was concentrating harder this time. Sweat dripped down his face by the time he finished.

"Excellent." Ryslind lowered himself into the room. Once the others had joined him, he said, "I suggest you do the same thing with the Necromancer's little trapdoor. Or do you require time to rest, to regain your strength?"

Even Jig could see the way Ryslind baited his brother, pushing him to admit that the magic was too strong for him. Every word the wizard spoke positively oozed compassion, as if it were all he could do to watch Barius shoulder this heavy burden by himself.

"We shall proceed," Barius said through gritted teeth. Again he used the rod, this time melting the throne itself into a ladder. Before he could finish, he cried out and fell. His hands pressed against his temples.

"Such pain," Ryslind muttered sorrowfully. "You must have triggered another backlash when your ladder pierced Straum's illusionary sky. A pity, for in most cases the rod's magic is easy to control. Only when it collides with other art does it cause this kind of anguish, and then only to the unskilled."

As Barius used the rod like a cane to push himself back up, Jig found that he actually felt *sorry* for the prince. Then he remembered being led around at the end of a rope, punched in the face, and threatened time and again for the past week. His sympathy faded.

Barius managed to finish the ladder without further problems. The rungs were a bit slippery, having taken on the glassy polish of the throne, but nobody fell off.

At the bottom, another of Straum's dragonchildren waited for them. "You have the rod," it said. This one was smaller and darker than the first. Female, Jig guessed. Or perhaps it was simply younger.

Barius drew himself up and forced the fatigue from his face. "I do."

He saw Darnak glance worriedly at their escort, and he could guess what the dwarf was thinking. Barius might, with luck and a great deal of help from the gods, be able to use the rod against Straum. But did the prince's plan include a way to deal with Straum's children? A lot of good it would do to kill the dragon if the dragonchild tore them apart a second later.

They couldn't retreat. The creature probably had orders to stop them if they tried. The only thing to do was march onward, through the gardens and into the cave, and hope Barius knew what he was doing.

When they arrived, they found that Straum had emerged from his lake. His body stretched across much of the cave, and rows of enormous wet footprints suggested that he had been pacing. His head perked up as Ryslind entered.

"You have it," Straum breathed. When he saw what Barius carried, he threw back his head and roared so loudly Jig thought his head would crack. The terrible sound went on and on, and when it stopped, the echoes continued inside his skull.

"I think he's happy to see us," Darnak said dryly.

Strong clawed hands nudged Jig into the room. He glanced back, wondering if Straum suspected something. Dragons were supposed to be the most dangerous creatures in the world, undisputed masters of trickery. When he thought about it, how could Straum *not* suspect something? With freedom so close, he wouldn't risk anything going wrong. Barius's plan would get them all killed.

Jig started to inch closer to Darnak. Maybe he would know what to do. Before he got close enough to speak, Ryslind walked up to the dragon's side.

"We have it, master," he said. "It was a close thing." His thin finger pointed at Jig. "The goblin attempted to betray us and take the rod for himself."

Jig froze. Maybe his ears were still recovering from Straum's roar and he had misheard. "I gave the rod to you," he said meekly.

Ryslind smiled, a cold expression of triumph. The slitted glow of his eyes seemed to burn into Jig's chest. As he had done once before, Ryslind spoke directly into Jig's mind.

I warned you that you would pay for humiliating me, goblin. Jig suddenly understood. Whatever Straum had done to the wizard's mind, enough of Ryslind remained to want revenge. He hadn't forgotten his promise to punish Jig. He had simply waited for the best time to exact that punishment.

"It wasn't like that, exactly," Darnak protested.

"Silence," Barius hissed.

Jig glanced over. Barius had begun to edge away from his guard. He glanced at Darnak, who tilted his head slightly. They planned to use Jig's execution as a distraction. A good plan, Jig admitted. The only flaw involved the minor detail of Jig's painful death.

"Did he?" Straum asked. His neck twisted around until he stared down at Jig. "I've always thought goblins to be cowardly, stupid creatures. Betraying me took more boldness than I'd have expected from you. For a goblin, you're quite the brave fellow."

Jig didn't breathe. He couldn't look away from those huge, gold eyes. He could see himself reflected in the slitted pupils, his body distorted on the curved surface. He watched the mirror-Jig raise his hands, as if to explain. He saw the wide-eyed expression of fear, the frantic trembling in his jaw.

He never saw Straum's tail rush through the air to smash into Jig from the side.

The last thing Jig heard as his body crashed into a wall was Straum's amused voice saying, "Pity, really. Had you been as cowardly as the rest of your race, you might have survived."

CHAPTER 17

～❖～

In the Blink of an Eye

"You lasted longer than I thought you would, I'll grant you that much."

Jig opened an eye, closed it again. He peeked out through the other one, just to be certain. Nothing had changed in the interim.

"This isn't Straum's cave."

"You can do better than that, Jig. If you were really this thick, I can think of seven times in the past week alone when you would have died. Use your brain. Figure out where you are."

Jig scowled. He knew who he was talking to, if nothing else. Somehow, Tymalous Shadowstar sounded less impressive when his words weren't reverberating inside Jig's skull. As for *where* he was . . . he sat up and took a good look around.

He noticed the sky first. Straum's illusionary sky was nothing compared to this. There must have been hundreds of stars here. Thousands, even. He didn't try to count, since his vision would make the task impossible.

Except that it didn't. Instead of round blurs of

light, each star was a clear pinpoint. He could even
make out individual colors. Some sparkled with a
blue tinge, others appeared yellow, and several
flashed red as he watched. *He could see!*

He stared at his hands. For the first time, he
could hold them at arm's length and still see the
layer of grime beneath his nails. Everything had
come into focus. This was wonderful! He looked
back into the sky, noticing one star that stood out
from the others. It was a large red star, which appeared to be a half-inch wide and shone brighter
than the rest. In fact, that star provided the only
illumination. The red light gave everything an
angry, flamelike tinge. His own skin had turned
purplish.

What had Darnak told him? Shadowstar was the
God of the Autumn Star, so the Autumn Star was
probably that big red one. He lowered his gaze to
survey the more immediate surroundings. Whatever this place was, it needed to be torn apart and
rebuilt from scratch. Crumbled walls traced a
roughly rectangular outline. Scorch marks blackened parts of the walls and the floor. The floor
itself was mostly dirt and clumps of yellowed grass,
and only the occasional ceramic fragment gave any
hint of what must have once been an impressive
temple.

There was no smell. Even the stink of sweat and
blood that had followed him for days was missing.
Jig glanced down at himself.

His boots and loincloth were the same as before,
only brighter, lacking any trace of grime. He didn't
even try to remember when he had last washed
the loincloth.

His body appeared whole. He couldn't remember
what had happened right before he came here, but

he had expected to find himself torn in two, or at least bent at a sharp angle. Instead, he was healthy as ever.

He tested his fingers, flexing each one individually to make sure the bones still worked. He checked the wrists and elbows next. *So far, so good.* As he pulled off his boots to check his toes, it occurred to him that he was stalling. Jig didn't really want to admit he was sitting here with a god. He might have grown used to the day-to-day oddities of traveling with adventurers, but this went beyond strange.

He cast a furtive glance at Shadowstar.

"You're not dead, so don't bore me by asking. Everyone always asks me that. Right after the 'Where am I?' bit. You'd think they could at least come up with something more original."

Jig straightened, confused, and so got his first clear view of Tymalous Shadowstar. His first impression was not a flattering one. *I thought gods were supposed to be . . . taller.*

"Not this god," Shadowstar said. "Big gods make better targets."

Jig absolutely refused to think about what it would take to threaten a god. Another god, presumably, but he didn't want to imagine fighting of that magnitude. Quarreling among the adventurers was more than enough for Jig. Instead, he took a closer look at Shadowstar.

He stood only a few inches taller than Jig. He could have passed for a short, skinny human, about thirty years of age. Assuming nobody looked him in the eyes, that was. The skin around the sockets appeared normal, but they contained a blackness as deep as the night sky. Red starbursts shone from the center, reminding Jig a little of Ryslind. But unlike the wizard, Shadowstar's eyes held no malice. As Jig stared, he felt as though he were falling into the sky itself, and his stomach gurgled in protest.

Jig forced himself to look away before he lost himself completely. As he took in the rest of the god's appearance, he deliberately avoided that face.

Shadowstar wore loose-fitting clothes of black silk. Strips of tiny silver bells ran down the outside of his pants and sleeves. The shirt was open at the chest, revealing a smooth, lean body. His skin wasn't quite white, but it was pastier than that of any other being Jig had seen. His silver hair flowed to waist-level, but the hairline appeared to have receded a bit over the years. A balding god? Even gods grew old, he supposed. At least Shadowstar hadn't acquired the swollen gut carried by most older goblins.

"Why am I here?"

Shadowstar grunted. "Another obvious question, but not quite as trite as it could have been." He chuckled. "Worship is a two-way deal. I'll help you out a bit, but it means I get first dibs on your soul when you and your body part ways. After the pounding you took from Straum, you came here."

"But you said I wasn't dead yet."

He ignored Jig's question. "Rule number one when dealing with dragons," he said, extending one gloved finger. "Never look them in the eye. It's distracting, to say the least. But seeing as how goblins don't usually go in for dragonslaying, I understand why you hadn't learned the rules.

"Unfortunately for you, ignorance makes a poor shield. At this moment, your body is upside down against the wall of Straum's lair. Your back snapped in two places when you hit, your ribs are gravel, and you're paralyzed from about here down." Shadowstar tapped his hand at the middle of his chest. "You also bruised your brain, which wouldn't make a difference to the average goblin, but you've shown yourself to be far from average, my friend.

"When faced with a choice between living in excruciating pain, albeit only from the nipples up, or getting a head start on death and avoiding that last bit of nastiness, you opted for the latter. This left your body in a coma and your mind and soul here with me."

"Oh." Jig's shoulders slumped. "What if Darnak heals me?" The dwarf had done it before. Maybe there was a chance Jig could still survive.

Not that this place was so terrible. At least he was safe. He had never thought much about an afterlife. Goblins believed that once you died, your body went to the carrion-worms, and that was the end of it. He didn't care what happened to him after he died, because he had never expected to see any of it. Goblins died, and then other goblins came along to steal their belongings and toss the body into the tunnels. He never imagined spending time with a forgotten god in the midst of a rundown temple.

Still, while Shadowstar might be good company, Jig wasn't ready to make this place a permanent home. Nor did he like the fact that Ryslind had beaten him. In a strange way, he had been having fun. Not that he enjoyed always hearing Death's footsteps follow him around, and he would have chosen different company if he could, and those dead warriors had been a bit much. But skipping between Death's fingers time after time gave him a strange, bubbling thrill in the middle of his chest. He had learned things, too. Things that could help the goblins hold their own against the other races. Or they would have, had he lived long enough to pass them on.

When Jig spoke, it was in a soft voice, full of wonder. "I want to go back."

He looked hopefully at Shadowstar, but the god was shaking his head. "You can't. Rather, you're already there. You've just taken a step sideways from reality, that's all. But I'm afraid Darnak can't help you. Things are about to get messy, and nobody is going to worry about a goblin they believe to be a corpse."

His starburst pupils bored into Jig's eyes. He was waiting for something. Jig didn't understand what Shadowstar expected him to do. That Darnak couldn't help him was hard to accept. Goblins, by nature, did not ask for help. To ask for help was to make yourself vulnerable. The closest word for "trust" in the goblin tongue was a word that meant either "gullible" or "dumb as dung," depending on context. So for Jig to admit he needed help was hard enough, even if Darnak would never know. To learn that Darnak couldn't help was worse, because Jig *knew* he would have tried to heal Jig's wounds if he could.

That was simply who Darnak was. He might not like Jig, but he would obey the rules of Silas Earthmaker. He would obey because he wanted to, not because he had to. If nothing else, Darnak was loyal. Loyal to the princes and their father the king, loyal to his god, and loyal to his fellow adventurers.

Jig grinned at that. He had thought of himself as an adventurer. At least he hadn't gotten tangled up with traditional hero traits like loyalty or nobility. Too much of that and he'd turn into another Barius.

His smile faded. He was still thinking like he was

going to survive, and Shadowstar had made it pretty clear that wasn't the case. Though if he was slated to die, why did Shadowstar watch him with that patient expression? Why all of the games, if he was truly stuck here?

"You want me to live, don't you?" Jig asked. Shadowstar shrugged noncommittally, jingling the bells along his sleeves. But his eyes literally twinkled, and Jig knew he was right. Darnak couldn't help him, because he didn't know Jig needed help. But Jig was a goblin, and if a goblin wanted help, he had better help himself, 'cause nobody else was likely to do it.

"Silas Earthmaker gives Darnak magic to heal people. Can you do that for me?"

"Maybe," Shadowstar said, drawing the word into a long drawl. "I've helped my followers before, back in the days when I had any. As I mentioned, worship is a two-way thing. You haven't yet committed to me."

Before Jig could argue, he held up a hand and said, "You picked out a god who would help you because he had nothing better to do. Darnak wouldn't even have remembered my name if I hadn't jogged his mind a bit. You wanted someone you could use, correct?"

Jig nodded. No use lying to a god, he figured. Still, it hadn't sounded quite so calculated when he first decided to follow Shadowstar.

"If I help you this time, there are things you'll need to do for me. Rules to follow, like Darnak does for Silas Earthmaker. Can you do this?"

"Sure."

Apparently Jig answered too quickly. Shadowstar smiled. "Remember, you come to me when you die. Betray me, and we'll have a very long chat once you get here."

Jig had heard many threats over the past few
days, but Shadowstar's cheerful warning made
them sound like the work of clumsy amateurs. In
a small voice, Jig said, "I can still lie to other people though, right? Telling the truth is a good way
to get killed."

Shadowstar laughed. "Fair enough. Now, let us
discuss the terms of our partnership."

Partnership. Awestruck, Jig watched as Tymalous
Shadowstar walked toward him. *Him,* Jig the goblin. The runt who hid in corners and cringed when
it came time to choose guards for patrol duty. This
goblin was about to partner up with a god.

What *had* the universe come to?

Smudge jumped in shock when Jig turned his
head. He had been peering into Jig's mouth, presumably seeking signs of life.

A good thing the spider had moved, because Jig
bit his lip so hard he expected the fangs to pierce
his cheeks. Shadowstar hadn't warned him how
much this would *hurt!* As he surveyed the damage,
he couldn't believe this was his body. This body
had too many joints in the legs, and the chest was
bumpier than it should have been. He didn't know
how his skeleton worked, but he knew he shouldn't
bend this way. To make matters worse, he was upside down, propped against the wall like a discarded doll. And why couldn't he feel anything
from the chest down?

I told you, you're paralyzed.

Right. That was probably a blessing, all things
considered. He had enough pain in the parts he
could feel. Even moving his head made him want
to vomit. Flopping onto his side was torture, and
he had to lay there for over a minute before he
could move again. His vision was worse than usual,

too. Outlines wavered and shifted, and he thought he saw two dragons arguing with two Bariuses. That couldn't be right. Unless he had angered Shadowstar somehow and this was his punishment.

Relax. That's the bump to your brain, remember? You're going to feel a bit strange, even when we start to heal you. Especially when we start to heal you. I can give you the magic, but you have to use it. We'll begin as soon as you're ready.

Jig tried to relax. The tips of his fingers grew warm, as if he had dipped them into a bucket of water. Was this magic? He could feel the sensation move through his wrists and into his arms. He pulled back involuntarily when it reached his neck. This was too much like drowning.

Trust me.

Back to trust again. Was Jig gullible, or simply dumb as dung? Probably a bit of both, but he didn't have much of a choice. Shadowstar wouldn't help him out only to drown him. He tried to relax, but he couldn't get enough air. His chest felt tight, and he breathed faster, struggling to inhale. Why couldn't he breathe? He heard himself panting like an animal, but the sound was growing distant. He was dying again.

You're hyperventilating. Stop it. Think about . . . whatever it is goblins do to relax. Killing and eating, or something like that.

Jig tried to concentrate on what was happening on the other side of Straum's lair. He forced himself to inhale and hold it for a few seconds, breaking up the frantic rhythm of his breathing. He exhaled slowly, turned his head, and tried to put Shadowstar out of his mind.

Very little time had passed since Straum flung Jig into the wall. His conversation with the god must not have taken as long as he thought. Barius and the others still stood in front of the dragon, apparently stunned by the attack on Jig.

Jig twitched an ear, which didn't hurt as badly as the rest of him, and tried to listen.

"You shouldn't have gone and killed him, not after he found your precious rod." That was Darnak. His protests were feeble, though. Did he expect an apology from the dragon?

"There are things you have to learn if you're going to live to see your five-thousandth birthday. One of the first is that when someone betrays you, you kill him. Preferably in a way that teaches a lesson to his friends."

That was a warning, to make sure the rest of the group cooperated. Jig wondered if Barius had noticed it. Not that he would change his plans if he had. In his own way, Barius was as loyal as Darnak. He might hate his brother, but he would still die for the chance to avenge Ryslind's destruction.

Jig had no problem with Barius dying. Indeed, he would have been far happier if Straum had chosen to break Barius against the wall instead of him. Barius could die happy and alone, knowing his had been an honorable end, while the rest of them crept quietly out of the lair and back to somewhere safe.

Instead he expected Barius to get them all killed when he tried to attack Straum. Unless he managed to win. Was it possible? He was a prince and an experienced adventurer. He had the Rod of Creation.

But Straum was an experienced dragon, and he had really big claws and a tail, as well as one of his children to guard him. Not to mention Ryslind himself, standing over there with those glowing eyes and all of Straum's magic at his command. At one time those eyes had frightened Jig. After seeing Shadowstar, he found them an annoyance, no more. He wanted to run over and pull tiny curtains over Ryslind's face.

"The rock overhead is almost a quarter of a mile thick." Straum's wings flapped in a quick, small movement. A nervous twitch? The sound reminded Jig of rugs being shaken clean.

"I'll need enough room to flap my wings. At least thirty paces wide. Once I'm free, you may help yourselves to anything you like from these walls." He shifted his weight from one pair of legs to the other. "Begin."

Are you ready?

"Yes." The voice in his head had startled him into answering aloud. Luckily everyone's eyes were on Barius. Nobody noticed the discarded goblin in the corner.

I feel bloated, Jig complained. The magic had filled his body while he watched the others. *All stuffed up and constipated.*

Please stop. Shadowstar sounded disgusted. *You'll get used to it. For now, what you want to do is place your hands over the worst injury. That would be the place where your spine takes a right-angle turn, right below the sternum.*

I know, Jig thought, annoyed. He touched the part of his chest that bulged worst. As long as he didn't think of it as a part of his body, he could keep from throwing up.

You'll have to push the bones down as the magic works.

Gross. Why does healing have to be so disgusting?

Why do goblins have to be so fragile? Next time you'll know better than to stand in the way of a dragon's tail. Now when you press down, imagine the magic inside of you flowing through your hands and into the spine. You need to visualize the flow.

The only thing flowing out of Jig's hands was

sweat. So he used that. He imagined the magic
seeping through his sweat and oozing into his chest.

Strange, but it'll do, was Shadowstar's reaction.

Overhead, illuminated by the blue glow of the
walls, a circular hole began to recede into the ceiling while the displaced stone formed a ring along
the outside. Barius clutched the rod in both hands.
His entire body had gone rigid with concentration.
Everyone watched as the hole began to grow.

That was good, because it meant they still hadn't
noticed Jig's struggle to put his bones back into
place. The pain really wasn't too bad. True, Jig had
never *felt* anything this excruciating, but he was
sure there had to be something that could hurt
more. He simply couldn't imagine what it might be.

Worse than the pain was the grinding sensation
in his chest, like rocks scraping against one another.
Sometimes he had to push with all of his strength,
and then something would pop into place, and he
felt a surge of magic seep through his skin to bind
the bones together again. "Next time I'm going to
stay dead."

*Next time, you should try to duck. You think it's
easy for me, trying to find all those bits of rib and
put them back together?*

Jig scowled and pushed another chunk of back-
bone into place. His toes had begun to tingle, which
he took to be a good sign. He could even wiggle
his feet again.

A heady rush of power distracted him from the
pain. He was fixing himself! The same as Darnak
had done. Jig the goblin was doing magic.

Concentrate, fang-face.

Jig snorted indignantly. But he paid more attention to the magic. Most of the bones were back in
place, though he could still feel things shifting and
moving inside his body. A bizarre sensation, really.

He wondered if this was anything like being pregnant. Goblin women generally gave birth to anywhere from two to five babies at a time. And Jig could feel at least three distinct places where his guts were rearranging themselves.

True, but pregnancy lasts eight months for you goblins. And you don't have to squeeze the kids out of your—

"I'm trying to concentrate," Jig interrupted quickly.

At the center of the room, Barius had deepened the hole. Darkness hid the inside, so Jig couldn't tell how high it extended. Presumably he would know when Barius broke through to the surface. Jig expected a dramatic beam of sunlight if nothing else. So far there was nothing but blackness.

Straum peered into the growing hole, his tail shivering with excitement. "Yes," he growled. "So close. To fly through real clouds again, to hunt real food. Faster, human."

Barius's attack came in silence. A huge spike of rock shot down from the black tunnel. He had used the rod to shape an enormous spear, one that he could release to impale Straum's skull. The interior of the hole was dark, and Straum shouldn't have seen the spear coming in time to protect himself.

Jig's eyes had reverted to their nearsighted state when he left Shadowstar's temple, so he saw nothing but a black streak heading toward the dragon's enormous skull. Halfway there, it broke into a cloud of dust and gravel. He twisted his face away as pebbles showered his body.

Barius lay on his back, clutching his head while his face twisted with pain. Ryslind bent down and plucked the rod from his brother's hands.

"You know, brother, if you had done as you were asked, we might have allowed you to live."

Ryslind cradled the rod like an infant. "Naturally we both expected you to betray us. You never were the smart one, were you?"

"Keep the bloody rod," Darnak said. His hair and beard had turned gray from the dust. "You've got your freedom. Let me take his highness home, and we'll not be bothering you again."

"Ah, Darnak. Do you really think it's so simple? My brother would insist on hunting us down. You know it as well as I. He couldn't live with this humiliation and defeat. We'd have to kill him sooner or later. Isn't it more efficient to finish him now and be done with it?"

Straum hadn't yet spoken. He seemed content to let Ryslind do the talking. Or maybe he was speaking *through* Ryslind, Jig wasn't sure.

Jig pressed against the wall and pushed himself to his feet. His legs felt like water, and he didn't know if he'd fall down as soon as he took a step, but this was a far cry better than he had been a few minutes ago. Even as he waited to see Straum's legendary temper reduce Barius to ash, a part of Jig's mind couldn't let go of his awe at the magic he had used to heal himself.

"A pity the rod can't be used to slay you outright," Ryslind said. "One of its few weaknesses. Though I suppose I could transform you into one of Straum's children. That might be a fitting end, to serve the one you tried to murder. Not forever, of course. Only for a few centuries. Or less, if you found the strength to rebel against him. You saw what happens to those who try."

Jig looked past them, toward the exit. If they focused on Ryslind, he could probably sneak past without being noticed. Even Straum's dragonchild appeared distracted by Ryslind's last comment.

After escaping from Straum's lair, it would be a

simple march through the tunnels, across the forest, and back up to his own home. Assuming his legs lasted more than two steps, he'd still have to face ogres, hobgoblins, and who knew what manner of creatures, but what did that matter? He had survived all of these things before.

He managed one shaky step before someone spotted him. Riana wasn't as enthralled by Ryslind's cat-and-mouse game as the rest. Her eyes constantly scanned the cave, probably waiting for the best moment to flee, just as Jig was. She jumped when she saw Jig alive and moving.

So much for that. Jig waited for her to cry out. The smartest thing would be for her to use Jig as a distraction to cover her own escape. He sighed. At least *someone* would make it out of here. She'd probably have a better chance at making it through the forest anyway.

The expected shout never came. Instead she watched the others to make sure they hadn't noticed, then began to nod at him.

Not at you, *dummy,* came the weary voice of Tymalous Shadowstar.

Jig looked over his shoulder. Nothing there but shelves bearing Straum's assorted junk. Some nice belt buckles, folded tabards in various stages of decay . . . oh. Jig stared at her. She couldn't mean for him to. . . .

But she nodded harder, both at Jig's comprehension and at the row of javelins lined up behind him.

Was she forgetting that Jig was a goblin? A half-blind one at that. He had never thrown a spear or javelin in his life.

Had he been a true adventurer, things might have been different. He could have leaped up, shouted a defiant battle cry, seized a javelin— probably that silver-tipped one with the finlike

flanges—and hurled it at Straum with all his might.
A true adventurer might even have wounded the
dragon, assuming he managed to pierce those scales.

But Jig was a goblin, and goblins had a different
approach to big, dangerous monsters. They ran
away. If they were fortunate, someone else would
take care of the heroism. That would either finish
off the monster, or at least create enough of a commotion for the goblin to escape unscathed.

Wait a minute. Jig gave himself a mental shake.
*The one thing adventurers and goblins share is their
ability to get into deeper trouble. Forget about what
goblins would do. Forget about what an adventurer
would do. I need to figure out what Jig should do.*

Running away still sounded appealing. If he succeeded, that would mean leaving the others behind
to die. Jig thought about each one, trying to decide
if he could live with that.

*Ryslind: Insane. Threatened to kill Jig numerous
times. Responsible for Straum snapping Jig's spine.*
Okay, he could stay here to die or live as Straum's
puppet. No problems there.

*Barius: Ultimately responsible for dragging Jig
into this whole mess. General twit, to boot. He
would probably kill Jig sooner or later on general
principles.* He was another one the world could
do without.

*Darnak: Decent fellow. Healed Jig's wounds. Still,
he hadn't stopped either of the humans from trying
to kill Jig. He had refused to kill Riana after she
triggered the Necromancer's trap, but he hadn't tried
to stop Barius from doing so. In the end, he was
still the prince's man.* Jig felt a twinge of guilt about
Darnak. But, Darnak hadn't put his neck on the
line when Ryslind betrayed Jig, so why should Jig
risk himself for Darnak?

Riana: Dragged into this mess against her will, the

same as Jig. Offered him the chance to escape, back in the beginning. He frowned. The others could stay here and die, but his conscience nagged him when he thought about leaving Riana behind. Sure, she hadn't been terribly nice to him all the time, but she had at least begun to treat him like an equal. Besides, Jig owed her something for that finger.

Still, she was one elf. Was she really worth risking his life for?

Shadowstar's voice whispered to him. *I expect better from you.*

"A lot of good it will do if I'm dead," Jig muttered. He glanced around. Ryslind was still toying with Barius. Darnak had turned his pleas from Ryslind to the dragon, who eyed the dwarf much as a tunnel cat might contemplate a plump mouse. Riana stood with her hands on her hips, watching Jig impatiently.

"Oh, hell." He pushed himself up and grabbed the javelin. *If you want me to try this noble stuff, you'd better help me out.* The god didn't answer. Jig shrugged. If this didn't work, he would have ample opportunity to complain in just a few minutes.

As he pulled back to throw, his movement attracted Ryslind's attention. The wizard opened his mouth to shout a warning. He needn't have bothered. His link to Straum carried the message faster than words.

Jig thought he could feel another hand over his own as he threw, one which guided his aim down and to the left. The javelin became a silver line, tracing a path from his hand to Straum's enormous eye.

Straum blinked.

The point hit the scaled eyelid and lodged there, quivering, as Straum snarled in fury.

Ryslind pointed at Jig and clenched a fist. Invisible fingers clamped around Jig's body, so tight he couldn't breathe.

"Wait." Straum's voice held no trace of pain, even with a javelin pinning his eye closed. "Hold him. I want to see this brave goblin who somehow survived my attack. I want to see how long his courage lasts." To the motionless dragonchild, he said, "Help me."

The dragonchild walked slowly to Straum's injured side, pausing only once when she passed the stained patch of sand where her fellow servant had died between the dragon's jaws. Jig wished she would hurry. His head pounded from lack of air, and his chest felt as if Straum had sat on him.

The creature placed both hands on the javelin. Straum's claws dug furrows in the sand. Jig looked to the others for help, but they hadn't moved. Maybe they were smarter than Jig had realized. Smart enough to stay away from an angry dragon, at least.

The dragonchild tightened her grip and *pushed,* forcing the length of the javelin through Straum's eye and into his head.

Ryslind screamed in pain. Straum's head dropped to the floor. His tail crashed into the wall, where it reduced several shelves to splinters and destroyed a five-thousand-year-old collection of oil lamps.

Then the dragon's body went still.

CHAPTER 18

❖

A Fatal Misstep

Jig was not happy. *Straum blinked. He blinked! I could have died!*

Tymalous Shadowstar's answer sounded grumpy. *How was I supposed to know? Even I can't see the future. Besides, you're still alive, aren't you?*

Thanks to a dragonchild.

It was a good plan. The eye was the only vulnerable spot large enough for you to hit. If he hadn't blinked, that shot would have gone right through the eye and pierced Straum's oversized brain. A weakness you'll never have to worry about, I'm glad to say.

Good, Jig answered without thinking, thus proving the god's point.

Ryslind was curled into a ball and crying like an infant. Barius and Darnak both bent over him, while Riana watched Straum's newly orphaned child. The dragonchild hadn't moved at all since plunging the javelin into Straum's eye.

Jig grabbed another spear and used it as a staff to help him walk over to the others.

"Nice throw," Darnak said without looking up.

"You might have had him, if Ryslind hadn't spotted you. I dare say I couldn't have done it better myself, though if you tell any dwarf I said that, I'll deny it to my dying breath."

He peeled Ryslind's eyelids back and said, "He's not dead. Don't know what it'll do to him though, losing Straum that sudden-like. Meaning no disrespect, but if he had any mind left, that might have broken it."

Riana grabbed Jig's elbow and pulled him a few steps away from the group. "You hesitated. That could have gotten you killed. What were you waiting for?" she said, her voice pitched for Jig's ears only.

In an equally soft voice, he said, "I only had one shot. I couldn't figure out if I should try to kill Straum or Barius."

Riana nodded in perfect understanding. "Tough choice. I think we need to get you away from these adventurers. Deciding to go after the dragon instead of your companion . . . you'd think some of their 'nobility' had rubbed off."

"Not really." He glanced at the prince. "Straum just made a bigger target."

The dragonchild straightened and walked toward Jig, who tightened his grip on his spear. Darnak rose behind him. The dwarf had lost his war club, but he held a large chunk of rock and looked ready to bash anything remotely threatening. On Jig's other side, Riana drew her knife and waited.

"What happened to the one who was here before me?" A long, clawed finger pointed to the blood-soaked sand.

"Straum killed him," Darnak answered. "Said he was getting ideas of his own, not wanting to follow his scaliness anymore."

The dragonchild's head drooped. "I assumed as much."

"Straum said something about being able to read your folks' minds," Darnak said slowly. "That's how he was knowing what your friend was up to."

"Of course. Straum was ever paranoid. We have wondered if he had some magic to sense our hearts."

Darnak frowned. "So tell us how it is that you killed him without his realizing what you had in mind?"

The dragonchild squatted down and grabbed a handful of sand. "When we were younger, a pair of ogres found our lair. The adults were hunting, and the ogres were confident in their ability to massacre mere children. They killed one of our cousins, as well as the old grandmother who had been left behind to watch for danger."

Wet clumps of sand fell to the ground. "We leaped on the nearest ogre. Our claws and teeth are sharpest when we're young. I doubt the beast felt anything as I tore open his stomach. The second fled, only to encounter the hunting party. He died . . . slowly."

Jig glanced at the creature's hands. Those claws might not be as sharp as they used to be, but they still looked powerful enough to rip a goblin in half.

"He and I were mated several years later." Glancing back at Straum's body, she said, "As you said, Straum knew our thoughts. But when I realized my mate was dead, I stopped thinking. I simply acted."

Her eyes turned back to Jig. "What should we do now?"

Jig blinked. She was asking *him*? The others looked as confused as Jig felt. Except for Barius. He looked angry.

"You ask this miserable coward for advice?" he said with a derogatory wave toward Jig.

Jig agreed completely with the sentiment, though he might not have said it in those words. "Me?" he squeaked.

"I lead this party," Barius said. "I brought us here to slay Straum."

The dragonchild's eyes narrowed. "You failed. Without this goblin, Straum would still live, and all of us would have died." With a flick of a black tongue, she turned back to Jig. "We . . . we don't know how to live on our own." Her head lowered, and that elongated, scale-covered face managed to convey a sense of embarrassment. "The others will be scared to go on without Straum."

Jig's ears picked up urgent whispers from either side.

"We can use them to help carry our treasure to the surface," Barius said. "Imagine returning home with a retinue of these creatures as an escort. Instruct them to begin gathering the gold and jewels."

At the same instant, Riana was saying, "Ask if they'll come with us. They could protect us." Jig didn't think "us" included the humans or the dwarf.

Darnak said nothing. A low groan from Ryslind had sent the dwarf running to his side like a worried mother.

What advice could Jig possibly give the dragonchildren? *Don't let a nervous fire-spider perch in your hair. If you're going to annoy a wizard, make sure you kill him when you're finished. Never steal a chef's spoon.* He had nothing to offer Straum's orphans.

He tilted his head, hoping for divine help, but Shadowstar apparently thought Jig should figure this one out on his own. All he picked up was a faint sense of amusement.

"Go home," he said. "Go back to your family."

The creature cocked her head. "But we have no home, not without Straum."

"Don't throw this chance away, goblin," Barius said warningly. He took a step closer, menace plain in his balled fists. He didn't manage a second step. The dragonchild slipped between Jig and the prince. One hand seized Barius by the shirt and lifted him off the ground before anyone else could move.

Jig grinned. He could get used to this. But it wouldn't work. Even if he could persuade the dragonchildren to follow him around as guards, like Riana suggested, he didn't think he could ever learn to tolerate the musty smell of dragon.

"You should leave," he repeated. "Find another home. There's a ladder in the clearing at the center of the woods. Another ladder in the throne room above will take you to the upper tunnels. Darnak will give you a map to lead you out of the mountain. You'll have a whole world to choose from."

"You're wanting me to give up my map?" From Darnak's expression, Jig might as well have asked him to shave his beard. But a glance at Barius, still dangling helplessly, silenced any protests. "Ach. Take it. I can draw it again from memory when we return."

For a long time, the creature said nothing. Jig began to wonder if he had said the wrong thing. Maybe they wouldn't want to leave.

"An entire world, you say?"

"I've never seen it myself, but I hear it's pretty big."

The creature nodded, her long neck exaggerating the gesture. "Thank you."

She dropped the prince and walked over to Darnak, who handed over his map. A few minutes later, she was gone, leaving Jig to collapse as the excitement wore off and his legs gave out.

Barius didn't kill him, though it was a close thing. There was a limit to how much humiliation the prince could tolerate, and Jig had obviously pushed far beyond those limits. Being told that a goblin had done more to kill Straum than the prince himself had been the breaking point, and finding himself helpless in the dragonchild's strong grip had added humiliation to rage. As soon as the creature left, Barius lunged to his feet with murder in his eyes.

Thankfully, Darnak intervened. As the prince stormed toward Jig, the dwarf shouted at top volume, "Your brother's awake!"

Ryslind looked as bad as Jig felt. His pinched features were more sunken than usual, and dark smears underlined his eyes. His eyes no longer glowed. Strangely, Jig found Ryslind's beady brown eyes even more disconcerting. He had gotten used to those twin points of red.

After a bit more healing from Darnak, Ryslind managed to stand up under his own power. He could talk, though his voice was raw, and he sounded exhausted. He could remember nothing beyond their encounter with the Necromancer, a fact that made Jig infinitely grateful, as it meant he wouldn't remember his oath to kill Jig.

They decided to rest for a while. With the dragonchildren gone, hopefully for good, this was probably the safest place in the whole mountain. As Darnak pointed out, "Would *you* go poking around in a dragon's lair?"

When Riana pointed out that this was exactly what they had done, Darnak merely laughed and said most monsters had more sense.

So they rested. Darnak shared a bit of his ale, which helped immensely. Ryslind found that he could still cast small spells, but most of his power had vanished with Straum's death. This also contributed to Jig's cheerfulness.

Smudge sat happily on Jig's shoulder, munching a small chunk of dragon meat Jig had cut from Straum's body. He had considered trying a bit of dragon for himself, thinking it couldn't be worse than human food, but decided against it. Even retrieving this small chunk had nearly broken his sword. Those scales were tougher than they looked.

Hours later, Barius decided it was time to depart. "Everyone carry as much treasure as you can. We will need to make at least a dozen trips to retrieve our wealth, but we must take the most valuable items now, to insure their safety."

Fortunately, among the odds and ends Straum had collected over the ages were a wide variety of sacks, pouches, and backpacks. Jig found himself lugging a small sack full of gold coins. He had tried to carry a larger bag, but that nearly destroyed his newly repaired spine. Gold was *heavy*.

He knew Barius was angry at him for not carrying more, but goblins weren't known for their strength. Had the sack been any heavier, Jig would have ended up with his knees jammed through his shoulders. He did tuck a jeweled dagger into his belt, though, and he shoved a few rings onto his fingers.

"I hope nobody tries to stop us," he muttered. If they were attacked, he planned to throw his gold away and hope the enemy stopped to snatch up the coins. It should work, if Barius's greed was any example. Jig's life was a lot more important than gold. Besides, he could always come back for more.

They made it unscathed. They found occasional footprints, but nobody saw any other sign of

Straum's children. Perhaps they had already left. Jig hoped so. They had saved his life, but he would still feel more comfortable if he never encountered another one.

Lugging their gold up the ladders was a chore, but with more of Darnak's rope, they eventually managed to pass the treasure up through the ceiling.

There they ran into two hobgoblin sentries. But the hobgoblins fled as soon as they spotted Darnak and Barius.

"Good to have a reputation, eh?" Darnak said.

The time they spent traveling gave Jig a chance to think. More than anything, he wanted to lie down and sleep for a week. A month would be better, but he'd settle for a week. That should be enough time for the aches and bruises to begin to heal. After that he wanted a real meal. A huge helping of stuffed lizard-fish, with those dumplings Golaka made from rats for dessert.

But thinking of home reminded him that, without the rod's magic, Golaka's cauldron would swiftly run dry. They could still manage. Probably. With Straum dead, there would be an influx of adventurers to prey upon. Enough to feed the entire lair? He hoped so.

Jig knew he was lying to himself. Barius would return, and he would bring an army to help him. They would march through the tunnels and kill anything that got in their way. They would gut Straum's lair, and Jig wouldn't put it past them to wipe out the goblins and the rest of the monsters out of sheer spite.

All for what? So Barius could prove himself? So his heroism would outshine that of his brothers? Was this the kind of hero all the songs celebrated? Barius's glory had come, not from his own courage and valor, but from the blood and sweat of the rest of the party. Ryslind's magic, Riana's nimble fingers, Darnak's strength of arm, and even Jig's blind, stubborn luck. Yet Barius would be the one about whom songs were sung. He would be the one who found the Rod of Creation, the one responsible for slaying the great dragon Straum, the one who discovered five thousand years' worth of treasure and claimed it for his own.

They stopped to rest in the shiny room before leaving the tunnels. Jig stared at the designs, losing himself in memories. Little more than a week had passed since he came to this room, clumsily trying to spy on the adventurers. Here he had lied to Barius, which had saved Jig's life but cost the life of his captain, which Jig considered to be a double blessing. Here they had debated whether or not to take Jig along, or to kill him and save themselves the effort. What would happen to him now?

"What are you going to do to me?" Riana asked. Apparently her mind had wandered the same trail as Jig's.

"I will permit you to assist us in retrieving the rest of the treasure," Barius said generously. "Afterward you will be turned over to the proper authorities. You are still a criminal, after all. Fret not, for I am certain they will take your cooperation into consideration."

Riana nodded glumly, as though she had expected nothing more. Jig, on the other hand, was stunned. After all this, they would throw her into prison?

"That's not fair! She helped us," he protested. "She picked the lock on the Necromancer's door. She showed me the javelins I used to try to kill Straum."

He shouldn't have brought that up. The prince

whirled on him at the mention of how Jig, not Barius, had fought the dragon. "The old worm was
weak and tired, and I would have killed him myself
had you not interfered. As for that lock, if you will
recall, she nearly died in the attempt."

Jig started to argue, then thought better of it. No
dragonchild would stop Barius from killing him this
time. He looked at Darnak, but the dwarf only
shook his head and looked away.

This started him wondering. If Barius planned to
throw Riana away once he had finished using her,
what did he plan for Jig? With Straum dead, Jig
had begun to relax. But Straum had never been
Jig's enemy. If not for Barius and the others, Jig
would have lived out his life and never once bothered the old dragon. Riana herself had warned that
the humans would kill him when they had no further use for their so-called guide.

He started to make plans of his own as he ate.
He held no illusions about the prince's feelings
toward him. Given the chance, Barius would kill
him. Darnak wouldn't stop him. Nobody would.

Could he run away? Abandon the treasure and
return to the lair? It might work. But if Barius were
angry enough, that could also bring the adventurers
right back to the goblins' cavern. Jig didn't think
he would be able to stop the slaughter a second
time. The only other choice was to kill Barius now,
before he had a chance to do the same to Jig.

He would have to be fast. An attack from behind. Barius was too good with a sword, so a fair
fight was out of the question.

Smudge, picking up some hint of Jig's plans,
hopped off his shoulder and crawled into a corner
of the room. There he began to build a web, which
reinforced Jig's sense of danger. Fire-spiders used

webs not only to capture prey, but also for defense. Smudge was building a place to hide.

If only he knew how Darnak would react. In combat, the dwarf would protect his prince. But would he still feel the need to kill Jig if the prince was already dead? Would he understand why Jig had to kill Barius?

He would have to kill Ryslind as well, he realized. An attack on one brother earned the wrath of both. Though the wizard was half-dead already. That should make things easier.

Jig doubted Darnak would forgive the death of one prince, even if he understood the reasons. If Jig killed them both, he knew what Darnak would do. But if Jig didn't act, the humans would eventually return, and goblins would die. Adventurers were like fleas. If you didn't kill them right away, soon the blasted things were leaping into everything.

Jig had to kill them both. But he couldn't be in two places at once, and Barius was clearly the more dangerous of the two brothers. He would have to kill Barius, then get to Ryslind before Darnak used the new club he had claimed from Straum's collection to smash Jig's skull. He had a feeling that this time Shadowstar wouldn't be able to help him if he failed.

Maybe Riana could help. But how could he get to her without making the others suspicious? Besides, she appeared to be lost in her own despair. Her food sat untouched on the floor, and her glazed eyes stared into nothingness.

Jig glanced longingly at Smudge. How nice it would be to create his own web and hide there until the worst was over.

His best chance would be when they prepared to

move out. Barius insisted on leading, which meant his back would be unguarded. Darnak had been walking with Ryslind to help support the wizard, which would make things a bit trickier. If he could kill Barius, then get to Ryslind fast enough . . . if Darnak hesitated for just a few seconds. . . .

Jig forced himself to finish eating, though his appetite had fled like a frightened goblin. His palms were moist where they rested on his thighs, but he didn't wipe the sweat off. He didn't want to do anything that might betray his nervousness. Anyone who grew up inside the tunnels would have known from one look at Smudge that something was up, but nobody here recognized that clue.

He waited while Darnak finished off his wine, while Barius chewed daintily on his meat, while Ryslind sipped at some water. Had they ever before taken this long to eat? Jig didn't think so. They knew he was planning something, and they intended to torture him by making him wait. How long could it take to finish a bit of bread and cheese? Were human teeth so feeble?

At last Barius rose to his feet. "Beyond this tunnel lies glory." He waved an arm at the tunnel. "At last I will be accorded my due respect."

Jig forced himself to wait. He stood with the others, tried to shake out the stiffness in his legs, and grabbed his bag of gold. He slipped into line behind Barius. Not his usual place, but it couldn't be helped. He had to act now. He shifted the sack to his left hand and slowly reached toward his sword. His fingers touched the hilt.

Had Darnak or Ryslind noticed? His body should hide the movement. He wanted to turn, to make sure they hadn't seen, but he didn't dare. If Darnak had seen, he would be raising his club to strike. He wondered if he would hear the damp thud of his own skull cracking, or if he would simply reappear in front of Tymalous Shadowstar, looking sheepish after his failure.

Would Shadowstar want me to do this? Jig hesitated. He had promised to follow the god's rules, but Shadowstar had been a bit vague as to exactly how those rules applied. *Respect the shadow and the light both, for both have their place in the world.* What was that supposed to mean? Was Barius the shadow or the light? Stupid metaphors. Still, Shadowstar had protested when Jig thought about abandoning Riana and the others to their deaths in Straum's lair. He seemed to think killing was something to be done only as a last resort. It was a strange philosophy, one that would take some getting used to.

With a silent sigh, Jig started to put the sword away.

The sound of the blade returning to its sheath caught Barius's attention. He whirled, and his eyes homed in on the half-bared sword. His lips tightened into a terrible grin.

"I knew one such as you could never be trusted," Barius said. He sounded merry. He finally had an excuse to kill Jig, something he had wanted to do from the beginning. He tucked the Rod of Creation through his belt and slashed the air a few times with his own sword. Not knowing what else to do, Jig pulled his sword back out.

Barius promptly knocked it across the room.

"Jig!" Riana took a step after him, but Darnak caught her arm.

"This is how it has to be, lass."

She struggled, but the dwarf's grip was iron. "Why? Because your noble prince can't stand the fact that Jig humiliated him time after time? Maybe Jig knows Barius means to kill him as soon as we reach the surface. Maybe he was afraid."

Yes, he had been afraid. Now he was terrified. His sword was gone, and as his back touched the wall, he realized he had nowhere else to run. Fangs and claws were no match for steel, and Jig had never been much of a fighter anyway.

He glanced over and saw Smudge's web right beside him, now waist high. Fire-spiders built quickly when they were frightened.

"I'm sorry," Jig said. He hadn't intended to lead Barius back to Smudge. He hoped Barius would ignore the spider. Was he so spiteful he would kill Jig's pet once Jig was already dead?

"A bit late for apologies," Barius said, misunderstanding. He raised his sword. "If it's any consolation, I will be merciful. A single stroke to sever your head from your shoulders. A painless execution, which is better than you deserve."

"If you want to be merciful, shut up and get it over with."

Barius's eyes widened. "Brave words from a goblin. Very well."

Jig watched Barius flex his strong arms. Posing for the others, Jig figured. Typical. Jig straightened, determined to be brave just this once. He might not make it into songs or stories, but at least when he saw Shadowstar, he could say that he hadn't flinched at the end. What would Shadowstar say when they met?

He remembered what the god had told him before. *Next time you should try to duck.*

Jig screamed and rolled out of the way as the sword whistled over his head. His legs kicked madly, knocking Barius back. He tried to get up, but Barius kicked him in the side. Jig rolled over, clutching his gut. Barius stepped away, and his boot brushed Smudge's web.

"Little runt," Barius gasped. He glanced down at his leg. "Disgusting." With his free hand, he reached down to brush the web free.

Any goblin would have known better. Even Barius might have known, had he stopped to think. Smudge's web, like that of any fire-spider, was highly flammable. With an angry human looming over him, Smudge reacted the way he always did in the face of danger.

Barius screamed as flames enveloped his leg. He swatted his burning clothes, then stomped at the web. Smudge scurried back, flattening his body to the floor. He darted one way, then the other. Jig could see his legs waving in fear as he tried to get away, but Barius was too fast. Snarling like an animal, Barius turned so his foot was parallel to the wall.

"No!" Jig lunged, but he was too slow. Barius's boot landed on the terrified Smudge. To Jig, the crunch of Smudge's body sounded as loud as a dragon's roar.

"No," he repeated in a whisper. Most of the flames had died, and Jig could see there was nothing he could do. Even if Shadowstar would have helped him heal a lowly fire-spider, it was too late. Smudge was dead.

Jig snarled as he attacked, leaping onto Barius and sinking his fangs into the prince's sword arm. The sword hit the floor with a ring. Jig's claws raked Barius's body. Barius punched Jig in the head, but he didn't even feel it. All he could see was Smudge's crushed body. Tears blurred his vision as he bit down harder. His nails struggled to reach the flesh beneath the prince's armor.

"Curse you," Barius yelled. He wedged a knee

against Jig's chest and pushed. Jig scrambled for anything to hold on to. If Barius got free, it was over. One of Jig's hands grabbed the prince's shirt, the other clawed at his belt.

Barius broke away. Jig flew back, still clutching a piece of Barius's shirt in one hand and something hard in the other. His head cracked against the floor. He wiped his eyes, and only then did he see what he had grabbed.

He had the Rod of Creation.

Barius saw it at the same time Jig did. He lunged for his sword. Jig scrambled to his feet and pointed the rod at Barius. "Stop!"

Barius froze.

"Look out!" Riana shouted.

Jig aimed the rod at Ryslind and Darnak, who stopped moving.

"You don't even know how to use it," Ryslind said. "Goblins have neither the strength of will nor the depth of mind for true magic."

"Neither do you," Riana snapped.

Jig felt his lips pull back into a feral grin. "*You* taught us how to use it," he said. He turned on Barius, who had begun to reach toward his sword.

"You can't destroy us," Barius said. "The rod is incapable of taking life."

"No matter what you do to us, we will find a way to reverse the effects," Ryslind added. "I've enough art left to see to that."

"Put the rod down, lad," Darnak said. "You go your way, we'll go ours."

Jig didn't have to look to know how the princes were taking that suggestion. "For how long?" he asked. "How long before they come back looking for more gold, or to get revenge on the goblin? When they get greedy for more treasure, they're not going to *ask* us to let them through. You know what will happen."

Darnak didn't answer.

"It's not as though you have a choice, goblin," Barius said. He had begun to smile again, believing he had won. "My brother is correct. You cannot kill us, not with the rod, even if you could control its magic."

Jig wavered. But then he saw the smoking web in the corner, and his arm tightened. "*You* controlled it," he said. He bared his teeth. "I bet I can do better."

The magic felt similar to the power Shadowstar had given him, but much more powerful. Jig felt as though his entire body were being crushed into the end of the rod and squeezed out the other side. He saw the prince stumble. His vision wavered, and his head began to pound. He concentrated on keeping himself whole. The rod tried to pull him apart, but Jig pulled back. He could feel the magic begin to work. He sensed the instant Barius's body started to reshape itself.

"Barius!"

Ryslind's voice, angry and panicked. He was trying to cast a spell of his own. Jig turned and pointed the rod at the wizard. Again the magic poured through him, halting Ryslind in midstride. White ice pierced Jig's brain as the rod's power broke through Ryslind's hastily erected shields. *Backlash,* he thought, remembering what had happened when Barius used the rod.

But even as Jig fell, he saw that it had worked.

He had just enough strength left to point the rod at Darnak. He didn't think he had enough strength left to use it, but Darnak wouldn't know that. So the dwarf stood helpless, watching the two enormous trout that had been Ryslind and Barius flop about on the floor as they suffocated.

"Go away," Jig croaked at Darnak.

The dwarf shook his head. Tears dripped into his beard. "I'll not leave them."

"I don't want to kill you, too," Jig said. *I don't think I can, for that matter.* If the other goblins heard him now, they'd think his mind had slipped. How could he not want to kill a perfectly good dwarf?

"They are family to me," Darnak said. "How can I go back to Wendel and Jeneve and tell them I watched their sons die?"

"Their sons were greedy fools," Riana said. She didn't bother to hide her satisfaction as she watched the gills of the Barius-fish stop moving.

"Aye," Darnak agreed. "But they were still family." With that he drew his club and walked toward Jig. He moved slowly, deliberately giving Jig time to use the rod.

Those few minutes had been enough for Jig to catch his breath. Was he strong enough to use the rod again? He didn't think so. But was he ready to die and rejoin Shadowstar?

Jig sighed and grabbed the rod with both hands. Once again magic ripped through his body. He struggled to control it. He didn't want to kill Darnak, and that made things harder. He figured out what he wanted to do and concentrated on a different shape.

Darnak fell. His body twisted and bulged. The walls spun, and Jig blacked out.

CHAPTER 19

❧❖❧

Parting Gifts

Jig woke up to find Riana's green eyes staring down at him. "My head hurts."

He still had the rod in his hands. She hadn't taken it from him. He wondered why. "What happened to Darnak?"

"You turned him into a bird," she said. For once no trace of sarcasm tainted her voice. She sounded impressed. "He flew away a few minutes ago."

"Good." He grimaced. The room had begun to stink of fish. He glanced down the tunnel, wishing he could have seen what Darnak had looked like. "Was it a good bird?" he asked.

She giggled. "Ugliest thing I've ever seen. Brown, with a dirty black crest and sunken eyes. He could talk, too. Said to warn you there'd still be people coming after this place. Barius and Ryslind had other brothers, and they'll want revenge."

"I know." He managed to sit up. "What will you do?"

Her eyes darkened. "What can I do?"

There was the bitterness Jig was used to.

"Go back to being a thief?" She gestured at the treasure scattered around the room. "If I take any of this, someone will only kill me to get it."

"You could always be an adventurer."

She snorted. "I never want to go on another 'adventure' as long as I live. I hate the dark, I hate the cold, I hate all the monsters from those ugly worms to that great hulk of a dragon. No treasure is worth this. If that's all I have to look forward to, you might as well kill me here and now. It would be a kindness."

Jig grinned. Only when she cringed away did he remember that his fangs were probably still covered in Barius's blood. Nor was his a reassuring face to begin with, even for a goblin. He looked around for something he could use to clean his teeth, and his searching eyes fell on the ashen remains of Smudge's web. His eyes stung.

"Oh Smudge," he mumbled. "I'm sorry." He shouldn't have let Barius get that close. An entire room, and he had led the prince straight to Smudge's hiding spot.

He crawled over and picked up the crushed spider. He stroked the furry head, then tucked Smudge into his pouch. He would take care of the body later.

Using the Rod of Creation as a simple cane, Jig pushed himself up. He didn't want to be here anymore. He wanted to go home.

"Wait," Riana said. She bit her lip, then said, "What about me?"

Jig shrugged. Why should he care? He wondered if she had meant it, when she said it would be kinder to kill her.

"I don't want to go back to that life." She grabbed the lantern Darnak had dropped and hurried after Jig.

"You've changed. You're not like the other goblins. Otherwise you would have killed Darnak. Well, I've changed too. I don't want to be a thief anymore, but I don't know how to be anything else. At least you can go back to your people. I've got nothing. I'm scared, Jig."

He stopped. He knew how hard it must have been for Riana to say that. "I can give you all the gold in the world, but you said you don't want it. What do you want?"

She began to cry. Why was everyone crying so much all of the sudden? First Jig, when Barius killed Smudge. Then Darnak, and now Riana. If this continued, they'd soon flood the whole mountain.

"I want to stop being afraid," she said.

"Fine." Jig grabbed the rod and used it before Riana could protest. A minute later, he was gasping for breath while Riana stared in amazement at her hands.

He had used Straum's children as a model, but made a few changes. Where the dragonchildren had been a dusky bronze, Riana's scales were pearly white. Her body was smaller, retaining her elven slenderness, but the muscles beneath those scales were as powerful as any dragonchild's. Anyone who tried to hurt her would be lucky to walk away with their limbs attached. The scales should turn most blades. Only her eyes remained the same. Jig hadn't wanted to change those wide green eyes. She glanced at her hands and laughed when she saw that Jig had restored her missing finger.

She craned her neck to see Jig's other addition. Two wide, white wings spread across the tunnel.

"Can I fly?" she asked. She spoke with the same lisp as the other dragonchildren.

"I think so. You'll probably want to practice,

though." He took a deep breath. "If you want, I can change you back. But you have to decide now. You won't have another chance."

She nodded slowly. "You're going to seal the entrance?"

"Yes."

Riana studied the sleek lines of her arms. Faster than Jig could follow, she punched a fist into the wall. Her delighted laugh echoed up the hall. "It didn't even hurt. Jig, this is beautiful."

He felt himself blushing. "Better than the bird?"

"Much better. I can go anywhere I want." Her voice rose with excitement. "I can fly through the clouds, I could cross the oceans, and nobody can stop me."

"You'll be lonely," Jig warned her. How could she not be? She was a monster now, and Jig had firsthand experience of how surface-dwellers treated monsters.

"I'm used to being lonely," she said. "Besides, if a goblin and an elf can be friends, what's to stop me from finding someone else out there?"

Jig had no answer to that, and he didn't know how to respond to her claim of friendship. He couldn't argue, either. Who ever heard of a goblin being friends with an elf? Who ever heard of a goblin being friends with anyone? But they had saved each other's lives several times, which was also unheard of. He blushed. If he tried to say anything, he'd probably make a fool of himself. Still, it felt surprisingly good to have a friend.

"I, um, I should go," he said. He blushed harder. "I have things I need to do."

"I understand." She rushed forward and pulled him into a hug he couldn't have broken out of if his life depended on it. "Thanks, Jig."

Then she was gone.

Feeling a strange mix of happiness and loss, Jig headed down the tunnel to close the entrance for good.

He took care of a few other tasks before heading back to the lair. He had a promise to keep to Tymalous Shadowstar. He took some time to redesign the shiny room. First, he shifted the glass tiles to form a clear image of the Autumn Star shining down on the best likeness Jig could manage of the god himself.

My nose isn't that big, Shadowstar protested.

I did the best I could. You're lucky I didn't stick with my first try.

That would have been even better. "Tymalous Shadowstar, the Cross-Eyed God."

The room itself remained empty, save for a small altar against the wall. For a while, Jig would likely be the only one to leave tokens of respect and thanks on that altar for the god. But he hoped to convince other goblins to do the same. If he could tell them of the things he had seen and learned, who knew what might happen? Shadowstar hadn't exactly been thrilled at the idea of a whole horde of goblin followers, but it was, in his words, *A hell of a lot better than nothing.*

At the base of the altar, an eight-pointed star marked the spot where Smudge had died. The fire-spider's body was buried inside the floor. A fine web traced the outline of the star. Jig didn't think the god would mind, and he wanted Smudge to have some sort of marker.

He left the gold and treasure where it was. What good would it do to bring it along? You couldn't eat treasure.

But you *could* eat trout. Jig had to stop several times as he lugged the huge fish along behind him.

He had strung a rope through their gills to make them easier to drag, but they still weighed the same as full-grown humans. By the time Jig reached the edge of goblin territory, his hands were sore and rope-burned.

"Who's there?" challenged one of the guards.

Jig's ears picked up the other one's whispered, "It's *him*."

He grinned. They were afraid of him. What a nice change. "I've got food," he shouted.

Not two, but four guards ran down the corridor. *Stupid move. I could have been the point man for an ambush.* He would have to see about improving the quality of the guards.

"What's that thing on your face?" one guard asked warily.

His grin widened. That thing was another of the rod's gifts. He had used the blade of Barius's sword for the frames, since the steel was harder than any other metal he could find. The lenses were made of amethyst. Jig had needed a long time to get the shapes right, but finally he had a set of elven lenses that worked. The bubblelike lenses covered his large eyes, the frames hooked lightly around his pointed ears, and for the first time in his life, he could *see*.

"Forget it," Jig said. "Someone help me with these fish."

Seeing the trout, the guards began to drool. Forgetting whatever their orders might have been concerning Jig, they ran forward and helped him carry the fish into the cavern.

"Golaka's gonna be happy to see *this*," one said.

"Yes." Jig bit his lip. Hopefully she wouldn't throw Jig into the pot along with the fish. He gave the rod a spin, admiring the way its gleaming new steel bowl caught the torchlight. After all, when he finished with his lenses, most of Barius's blade had remained. What better use than to repair Golaka's spoon? Maybe this would help calm some of her rage.

"Pickings have been pretty lean this past day or two," another guard grumbled.

"Don't worry," Jig said. "I have some ideas about that." He would have to talk to other goblins, but he thought everyone would agree with his plan. Especially if it meant finding more food.

Straum's forest had continued to exist after the dragon died. According to Ryslind, the trees, the animals, and most of what lived down there were real. Poor imitations of the genuine articles, perhaps, but still real. That meant they could be eaten! All Jig had to do was convince a group to go hunting with him. Once they brought back their first deer, there should be no more arguments. He looked forward to finding out if venison tasted as good as Riana had promised.

Something brushed against Jig's foot, and he stopped.

"What is it?" one of the guards said. Jig waved them away as he stooped over to investigate. A tiny spider, black with red spots, waved its front legs in the air at him.

"Smudge?" Jig said in disbelief. The spots were the same, though the spider itself was much smaller. This was Smudge as he had been two years ago, newly hatched. But it couldn't be Smudge. He had buried Smudge only a few hours ago.

Goblins . . . no faith whatsoever.

Jig glanced upward. If he took the rod back and opened up the stone in front of Shadowstar's altar, would he find Smudge's body gone? The god didn't give an answer, and Jig didn't really want one. He placed his hand on the floor and waited while the spider crawled onto his palm.

When the fire-spider went straight to the leather pad on Jig's shoulder, he began to giggle with delight. He scratched the spider's head, feeling that things were finally right with the world.

A shriek stabbed his ears. "What? He's *here*? Where is he? I'll teach him to mess with his betters. Boil him until his skin peels off, I will."

Jig sighed. "Come on, Smudge. Let's go give Golaka's spoon back." Together they walked down the tunnel toward home.